Second Edition

— *A Novel* —

JAGGED EDGES

One Moment of Betroyal Leaves So Much Torn

DORIS H. DANCY

Lightning Fast Book Publishing, LLC

www.lfbookpublishing.com

ISBN: 979-8-9852917-8-0

CONTENTS

DEDICATION

To my husband, Willie,
and my two beautiful daughters, Monica and Tara:

Thank you for your never-ending prayers for me,
for your support, your respect, your patience,
and most of all for your unconditional love.
You are my life.

POSTHUMOUSLY

To Mom and Grandma,

Thank you for your love and daily sacrifices
that have made your dreams my reality.

ACKNOWLEDGEMENTS

If you have ever had the opportunity to sit down and glare at a blank sheet of paper for more than what seems like an eternity, waiting for the inspiration to come, then you will understand my next statement as much as I do. Writing is difficult, and by no means is it a solo task. If it is to be effective, it requires lots of attention from many others. I have had the honor of a multitude of attentive friends who helped me make my dream come true, and I take this opportunity to say thank you.

First of all, I thank and praise my Lord and Savior, Jesus Christ who is always my moment-by-moment inspiration. He is the one who NEVER breaks a promise, and the One who allowed all that I have written here to come to fruition to glorify Him.

My Husband, Willie, is always there to support, encourage, and defend if necessary. He is the love of my life, my best friend, and together we have discovered the tools that make us almost experts in developing a good and healthy relationship...one that flourishes so that marriage for many years is a God-given, golden treasure to be nurtured and valued. He is my constant friend.

My daughter Monica, my inspiration, gave me those special moments of reading time when I called on the spur-of-the-moment. "Listen to this," was a frequent phrase. There were times when you stopped Tali's homework, Zoey's bath, Marc's dinner, and your own personal minute for yourself to read a chapter, write a passage, create an idea, or just tell me what I needed to revise. Thank you for the invaluable moments given to me that you can never get back; that makes them all the more special. You are the light of my life.

My daughter, Tara, my inspiration, and my no nonsense quote expert. "Mom that's too long...too cumbersome...doesn't make sense...change it! You gave me your patience, your understanding, and your COMPLETE honesty. Thank you for the long talks of encouragement, your help with photography, design, and technology. Thank you for just being there when I needed you. You are the light of my life.

The Reverend Barbara Dudley, my friend and writing consultant...where do I start? You encouraged me when I just had a dream in my hand and had no idea where to begin. You helped me fling it toward the stars where my ideas caught the light and burst into flaming reality that still finds me pinching myself. You are the personification of the scripture: "I can do all things through Christ Jesus that strengthens me." You read my chapters, reread my chapters, and reread them again. You pushed me, nudged me, questioned me, praised me, reminded me, and cared for me enough to let me know that God is standing in our midst for gigantic things, and that He forever holds my hand as I walk the path He ordained just for me. Thank you is simply not enough.

To my Editor, Catherine Y. Horne…you are truly a light in my life and have been for many years. I wanted to say…for *so* many years, but knowing how much you hate the word "SO," I left it out. There is nothing of importance that I do in my life without your being a vital part. Thank you for you attention to detail, your honesty, and the hours and hours you spent pouring over the passages, sentences, and diction. To the readers: if you find mistakes, and I am sure you will, it is not Catherine's fault. Sometimes, she told me, but I just didn't do it. (LOL) I love you, Lady Catherine.

My sister-in-law Elesta White has been a major encourager. You were my first reader, and when you called to tell me that what you had read was a page turned, it gave me something that I did not already have: the drive to continue and the belief that I could really do this. You have been there for me from the beginning, and your time and words of encouragement, as you can see, were invaluable.

My Best friends, Joyce AR Weeks, Catherine Y. Horne, Marion P. Wright, and Debra Hamilton Farley…Since we met, you have never left my side. Whatever I do you are always there to encourage, listen, offer your talents, and just remind me that there is nothing I do that you won't be dead center to help me. You have talked and prayed me through this, let me know that whatever I need you are willing to do, and just been what you have always been to me…my strong, unyielding support…THE CHRISTIAN LADIES BY MY SIDE. There are no adequate words to express how grateful I am that Our Lord placed you all in my life.

At **Red Lobster in Newport News, VA** I thank George J., Fabio, Rachel, and Kelly and at **Ruby Tuesday in Hampton**, I say thank you to Ashley Tunno for your support. I needed the **CLEAN SLANG LANGUAGE OF YOUTH,** like "been a minute" and you helped me so willingly. Thank you.

To God Be The Glory!

Doris

A PROLOGUE

~ The breaking of dawn is the best keeper of secrets I know;
it has a pact with the close of day. At sun's first peek,
the confidence is safe, and one has no evidence at all
how altered life might be by eventide~

The library at the university is quiet except for multiple pages turning and a stupid unnecessary clock facing me. I might just waste a star wish to get that annoying thing smashed. I'd do it myself, but I'd get caught, and be a greater disappointment to my parents than Ruff who still can't sit up, roll over, or even bark like a real dog. I sigh. Deal with the clock, Arianna. You're twenty-four years old, already have your MBA in Fashion Management and Entrepreneurship and almost ready to start your own Fashion House for goodness sakes.

All you have to do is complete this little research, and you're on your own. You're not five. Anyway, you have far more important things to think about at 8:15 on this lonely Friday night, like how to meet that gorgeous guy sitting at the table across from you.

I sit back in my chair and just stare at him, counting how many times he glances up and quickly looks back at his work. He is doing a very poor job of pretending he hasn't noticed that I'm staring at him. He's on his eighth under eyed glance at me when he puts his laptop down, folds his hands, sits back, looks straight at me with a smirk, and holds the stare. I smile what I think is my very best smile. Let the games begin! After a minute and a half of staring, I'm just getting comfortable, and there is no way I'm giving up. He begins packing up his things slowly. Still staring, never glancing down to see what he's doing, he meticulously places his laptop in his black leather attaché case. I can tell he is purposefully taking his time, and for some strange reason, his deliberate movements, to me, are extremely sensual. I almost have to break my stare when I think to myself: *any man that sexy ought to be locked up and the key thrown away.* He leaves his case on the table, returns two books to a nearby shelf all the while looking into my staring eyes, and then he brings his fine self over to me.

He pulls out the chair that faces me without saying a word, turns it backwards, and tries to stifle his grin from becoming a full face all teeth showing spectacle. Of course, he's far too cool for that.

"OK, you've been staring at me for the last ten minutes so I thought I would just come over and ask if I have spinach in my teeth or a booger up my nose." I laugh. He smiles.

"What if I say both?" I grin, cupping my hand under my chin and looking directly into his brown bedroom eyes.

"Well, I'll know that's not true," he taunts matter-of-factly.

"And how would you know that?" I question cynically. *This man is about to make my heart jump out of my body.*

"Simple."

"Simple?"

"Yeah, simple. It's a trick question." He rocks back in the chair. "I didn't have spinach today." We both laugh as quietly as we can since we are somewhat aware that we are in a library, and there are a few people still pretending to study on a Friday night.

"Well, to be quite honest with you, umm…Peter? Ah…Paul?" I lift one eyebrow and continue. "…Mary?" He gives me a closed mouth smile, and plays around his mouth with his thumb and index finger.

"Well, definitely not Mary. Derek. Derek Wellington." For the first time in my life, I hear the sexiness in that baritone voice of his that will drive me insane for years to come.

"Well, to be quite honest with you…Derek, Derek Wellington, your hair caught my attention.

"My hair?"

I bite my bottom lip to cover my grin, and nod my head yes. "Yes, your hair…and definitely your eyes too," I say with mocked serious-ness…"and then there's that mouth," I giggle.

"Oh, is that good or bad?" he chuckles.

"Oh, that's *real* good," I admit with a flirtatious grin.

"Good. Good," he nods in mock approval.

"So, you…this beautiful woman sitting here toying with me, you are…Gracie?"

"No, not even close," I laugh.

I opt here for a more serious tone. My hazel eyes, my windows to the soul, touch his. "My name is Arianna…Arianna Channing."

"Ah, a beautiful name for a lovely lady."

"Well thank you kind sir." I bat my eyes playfully.

"You are quite welcome, my lady." And then he does something totally unexpected. He reaches across the table, takes my hand in his, and slowly brings it to his beautiful lips. That is how it all started with Attorney Derek Chase Wellington, III and me.

I would say that we had a whirlwind summer romance. We were inseparable. Both of us were taking a break of sorts before starting full force into our careers. Derek had studied for the Bar, passed it, and in September would join a private law firm in Virginia. I had completed my studies in Fashion Management and Entrepreneurship in New York City, and studied an additional two years in Paris. Coincidentally, I was also moving to Virginia, after the summer, to start my own *Channing Fashion House*, the first one in the Tidewater area.

Our connection, from its inception, has that magic touch----that something special; however, there is this one thing that tears our bond, interferes with our solidarity, and will forever puzzle me. Throughout this disappointment, I am honest with myself. Common sense and life's experiences have taught me that it will be impossible to know the essence of the truth surrounding a very deep, but damaged, relationship in Derek's past, but that is not my issue.

From the inception of our brief courtship and after we marry, Derek and I are always completely honest with each other. We trust each other explicitly, or so I am led to believe. That is what makes my discovery so perplexing----so hurtful and a huge issue for me. The mystifying thing, now that the real truth irradiates, is that my friend, my boyfriend, my fiancée, my lover, my husband never mentions Morgan Shay LaRue to me. Not once, that I can remember, does he ever even call her name.

Derek

Chapter 1

MY MORGAN

*~Disappointment weights on the heart
like an uncomfortable wet blanket~*

I glance at my watch just before I raise my umbrella and make a mad dash for my car parked in the gym parking lot. I still have almost an hour before I'm supposed to pick up Morgan. I race to the car and get soaked fumbling with my keys, this big bulky fraternity umbrella, and my gym bag. I slide into the driver's seat, grab the towel out of my bag and try to do the impossible: dry myself off while seated in car. That's a tough job. I turn on the radio to check the traffic and listen to some of my favorite music when I feel my phone vibrate. When I slide the phone on, Morgan's beautiful face appears on the screen, an automatic smile slowly forms on my lips, and I take a deep breath.

"Hey babe. I can't *wait* to see you."

"How's my favorite man?"

Her voice is soft, sultry, and engaging, but because I know her so well, I already hear what I don't want to hear.

"I'm fine…a little wet," I respond. I still haven't mastered the art of opening car doors with big umbrellas and gym bags. Even four years of college and three years of law school haven't taught me that.

"I know, right?" I hear a slight familiar giggle. "It seems like this rain just won't let up, and it's making everybody so depressed."

"Well, I'm not depressed, and far from it. In less than thirty minutes, I'm about to see the most beautiful girl in the world and the love of my life, so rain is the last thing that can depress me. It seems like it's been a long time, babe. It's been something every week, so now I can barely wait. I'll be out front in a few, O.K.?"

I hear Morgan take a deep breath and hesitate so I know what's coming: the same thing that has been coming for the last three times I've tried to see her, even though I never fail to show up. I never fail to hope that I will actually see her. I never fail to believe that this time will be different.

"Baby, I…I don't even want to tell you this, but I…I still can't meet you tonight, and I probably can't meet you before your plane leaves tomorrow either. I have another rehearsal after this one, and there is no way I can get out of it. We're meeting early tomorrow morning too, and I have to be here. I hate disappointing you again and again, but I just don't have a choice."

Suddenly it seems that the rain is pounding the roof of my car, the windows are fogged, sheets of water blind my view of the outside, and except for the noise of nature in command, there is a *very* long silence. I guess the silence is for a lot of different reasons: silence because I've flown on a crowded uncomfortable plane for nothing, silence because my hopes are shattered AGAIN, silence because I'm beginning to wonder if what Morgan tells me is really the truth or if she's hiding some new guy. There is silence because I feel used and because I just don't want to say something that I'll want to take back even before it spills out of my mouth.

"Morgan, you have a choice. You're just making the one I don't like again."

"How do you think I have a choice? I have responsibilities Derek just like you do."

Her voice is snappy and short and communicates to me that she does not have much patience with my complaints even through she has done this to me repeatedly for quite a while.

"Don't do that, Morgan. Don't...don't do that." My voice is quiet, but edgy and I am mad.

"Almost every other week for the past seven years, I get on a plane, rent a car just so that we have some time with each other....just to help us hold this long distance thing together. I've done this through undergrad, law school, and studying for the bar. I've never asked you to come to me one time. And what do you do when you know I'm coming? You let me spend money unnecessarily, make this uncomfortable trip, and after I get here, then you tell me, four times straight now, that you can't see me, not even for a stupid lunch, a quick dinner, or a minute after you finally get home. What am I suppose to think? I love you Morgan, but you can't expect me to keep doing this."

My anger is rising fast and furious, and I bite the corner of my bottom lip trying to control my words---trying to control the temper that I know is about to go berserk. I know I am at my limit with this.

"Derek, you just don't understand. It's not that I don't *want* to see you. I do. I *really* do. The bottom line is I just don't have time to see you right now. Personally, I think that you ought to get that."

I hear the tremble in her voice, and I know she is about to cry, but even that does not stop me this time.

"No, I don't get it," I snap. "I don't understand how you can keep blowing me off like this. I don't understand how you can just let me waste time and money coming here week after week while you dial me on a phone at the very last minute and call everything off. No, I don't understand."

My words are coming fast, and I am on the verge of being out of control. I can feel the heat coming off my neck, beads of sweat already popping out, and I feel my head beginning to ache.

"You're selfish, ungrateful, and don't care about anybody but yourself and your career. Morgan, this is just inconsiderate, plain and simple, and to be perfectly honest and clear, this is not going to keep happening to me."

"But Derek…"

"No, no buts…you think I'm going to always be around, right? Well, think again. I'm not. Yes, we've been together for a long time, but maybe I'm fooling myself about that too. Maybe the real deal is that I'm just an old habit to you."

"Derek, stop."

"No, I'm not going to stop 'cause I'm not going to be treated like one of your old worn out, comfortable shoes or something that you can choose to wear or throw in the back of your closet. It's not going to happen."

I can tell that Morgan is trying to interrupt my tirade, but there is no way I'm stopping now.

"If you don't care about us any more than this then just tell me, and I'll be out of your way. You won't have to worry about Derek Wellington interfering with your precious rehearsals or coming between you and your career; I can guarantee you that. You can just dance yourself right out of my life and be done with it. Do you hear me, Morgan? Do you hear me?" I am shouting in the phone and feeling miserable, and I want her to feel worse.

"Derek, everybody in Virginia hears you. Yes, I hear you."

When she speaks, her voice is calm, cool, and distant, and that makes me even angrier.

"The bottom line, Derek, remains the same: I can't see you today, tonight, or tomorrow, and that's just it. You can understand or not understand. I really don't care. Yes, dance is my career, and I can't just walk away anytime I want just because you come in town. A lot of people depend on me, and I have to be responsible enough to be where I'm supposed to be when I'm supposed to be there. So, your little temper tantrum is not going to work."

She slows her speech down now as if she is talking to a very small child, and as I listen, I feel my temper soar.

"I have to be at the studio this weekend, Derek…no ifs, no ands, no buts about it."

I try to interrupt but she hurries on.

"It is what it is, Derek. So, bye. I've got to go. People are waiting for me, and my break is over. I'm sorry to have inconvenienced and disappointed you again."

I hear the dial tone. I take the phone from my ear and look at it in disbelief.

"Incredible! I know she didn't just hang up in my face," I mutter to myself.

I probably turn the ignition a little too hard and pull away from the curb a little too fast, but there is no way Morgan is getting the last word on this. I swerve in and out of traffic and I'm just begging for a speeding ticket as I move at break neck speed down the highway, muttering to myself, honking at innocent drivers, and generally being an inconsiderate, obnoxious jerk just to get to the studio before my common sense kicks in again. I put the car in park under a "No Park" sign in front of the studio, jump out, and take the steps two at a time. I swing the door open and follow the sounds of music coming from the far end of the hall. At the door, I take a deep breath, snatch the door open, and immediately spot Morgan and her partner, Peter, executing a lift that, even in my anger, I see is absolutely beautiful.

"Morgan! Morgan!" I hear my booming voice out of control now, and I don't care that every dancer is frozen in place…that I am perhaps embarrassing the heck out of Morgan…that my career is based on upholding the law and this is far from it. At this moment, I don't care about anything but getting what I want. I see Peter finish the lift and bring Morgan to the floor. Now, out of his arms, she moves with defiance over to the music and snaps it off. I see her mouth tighten and her shoulders hunched, and I know she can just about kill me. At the same time Pierre, the choreographer, is yelling something at me, but for the life of me I don't know what it is nor do I care. For a new lawyer, it is blatantly obvious that I have thrown caution to the wind. Peter moves over near the door and attempts to calm me down, and at the same time encourages me to move back outside the door, but I'm resisting. By this time, Morgan is at my side pushing me out too, and little Pierre is behind holding on to Peter's shirt. Nobody seems to be worried about Pierre who is peeking around Peter yelling about calling the police and how I have no business coming into his studio or trespassing on his property.

Peter is trying to pull Morgan out of his way and winning in his attempt to get closer to me. Even in this confusion though, I can see that he is being careful not to let Morgan get hurt in anyway.

"Hey, hey, take it easy, man. Let's just chill for a sec."

I know that I am a bit out of control, and that somewhere common sense is also attempting to play a role, but even so, I still can't stop myself from insulting this clown.

"You need to mind your own business, ballerina. I just want to talk to Morgan, and you need to stay out of this."

Peter holds up his hands to indicate that he wants no trouble. "Come on man; it's all right. Be easy."

Peter is making sure that things are calm before he even thinks about leaving Morgan alone, but she knows that there is no danger, and she steps between us.

"Peter, I got this. You go back inside. I got this." I can tell that Morgan is totally in control.

"Yeah, Peter, she got this," I mock never letting my eyes leave his.

He moves away slightly, but is standing at the door in protection mode. As a dance partner, as I understand it, he is always in protection mode with her. The jumps, the moves, the lifts and just walking her to her car, he is her protector, but he can't be that right now.

"Let me know if I need to call the police." Peter is standing with his cell in his hands ready to dial the magic three that can bring assistance in an instance.

"No. Please. I'm fine. I'll handle this. Just go back inside, and I'll be back in a minute. Everything is fine."

Peter and Pierre reluctantly open the door to the studio and leave us alone to talk. I can tell that Morgan is very angry. I'm angry too, so I know that this is not going to be a good scene.

"What the heck is wrong with you, Derek? Are you crazy?"

"No, I'm not crazy, but you can't just blow me off like you did and then hang up the phone in my face. It don't work like that, babe." At this point, I toss professional grammar to the wind.

"Well, how does it work, Derek? This is my job. This is where I make my money. This is my career. This is what I have been working for all of my life. I am trying with everything in me to compete for one of the biggest dance leads in the country, and here you are trying to mess that up. I'm on the brink of getting everything I want, and now that it's here…close enough for me to taste, you have to storm in here acting imbecilic. What is wrong with you?

"No, you're the one acting im- be- cil- ic," I shout emphasizing the word far too much as if I'm testing its syllabication.

"Morgan, you think I like never being able to see you, missing you like crazy, and finally thinking that I'll be with you only to be dismissed repeatedly like some errant child? Do you think I like going through security, getting on a crowded plane, renting a car and coming here for nothing? I understand about your job, Morgan, but can't I get a couple of hours if I do all of that?"

Both of us are standing our ground that the other owes us some respect, some space, some consideration, and neither of us is willing to back down even a little.

Morgan folds her arms, steps back, and ethnicity takes over.

"If I say you can have a couple of hours, Derek, then you can have a couple of hours, but if I say I don't have time, then I don't have time, and you have to respect that *for me*. You claim you love me. Well, prove it! Stop trying to wreck everything for me before I can even get it off the ground, Jerk!"

Her words are coming faster now, those beautiful green eyes of hers are flashing a weird grey color, and now one hand is planted firmly on her small hip and the other hand is waving, without any particular pattern, all over the place.

"Do you have any idea how many girls are in that one room right now wishing they were in my place with the chance I have to nail this part down? No, you have no idea. You have no idea that every girl in there with the exception of one thinks I have this in the bag. Why doesn't that one think the same thing? ...because she thinks she has just as good a shot at this as I do. Does she? Not until you pulled this little stupid stunt; now she might be able to grab the brass ring just because *you* had to be so selfish and stupid."

I'm calming down now, but not enough to just walk away without that last little stab that lets Morgan know she can't treat me like trash...without letting her know that I am my own man, and nobody is going to change that.

"I understand about your job, Morgan. I understand what you've worked for all of these years because I'm doing the same thing. I even understand why you're furious with me right now. But what I don't understand is how you never make any sacrifices for us anymore, and you no longer seem interested in me at all...in what is happening in my life. You can cancel on me at a moment's notice, and it doesn't even phase you. You know that we only meet every other week, and for the last three, now four times that I've come, we haven't even laid eyes on each other at all, and you never even ask one question anymore about how I'm doing...what I'm doing, or where I'm doing it." I take a deep breath, and both of us just stare at each, me with my hands on my hips and her with arms folded in front of her. Both of us are wondering what to say next that will make any difference. Finally, I decide to tell her what I have wanted to tell her, in person, since February.

"Since I won't see you later, and I will probably leave tonight, I'll let you in on a little something now. I had planned a big celebratory dinner for us tonight with reservations, candlelight, roses, everything... the works.

"Celebratory?"

"Yes. I passed the bar on my first attempt in February, but I wanted to share that with you in person….not over the phone…not in a cold hallway…so I've kept it to myself trying to have a special weekend just the two us celebrating together. That, as you know, never happened. So, I'll tell you now, out here, with you anxious to get back to your group. You are looking at, arguing with, and basically blowing off *Attorney* Derek Chase Wellington, III. I have joined Brollen and Brollen Law."

I see her eyes soften and a glimmer of excitement, but nothing like the excitement she would have expressed a year ago. That kind of expression is, without a doubt, missing.

"Wow! Derek, I *am* really proud of you, even if you don't believe me right now, but I have always known that you would be successful….a Defense Attorney…that's great!"

We are both calm now, and I take Morgan in my arms. Outside of her dance studio, she puts her arms around my neck and pulls me to her and our lips meet. It is a sweet kiss, but nothing like what I had expected for this weekend.

I touch my baby's beautiful face, and I lean down and passionately kiss her this time.

"Babe, I hope I didn't mess anything up for you, but please know that I love you, and I miss you so much it makes me a little crazy."

I pull her even closer to me and hold her tightly for a brief moment. "Take care, and I'm sure we'll be in touch soon."

I take her hands in mine, and do what we have done more times than I can count. Looking into each other's eyes, we share our special little hand squeeze that simply says, "I love you." I bend over and kiss her forehead. With that, I quietly leave the building, disappointed, and drive back to the airport.

Chapter 2

EYES WIDE OPEN

~Time, that old mystical man, is ever fleeting,
altering life with each tick tock of his hand~

I won't lie. When I finally board the plane leaving Virginia to return to Cambridge, to Harvard, to all that I have known for the past seven years, I'm a wreck. Yes, the plane is crowded, I feel cramped and still damp from the heavy downpours of rain, and I don't even want to think about the lay over for three hours, but none of this is the source of my misery. For reasons known and unknown, I have this horrible sinking feeling. I know this weariness I sense is not all about what happened today with Morgan. It is more about my own heart sensing that the cruel tick tock of the clock is moving us on to other people, other places, other things and my Morgan is slowly but clearly slipping away. Time and distance have taken their toll, and somewhere in the depths of my heart and in the recesses of my mind, I am allowing myself to acknowledge, for the first time, what I have known for at least a year…that something drastic is changing in our relationship.

"Derek, maybe if you come back next week, that would be a better time for me. Right now, it's not." That's what she said to me on the phone, three weeks ago.

"I just have so many things to do right now that I wouldn't enjoy myself or relax." I got that one at least four times during the year. Now today has been no different. I guess today she was saying, *"give me another three weeks, Derek, then maybe, just maybe, I'll be able to fit you into my very busy schedule, Sucka!*

"Come on, Derek. I love you so much. Don't be mad." Now THAT one…that one, with those beautiful eyes looking up at me…that one has been her favorite…her mantra…and now those words, to me, are cold and reverberate in my mind like an echo at the top of some icy remote mountain. From the time that they were spoken until now, her words of rejection continue to take random and ruthless cuts at my very core, and what is left now is a heart with jagged edges. Just thinking about how many times in the past year she has pushed me aside for her career, her need to rest, her appointments to adjust costumes, choose costumes, take classes, exercise, attend extra practices…all of her many excuses burn in my mind now as I find my seat at the back of this crowded uncomfortable plane. Seated, isolation surrounds me, despite excited college students heading home, despite babies crying in their mothers' arms, despite the rattle of newspapers, or attendants checking for safety. I sit alone in my thoughts pondering

if any of Morgan's excuses are the real truth. The lawyer in me profoundly doubts it, and that makes a deeper cut in my heart.

Regardless of the fact that the overweight man on one side of me is already snoring loudly, and I can smell the staleness of his breath, and the slender redhead teenaged girl on the other side of me is frightened to death and grabbing my knee every time the plane shakes a little, I am still in my own microcosm with this sinking feeling of pain. I'm thinking about how I saw Morgan today when I opened the door to the studio...beautiful and graceful, leaping in the air like a bird in flight, but mostly I see in my mind's eye the immediate and profound change in her eyes when she sees me at the door. The look is not that of my old Morgan...the one who runs to me smiling and grabs me around my waist like always...the one whose eyes never seem to lose the little sparkle that is just for me whenever I enter her presence... the one who throws back her head and laughs at the corniest of my jokes, but mostly the one who cannot wait to hold me, kiss me, make love to me, and lay cuddling in my arms for hours. That Morgan is not the one I met today. Perhaps the impact of this realization is hitting me hard now because on the other four or five trips, we never connected; therefore, I could continue to deny the truth that, for months, never stopped staring me in the face. Today, however, is very different. Today our eyes did meet, our bodies did touch, and in those few moments, there is this unspoken, palpable sense of distance that stands between us; I know that we both sense it, feel it, but we both leave the words unspoken that will touch it and make it far too real.... the words that would bring to unbearable life the reality that time, distance, and different directions in life have all cut into Security; Security stands now with its back turned to us, introducing Reality, a reality completely separated from Dreams and Desires of the past. Sitting here on this plane filled with people, I am sad and detached with my heart wrapping itself in knots at this near death experience.

The three-hour layover is a blur to me. People passing, the noise of idle chatter, the calls for boarding, the smells of travel all escape me on this return trip. What does not escape is the silence of the cell phone in my hand. I keep waiting to see Morgan's smiling face appear on the screen to just say hi or that she's sorry we couldn't meet, or that she does miss me, or that she wishes I could have stayed longer. I so desperately want to hear her voice filled with pride for my success, but mostly I want to hear that the man who lifts her everyday in dance… the one who touches her body to musical strands is just a partner and no more….something…anything to say she still loves and cares about me, but the phone remains dark and undisturbed from her like it has for months. I dial her number six times during the wait, but to no avail. The last call is just to hear her voice again, to hear that message that use to make me smile because it is so Morgan: *Dance to the beat, and catch me on the fly. Later.*

Back at Harvard, I turn the key in the lock and enter my house. Toc…toc…toc…the steady drip of a faucet that should have been fixed seven years ago does not fail to greet me. Its sound is the only one I hear, and immediately loneliness floods me. It is very dark, and there is no expectation of company here since my housemate, Zack, has been back home in New York now for quite a while. I snap on the lights, drop my overnight bag at the door, flop down on my worn out sofa and let the hurt envelop me. It wraps itself around me like a quilt with no pattern, no design and no warmth. Despite my efforts to stop them, tears sting my eyes.

"I lost her," I utter to myself in the quietness, and while my sound is barely audible, the words take flight and launch life to loss.

I pull my cell phone from my pocket and check it again to see if I missed a call, and there is nothing but the time staring back at me. I see it is late, but sleep evades me. I sit thinking about another time…a time when Morgan was everything to me, and I was everything to her…. a time filled with laughter, and anticipation for the future when we would have our beautiful house with the picket fence, a dog, and five kids to drive us joyfully insane. Well, anyway, that was my dream. Hers has always been slightly different especially about the five kids, but we were always able to meet each other somewhere in the middle, merge our dreams, and seal the future with a kiss, a hug, and a smile. No more. The distance has taken its toll, and now we are moving in vastly different directions. I am leaving in a day or two for New York to visit Zack and to just stop for the summer before moving back to Virginia and starting my career with *Brollen and Brollen Law*. Morgan is more than likely going to be the star in a long running performance with her dance company which will require a little travel, but a lot of time and dedication. We will again live close to each other, but distance will not be the issue, and sitting here on my beat up sofa, I know that is a truth I have refused to accept until today.

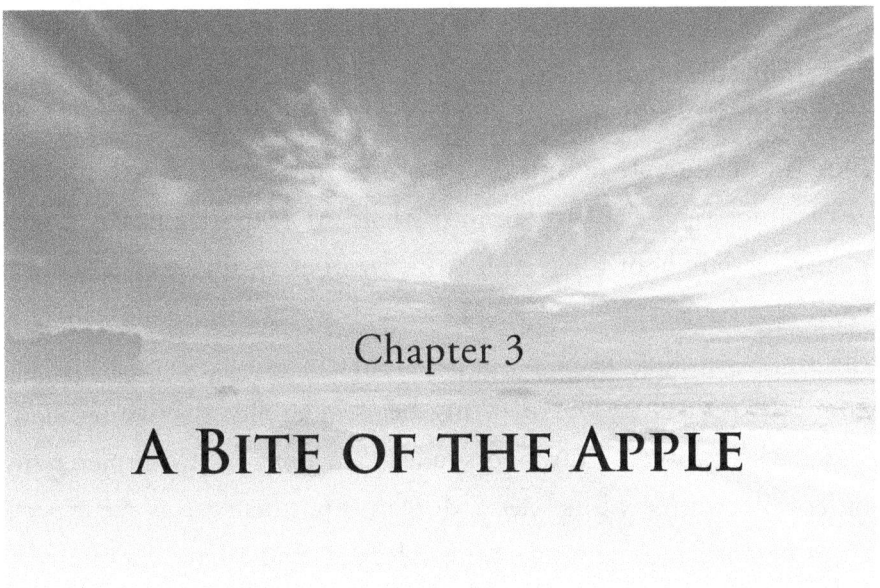

Chapter 3

A BITE OF THE APPLE

~Enjoy today, and take advantage of its offerings,
for there is no promise of tomorrow~

The sights, sounds, and smells of New York City never disappoint. The ride from the airport to my hotel captures the hustle and bustle of the city even at the late hour of my arrival. The lights that illuminate the night and the skyscrapers that seem to touch the sky are as alluring to me now as they were the very first time I experienced the energy and life of this captivating place that never sleeps. I lean over looking out of the cab window at the city's exuberance, watch the multitude of colorful lighted ads whiz pass, hear the honking of horns and the expletives of impatient drivers, and inhale the smell of my passion…New York pizza.

At the door of my hotel, the bellman, almost sparkling in brass and immaculate attire, snaps to open doors, take luggage, and make me feel like I am the most important person on earth. My penthouse suite is unbelievably beautiful, and every amenity you can think of is at my fingertips. The view from my balcony is spectacular. A multiplicity of stars light a navy blue sky creating an undeniable natural wonder. I have everything anyone would ever want, but still there is this sinking feeling in the pit of my stomach, and the ever-tightening knot that refuses to loosen in my heart. The city is bursting at its seams with people, sights, and sounds, but none of it can pierce my inner isolation…my loneliness. Morgan is not here nor is she expected to come. I look around at the splendor, and I have no one with whom to share this with me. I have been graduated at the top of my Harvard Law Class, passed the bar with one attempt, and looking forward to practicing law in Virginia. Yes, my parents are proud, and my friends wish the best for me, but the person who means so much to me…the person who has shared every moment of importance with me since I can remember is missing…missing from this room, missing from my arms, but definitely not yet missing from my heart. I dial her number once again, my fifth time today, and I get the same sassy message that no longer makes me smile. I feel the anger rising in my chest, but at this point hurt overcomes anger, and I flop on the bed, kick off my shoes, rest my arms on my forehead, and stare at the ceiling. After what seems like an eternity, I come to the awareness that I am in the same position and wonder if I have gotten any sleep or if I have done what I think I've done…stared, almost void of motion, at this soft white ceiling for more than an hour.

I feel exhausted, but I will myself off of the bed, open the draperies and let the morning light flood the room. I shower, pull my hair back in a knot, and dress in a gray three piece suit with a black shirt and gray and black striped tie. I get a cab to the only revolving restaurant in New York City, grab a newspaper from the rack at the entrance of the dining room and wait to be escorted to my table. The panoramic view is unbelievable. The skyline, and the miniature people below make me smile for a second. When my phone rings, I'm almost under a New York spell, and I think I fail to hear it on its first ring.

"Morgan?" My voice is anxious, and I feel my heart skip a beat.

"You wish, lover boy. I see you're still dreaming." The chuckle at the other end of the phone is so familiar. I cannot tell you how many times in the course of seven years I have heard that teasing voice and seen that quick smile cross my housemate's lips.

"What's up, Zee?...been a minute. An immediate grin spreads across my face, and I am genuinely happy to hear his voice.

"I can't call it. It is what it is. How long have you been here?"

"Hmm, couple of hours, I guess. I got in late."

"What's the plan?"

Zee always needs a plan. Nothing changes with him. He is as steady as a rock, but with him, you have to have a plan.

"You're the New Yorker. How do I know?"

"I got you, man. Actually, I'm almost at the hotel. Where are you?"

"Having a little brunch on your dime," I laugh.

"That's cool. Dinner will cost more so that's on you. You on the roof top?"

"Hmm…Not exactly," I laugh. It's a *classy* revolving *dining room* at the top of the hotel….*very* classy. I know you've never been here." We both laugh and relax in that old familiar way we love to tease each other.

"Oh, you think I haven't been there, huh?" He smirks. "Well, actually, I know *exactly* where you are. I'll see you in a sec."

The phone goes dead, but not before I can detect that slight air of insecurity that always seems to sneak into Zack's demeanor when he is around me; however, despite that little flaw in his character, in a few minutes I see who I think is my friend for life. Zack has passed the New York Bar, gotten a job on Wall Street and is now already looking like one of the Wall Street boys. Heads turn, and he stops the room standing in the doorway, scanning the area and exuding success, confidence, and narcissism. I see him in his three -piece black suit, matching tie, diamond cuff links, Rolex watch, baldhead, and that winning smile that can sell you anything. He is letting what he calls his baby browns scan the room, and I smile at my ostentatious friend, as he makes his way over to me. Of course, eyes follow him, and I wonder to myself how many people are thinking that this is the Hip Hop artist and movie star, Common, about to sit at my table. That mistake almost happens on a daily basis, and we have laughed about it for years. Based on looks alone, the two could be identical twins. When he gets to me, I stand immediately, and we greet each other like long-lost brothers.

"Dag, man! You're sharper than a tack. What's up, Zee?"

"Nothing to it, Bro, but to do it. I can't call it. You just getting back from Morgan?"

I take a deep breath, slightly shake my head no and look my friend directly in the eyes as we take our seats. "I don't know what's going on with that, man." I pause. "I don't want to talk about it."

"Hmm. You two break up?"

"See, like I've told you a million times over seven years. You don't listen. What part of I don't want to talk about this don't you understand?"

"Ah, the part that says, "I don't want to talk about this. Come on man, this is me. What's up, D?"

"I don't know. Lately, every time I go to see the girl, she's too busy to give me the time of day." I swipe my hand over my mouth and look directly at Zack.

"This mess hurts, man. I mean, I don't know what happened."

"Is she with somebody else?"

I take an exhausting breath and exhale loudly.

"I don't think so. Unless…" I stop, shake my head, and slightly bite down on my bottom lip because I don't want the words to come out of my mouth. The thought is too real, but Zack won't let it go.

"Unless what?"

I sit back in my seat and feel the weariness take over my body again…I feel the sadness envelop me, and I see that inevitable Reality staring me in the face. I drop my eyes to the tablecloth and rub my thumb across its smoothness.

"Unless she's having a fling with her dance partner, Peter."

"Peter?" His voice is almost too loud, and he quickly leans in to me, and it startles me a bit.

"Come on, man," he chuckles at the end of each word and sits back in his seat.

He moves back in closer to me and quiets his voice. "Huh! You can guess better than that. She wouldn't be interested in him."

"How you know? You don't even know her or Peter," I respond with some irritation.

Zack has one finger covering his lips, but I can still sense the sarcasm in his smile. He sits back in his seat and looks at me with this odd quizzical stare.

"You think Peter, huh?...a dancer."

"Man, I don't know. Just drop it."

He is already doing what Zack does best...irritate me.

Somewhere between the conversation, the mesmerizing elegance of our surroundings, and the pleasure of just being together again, we enjoy our Sunday brunch. We have a lot more to catch up on since we haven't seen each other in over four months.

As I expect, Zack has the week mapped out. We are scheduled to bar hop at night, go to a couple of late night shows, and hit the casinos in Atlantic City during the day since he knows how good I am at Black Jack. Leave it up to Zee to find a way to make money and spend as little of his as possible.

After breakfast, in the parking garage, I see for the first time the success that my Bro has already attained. I hear the squawk of the car to open the doors, and then I see the lights flash on one of the most beautiful vehicles I have ever laid my eyes on. It is a white convertible 911 Carrera S Cabriolet Porsche with a black hood.

"Wow, Zee! Man, this is awesome! How long have you had this little beauty?" I ask as I walk around the side to look at this work of art. It is low, wide and has an elegance about it that personifies sophistication. It is any man's crazy dream.

"…just got it last week, and I'll be honest with you. When I drove off the lot, I was more nervous than I was taking my driver's test at 16."

We laugh and he opens the hood so that we can examine the inside more closely, and he demonstrates an acute knowledge of every nook and cranny. The car oozes the idea of money and looking at Zack now standing on the outside showing me every detail with pride, I see him in the corner of my mind in our little apartment hunched over his books and papers determining and willing this dream to come true. He has moved a long way from the three- room house that suffocated him as a child, angered him as a teen, and catapulted him into success as a young adult.

Inside, the new smell of black leather upholster is calming and the quietness is unbelievable. As we pull out into traffic I can tell that the pick up is amazing, and I experience one of the smoothest rides I have ever had in my life. The trip to Atlantic City is fun. We reminisce about a thousand different things, and laugh at ourselves. We talk about all the crazy things that have happened to us in the course of our college years together. I talk specifically about how hard it is to actually get to know Zack, and how sometimes I still feel like he is a mystery man to me. He talks about how I worry and analyze everything and everybody, and how I definitely always have to solve a problem before I can move on. All of it is true to some extent, but re-gardless of our personal idiosyncrasies and some difficulties over time, I feel that we love each other like brothers.

At the casino, I start out feeling lucky at the Black Jack table, and I am right. Zee plays around with the slot machines and hangs around me for most of the day watching my skills at the table. I enjoy watch-ing the different styles of players, the sounds of the chips falling, the roulette wheel, the callers and the general smells that come with min-gling perfumes, colognes, money, and casino furniture. My winnings are unbelievable, and I'm exhilarated with a lot of new money in my pocket, my "brother" by my side, and the excitement of the summer to do whatever I want.

"Wow! It's hard to believe…no more classes, no more exams, no more stress to read and comprehend an inordinate number of books and textbook cases in a few hours with no sleep. There are no more interviews, applications, networking, or trying to decide which firm best fits me. It's all done, and I rejoice looking over at Zack. The idea is sheer joy.

Zack looks at me with a slight smile curling his lips. "As hard as it may be to believe that I've made it, I have. You? It was just what was going to be.…a certainty.…but me? Wow!…a very long shot.… passing the bar on the first try…incredible. I could have gone either way, D."

His words flow out slowly. Memory is interfering when he flashes a look at me.

"Sometimes…in the middle of the night, I still pinch myself."

Zack's eyes are far away from the road we are traveling, and I can tell that he is back in time remembering scenes, voices, and people that he may or may not want to forget.

At that moment the mood is serious, and we glance at each other knowing some secrets, some moments of joy, some hours of sorrow, patches of anger from misunderstandings, points of confusion, encouragement, and even pain. They all bind us together forever in this strange brotherhood.

I recline my seat, lay my head back and let the wind free me from stress, sadness, loneliness, Morgan, and every other negative thing that has found its way into my body in the last few days. I feel myself sink down into the plushness of these expensive seats, and allow sleep to take over my aching body. In a short time, we enter the city, and run into lots of traffic jams that finally clear. If we hurry, there is still ample time to shower, dress, have dinner and get to the late comedy shows. I'm awake now, and we're laughing, joking, and just feeling the beauty of the day when I hear a blood curling scream coming from the depths of Zack's being. It's a voice totally out of control.

"Whoaaaaaaa!" In a split second, time alters, and we are in slow motion. Zee is fighting the wheel with every fiber of his being, and while time stops, I see every twist and turn his body makes. Simultaneously, out of the corner of my eye, I see death...a red car has jumped the medium, is airborne and careening backward like a feather precariously carried on the wind; it is floating toward me....then the crash. I hear the crush of metal, the breaking of glass, and the scream that may have come from me; I feel the sudden power of airbags, the sharp pains everywhere in my body, but in the midst of this chaos, there is an unnatural hush. In the still sounds of silence, there is nothing but blackness.

Chapter 4

IN THE THRALLS OF TRUTH

~Betrayal sucks the life out of Promise~

Somewhere in this tunnel, I hear a humming sound, a ticking clicking noise, something dripping, and the very soft whisper of someone familiar. I am confused, and I want to open my eyes but sleep won't allow it. My head is aching like crazy. It feels heavy, and I can barely move it if I can move it at all. I feel someone slightly elevate my arm, and I feel a cool metal thing and something squeezing my biceps, but my eyes remain closed, and my mind is in a fog even though I'm trying so hard to concentrate and will myself awake.

I smell her perfume, and I know that it's Morgan. Morgan is here. I want to talk with her. I want to see her. My breathing is coming fast now, and I'm excited. Why can't I open my eyes? Come on. Open. I hear her now, and I hear Zack. They are both here. I force myself to relax a moment, and I try to take a deep breath. Am I dreaming one of those too real dreams, and when I wake will it all be just a crazy nightmare? I'm nervous. The squeezing thing is gone now and so is the cool metal, but the voices are still here and the perfume is closer... stronger. My eyes barely open briefly, but in those moments I see a blur of Zack too close to Morgan who is dressed in blue, her favorite color. His arms are around her waist, and I see him kiss her, and I see her slightly push away, too late to miss the kiss. There are voices in the tunnel, and the sound is weird...muffled.

"Zack, behave yourself. Derek is right there." The words come out like slow motion.

"Yeah, but he's not awake. You didn't push me away in V A." Zack is swaying with her and holding her at her waist in blue.

When did he go to Virginia? How does he know my Morgan? Why is he holding her at her waist? Where am I? I don't think I'm dreaming, but this is confusing me.

"I should have pushed you away." Morgan is leaning back looking at him and swaying with him to a private rhythm. My eyes close again.

I hear Morgan through the fog in the tunnel, and she is laughing in his arms.

"Should have, could have, would have, but didn't," Zack teases.

I hear the giggle that is so familiar to me, and the sly cool chuckle that I've known for all of my adult life.

"You had a good time, didn't you, girl? I taught you some new tricks....too advanced for your Derek to try, right?"

"Let's just say that the two of you are very different, and leave it at that."

"Hmm…different. That's a good word for it, I guess," he chuckles.

"You left without saying goodbye, Zack."

"No need, Baby, because it wasn't. What we do is never going be goodbye. Just see you later."

I can't really open my eyes again, but with everything inside of me, I manage to make a sound. In a second, the perfume is almost on top of me mixed with familiar cologne that I recognize even in my confusion.

"Derek? Derek? Can you hear me, Babe?"

"D. Open your eyes, man."

They are both hovering over me, and I can feel their hands on me in different places. Morgan's hand is on my face and Zack is touching my arm, the one that had the squeezing thing a moment ago. I want to open my eyes; I will open my eyes; I do open my eyes, and there she is…my Morgan, but I'm confused about why she was letting Zack kiss her. I stare at her. She has on the blue dress I saw in the dream. I know it wasn't a dream because she looks the same. How long has Zack known her? What happened to me? A thousand thoughts run like wild untamed horses through my brain kicking up dust so that I can't see clearly. I feel like I'm in a fog.

She's talking to me in the tunnel again, and I'm trying so hard to concentrate.

"He's awake, Zack. Get the nurse." Her voice sounds anxious.

I hear him scurry, and I see Morgan looking at me with tears in her eyes.

"Derek, you were in a car accident, and you have a concussion, but the doctors think you will be fine. You'll be fine, Babe. There is no bleeding in or around your brain and that's a very good thing."

I swallow. My mouth is dry, but I want to speak. It's hard. The nurse is here, and I see her wrapping my arm again. Now I know that she is taking my blood pressure. Zack is back. My eyes close again, and sleep takes me away in the midst of antiseptic smells and the squishy sounds of rubber soles on a tile floor.

The following days are a blur of doctors, nurses, X-rays, tests, and visits from my Mom and Dad who hover over me like I'm still an infant. Morgan and Zack have been with me throughout the week off and on and decide that my irritability is caused by the concussion. In reality, that is not true at all. They are the cause of my irritability. I can't get that kiss out of my mind. I can't get their words out of my mind. It all keeps playing like a repeated sad song. Despite it all, however, I'm feeling pretty good and have actually taken walks in a beautiful garden on the hospital grounds. I hear about how blessed I am that the car basically missed us, but it did manage to skirt my side and cause me to hit my head rather hard, but the airbags and seat belts saved me from greater injury. Zack escaped with a little soreness, but miraculously injury free. I remember none of that. While I am grateful for Morgan's and Zack's attention to me, I still ponder that first day I saw them in my hospital room. The problem for me is determining if it is real or just a dream.

My room is quiet and Mom and Dad have returned to Virginia earlier in the day, reassured by the doctors that I will be just fine. I expect to be discharged in a day or two. After what has become the routine of my hospital day, I feel tired, the room is quiet, and I doze off. When I wake, I wake slowly, and feel myself stretch a good stretch. I smell Morgan's loud perfume, and then I see her. Things are much clearer to me now. The dim light over my bed no longer hurts my eyes, the bags of fluid no longer hang from the pole that is still stationed close by, and there is Morgan sitting on the edge of the bed looking up at the TV on the wall. The sound is very low, but I still hear the laughter and see Lucy stuffing her mouth with candy pieces that rush pass her on a conveyor belt. I lightly touch Morgan's arm, and she turns quickly to see me staring back at her. At first, there are no words, just looks of love, and then she leans over and brushes my lips with hers.

"Hey, Babe.…feeling better, today?" It's almost a whisper.

I don't respond verbally at first, but I take her hand in mine and entwine our fingers.

"You're going to be all right, Babe. You know that, don't you? The doctors say you have to take it easy for a while, but you're going to be just fine."

She is staring at me…waiting for a response.

I'm playing with her fingers when I ask her.

"When was the last time you really took us seriously, Morgan?"

I am not looking at her. I am looking at the fingers that I have seen for a lifetime…the fingers I have seen change from childhood to young adult…the fingers that I know so well. I've seen them cut paper dolls, and balled in a fist above her head in a cheer. I've seen them gracefully tell her story of dance. I've seen them embrace me in love. I've seen them slowly, but with intent, come to my lips and touch them before the kiss that sends me into another world. I know these fingers. Now, I realize that I know the fingers better than I know her.

"There's never been a time when I wasn't serious about us, Derek. Why are you asking me that?"

Despite her efforts, I hear the caution in her voice and feel the instantaneous unbridled fear in her touch. I know she is gazing at me with those beautiful alluring green eyes....and me? Without looking, I know that long crinkled hair, falling just right, frames her bewitching face....so, I keep my eyes on the fingers, lest, even as an astute lawyer, I lose the battle of inquiry.

"I saw you." My voice is quiet.

"You saw me?"

"Yes."

"What do you mean you saw me?"

"With Zack...I saw you with Zack."

"He just picked me up from the airport, Derek, and brought me here, and sometimes he's here when I visit you."

She takes her hand from mine, and for the first time in the exchange, I look at her, knowing that she is trying to cover a lie... knowing now that she has secrets. I hear it in the voice attempting to disguise truth. I turn my head away and look at another part of the room. I don't want to see her tell me. I don't want to hear. I want to shut off the voices in my head telling me that this thing that we have

44

had for so long is probably over. I look back at her, and she looks puzzled.

"I woke up while Zack was kissing you. I saw his hands around your waist. I saw him lean over to kiss you, and I heard him talk about a trip to Virginia to see you. So, when did he come to see you?"

"Derek, we don't need to talk about anything like that now."

"I need to talk about that now. When did he come to see you, Morgan?…and don't lie to me."

"Derek…"

"When did he come to see you, Morgan?" I insist.

I am looking directly at her now, noticing the quick subtle flinching of her lips, the steady but slow blinking of her eyelids and the way she is slightly, almost unnoticeably, twisting and untwisting the fingers.

"It was the week you had your interviews with Fitchett and Law." He knew you would be in Arlington and wouldn't be coming to see me, so he showed up on my doorstep unannounced."

"…and you had time to see him?"

"Yes." Her answer is a whisper. I barely hear it.

"No rehearsals…no practices…no classes…no bone tiredness that week? Wow! Zack's a lucky man."

"Derek, it's not what you think."

"It may not be, Morgan. I don't really know what I think. I'm thinking maybe you're messing with my best friend."

She starts to interrupt me, but I keep on.

"Knowing Zack, I'm thinking maybe he took advantage of you. I'm thinking maybe you betrayed me…that you've been trying to tell me for a while that it's over. I don't know what I'm thinking, but I can tell you this: I don't like it. I don't like it, Morgan. It hurts. You think this hurts."

I point to my head.

"No, this hurts."

I point to my heart.

She turns away, and stops looking at me. Her concentration seems to be on her fingers more than on me.

"It's not what it looks like, Derek."

"Well, I saw you kiss him…"

"No," she interrupts emphatically. "You saw him kiss me."

"…minor technicality…you two were kissing. I even remember the swaying back and forth in each other's arms. My concussion didn't make me not see that, nor is it making me not remember that."

"Well, I still say it's not what you think. That day was very hard for me. When I first got the call, I was scared to death that you wouldn't be all right. When I got here, Zack met me at the airport and drove me to the hospital to see you. You were a mess, Derek. You were out cold, and the doctors didn't know if or when you might wake up. They didn't know what damage had been done, and I was scared. Zack was just comforting me, that's all."

"And was he comforting you the week he spent in Virginia?"

"He didn't spend a week."

"A week...a day...an hour.... It doesn't matter, Morgan. You two were together behind my back, and you never would have told me if this had not happened. My voice is a little loud. I am extremely upset, and my head starts to hurt again.

Her mouth is pouty, and I see the tears on her cheeks. I want to pull her to me and tell her that I still love her so much, that I want things to be the way they used to be, that everything is all right, but I can't because everything isn't all right. It is far from all right with me. How many times can I let her keep hurting me, and I let it be all right?

"Morgan, I know Zack. I know him very well, and I know his capabilities. I learned a long time ago about his insecurities, his anger, his will to get back at the world, and that he wants everything that I have and have ever had."

I take her hands in mine again, and I look at the tears staining her face.

"Babe, with all that I know about him, and it's a lot, I have to know first that I can trust *you,* and right now, I don't think that I can. I saw you playing in his arms. I heard your words, and I heard his."

I see the tears escape the well of her gorgeous eyes, and my thumbs wipe them away. She takes my hands from her face and brushes them with a kiss.

"All I can say, Derek, is it didn't mean anything. When he came to Virginia, he spent one night at a hotel some place, and he took me out to dinner. Yes, he tried to kiss me goodnight at the door, and he asked to come in, but I said no to both and he left. That's it."

She's lying. I heard them, and I remember the words…"should have…could have…would have, but didn't…" I feel my own tears now stinging my eyes and this intense ache in my chest. I take a deep breath.

"My girl and my best friend…behind my back. That's unacceptable, Morgan. I think…"

There is a pregnant pause, and I take another deep breath.

"I think it's all right…if you go back to Virginia now. I'll be fine."

"Derek…"

"Morgan, I'll be fine."

Chapter 5

DIFFERENT WORLDS

~While experiences may differ, the common desire of the heart
for all is a perfect match~

Being back at the hotel, I feel displaced. It's not home. It's not even close to home, but I'm not ready to leave for Virginia. I still need my time, and I think I need it more now than ever. Most of my bags are still at the door, and the room is as I left it. I go out on the balcony and look out at a splendid day, and I have no idea what I plan to do in it. I think of Morgan, and I know that without the accident she would never have been here, and now after the accident and after the incident, I have sent her away...for good?...I don't know. What I do know is that I love her.

I look out at the city below me, but I really see none of it. My thoughts close off my present, and I see only our past. In my mind's eye, clearly I see our childhood, our first dance, football games, the prom, and the last day we lived on the same street. Hmm, the last day we lived on the same street...that thought sparks an indelible memory. I take out my wallet and move aside the money. I see it. I pull out an old folded piece of paper that has seven years of wear and tear...seven years of taking it out...seven years of unfolding and reading it again and again...seven years of putting it back in its rightful place in whatever wallet I have at the time. I unfold it again, carefully now not to make another tear. It is special, and somewhere in my mind and heart, I know that it always will be. I read:

My Derek

It was high school when you stopped my heart, baby.

As kids, we played running games in our backyards,

And tried piano and violin together,

But high school was when you stopped my heart.

One day, you entered a room and somehow I really noticed *YOU,*

And when I did, the world, for a second, stood still.

In that special silent moment,

My eyes requested a kiss.

You looked at me with questions,

Then, in agreement, bent your face to mine,
and our lips met for the first time.

Now, your eyes catch and hold mine in a majestic gaze.

You charm me, love me, and help me trust the world.

You reside in my heart with purity, an undeniable authenticity.

Our love is an exquisite kaleidoscope of vast shapes,
colors, and views,

And even here, in the language of poetry,
words elude the essence of our bond.

Today is sad. We part for places far from one another.

This is a defining moment, but with hopes and prayers
I beg it never be our definition.

I know that if I am blessed, I will capture your heart and hold it,
and you will keep mine secure for an eternity.

With All My Love,

Your Morgan

"Wow. What have I lost?" I muse. My mind is a barrage of flashbacks when I hear a loud knock on the door, and I know exactly who it is. Silently, I ask myself if I'm ready to do this. Am I strong enough to do this now? The knock comes again, and I have little choice. I open the door.

"Why didn't you call me to pick you up?"

Zack pushes past me, and then turns around with hands on hips to look at me still at the door. I close it quietly and walk over to face him.

"Why did you do it, man?" I try to ask as calmly as I can, recognizing that I just brought my woozy head home. At the question, Zack turns away, puts his hand to his mouth like he does whenever he's nervous and cautious, then turns back looking directly at me. His eyes tell me that he knows exactly what I'm asking.

"Huh. The short answer to that, Bro, is because I could."

He moves away and looks out of the window.

"You know that saying, Zack, 'you can take the boy out of the country, but you can't take the country out of the boy?'" I ask looking at the back of him.

"Huh."

He turns to face me.

"Harvard can't change my bad behavior? Is that what you trying to say, D?" His grin is sly, and I see that evil glint in his eyes that he gets every now and then...his victory grin.

"...Something like that. You know what Morgan means to me, Zack, and you may have ruined it for nothing, but a cheap shot. I know you don't love her."

I move over and sit on the sofa and just look at this man that I have spent seven years living with, seven years befriending, seven years trying to make him my brother...trying to make him see a different world.

He leaves the window and comes to sit beside me.

"Derek, you probably won't believe what I'm about to say, but I'll say it anyway. What I did has nothing to do with Morgan, and really, it has nothing to do with you. You never will understand me, D, no matter how hard you try, and you have tried hard. Likewise, I probably never will understand you. We are from two very different worlds."

"I've heard all of this, man. Remember our freshman year? You told me this when you hid one of my major essays so you could get a better grade than I might get. I don't need to hear it again."

"Well at least let me say this uninterrupted, and then you can say whatever

you want."

"I don't want to say anything else to you, Zack. I'm done talking to you and with you."

I shake my head because he is one arrogant, incredible jerk. First of all, he has invaded my space by coming here. Now, he wants me to sit here and listen to him expound on why he has betrayed me with a person he knows means the world to me, and then tell me to let him explain his betrayal without interruption. Unbelievable!

"Zack, do us both a huge favor, and just go, please."

"No, I want you to hear this, and then I'll go. I promise."

He pauses and seems thoughtful.

"I look at you and anything you have, D, I think you can have it again, no matter what. You have wealthy parents who have given you everything.

"Man, just get out! I don't want to hear this." My head is down. I can't even look at him.

"Admit it. You got the silver spoon, Bro, and you eat from it daily whether you want to face it or not. I'm not trying to say you don't work hard because you do. You work very hard. You earned every-thing in school that you got. It's just that if you didn't work hard, you wouldn't be at a loss. Look where you're living right now for at least two months…a suite in the Waldorf Towers, and you haven't worked a day yet….a trust fund? Huh! Man, I didn't even know what that was until I started paying attention to finances, and even then it was hard for me to believe that something like that really existed….that people put aside that kind of money when you're a baby. You see D, the difference between you and me is that you could lose everything today, and have something ten times better tomorrow. Me? Not so much. I'll always have to face my past, and deal with a family that could try the patience of God, a family trying to scheme everything I get my hands on, always fighting me, never looking out for me, showing up just to start trouble…their baby brother. I'm always in the protection mode, baby!…crouched down, ready to rumble."

Zack is back at the window now looking out at something that I'm sure is a blur to his real vision. He's looking behind the eyes remembering a different time and place and determined to move out of it no matter what it takes, no matter who he hurts or how many times he inflicts the pain because he still has pain. He has the misguided notion that if he can inflict enough pain on someone else then he will have much less, and it is beyond me at this point to tell him, yet again, that his theory does not work.

"Yep, I'm still running from my past, D…. the valedictorian of my high school class, the guy with a full ride to Harvard, the one who graduated at the top of his law class, lands a sweet gig on Wall Street and, the same guy who had to fight and scratch every day for a scrape of food, sneak and take a bath in the boys bathroom in elementary, middle and high school, sleep in a bed with four other siblings until I was twelve years old, and fight almost every single day coming home from school just to survive. That dichotomy, D, is who I am."

He turns around now and faces me.

"Yes, I've always been smart, and that attracted excellent teachers and put me in the best classes where most people said I didn't belong. I was smart enough to outsmart the system, the good part and the bad. I had to fight for everything I ever got, and it made me determined that no one will ever again beat me *at* anything or *with* anything."

His tone changes, and I hear a deep sadness. It's almost vulnerability, probably as close as he can come.

"I wasn't really trying to hurt you, D. I'm just always fighting to find out if I'm good enough...if I can beat everybody else at everything. You are the only person on earth I trust enough to be this honest with."

"See, Zack, you don't get it. I don't care anymore how honest you are with me, or what excuses you come up with this time. You always have a reason why you do something stupid. I'm tired...tired of your mess...tired of trying to get you to help yourself! I give up!

"Don't give up on me, D. You're really all I've got." His voice is distant...almost like he's not even in this room...almost like this is the last struggle before he goes off the cliff and succumbs to defeat.

"I have to Zack. You wear me out. Morgan is the last straw. For you to sneak off behind my back and see her, and then to seduce her is unforgivable. Then you sat in my face at the restaurant, seeing my confusion and pain knowing what you had done...knowing what you had taken from me. You sat there with that smirk on your face saying to yourself, *Fool, you think its Peter?* Huh! No wonder you were so smug. All you want to do is hurt me because you hurt. I'm tired, Zee. I can't do it anymore."

"I told you, D, I don't want to hurt you."

"Yes, you do…over and over and over again and every time is worse than the time before. Track your record, Zack. You started with stealing my classwork, then my college friends, tried to take away my reputation with my professors with your lies, and now the finale…my precious Morgan."

I can no longer stop the tears from moving down my face. I want to because he does not deserve to see them, but they're stubborn and won't stay put. I can tell that he feels every cut that he has inflicted on me. The words bring a certain reality to the situation, and he can't escape that pain because in his own warped way, he wants so desperately to love me as his real brother, and the words reveal how incapable that is for him. Now my words sound distant as if someone else is speaking them. My voice is low and the words come slowly almost like the two of us are in some hallucinogenic dream. I'm tired…very tired…exhausted.

"Zack, you have everything you need to be anything you want to be right now, but the odd thing is you can't accept your present because you can't escape your past. If only you could just bring your mind out of that dark alley…away from that stubborn force that wants to lock you in place cowering on your knees in the corner of that filthy kitchen while you face a monster with an ironing cord or a hot iron threating you."

Still seated on the sofa, I look up at him and meet his eyes and hold them.

"…but you can't. You can't seem to do that, and you won't get the help you need. So, you'll always be running as fast as the roaches you hate and the rats that still live in your nightmares. You're never going to stop screaming at night, Zack, no matter how high you climb because you can't let go of your horrible past no matter what else you do in your life. You want to take everybody else down with you, especially me, but you will never be able to accomplish that no matter what evil things you design because I believer deeply in One far greater than you, Bro…far greater than us all. He will never leave nor forsake me. He promised."

I stand up and move closer to him because the next thing I have to say, I really want him to hear this time even though I have said it to him different ways a thousand times over the seven years that I have known him. As of this moment, he has not heard my words, and this is possibly my last ditch effort at getting him to understand. I have come to the realization that maybe I'm not the one he can hear on this subject. Maybe there is someone else.

"You only seem to be able to answer to those demonic voices of your past. Never to the voice of God who continues to show you over and over and over what He can do for you, what He will do for you, and what He has already done for you. You're stubborn, Zack. You refuse to look into that theory no matter how many times I remind you of it. You can't seem to believe God. No, you're bound and determined to believe the old demons in your head, and I keep wondering why because they have done absolutely nothing for you for your entire life, except continue to hold you prisoner to their own insanity. Whatever is negative is their greatest reward, and you keep accepting what they offer you. So, it makes no sense to me why you continue to listen to them and act on their impulsivity; I don't get it."

He walks away now, back to the window, ashamed to face me with the tears burning his eyes.... the tears I've already seen coming to the surface. I talk to his back, now.

"You're going to keep on throwing it all away until there are no more chances, and, in your head, you'll still be living in that three-room house in a Harlem alley getting your beating everyday no matter how good you try to be. For me, your excuses have run out, partner. Maybe I was born with a silver spoon, and maybe you did have a hard time growing up, but at some point, Zack, common sense ought to tell you that you have to forget what is behind you and reach for what is right in front of you."

He turns and faces me.

"You can't seem to do that nor are you in a place where you can take full responsibility for your own actions. I'm not going to be that little boy for you anymore. I'm not going to let you transfer that hate...that hurt...to me anymore. I'm not going to let you keep holding the hot iron to my back. I'm not going to take the eternal beatings for you. I've done it long enough. Your excuses are now falling on deaf ears, Bro. What you've done to me now is unacceptable."

I turn away from him now and move over to stand near the window and look out on the sunshine in this day that cannot brighten the darkness in my heart. "I think I love Morgan more than I love myself."

I turn and face Zack, and look in his eyes.

"...and now you're ruined it, so I'm done. I need you to leave, and just so you're acutely cognizant of what I think of you...No, you're NOT good enough, and I don't think you ever will be."

"Come on, D. It doesn't have to be like that. I'm sorry, man. I'm really sorry."

He crosses the room and reaches to shake my hand, but in my fury and his surprise, I take him to the floor.

"Come on, man. Stop! I don't wanna hurt you, D."

In the tussle, I hear his shouted words. I hear his emphasis on the word hurt, but I pay him no attention. I land two hard punches to the left side of his face, and I immediately see the blood.

"This one is for me, and this one is for Morgan," I say through clenched teeth as I bang into his face. The licks are hard and hurt my fist.

In a flash, quicker than my mind can think, I am on the bottom, and. Zack is straddling me holding my hands above my head with one hand. His other arm rests heavily on my throat.

"Man, you don't want to do this. I don't want to do this. Morgan doesn't mean anything to me, and I don't mean anything to her. Nothing is ruined." He pauses and is still holding me down. "I'm gonna let you up now, but you better be cool. My reflexes react before my brain. You understand?" His words run through my mind… *crouched down, and ready to rumble."* I shake my head yes.

"You cool?"

…*ready to rumble*…I shake my head, yes as I see a little blood trickle from his cheek to my shirt.

Zack pats my face twice. The licks are almost slaps. He moves off of me, and pulls me to my feet.

"Your head is not ready for this, Bro. You need to be cool." He takes a white handkerchief from his pocket and wipes the blood from his face, and I notice that he checks his sweater to see if it's stained.

"Get out," I growl through my teeth. I want to scream at him, but my head is screaming back at me, and I don't have the strength to fight.

"I'm done with you, Zack."

I'm breathing hard, but I spring to the door, open it, hold on to the knob, and wait for his exit.

I see Zack take a deep breath. He looks at me and somewhere, beneath his surface, in the window of his eyes, I see, as clearly as the day, the little boy, scared, but ready to fight…sad, but defying tears to flow, helpless, but unable to ask for a hand. On the surface, the man is dressed in a dark blue shirt layered with a still immaculate white pull over V-Neck sweater, perfectly creased navy blue slacks, Italian soft black loafers and a sparkling diamond cut bracelet. The only flaws now are a tinge of blood coming from a small cut on the side of his left jaw and the tail of his navy blue shirt, no longer neatly tucked into his slacks, but rather peeking out from under his white sweater. Fused together, the man and the boy move reluctantly through the door, stop, turn, look directly at me, and one of them winks.

"Stay cool, Bro."

I say nothing in response. With force, I slam the door on the man I thought would always be my very best friend…my only brother.

—◊—

For the last two days, Morgan has been blowing up my phone, and I've ignored every call, but when it buzzes now, I decide to answer. The conversation is not good.

"Hi Derek....forgive me yet?" Her voice sounds cautious.

"Hi, and no."

"Do you think you can?"

"I don't know, Morgan. You've made me doubt you, and I've never doubted you before...not in all of these years."

"Nothing happened, Derek. How many times do I have to tell you that?"

"If Zack was involved, something happened. I know him, Morgan," I state emphatically.

"Maybe you only think you do."

"So now you want to run a second game on me, huh? Why can't you just admit the truth, Morgan? Lying makes it even worse."

"I'm not lying; you just need to stop being a lawyer for a minute."

"Oh, you're lying all right. I don't have to be a lawyer to know that because I know Zack, and he is all about winning. He doesn't stop until he does. He knew the outcome before he left home. If he had had any indication that you would reject him, he never would have gotten on the plane. It's as simple as that, Morgan. I know him; I know what he *can* do, and I know what he *will* do."

"Derek, I don't care what you think you know about Zack, and I don't care what you think happened. I'm telling you that nothing happened. I simply went to dinner with him. I just need you to believe me."

"Well, there's your problem. I don't. I just need you to tell the truth. There is no way that Zack Belford traveled on a plane all the way to Virginia, and stopped at just dinner." My voice is filled with disgust, anger, and impatience.

"Why can't you listen to reason?"

"Oh, Oh! It's me...I get it! Unreasonable me...I'm sorry...not reasonable when my girlfriend is secretly building a romantic relationship with my best friend for a year. Unreasonable when my girlfriend allows him to pay her a visit all the way to Virginia when he knows that I'm occupied trying to start my career so I can ask my girlfriend to become my wife....not reasonable when I wake up from a coma to see them together in each other's arms talking about would have, could have, should have, but didn't...unreasonable because I won't accept your lie? Oh, unreasonable me! I'm sorry."

"Derek, it wasn't like that, and for goodness sake, stop being dramatic. I'm not lying. That little visit didn't mean anything."

"Well Morgan, it did to me. It meant a lot and lest I fall back into dramatics, I got to go," I snap.

"Derek, don't. We need to talk about this."

"No. I need some time, Morgan. I'll...I'll talk to you later."

"You sure?"

"No. Bye."

I slam the phone down and look back to see if I'll have to pay hotel damages, but the phone seems all right. I look around the room and quickly decide that I can't stay here alone right now. I just want to feel better, and get prepared to start my career in a few months. I don't want to think about Morgan and her betrayal or Zack with all of his mess. I'm positive that Zack has been talking to Morgan for a while. I'm sure of it. I just don't know exactly how long. I also know he did not fly all the way to Virginia and leave without doing something, and he didn't fly there without some major encouragement because he refuses to fail at anything. Failure doesn't happen with him because he prepares for things…he plans everything.

To keep my imagination from running completely wild with no barriers, I decide to take a trip to the library to look over a few notes that I have from *Brollen and Brollen*….Oh, happy day! I sigh loudly. It's a sad state of affairs when you have to spend a Friday night in a strange city alone in a library, but I really have nothing else better to do than research the life of an alleged serial killer….so off I go.

After two hours of keeping my nose and eyes glued to my laptop, I glance up at the clock in front that reads 8:15. I let my eyes move from the clock and look straight in front of me, and that is the first time I see her face. She is looking at me, and our eyes meet. I quickly avert mine, and look back at my laptop, but not before noticing the allure of her gorgeous hazel eyes and beautiful dark brown hair. I take a few more notes, pretend to be very engaged in my work and look up again. She is wiggling a pen between her fingers and still staring straight at me. I look down again, and sneak a playful peek and see that her gaze has not moved. *I'll play the game.* Without taking my eyes from hers, I slowly pack up my things, put some books back on the shelf, and saunter over to her table. She is playful, flirtatious, fun, and exactly what I need at the moment. In addition to all of that, Arianna Channing is absolutely beautiful. Talking with her, I can barely believe how quickly I've relaxed. At one point in our conversation, I take the liberty of picking up her hand and planting a kiss on the back. I'm glad that she liked that. After about forty-five minutes of banter, I get the nerve to ask.

"There's a coffee shop down the street. Would you like to accompany me for a quick cup or two on a Friday evening, Miss Channing?" My voice is playfully formal.

She sits back in her seat, looks at me under eyed, and hides behind her hands twisting the pen around and around in circles.

"I don't know you," she giggles.

I lean over closer to her, lace my fingers at my chin, and look into her eyes.

"Well, let's see if we can solve that," I say in the sexiest voice that I can manage

without cracking a smile.

"I've been here in the city for about eight days. I'm staying in a hotel suite alone, haven't met anyone new, don't have any New York friends, and came over here to the library on a Friday night cause I had nothing else to do. How about that?"

"Well, I think that's pretty sad, and it almost makes me cry." She giggles at first, but then her laughter becomes hardy and a bit uncontrolled in this quiet place.

I fold my hands in front of me, get the most serious look I can muster on my face, and look directly into her beautiful eyes.

"I can see just how much it's tearing you up inside. Your sadness is absolutely overwhelming." I reach across the table and lightly draw circles around the back of her hand with one finger.

"So, what do you say? Will you go with me and maybe cheer me up in the process?"

She takes my hand in hers.

"I think you have just met your first brand new friend in the Big Apple; but we have to walk," she hastens. "I'm not getting in your car."

"That's fine," I say with a touch of sarcasm. I let a slow smile crawl across my face. "I don't have a car."

We both laugh, gather up our things and head down the street to the little coffee shop on the corner.

Inside, there is somewhat of a crowd. The lights are soft and the tables are small and inviting for two people. We find a table, order two Frappuccino blends, and begin, at first, to talk silly talk.

"So...what's a pretty girl like you doing all alone in a library on a Friday night?"

"It's an amazing thing! It's the exact same reason why a handsome lonely Virginian is at the same place on the same Friday night in the same old New York library. The difference is, he doesn't have a single friend," she laughs.

"Oh, but I do now. The pretty lady and the handsome gentleman have decided to hook up in a coffee shop, and play footie under the table. How about that?"

"Oh really? Does she know that this footie thing is in the bargain?"

"She does now."

"Did she agree to this or does the handsome Virginian just make up rules as he goes along?"

"…makes up rules as he goes along." We both burst out laughing.

"Well now…that may explain why he's friendless."

The laughter is contagious, and I play with her foot under the table, and she pretends to try to escape my little game.

Later the conversation becomes engaging and a little more serious. It's one of those times when you hit it off just right with a new person, and there's no problem discovering some of each other's dreams, desires, fears, and expectations. Our exchange is so easy that we find ourselves acting as if we have known each other for years. My biggest challenge is to keep Morgan out of the conversation, and I accomplish that with flying colors.

"So, Derek, when are you leaving for Virginia?"

"…in August, I guess. Recently, I bought a beach cottage, and I want to give myself time to settle into it before I really start my job in September. Actually, I'm doing a little work for the firm now, but it's not much. I asked for this time before starting, and they have been most gracious to let me have it. I've spent the last three months traveling to find just the right place for me. Now, that all the stress of being accepted by a firm that fits me is over, I'm tired, and just need a short break."

"It's so funny how we're practically doing the same thing. I've been studying in Paris for two years, and I came here about two weeks ago just to relax before I completely open my fashion house in September. I'm excited about it, but I need the rest…I need a vacation."

"So, when are you leaving?"

"In late August. That's what is so funny about our meeting. Both of us have finished our studies and are just about ready to embark on this great life adventure, but we both need a break for a while. I am here for the exact same reason that a handsome lonely Virginian is at the same place on the same Friday night in the same old New York library. The difference is, he only has one friend," She recites with mock seriousness.

"Wow! What a memory. I can't believe you can say that line all over again exactly like you said it before," I laugh and reach for her hand.

"I bet you could do that,' she smiles.

"Yes, I could, but lawyers get paid to know minute details."

"You'd probably be shocked at how many details haute couture requires. Just think, there's the face, the shape of the face, the eyes, the color of the eyes, the shape of the eyes, the mouth, the size of the mouth, and the clothes that have to accentuate these features, and the…"

"Yeah, I get the point," I interrupt.

It is a great night, a wonderful first meeting with lots of laughs, and a new friendship that screams *I don't want this night to end. I don't want to let you go.*

Around midnight, we see the shop owner sweeping up and putting chairs on top of tables. We finally notice that the crowded shop that we entered a few hours ago is empty except for the three of us. We pay our bill, leave, and I walk Arianna to her car. Under the blaring New York lights, she unlocks her door, and leans against it. She looks stunning with her long fishtail braid, those eyes that draw you in, the sexy skinny white jeans and heels that accent her long slender legs, and the sunny yellow tank that leaves her flat midriff exposed. She is a knockout, and I can't take my eyes off of her.

"Since you don't have a car, and I am your very first and only friend in the Big Apple, would you like a lift someplace, sir?" she asked with a sly smile.

"So, you're willing to get in a car with me now?" I grin.

"Yeah, but I'm driving."

"Hmm…" I slowly lick my lips. "The offer is tempting."

"Well, take it then." She laughs and playfully pokes me in my chest. "New York cabs are just not as good as this ride. I can promise you that."

"OK. You're on."

I feel comfortable in her silver convertible BMW as she pulls out of the park, lets the top down, and heads South to the hotel.

"This is a really nice night," I volunteer.

"Yep, it is, in more ways than one. You know I love to watch the stars at night. I have this place I visit sometimes where you can sit on a mountain of rocks and relax. The stars are so bright there that I always feel like I have to make a wish or say a prayer. It's like it would be criminal if I didn't. I always say it's my place to touch God's face."

"Hmm, sounds like a really beautiful and serene place because He is the Master Artist."

"It is beautiful. Too bad it's all the way in Virginia on the ocean. Otherwise, I'd take you there tonight, but too bad, new friend," she giggles.

"Well, since both of us are headed in that direction, you can take me another time."

"Now that sounds like a plan. We'll have to do that."

"Yes, we will."

I enjoy the ride in the warm night breeze, the sight of a bright moon overhead, and the white twinkling stars that seem to leave no room for the navy sky. I love the talk, the laughter, and most of all the company that has taken away my stress and left me feeling relaxed, serene, and happy. At the hotel, Arianna pulls into a park, turns off the motor, and shifts her position to look directly in my eyes.

"Well, Friend, you're home, and a nice expensive one to boot. You have excellent taste."

"Yes, I do, in homes and women."

A slight smile crosses her face, and I can tell that she doesn't want to leave me any more than I want to leave her. I am not exactly sure, but I think her eyes tell me that she is waiting for my next steps. My look is serious when I take her hand in mine, and look into her eyes.

"Will I see you again?"

She is silent for a moment, but she uses the moment to look in my eyes and down to my mouth. When she speaks, her voice is sexy, her words are slow, and slightly above a whisper as she finds my eyes again.

"Wild horses couldn't keep me away, Derek Willington. For some strange reason, I think we're going to be friends for life."

I feel my lips curl into a kind of sad smile. Morgan flashes across my mind for the first time in hours. I desperately want to kiss Arianna, and feel those beautiful full lips covering mine, and watch her pull back and look at me with those bewitching eyes wanting more of me, but I know I'm already confused about Morgan, and I don't want to

betray anyone in my confusion; therefore, instead of the kiss, instead of inviting this beautiful woman up to my suite for a nightcap, instead of gathering her into my arms and feeling the comfort of her embrace, I simply smile and say, "I think you're right....friends for life. I'll call you tomorrow."

Without another word, I open the car door, walk into my hotel, and ride the elevator to my suite at the top of the building with both Morgan and Arianna on my mind.

Chapter 6

MEETING A DREAM

*~Infatuation! Who do you think you are invading my stomach
with butterflies and my eyes with make-believe stars?
Infatuation! Who do you think you are? ~*

I roll over and glance at the clock. It's 9:10. I shift on to my back and stare at the ceiling, for a time, in deep thought. Arianna is still on my mind. She is so beautiful....tall, slender with curves in all the right places, and an obvious mixed racial blend that has turned out perfect. An involuntary slow smile crosses my lips. Impulsively, I reach for my cell on the nightstand, scroll to the number that she has given me and call. After three rings, I hear that unmistakably seductive voice.

"Well, hello, friend."

"Good Morning. Am I calling too early?"

I ease down into the covers and make myself more comfortable.

"No, not at all. I'm just coming back from my run."

"Really? I'm still in bed. I guess you would call me pretty lazy."

"No, not really. Aren't you on vacation?"

"I am. Listen, if you're not too busy, I was wondering if we could spend the day together."

"Now, that is what I call a very good idea. I would love to spend the day with you, Derek." Her voice is low and oozing a titillating allure.

"So, what time does our day start?" she asks.

"How fast can you get here?"

"Hmm…Anxious, are we?"

"Quite."

"I'd say about an hour."

"I have to wait a whole hour?" I chuckle. "Well, You know where I am. I'll meet you in the lobby in an hour."

"I'll be there."

I throw the covers back, dash in the shower and dress in black slacks, a silver belt, a black shirt, white sport coat, and black socks and shoes. Slicking back my shoulder length hair, I tie it in a knot, slap on a hint of my favorite cologne and head to the lobby. Downstairs, I wait and make casual conversation with different guests.

Out of the corner of my eye, I see my beautiful date across the room, and her very appearance electrifies me. I feel that thing that happens in my stomach, like butterflies taking flight. I'm surprised that they are there so fast, but I don't have time to think about that now. My eyes are almost popping out of my head. When I see her, it's like a movie in slow motion. She moves with grace and looks like a model in her silky one shoulder white blouse with an asymmetric hem. There is only one long flowing sleeve and her matching white silk slacks flow with her every movement. I see the red sparkling earrings, long necklace and perfectly matching bracelet adding that touch of color to accent those haunting eyes and beautiful smile.... then she reaches me.

"How do you do that?" I ask as she nears me.

"What?" Both her eyes and hands ask the question.

"...dazzle me like you do." While the voice is playful, my eyes, I am sure, speak another language and that is not lost on Arianna.

"Do I now? You're not so bad yourself, Mr. Wellington," she laughs and gives me a friendly hug. She breaks the embrace and looks up into my eyes.

"Now where are you about to take my dazzling self?" she grins.

"...Right here, actually, to brunch. I smile and hook my arm into hers and escort her into the dining room at the *Waldorf Towers*. The brunch is delicious, the presentation of the food adds a special touch, and this woman sitting across from me, in all honesty, is rocking my world every minute of my day!

"So...tell me...how is a woman as lovely as you, free...not engaged...not married? How is that?"

"Well, I could ask the same question of you. Here you are a handsome, charming, and successful Harvard man, obviously with at least a little money to throw away...not engaged...not married."

"Yes, you could ask me that, but I asked first." Immediately, Morgan flashes across my mind, and I push her away as quickly as she comes in focus. No time to risk a reaction to sadness and disappointment now.

"For the past two years, I've been studying in Paris, and I've tried to put most of my concentration on my career. As I told you last night, I just got back to the States two weeks ago to finish up some research and get some rest before starting my fashion house in Virginia. So, I haven't really had much time for dating or, you know, getting serious with anyone."

She fidgets telling me this, and the lawyer in me says it's not completely true...so I push.

"No French guys left behind pining away?"

She hesitates. "No, no French guys pining away at all."

"Hmm."

I notice that she conveniently omits the words "left behind" and concentrates on the "pining away" part. She seems a bit embarrassed now and looks down at her food and then away at the other diners. Her body language speaks volumes, which heightens my intrigue and provides momentum to my somewhat playful investigation.

"...and...now?" I realize I am walking too close to the edge, but I can't seem to help myself.

Arianna's smile is coquettish. "Why are you asking about *now*? Are you asking for yourself?"

"No." My answer is a bit too quick and a lie. "I'm just asking."

"Well, Derek, I'll answer that when you're asking because you *need* to know. Until then, let's just leave that blank."

The answer catches me off guard so I reach across the table and take her hand in mine hoping she won't notice my discomfort at her evasive answer.

"May I call you Ari?"

"I like that…it has a friendly ring to it."

"I like you, Ari. I like you a lot."

"I like you too, Derek, but that does not mean I'm going to sit here and play truth or dare with you. You like games, and I don't."

"I see."

"Let's be honest, Derek. You're a lawyer, and I'm sure a darn good one having been graduated from Harvard and already set up with a well-known law firm, so you're always digging around for some truth. Well, let me give you some so that we understand each other perfectly. If the time comes that you need to know all of my truths then I will not hesitate to tell them, but we will do this on a need to know basis, and right now, you don't need to know anymore than I'm willing to tell." She knows that she has gotten the upper hand, and has wiggled out of telling all of her secrets, but she laughs, and that lightens the mood.

We finish our brunch, and take a cab to the Guggenheim Museum. To avoid the long lines, I present two New York passes to the attendant, and we're free to enjoy this fantastic place.

"You have two passes? Why?"

"Well, I got them for my friend, Zack, and me. He was going to join me here, but something came up, and he couldn't make it."

"Oh, I see…His lost, my gain."

The day is outstanding and passes far too quickly. The architecture of the building and our discussions of Picasso, Van Gogh, Monet and others verify for both of us how much we have in common. We take our time enjoying the art, the surroundings, and each other.

"I absolutely love this Picasso piece, Derek."

"That's funny. It's my favorite."

"No, it's not," she laughs and hits me on my arm.

"It is…it most certainly is."

She runs behind me, and covers my eyes.

"What's the name of it, Derek?"

"Now that small slice of information momentarily slips my mind," I laugh. "Wait a minute. I got it. It's right on the tip of my tongue. It's ah…"

"An astute lawyer as yourself can't remember the name of your favorite art piece by a master artist? We could get a third grader to name this piece," she teases.

"Then I'm in an immediate need of a third grader. Let's see if one is available. There must be one handy that can refresh my vapid memory." I try looking around the room desperately searching for the third grader with her hands still covering my eyes.

We laugh, she uncovers my eyes, and grabs my hand to pull me away to another area.

"Why are we skipping all of these paintings?" I ask. "Are we going to look at another one of my favorite pieces?" I put my arm around her shoulder. "Take me, darling, to my favorite places. Lead the way. I'll bet they're all your favorites too. Copy cat!" I laugh.

"You are so silly." She grabs my hand hanging over her shoulder and begins to explain some of the new pieces as if I'm five years old.

"There's something about your voice that makes me want to say, 'yes, Mommy.'"

"Well don't." She hugs me and lets her mouth come close to my lips. "Let's see if this can stifle your Mommy thoughts."

"Yep, that does it immediately." I attempt to smack her lips with mine, but she moves quickly away and laughs at me. We are so easy with each other, and the day passes quickly. Together we just have a lot of plain unabashed fun.

Around four, we head back to Time Square where Ari dashes into a couple of stores to buy a few items, and we go back to the hotel where we freshen up, change clothes, and head down to the hotel parking garage.

Half way into the garage, Ari stops in her tracks.

"Did you lie to me last night, Derek?"

"Lie? No. Why?" The question startles me, and for a moment, I'm very serious.

"You said you didn't have a car."

"I don't really," I chuckle relieved. "I rented this one through the hotel just for tonight."

"Oh, I'm glad. I don't want to think that you would lie to me."

"I wouldn't." Morgan flashes again, but we are at the car, and I have something else to replace her face in my mind.

We reach the black CTS Cadillac with all of the bells and whistles and drive away to my surprise destination.

"Do you want to guess where we might be going?"

"You're funny, Derek. No, I don't want to guess. Surprise me. I like surprises."

"OK. A surprise it will be."

After a short time, we join a three- hour sightseeing cruise on the Hudson River and Manhattan Harbor. I have arranged for the Gold Preferred Package and a window seat so that we can really enjoy the breathtaking skyline of New York City at night and the best food they have to offer.

"Wow, Derek. You really know how to entertain a lady. This is awesome. For once in my life, I don't know what to say. You can ask anyone in my family. That has never happened before."

She laughs and I smile, but I can tell that she believes what she is saying. I pull out her chair for her to be seated, come around to my seat and marvel at what Ari has been able to do with a few quick purchases. The white pant ensemble she wore during the day is now the silk white pants, a tucked in silk white shell with lace at the top and a beautiful long sheer red flowing coat with splits on both sides. She is a sight to behold across the table from me. I reach over to hold her hand.

"I hope you enjoy every minute of this night, Ari. I certainly plan to."

We both look out at the stunning skyline and enjoy the commentary as we view the Statue of Liberty, the Chrysler, and the Empire State Building when we pass them. The food is superb, the music soothing, and they both put us in a mood for romance.

"I love this song."

"I'm hesitate to say that it's one of my favorites, but it's true this time," I say as I reach for her hand to join me on the dance floor.

"The first time ever I saw your face," she looks up and smiles at me.

"Yeah, you examined every inch of it: my eyes, my mouth, my hair."

"Well, I stared at you long enough." She leans back and looks at me with that cute smile she has when her lips spread and her eyes sparkle.

"It was a blessed night for me the first time I saw your face, Ari."

"Really?"

"Yes, really. I was very depressed when I saw you." *Now that was a slip up.*

"Why?"

I take a deep breath to give myself time to think of my answer.

"I don't know. I guess that's what sitting around in a hotel suite with no friends will do to you. I was kind of lonely."

"Well, Mr. Wellington, I'm glad I could liven things up for you."

"Me too."

I pull her close to me, and she comes willingly. She looks into my eyes, and I can tell that she accepts my words as truth. She smiles up at me, wraps her arms around my neck, and lays her head on my shoulder. The music takes us both away from the cruise, away from the tables and food, away from all of the other guests, and for a brief moment, we are the only two people on this small spot of the world, and like the song, I, too, feel "the earth move in my hand." I kiss the top of her head, and I feel her pull me closer to her as she and I sway to the music; I can feel it all binding us together. For three hours, we live almost in a fantasy world of beauty and romance, and when we take a picture together, for some reason, I instinctively know that the picture is a display of our future on some level.

At the end of the night, we return to the hotel, and I walk Ari to her car. Standing at the door, she looks up at me, and I bend my head to her, but she takes a small step back. I have this feeling that we both know we're moving fast…that there could be something with us more than a causal relationship, but I can't let that happen, and obviously she can't either. Not right now. I have to know for sure how I feel about Morgan, and maybe she has someone. I don't want to ask, and I don't. For some reason though, I need something from Ari, and I can sense that she needs something from me. I brush her lips lightly, and then straighten and look at her beautiful face. She pulls away, reaches up, and moves a loose strand of hair out of my eyes…a very intimate act.

"Derek?…What are we doing?"

"…becoming friends."

"What kind of friends?"

"…just friends."

"Well, just to clarify: I don't do the friends with benefits thing."

She moves out of my arms, opens her car door without taking her eyes from me, and gets in.

I take the few steps to the car door and lean over.

"I'll call you in the morning," I promise.

"I can't wait." There is a slight air of sarcasm in her voice.

"Are you upset about something?"

"Absolutely not. I just want you to understand what I do and what I don't do so that there is no misunderstanding if you spend a dime on me."

"That's not fair, Ari, but I got it. No friends with benefits."

"Right."

I close the door and watch her drive away leaving me feeling alone and a little weird about this last conversation. It is a bit cold and serious. That is the first time I've seen this side of my new friend.

Up in my room, I undress for bed. I feel a light headache, but that does not stop me from getting in bed and reaching for the phone.

"Hi, I thought you said you would call in the morning."

"I did and according to the clock here in my room, it's 1:00 a.m. Are you in bed?"

"Yes."

"Were you asleep?"

"No. Not yet. I have too much to think about," her voice teases.

"What are you thinking about?"

"You."

"What about me?"

"Your hair."

"My hair?"

"Yes, your hair…and definitely your eyes too….and then there's that mouth."

"Oh, is that good or bad?"

"Oh, that's *real* good," she giggles.

"Good." We both laugh remembering our first conversation almost verbatim.

"Good night, Derek."

"Good night, Ari. Dream of me," I quickly add.

"Do just friends dream about each other?"

"Sure, they do," I laugh.

"OK. Then I'll think about it.

"You do that."

I hear her giggle again, and the phone goes dead.

I feel much better about that ending conversation. I click off the lamp at my bedside, snuggle into a comfortable position, and I have no doubt in the world that Infatuation will visit both hearts tonight.

Chapter 7

GETTING TO KNOW YOU

~Nothing is more honorable than being true to oneself,
even at the risk of lost friendships~

Sometime during the night, my headache is no longer just a head-ache; it's a torture chamber. I move to a cooler part of the pillow and immediately see that that is not a good idea. The coolness is great, but the movement is definitely a no. I feel a little confused and that's frightening, but I steady my nerves and talk to myself.

"So, you should have taken your medicine yesterday," I mumble aloud. "You should not have done so many things."

I try again to go to sleep, but that, too, is frightening. Suppose I don't wake up. I take a deep breath and try to think of Ari and how beautiful she is, but the pain is stubborn and demands my attention.

I feel the heat off of my body and the perspiration soaking the sheets. Somewhere in the midst of my confusion, my fever, and my pain, God gives me grace, and I manage to sleep.

The buzz of my cell wakes me, and at first, I almost don't know where I am, but then I do and reach for the phone. I glance at the clock as I answer, and see that it is shortly past noon.

"Hi, Ari." I can hear that my voice is slow, weak, and sleepy.

"Hey! You sound like you're still in bed." Her voice is too loud for my head, and I pull the phone away from my ear.

"I am." I can barely get the two words out at first. I have no energy, and the pain is harsh.

"Why? Are you all right? You sound funny."

I am silent, trying to figure out exactly how to answer the question with the least amount of words.

"Derek, are you there? Are you all right?"

"No, I'm not. I have to…tell you something." My words are halting and slow.

Oh, Derek, don't tell me you're married."

I can hear the disgust in her voice. I want to laugh, but I don't dare risk that kind of pain.

"No, silly. I'm not…married. Right now, I'm sick. I should have told you…what happened to me recently."

"Well tell me now, and stop making me wait. You scare me."

"Friday night...when I first met you, I had just gotten...out of the hospital. I was there for...about three days...I think. I had...a car accident and a concussion...that knocked me out for a while."

"Derek!"

"Yesterday, I probably...did a bit too much and...the headache resurfaced...with a vengeance last night."

I can barely move my mouth so I'm talking through my teeth.

"So how are you now?"

I can hear the worry in her voice, and that is not at all what I want.

"I'm going to stay in bed today. As soon as I can get up, I'll take my medicine."

"When was the last time you took it?"

"Friday night when you brought me home.

"You didn't take any yesterday?"

"No. I wanted to be with you."

"Derek! I'm coming over."

Before I can say no, the phone goes dead, and my common sense makes me glad that she's on her way.

I doze off again, and when I wake, she is here. I remember I gave her my extra key when we changed clothes for the cruise. Both of us were in and out of the suite for different reasons, and I handed her a key to get in in case I was in the shower when she got back with the ice. I'm glad she has it. As soon as my eyes open, she is all over me asking questions without giving me a chance to answer any of them.

85

Are you all right? Should I get you to a hospital? Where is your medicine? Have you eaten anything? I manage to raise my hand, and she
stops, thank God.

"My medicine...is on the counter...in the bathroom." She goes to
get it, helps me sit up and hands the pill to me with a glass of water. I
take it, lie back down, and notice her beautiful face for the first time
since she came.

"Derek, do you want something to eat....maybe some chicken
noodle soup?" The words alone make me feel sick, and I shake my
head.

"I think you should eat something even if it's just a little."

She picks up the phone and calls room service and orders the
soup, and tells them its an emergency. The word soup makes me want
to throw up, but I don't have the energy to argue. She goes into the
bathroom and brings back a cool wet cloth for my forehead and puts
an additional pillow under my head and one under my feet. It feels
good to have her here. The soup arrives shortly, and I groan.

"I heard that. If your headache is still really bad after a half hour,
I'm going to get you back to the hospital. This doesn't sound like
anything to play with, Derek."

She comes over to the side of the bed.

"Can you sit up?"

"Yes."

"Just take a few sips of this soup, and I think you'll feel better."

"I think I'll feel better if you don't say 'soup.'"

"OK I won't say it if you eat it. Deal?

"Deal," I manage to repeat.

To my surprise, the soup is delicious. I guess I am hungry. I eat half of it, and I am actually feeling better.

"This is not how I want my new friend to see me. I think it might scare her away," I confess.

"Just try getting rid of me if you dare," she says as she checks my forehead for fever. "I think your fever broke." She smoothens my hair away from my face, and runs her hand down its length.

I think so too. The headache is almost gone. I get out of bed, head to the bathroom and decide to take a shower and put on a pair of gray jogging pants and matching tee. When I come back to the bedroom, Ari has spread the bed up neatly and is sitting in a nearby chair thumbing through a magazine.

"Feeling better?" she asks.

"Yeah a lot. Thank you so much. I was a mess when you came. I couldn't get up for the medicine, but when I took it, it really did do the trick."

I sit up on the bed with pillows at my back and look over at Ari. Her head is down looking in the magazine, and I realize that I'm staring, but I can't help myself. Gosh, she's lovely.

"Come sit with me, Ari." My voice is quiet, and I'm sure my eyes invite her.

She looks up from her magazine, and studies my eyes.

"No."

"No?"

"No. I'm not going to sit with you on your bed. Your eyes are talking, and I know exactly what they're saying. What did I tell you last night?"

"I don't get you." My voice has a tinge of irritation.

"I know you don't, but I think I'm pretty clear…no friends with benefits."

"You act like you like me. You act like you have fun with me, but then you put up this wall the minute I get close to anything intimate."

"You want me to come and sit with you on that bed, but where is that supposed to lead, Derek? What do you expect after I come over?"

"Why don't you come over here and see," I say in my most flirtatious voice.

"I can't take that chance. I asked you last night when you tried to kiss me, what are we doing. You said, 'we are becoming friends.' I agree with that, and to me, that doesn't mean intimacy. It doesn't mean I owe you any kisses, or hugs or special favors just because you take me out and show me a good time. Derek, I'm nobody's prostitute."

"Wow! Where did that come from? Have I ever treated you like a prostitute, Ari? Why are you so harsh when it comes to sex or a simple kiss? You got something weird in your background?"

"No, I wouldn't say weird, but I would say I have some experiences that make me cautious…very cautious. Some mistakes, Derek, are extremely hard to correct, and when you give the wrong impression, it's hard to change it back.…so, I've learned that you get it right from the beginning, and it saves a lot of future headaches. I think you ought to get to know me well enough to know what's in my background without speculating. I just want to send the right message this time."

"...this time?" I question.

"Yes, this time with you. I haven't always sent the right messages. Sometimes guys get confused, and think they own you....think they can dictate every minute of your life."

"Hmm. That sounds like you've had a rough time. So, what is the right message now?"

"Well, I want us to be sure about what we're doing and secure about our feelings before we start kissing and holding each other. That's the stuff that can get you hurt if it doesn't have any real meaning, and, simply put, I don't want to get hurt anymore.

"Neither do I."

"Well good. We understand each other. Derek, I don't even know if you have a girlfriend somewhere."

I am guarded now, and I don't want to talk about Morgan and Zack to her. I don't want her to know about the betrayal, so I say nothing. It's too embarrassing.

"I don't want any misconceptions, Derek. I don't want to be known as the other woman, and I want us to know for sure that intimacy means something significant to both of us if that is a direction we go in. Kissing is very important. It means something. It's not a passing greeting. To me it is the beginning of something very significant. If we don't view it that way, then we send mixed signals that cause pain, and I've had enough of that in my life."

"Have you, really?"

"Yes I have, really."

I get off the bed, and I take her in my arms carefully, and she lets me. We stand together quietly. The quietness is comfortable, and at first, there is no need for words.

"Stay...stay with me tonight, Ari."

"No, Derek."

"I don't understand why you can't stay," I whine, whispering in her ear, and I know it would sound sexy to most women, but not Ari.

"Stay and do what Derek? She pushes away...act like a tease? I'm not ready for a sexual relationship with you, and if I spend the night, that is what you will expect, and I know it. I don't know any other way to say this. I think we need to be sure about what we're doing. There's a big difference between lust and love. I'm not interested in lust. I'll be very honest and up front with you: I want the fairy tale, Baby. I want the Knight in shining armor who sweeps me off my feet, and that is all I'm willing to accept. I'm looking for the man who is willing to be patient with me and give me happiness. If you can't, then we'll just be friends. No kissing, no intimate hugs...just friends, and I can accept that if that's all we can give each other; you want to rush into this sexual thing, and I'm telling you as clearly as I possibly can, it's not going to happen. You are a handsome, intelligent, and attractive guy. Why are you so free? You may be trying to rebound with me for all I know, or have a secret love someplace."

I stare in Ari's eyes, but I immediately envision Morgan invade the space.

"We've known about each other for less than three days, and you think I should let you kiss me and hold me and probably even more. I want a man who will take care of my heart; I need more time.

"Ari, take all the time you want." My voice is irritated and resigned.

"Are you dismissing me? What does that mean?"

"It means what I'm saying. If our friendship develops into something more serious then so be it, if not, whatever..." I make no attempt to mask my anger at this point.

"I just want you to understand that I value myself, and because I do, I'm not going to sell myself short for a fling that won't last any longer than it takes me to blink my eyes. Derek, I'm nobody's rebound, or one night stand, or convenience, or friend with benefits, and definitely not a mere distraction until you wait to start your career and possibly go home to the woman you really love. I want to be your friend *before* I'm your lover. If there comes a time when we are in love and become intimate, I want to know that these feelings are real for both of us, and I promise you, I'm not going to make a move until we're sure."

"Well, I guess I got that message, and that's that. Take forever for all I care...until the end of time. I think you've got some major problems, lady."

My tone has now passed any evidence of politeness and expresses the pent up tension and anger I feel from Morgan, Zack, and now my new friend who has accused me of treating her like a prostitute twice. I think I have treated her like a queen.

"So now you're angry when I tell you my truth?" Her voice is soft and inquiring, tiptoeing with caution passed a friend she does not really know who is definitely expressing anger. I think I see a little fear in her eyes when I raise my voice, but I'm not sure.

I don't answer her. I put distance between us, and move away from her to sit back against the pillows on my bed.

Ari looks at me in all of my arrogance, gathers up her things, goes to the door, and stops. She turns in her white high heels, those sexy blue jeans with a little short white off the shoulder top that's driving me insane, and looks at me again. I look at her too, all of her, but say nothing.

When she speaks, her voice is quiet and sincere.

"Derek, this fast track you want me on, scares me. It scares me to death. Yesterday, for me, was magic, and showed me how easily I can fall in love with you, but I don't want to get caught up in my own imagination, and I definitely don't want to be caught up in your fantasies. If you're angry, I'm sorry, but I'm looking for the real thing. For me to be me and stay me, I can't accept anything less. I'm sorry if that doesn't work for you, Derek. I'm glad you're feeling better…and just so you know, your looks take my breath away even when you're sick….your hair…your eyes…and that mouth."

She smiles a very slight almost sad smile.

"Good night. You take care of you."

"Ari, wait." I don't get off the bed because common sense tells me that I have no business asking her to wait when I can't control Morgan from roaming around freely and constantly in every corner of my brain.

"No, I'm going to go. I think I need to go before I completely lose my new best friend. Good night, Derek." With that, she smiles slightly, closes the door, and is gone.

My irritation showed a lot, and now I think I've caused a problem with my new friend. Intellectually, I know she's right, and if the truth be told, I have no right trying to start a new relationship, sexual or otherwise, in my present confusion. I really don't know what to do about Morgan because I am so mad with and disappointed in her, but I know I'm still very much in love with her. I pick up my cell and think about calling, but before I can, the phone buzzes and disturbs my thoughts. I answer and Zack's photo stares back at me. I hesitate and then slid the on button.

"What?" My voice is beyond irritated.

"What's up, partner?" He sounds lively and in a very good mood.

"Not much."

"I just called to see how you're doing. That's all."

"I'm fine."

There is a long pause.

"Look, D, I've been thinking about what I did. I just want to say I'm sorry, and I hope we can get past this."

"I don't think so, Bro....not this time."

"Well, will you at least think about it?"

""Huh! I think that's a waste of brainpower. I don't plan to change my mind, Zee; you don't change. We've already been through this several times, and there's one thing about me in case you haven't noticed.

It doesn't take me long to learn something, and you have taught me well. You're a thorough teacher. I can't trust you, Man, and you do too many disrespectful things that hurt other people, and you don't even care, and you certainly don't consider the consequences."

"I do care. Why do you think I'm begging you now to forgive me? I let you bust my face open, Man. That didn't have to happen. I hate that I did this to you, and I am very sorry about it."

"...and how long will you be sorry? The minute this is over you'll start something else even worse if that's possible....and where does that leave Morgan now that you have messed things up with us, and you're so sorry about it?"

"It leaves her wherever she wants to be. She had a choice."

"...and so did you."

I don't have the energy or desire to do this now so I find a way to cut it short.

"Look man, I can't hear this now. I'm out."

Before I can put the cell on the nightstand, I feel the buzz, and without looking, I answer it.

"Zack, I'm not dealing with this tonight. Stop calling me." My voice is tight and angry.

"Ah, Derek, it's me."

"Oh...Sorry, Babe."

"Wow," she laughs. "That's a tone change if I've ever heard one."

"Yeah. Sorry about that, Ari. Sometimes people just get on my nerves."

"I think I did too, tonight, but I didn't mean to get you angry. I'm just calling now to let you know that I'm home safe and sound."

"...and that's very good news."

"Look, Derek. I didn't want to leave, and I certainly didn't want to leave the way I did, but I had too. I'm not a tease, and I wasn't going to stay and give you hope for something that was not going to happen. I hope you understand that."

"I do. I understand."

"Do you really?" Her question has a note of uncertainty.

"Yes, I do. You want the fairy tale, Baby, and you're not sure this soon if I'm your Prince Charming... your Knight in shining armor. I get that." My voice is serious, low, and intentionally sexy.

"Yes....something like that, and I will say this: I think I would love it if you were my Prince...my Knight in shining armor."

"...and I will say this: I think I would too. We'll see what the future holds, Ari. I just hope I pass the test. It's one of the most important ones I think I will ever take, and I think someone in your past has made it harder than it used to be."

"Good night, silly. I'll let you go study your crib notes for what you say is a difficult test," she laughs.

"Oh, I'm a lawyer, Baby. We never use crib notes....too risky. When we pass, we pass on our own merit. Good night, Sweetheart."

I put the phone down and sit on the side of the bed. It's still early, and I'm feeling a lot better and not sleepy at all. I switch on the TV and do a rapid fire channel changing, but nothing seems to interest me. I look at the clock trying to decide what to do with myself when the phone buzzes again, and I am hoping it's Ari not being able to sleep, but when I pick up the cell, I see my Morgan's smiling face.

"Hey."

"Hi, Derek. How are you?"

"I'm fine. What about yourself?"

"Fine...just tired. We had our dress rehearsal tonight. I got the lead."

"I knew you would. So, congratulations are in order. Congrats."

"Thanks."

Her voice is quiet and subdued. The excitement that I'm so used to hearing when she talks about dance is completely missing. There's a pause, and I hear her take a nervous breath.

"Babe, when are you coming home?" I hear a longing in her voice.

"I don't know. Why?"

She is slow to answer. "...because I miss you."

There is silence, and I'm not really sure what to say.

"Well, my office opens in September, and I'm moving to the beach so I have to get home and settled. They're decorating the cottage now, and it's almost finished. It won't be too long."

"May I come back to New York to see you?"

"No." My answer is quick and final.

"Will I see you when you come home?"

That question stabs me in the heart, and I feel a strange quick pain, and an overwhelming sadness that seems to wash over me. The question communicates, all by itself, how much we have lost in this short time.

"I'm sure you will at some point." My tone is sarcastic, urged on by my anger and my attempt to fight the sadness.

"Derek, don't play with me. You know what I mean."

"There's nothing about this playful, Morgan. You hurt me….my best friend? How could you?"

""I never meant to hurt you, Derek. It just happened."

"Nothing just happens, Morgan, especially with Zack."

"Well yeah, he had been calling me for a while."

"You never told me he was calling you, and he never told me he was calling you. Things don't just happen."

"Well, that day they did. He just showed up out of the blue. I had no idea he was coming. One minute he was standing at my front door, we went to dinner, and when we got back, I guess somehow, the truth is, we just lost it."

There was more silence, and a greater ache in my chest…and then…

"Good night, Morgan."

"Derek?"

"I let my thumb slide the phone to off, and I throw it and myself on the bed. Every bit of energy seems to drain from me. I have the answers to a lot of questions that I wasn't completely certain about before this two- minute phone call, and those answers tear at my heart, and the jagged edges become even more pronounced.

Sleep, on this night, is cruel; it absolutely refuses to come.

I get up and open the draperies to let in the sunshine. The day is beautiful, but despite the sun, I'm sad and still trying to put Morgan's phone call out of my mind. The words continue to sting…"somehow, we just lost it." I shower and go to the dining room for breakfast and decide to walk around the city to get some fresh air. I stop in a few stores and make a purchase for Ari that finally makes me smile. It's a gag gift, but it makes me think of her, and I want her to know I hear what she's telling me, and I respect it. I walk back to the hotel, unlock the door and hear the hotel phone ringing, and hope it's not Zack or Morgan. I can't deal with either of them right now.

"Hello."

"Derek?"

"Hi Mom. How are you?"

"I'm fine, but I called to see about you. Are you taking care of yourself?

"Yes, I am.

Have you heard that Morgan got the lead role with her dance company, and they open tonight? Dad and I will be front row and center. They had the dress rehearsal last night."

"Yes, she told me last night when she called."

"I am so proud of both of you kids….my two very successful children. I thought surely you would be here for opening night. This means so much to Morgan. When are you coming home?"

"Ah, Mom, I met somebody else, and I want to take a little time to get to know her better. The good news is she's starting her own business in the Tidewater area, so we probably will come home together."

"Wow!" Now, that's some news! Does Morgan know this?"

"No."

"Derek, don't tell me you're going to break that girl's heart after all of these years, and break mine too." I hear the Mom voice, and that's the last thing I need when she doesn't know the details.

"I don't think so. She's already moved on," I reply with some resignation.

"If she's moved on, I don't think she knows about it. She called me last night to find out when you're coming home. She sounded sad, and when I asked if she was all right, she said no, but I could tell that she didn't want to explain."

"I bet she didn't. What did you tell her?"

"I told her to call you, and from what you just said, I guess she did."

"Yes, she did, and I told her that I didn't know when I was coming home."

"Well, It's not my place to get into any of this, but I do want you to take care of yourself, and make good choices. Derek, don't ever forget that there is a lot of money involved here, and you can't just pick up any girl and decide that you're interested in her. You have to be careful. I have to trust whatever your decisions are, but I don't want my Morgan to get hurt either, and you know that, don't you? I love Morgan, Derek, but I love you more."

"Well, that's good to know," I joke. "I love you too, Mom, and I still love Morgan very much, but, at this point, I just don't know how it's going to end. It's like you told me a very long time ago: sometimes all the king's horses and all the king's men can't put Humpty Dumpty back together again. But then sometimes you don't need Humpty put back together because life gives you something better. We'll see what happens….and just so you know, I don't just pick up any girl. I know what is at stake."

"Do you want to tell me what happened with Morgan?" Why are you trying to give up on her?"

"No, not now. I don't want to talk about it." My voice is very sad.

"All right, but you know where I am if you ever need the best advice in the entire world," she laughs.

"I do know, Mom, and I'll remember that.

"Well, you take care of yourself, Son, and be careful about those New York gold diggers. There are plenty of them out there just waiting to snag a wonderful young man like you."

"I will. I got all gold diggers on my radar, Mom," I laugh. I'll see you in a few months. Tell Dad I'm looking forward to taking his pitiful golf game on when I get home."

We both laugh because we both know the secret, and Mom can't help herself. She has to say it aloud.

"Well, since you still have your first time to beat him, I'm sure he'll be up to whatever challenge you throw at him, and he will get a huge laugh out of your message. Bye, Son."

"I love you, Mom. I'll see you soon."

I hang up the phone and glance at the clock and see that it is almost 4:00 and Ari hasn't called once, so I dial her cell.

"Hey You, It's about time you called. I was getting worried."

"…but not worried enough to call me, huh?" I chastise.

"Well, I don't want to wear out my welcome, but I was getting worried. I thought you might still be angry."

"I wasn't angry, Ari. I think disappointed is a better way to put it. You're a good- looking, sexy woman. You can make any man beg and be a bit unreasonable," I laugh. "Anyway, it's good to know you care about me a little."

"You have no idea how much I care about a man I've only known for four days. I think I'm losing it," she laughs. "Have you been resting today, and have you taken your medicine?"

"Yes, to both of those questions. Look, I was thinking maybe tonight we could go out for dinner together."

"That sounds great, but are you sure you're up to it?"

"Yes, very much so. I can't wait to see you again."

"OK. What time?"

"How about I pick you up in a couple of hours."

"That works for me. I'll see you then."

"Oh, wear something after five like. OK?"

"Derek, please don't tell me what to wear. I'm capable of figuring that out since it will be after five," she snaps.

"Sorry, I was just trying to tell you the type of place I'm taking you. Touchy…touchy!"

"No, I'm sorry. I was out of line. Old bad habits surface some-times...Well, never mind. I'll see you soon."

I hang up the phone, and try for a split second to figure out that last exchange, but I quickly forget about that and just try to slow my heartbeat. Wow, that girl excites me even with her craziness, and I try so hard to be cool. I'm not quite sure how she does it when I know I still love Morgan...but then Morgan is making me mad, sad, and totally disappointed in her. Somewhere in the back of my mind, I already know that getting over this and forgiving her is going to be almost impossible. On the other hand, I can't imagine what my life will be like without her in it. I can't imagine not kissing Morgan again, not holding her in my arms, not making love to her again. I wonder if I'll see Zack every time I touch her. Those are questions that scare me, and questions I can't seem to answer for myself. I push those thoughts out of my mind for now and concentrate on dinner with Ari, a much more pleasant way to occupy my time and thoughts.

I shower and dress, then call the concierge to check on the limo for 6:30 and the reservations at the restaurant. Everything is in order. I dress in a black suit, a white shirt, black bowtie and add my dia-mond cuff links and black patent shoes for the elegant touch. I slick back my hair and put it in a knot at my neck. I feel good, and I am very anxious to see Ari. I can even say I'm excited.

At her door, I knock, she opens it, and, for a moment, I can't breath. Of course, I see those gorgeous hazel eyes first and then the rest of her leaning up against the door jam. Her black dress is stun-ning, fits her tiny waist perfectly, and the soft material flows into a beautiful handkerchief hemline. Her honey tone skin is glowing with its youth, and perfect makeup. Her shoes are clear with a high silver heel, and her dark brown hair is done in a loose braid that flows down over her right shoulder. There are tiny diamond studs throughout that accent her teardrop diamond earrings.

"Close your mouth, Derek," she laughs.

"Really? Ari. Tell me how. You are one beautiful woman. You make me want to…"

"How about you whole that thought and tell me all about that at dinner," she interrupts as I try to move closer to her. "Right now, I'm hungry and you're late, so let's go."

"Wow, we really are just friends. No new girlfriend would ever act like that…bad impression for a girlfriend, but just right for a friend."

We laugh, and I take her arm and escort her to the limo. I can tell she is slightly impressed, but not overwhelmed like I want her to be. She's a silver spoon kind of girl so I take what I can get. Dinner is elegant and the conversation is stimulating and impressive as we listen and talk about what we anticipate about this newfound friendship. Ari is intelligent, inspiring, motivating and has an humble spirit that makes her beauty beyond skin deep. To say the least, I am extremely impressed. At the end of dinner, we go back to her hotel for a night-cap. She orders some fancy non-alcoholic drink that looks like an expensive smoothie you should drink with a straw. She encourages me to try it. I do, and again she hits the mark. We enjoy our drinks, more pleasant conversation, and I walk with her back to her suite. Inside, I put my arms around her waist.

"I've wanted to do this every since I saw you standing in the door-way. You told me to hold that thought. I did."

"You've wanted to do what?"

"This…"

After about ten minutes of "this," we come up for air.

"Never let it be said that you don't get an A plus in show and tell," she whispers in my ear.

"…never have missed an A plus in that skill." I smile and touch the tip of her nose with my index finger.

"Ari, let me stay the night," I whisper close to her ear.

"Derek, don't do this." She pushes out of my arms and walks away.

"What?" I say to the back of her.

She turns and faces me.

"Derek, you're an intelligent guy. What part of 'no' don't you understand? I thoroughly explained all of this last night, I thought. Remember the fairy tale and the Knight in shining armor?"

"Yes, I know all about the fairy tale and the Knight. You've given me at least five crash courses in them already." I laugh to lighten the mood, follow her, and take her back in my arms. She is looking directly at me with those alluring eyes.

"I am very serious about waiting. It's not a laughing matter to me. I need you to know who I am Derek. I'm not a person who can jump in and out of beds the minute I feel desire or something special in my heart. I need to know *You* before that happens. I don't want us to be strangers waking up in a bed together. Call me old fashioned…the little church girl, whatever, but I am who I am. My brain speaks, and for a change, I'm listening because I know my heart will let me down."

"You don't trust me?"

"Come on, Derek. You can give me a better line than that, Mr. Harvard Lawyer," she smirks. "I trust you as much as I know you, but my decision has very little to do with you. It's mostly how I view myself, and what I expect of me now. If we decide to take this relationship to another level, I want it to be a mutual decision. I don't want to be pressured into anything feeling that I will lose you if you don't get what you want from me. If we ever go that far into this relationship, I want to know that you are feeling what I'm feeling, and right now, I think neither of us knows what we're feeling. Our emotions are all over the place with excitement, allure, fascination, charm, and definitely pure unadulterated heat. The proof is in your little kissing session that almost pushed me kicking and screaming into another world." She playfully hits at me.

"I can take you to that world if you let me. It's nice. I promise."

I see her sigh.

"It's only nice if both parties go willingly," her voice teases.

She alters her tone now and looks directly at me. She touches my face and brings my eyes in direct line with hers, forcing me to meet her at the place where she stands so that I might discern the depth and gravity of her sincerity.

"I don't want to mess this up, Baby, because I think we have something special...something rare...something that can be real if we are just patient enough to wait and discover it. I don't want to let lust confuse us, destroy us, and steal away from us what could be beautiful and lasting. There's something about you that I've loved from the moment I first saw you, and I think there is something about me you love. I don't believe that this is coincidental. I believe that things that feel this good are spiritually planned and designed. Derek, please... please...please don't mess this up for us."

I can see her tears coming to the surface. I can see that she is almost begging, and instinctively, the lawyer in me knows somewhere in France, somewhere in her recent past, serious mistakes were made, tears were shed, and at least one heart was shattered.

"Well, I guess this is the perfect time to tell you that I have something for you." I kiss her cheek.

"You do? What?"

"I have something for my new friend....something to show you that I am your friend and understand you better than you think I do...something to prove that I mean what I say too. You take as much time as you need, Baby. I'm not going anywhere."

I reach in my pocket and pull out a very small box and place it in her hand. She looks at the box and then back at me.

"When I open this box is a clown going to jump out on a spring and spray me with confetti?"

We laugh, and it feels good.

"Well, if that happens, Sweetheart, take solace in the fact that it has to be a very small clown, on a very tiny spring, with only a sprinkle of confetti," I smile and kiss her hand. She unties the ribbon, opens the box, and pulls out a silver stopwatch on a chain.

"Ari you say you need time, and I have said that I am willing to give you all the time you need. I want you to understand that *you* have the controls, not me....but if or when you're ready, push right here on the top. The waiting will stop and we will know that we belong together."

I kiss her forehead and her cheek, and I look into her eyes so that she will believe what I say next.

"I love and respect what you stand for, Ari, and, if you want me to, I will wait for you.

I kiss the tip of her nose and the top of her head.

"Thank you, Derek. I want you to know that I had a wonderful time tonight. You make me feel so special every time I'm near you."

"That's because you are, and I've known that from the moment I saw you."

I put my hands on each side of her face, and pull her to my lips. The kiss is slow, soft, passionate, and meaningful. I feel my heart leap and static electricity fire through my body. I release her, look into her eyes and start for the door, but, at the door, with my hand on the knob, I have to look back. I never want to forget how Arianna Channing looks at this exact moment in time. I take a mental snapshot of this beautiful woman standing in front of me; I ride back to the hotel, placing her picture in an eternal special spot in the corners of my mind.

Arianna's Story

Arianna

Chapter 8

A SECRET PLACE

~Life pays benefits when we take the time to honor it~

Derek is like a whirlwind. In New York, he takes my life in his hands, with all of his energy, charm, intellect, charisma, and down right determination, and I let him. I almost feel helpless under his spell, but even with his strong influence, there are lines I refuse to cross or allow him to cross. I've learned that lesson, made that mistake, and now, I'm not about to act impulsive and foolish like some inexperienced errant schoolgirl. I've been there, done that, and know that traveling such a road can be very dark and lonely. Yes, three years ago, I thought I fell in love, and I gave far too much far too soon. It ended badly. With Derek, I'm determined to know this man and give him time to know me as well. The lesson is clear to me. Relationships don't work when you don't know much about each other, don't have much in common, and really don't like each other very much. That whole thing about, I love you, but don't like you, does not work for me. I want a best friend in my husband, someone I can depend on and who will allow himself to depend on me. I know now that it's virtually impossible to find out if that can happen if I'm blinded by vacuous infatuation and carefree sex. I'm determined to get Derek to see how important this is for building a strong and effective relationship, and today I have planned Lesson #1.

I finish shopping, pack a picnic lunch, and now all that's left is to pick up my student who has been instructed to be ready by 11:30 wearing very casual clothes like shorts and sneakers. I jump in my car and make my way over to The Waldorf Towers. Just like instructed, he is waiting at the front entrance in his casual attire.

"Hey you," I smile as he gets in on the passenger side.

"What's up? Are you going to tell me now where we're going?"

"Nope."

"I thought you didn't like surprises," he jokes as he adjusts his seat to almost a bed position.

"Well, I've learned that one or two won't hurt; sometimes they might even give a person a new perspective on life. You never know," I giggle.

"Ok."

I pull off and head out of town, and when we reach our destination, I find a park, which is very easy since no one else seems to be here.

"Can I know now where we are?" he laughs.

"To be honest with you, I don't actually know. I was driving one day when I first arrived, got lost and ran into this place. I liked it, so I stayed a while and fell in love with it."

I grab the basket and some blankets off the back seat, take my student's hand, and lead the way. We take a very short hike through a rather dense area of trees and come to a beautifully shaded spot. It is luxuriant with beautiful wild flowers and a lovely babbling brook that create what I refer to as nature's private sanctuary.

"Wow!" Derek stands with hands on hips taking in the beauty of this secluded paradise while I take in the beauty of him.

"That was my first response, too."

"How did you find this place?"

"I told you. I was lost. I got out of my car and was walking this way to see if I could find someone who could help me get back to the city when I stumbled on this spot. I sat for a while and just said a few prayers because it is so serene and beautiful. I feel closer to God here."

"I certainly see why."

I spread the blankets, and we walk over to the brook hand in hand.

"If we walk a little further, there is a cemented path, some swings and a few picnic tables, but I like it here best."

"Then this is where we will stay."

The two of us sit cross-legged down by the brook, facing each other, and he takes my hand in his and kisses it.

"Derek, look at this blade of grass," I say holding it up close to his eyes.

"All right," he laughs. What is so special about that blade of grass, Ari? Enlighten me."

"Did you know that this one blade of grass is a replica of every other blade on the ground? Just like if we pick one leaf off of that tree over there, it will be a replica of every other leaf on that tree...they, too, are all shaped the same? It's amazing. We can see the shape of all of this grass just by looking at this one small sample?"

"So, I guess you're saying that God creates one shape of something and just keeps duplicating it until He gets so many that we can't count them, huh? He chuckles.

"Yes, you make that so simple."

"Well, I know a tad about fractals. I'll never tell anyone that I'm a master of geometric figures, but when I studied this scientific phenomenon, I was fascinated too."

"You know, Derek, I don't think we ever take enough time to come to a place like this to see what life is really about or to even notice this kind of miracle. We get so caught up in being busy and rushing our lives away that we miss it."

"What do you think should determine our way of life, Ari?"

"...Love....Real love."

"Are you just talking about romantic love?"

"No.....all kinds of love...Agape, romantic, even unrequited love."

"I think you're right." Derek runs his fingers back and forth casually through the water.

"I love the sights and sounds here," he murmurs. I can tell that he's thinking about what I've said. I see him look up through the trees and then at the pattern of the shapes dancing on the forest floor.

"Shh...Listen, Derek," I whisper. We hear the sounds of various insects and birds mingling with the babble of the brook.

"See, if you never come to a place like this and slow down, you never get a chance to experience these amazing gifts from God."

Both of us are quiet now enjoying the sounds, taking in the natural sights, and mesmerized by the peace of it all. Derek breaks the silence first.

"Ari, I've never met anyone quite like you." He's looking at me with that look that drives me crazy in a good way.

"What do you mean? How am I different?"

"Hmm...in so many ways, important ways."

"Like what? I like specifics," I smile.

He pauses.

"You're deep. You don't just glance at life. You delve into it...take it up in your hands and touch it. You look for the details and for what is beneath the surface. That's why you need so much more from me. You want authenticity...validity...nothing contrived. You see things in term of what God intends for us, what He has created for us, and how it shapes our morals and purpose; you live your life according to those terms. The way you treat love makes you different from a lot of people that I know, including myself. I respect that so much, Ari. To make it simple...you don't want the quickie," he grins.

"No, Derek, I don't. I had that, and I hated it, and I hated myself for allowing it to happen. It was so unfulfilling. I want to grow in love with somebody, and feel his heart entwine with mine and know for sure that there is a total sense of mutuality. When a man kisses me, I want to know that it's an expression of all that is in his heart for me, and he can write that expression so clearly that I have no trouble reading it. I'm not perfect by any means. I make lots of mistakes like everyone else, but I always want to learn from the mistakes I make. I've learned some very hard lessons about love or the lack of love, Derek, and sometimes I still feel the pain of my losses…mostly losses in myself. What I know now is that it takes time to really know if what you are feeling about someone is real, and I want the love that I feel to be as real as these blades of grass, this brook singing its natural song…as valid as it can possibly be. Is that too much to ask?"

"…not from Prince Charming." He smiles that quiet smile looking up at me.

There's that sexy look again, especially since his hair is loose falling just right over his eye, so I avert my eyes so I can concentrate, and I totally ignore his attempt at a joke because I am about to tell him something very important to me, and maybe to us.

"You know, Derek, I sold myself very short once, and I made a promise to me. I promised that if I got out with any semblance of myself in tact, it would never happen to me again. I thought I was in love, but more importantly I thought he loved me. His actions proved he didn't, even though everyday he said he did. He wanted to possess me…own me….put me on his pedestal and make me stay there. When I escaped him, I left a part of myself behind…the part that would allow that to happen to me again. I want the man who says he loves me to know that my heart is no plaything; it's nothing for him to toy with, take risks with, own, or bargain with. It should never be something he can destroy at his will."

"Ari, for some strange reason, we...we don't demand that, and we should." Derek looks up at me, and it seems that his thoughts are here, but also someplace far away touching a bad memory.

"No, you can't demand it. It comes naturally with real love. You just have to wait for it, and therein lies the problem. So many times, we're not willing to wait, and so in our haste, we ruin what could have been."

Memories begin to flood my mind now, many that I don't want to share, so I get up from where we are seated, and walk over to the blankets and spread out the food. Derek takes a very short stroll around the perimeter and then comes to sit with me.

"I'm glad you brought me here." He touches my face on his way to sit in front of me. "I understand a lot of things I didn't get before today. You're a very special woman, Ari. The man who loves you and gets your love in return, will be extremely blessed."

"Well, I want more than anything to be a blessing to him too."

"I'm more than sure you will be."

We feast on fried chicken, potato salad, cheese, crackers, fruit, pound cake and iced tea.

"This is finger licking good, girl, and it would even be better if I thought you could cook like this," he teases.

"Who says I can't? My Mom started teaching me how to cook when I was seven years old. We use to spend a lot of time together in the kitchen. I can throw down, Baby."

"Can you?" He lifts an eyebrow and grins at me with a large chicken breast half way to his mouth....as good as this?"

"Better. My grandma gave me recipes when I was a little girl, and I kept them all in a special tin, and I still have them to this day. When I want to feel very close to my Grandma Lillie, I cook one of them."

"Really? What's your Grandma Lillie favorite?"

"Peach cobbler without a doubt. She used to make it often, and let me help her take the peach skin off after she put the peaches in hot water. We would sit and talk and laugh and peel those sweet peaches together. She would cut them up and make the dough. My job was to roll out the dough and make dough stripes. I'll never forget how good that dough would taste after it cooked in all of that sweet peach juice. Hmm...so good."

"Maybe you can make that for me one day if I'm lucky."

"I might. We'll see. I only do that for *very* special friends," I grin.

"So, how does one get to be one of those very special friends? He leans over close to my face.

"It's a secret," I wink and smile at him.

When we finish our lunch, I start packing the food up and cleaning our blanket space when I notice that Derek is lying on his side now staring at me almost without blinking. At first, I act like I don't notice, and I continue to put things back in the basket.

116

"Do you want me to dump that ice or are you still using it?" he asks.

"I'm still using it."

He hasn't moved, and he is still staring.

I sit back on my heels.

"Derek, you're making me nervous."

"What am I doing to make you nervous, Sweetheart?" He asks in mock seriousness.

"Staring."

He is smiling slightly and continuing to stare. "I thought you were the master of the stare game. Why would staring make you nervous? Before I even knew your name, I was calling you the Stare Master."

"Stare Master? You're crazy," I giggle.

I throw a cloth napkin at him and he catches it and before I can think he playfully grabs me and tickles me on the ground.

"You dare throw something at me, girl? Huh? Huh?" I am laughing so hard and pretending to do everything I can to get away from him.

"Stop! Stop! Stop, Derek! I'm not playing," I giggle as I twist and turn to get out of his grasp, but he pins me down, and is leaning over me with a grin that is quickly fading into his most serious look. His eyes find mine, and we stare. There is silence. It's almost as if time has stopped. I see his face move closer to mine, but something stops the magic moment. He smiles a little and helps me up.

"See what you do to me? I was just about to lose my mind."

"…and do what?…tickle me to death?" I laugh.

"See you think it's funny. You play too much."

"What? You want a little kiss, Derek?" I tease in a very silly voice.

"No, not from you, friend. Friends don't kiss."

"Are you sure?" I ask teasingly seductive.

"Well, it's what I've been told."

He is on his knees, and I am on mine in front of him. I look at him, and he is looking at me. His face is serious again.

"Maybe I heard wrong." His misty eyes are even more dark, dewy, and alluring.

"Maybe you did." *I can't help myself. I want this man.*

He cautiously reaches for me and takes me in his arms, exactly where I want to be. He cups my chin under his curled fingers and lifts my face to his, and our lips meet. The kiss is brief, but I can tell we have moved another level, and I feel very good about it.

We go arm in arm and sit by the brook again, and listen to nature and each other. When we look out, we see that the sun is setting and in the sky is a red and orange glow that creates an atmosphere of serenity.

"Did you have a good time today?" I ask.

"Ari, I had a wonderful time, and I thoroughly enjoyed this place, but most of all I enjoyed you. We'll have to come back here again sometimes."

"Yes."

"Derek, I have one more surprise before we leave."

"...and what is that?"

"Come over here."

We move back to where our things are, and I pull from the basket my phone, and play one of my favorite songs. I take this gorgeous man into my arms, and we dance under the setting sun, wrapped in the embrace of our private paradise. I feel Derek bring me closer and closer as the music plays, and I'm a willing participant. The music comes to an end, and I look up at him, move aside those naughty strands of hair that always flirt with his eye, and I kiss him.

"Now I've shared my favorite place, my favorite song, and favorite feelings from my heart.

"Adele, huh...*Make You Feel My Love*. Nice song."

"Yes, I'm looking for the man who wants to feel my love, and I feel his."

"Do you think you've found him?" I feel him pull me a little closer to him.

"I don't know...but we'll see."

"Yes, we'll see." He taps my nose playfully.

Standing behind me with his arms wrapped around me, he kisses the top of my head and my bare shoulder. He turns me to face him, looks at me, slowly smiles that half smile of his, and winks. It is the sexiest thing I'd seen him do all day, and I almost melt in his arms.

He hugs me and we gather our things and reluctantly ride back to the city.

—⟋⟍—

119

Derek and I become very good friends, and take New York by storm. He makes sure that no grass grows under our feet. We act like kids with new toys. There are the stage plays, the glitzy musicals, and the exciting fashion week in New York. There are the lazy days, too, when we just hang out together at a movie, sit in a beautiful place and get to know each other or take a hand in hand walk or a run through Central Park. We have so much fun together, and it becomes hard to remember when we didn't know each other. I don't think I will ever say again that someone is falling in love. I believe that we *grow* in love, and, to me, there is a big difference. Yes, there are the stomach butterflies that take flight every time we touch or see each other. There are the times of being on our very best behavior and hiding what we really feel at the moment as we learn to pick our battles. There are also the times of complete honesty when we are both put in check because a line has been crossed or because a word, stated in jest, is too much for laughter. There is something very deep about this blooming love thing, and both of us feel it, realize it, embrace it, and value it.

We all know that life and time never stand still no matter how much we want it to, so there is that day in late August when we end our vacation, pack up our things, and drive together to Virginia to begin our new careers. My mom would say that we're running on to see what the end might be.

Morgan

Chapter 9

THE IRREPARABLE ACTS

~Thoughtless actions: initial steps toward irreparable damage~

"Five, Six, Seven, Eight," Pierre taps the rhythm out with the stick that seems never to leave his hand. This is the fifth time the dancers have done this routine in the last hour. They're tired, especially since this is a dance that everyone seems to know except me.

"Ah, Morgan!" he screams. "Stop! Everybody just stop! Morgan, you missed that count again!"

Pierre slams the stick down to the beats, "**Six,** seven, eight. The change is on **six.**"

The stick slams again. ". . . not seven!" The stick slams on beats seven and eight.

"You can't be late!"

On the word 'late' the stick hurls in the air and lands close to my feet. Everybody knows this is Pierre's last straw. This is the fifth time today I've made a critical mistake in a dance that I can do with my eyes closed and my hands tied behind me. Earlier, I miss a jump that almost costs me dearly, but Peter catches and saves me despite my error.

"What is your problem?"

Pierre is screaming almost out of control. His eyes bulge, his nose flares, and he is less than two inches from my face. His free hand is balled in a fist; spittle is forming in the corner of his mouth. He is totally exasperated. There are three more dances to learn, and this one has been finished for over two weeks, yet here we are going over and over this one because I keep missing jumps and beats. Today has been a complete waste of time for the rest of the company.

I stand in front of Pierre with my shoulders slump, my head down, and my feet in a position never thought of by a dancer. My entire look is one of defeat. The tears are coming now, and I'm a total wreck. The group is milling around quietly not knowing whether to go or stay, whether the rehearsal will go forward or end for the night. I have been a mess for the last few months, but really falling apart during these last two weeks. Reality is sinking in that no matter what I try, Derek is not coming back to me...he is refusing to forgive me. For the last few days, he won't even talk to me.

"Morgan, this is completely ridiculous. Do you want me to replace you? Are you begging for me to replace you?"

Pierre is leaning forward just inches from my face with his hands on his hips. He is mad.

"Are you giving up on your dream? You have patiently waited for your turn to take this lead, and now that you have it, on Broadway no less, you're about to blow it all, for what? Do you even know?"

He is getting some control, but not yet able to speak in a civil tone, so he stands in front of me breathing hard, and trying to get some answers. I look down at my feet shuffling one of them back and forth and see Peter out of the corner of my eye ready to protect me, if necessary. Then without a word of explanation or apology to the company, I basically run from the room, grab my bag from a locker just outside the door, and head for the stairs.

"Morgan! Morgan! Where do you think you're going? Morgan, come back here right now!"

I hear Pierre calling my name as I run down the steps at break neck speed…a very dangerous move for a person who depends on her legs and feet for a living. I know the show must go on, and I know that Samantha is probably standing in front of Pierre right now ready to replace me, and I'm not yet out of the studio.

The cars, the people, the noise on the street are a complete blur, and finding my own car is proving to be a bit of a task. Up until a short time ago, I would have been able to walk out of the studio and have the car door already open and waiting for me. The love in my life would be standing there with a big grin on his face….but something has gone wrong with that…something has gone drastically wrong, and it's all my fault. I was so used to Derek being there for me that I know I started to take him for granted, but never in my life did I think we would be in this place. My actions were bad. I admit that, but Zack was so different...so sexy, so attentive, and alluring. He was just fun for a while...mysterious, and even a bit dark. I was instantly attracted to him. I know now that I was just infatuated and seeking a thrill I had never dared. Derek has been my only boyfriend, and I guess I was just looking, for a moment, to experience something different. In reality, Zack means nothing to me. That little time we had together is very empty now. It looks, however, like this discovery has come a bit too late for me to fix things with Derek. There is someone else in his life, and even though he won't confirm it, I can feel it, but I refuse to let it continue. Derek is mine. He always has been, and always will be.

After about a thirty second walk down the block, I realize that I'm walking in the wrong direction for where my car is parked. I turn around and find my little red sports car right where I left it this morning. I throw my bag in the back, get in the driver's seat, start the ignition and zoom off toward the beach. My face is tear streaked, and I can feel the wetness drying on my skin. My green eyes have taken on that color somewhere between a blended green and gray, and all of a sudden the tight bun at the base of my neck is a bother. I reach up with my free hand, pull out a few pins, and sling my long light brown crinkled waves free. I put the top down and let the humid September breeze take control of my hair, my eyes, my tears, and me.

In my mind, I hear my voice persisting, "Let's try it just one more time. I'll get it right. I know what I did wrong." I say those lines at least eight times during the day, and my company looks puzzled every time. What I don't say is that my concentration is far from this rehearsal, far from these dance moves, far from everything that is not Derek. As my mind replays these events, I suddenly become aware of how wet my clothes are as the warm breeze brings me to some consciousness.

I started my day around 7:30, and took about an hour for lunch, but the rest of the time was consumed with warm-ups, dance classes, and rehearsals except for the few minutes when I called Derek on his private office line this afternoon. The conversation was very upsetting to say the least. I called. He answered. We talked. I fell apart.

"Hey Babe." I try to sound light and full of energy, which is not the real truth at all. I'm burdened, sad, and desperate.

"Morgan, why are you calling me?" His voice is impatient with a tinge of anger.

"…because I love you…because I miss you….because I won't ever give up on us."

There is a deafening silence.

"Derek, don't you think you've punished me enough for one mistake?"

"Morgan, a mistake is a careless error on a test paper. A mistake is calling a wrong number. It's not a mistake when you sleep with my best friend and sneak behind my back for months having regular conversations with him on the phone. You were secretly building a relationship with Zack. While he and I are housemates, and, stupid me, I think best friends, you two are keeping your secrets and making me look like a complete idiot. Those things are not mistakes, Morgan. It's called betrayal. I know that's Zack's game, and he loves to play it. I can get prepared for that; I'm used to that, but never in my wildest dreams did I think you would ever do anything that hurtful and down right mean to me."

"Derek, it was just a thing to do. How can I convince you that it was meaningless? I didn't think I would ever hurt you."

"Just a thing to do? Are you kidding me? Did you think I would never find out? Error...Zack loves to gloat? He would not have been able to help himself from telling me at some point. ' Man, I even got your girl.' He mimics Zack's voice and I can tell he is trying to keep his voice down since he is at work.

"Did you think you could deceive me and put some kind of notch on your own belt for continuing to make me look like a fool?...pushing me further and further in your background...letting me fly all the way here four or five times without one glimpse of you. Error...I would have come to my senses at some point and realized what you were doing." I hear his impatience with me in the edginess of his tone.

"Look, I don't have the time or the energy to rehash all of this with you. I'm due is court in a couple of hours. I have some last minute notes to make and a few people I need to see before I go."

"Wait, Derek! Can I see you?" My words are rushed.

"No, Morgan. I'm busy." His words hold finality.

There is a blaring silence. We are both still holding our phones, and in our own separate ways holding on to the last thin thread that still connects us, but I break the silence and speak the line that has the capacity to sever all ties.

"You have someone else, don't you?" My voice is quiet, and scared, but his is still on the attack, and his words are rapid fire fast.

"Think whatever you want to think to ease your own conscience. I was faithful to you, Morgan, and loved you....and in some small moments when I'm quiet and honest with myself..."

His voice breaks and he pauses.

"...I know that...I still love you, and I probably always will, but things are different now and you changed them, and now, you can't change them back. To me, you're gone, and I'm free to do whatever I damn well please. I've got to go now, and by the way, in case you haven't noticed, there is no 'us'."

I hear the dial tone and he's gone. For the first time in my life, I feel that I cannot reach him. I look at the phone in my hand, absent-mindedly move it to my side, and with no thought of motion, walk a very tiny circle around the space that holds my suddenly exhausted body. Somewhere in that space and time, I totally lose it, crumple to the floor, and break down in uncontrollable tears for more than a half an hour.

Driving is freeing me now for the moment, but the recap of that telephone conversation is tearing at my heart again, and the pain is almost unbearable. The thoughts are too hurtful and sad, and they are causing me to lose my will...lose myself. I have no idea how I will go on without the person who has been by my side, encouraging me, supporting me, the person who has loved me for all of my life. I have lived very few moments without having Derek with me....and now... we find ourselves at this crossroad. He refuses to tell me he is with someone else, but every time I've called him in the past two months, I instinctively know why he hurries so quickly off the phone. *The other woman is there.* I know why he makes those flimsy excuses of not being able to take me out. *The other woman is occupying his time.* And I know now, somewhere deep in my spirit, that he has already left me. *The other woman has taken my place.*

I park the car, walk to the house, open the door and know immediately that this will not be the night for bright lights. I turn on two lamps in the living room, lower the chandelier light and slump down on the floor pillows across from the sofa.

I look at the corner wall and see the framed picture I painted of Derek and me in the fifth grade...so long ago, but it still makes me smile. Everyone thought it was beautiful and the artistic ability far beyond my years. My Mom had gotten it professionally framed, and for a long time it had claimed a place of distinction on my bedroom wall.

Since the eighth grade, almost everyone says that one day Derek and I will be husband and wife. We have always been considered the perfect pair. Even in first grade I force Derek to play with my dolls, Morgan and Derek. Our parents take us to Disney World together when we "fly up" from elementary school. When we are fourteen, my Dad drives us to our first date...a movie and a game or two at the bowling alley. In high school, when things begin to get serious for us, Derek plays football and I cheer for him as Captain of the Varsity Cheering Squad. We are Prom King and Queen, and the only time we separate is during our college years; even then, we manage to see each other almost every other weekend for the entire time until I, like many before me, fall prey to Zack's smooth talk, sexy looks, and down right irresistible total package.

Somewhere, somehow in my own stupidity, another woman has done what no other has been capable of doing....has accomplished what everyone thought was the impossible. Because of Zack and me and our foolishness, because of a night that meant absolutely nothing, the mystery woman has found an opening, and Derek has lost faith in me, and probably thinks he has fallen madly in love with her.

I sit on the floor clutching a pillow. In the secret place of my mind, I admit and regret the lies that I have told Derek. I am feeling very sorry for myself, and remembering, in great detail, that night with Zack. In my mind's eye, I can still see and hear us so clearly. I think it's more real to me now than it was then. At the time, it had the feel of some crazed hallucinogenic like dream that held me willingly captive.

I hear the doorbell, and I open the door. When I see him, I have to catch my breath and steady myself. He is beyond handsome.

"I bet you don't know who I am." His voice is sultry and very masculine.

"I know your voice, so I know who you are."

"Do you now? So, what's my name?" He is playful and dangerously charismatic.

"You're Zack," I laugh.

"Bingo! Smart girl." He winks.

"I know." I try to return the flirt, but I don't come close.

"So, you're going to let me fly all the way to the big V A, and not even invite me inside, huh? Now, that's cruel."

He is standing on my porch in black slacks, a red V-neck sweater, an expensive gold chain that draws me to his neck. I notice immediately that he is shirtless. Leaning against the post grinning, and chewing on a toothpick, I don't miss the fact that his every word almost hypnotizes me, and every movement he makes is openly seductive.

"I never said you couldn't come in. I'm just surprised you're here. You never said anything about a visit in all of the many times we've talked on the phone."

"Maybe I like to surprise my ladies."

I smile and push the door open for him. He purposefully brushes my breasts as he passes through the door, and then turns with a boyish mischievous grin to look at me.

"Girl, you are fire! I didn't think you could look any better than that picture Derek has on his table, but you are something else."

…He audibly sucks in his breath, "Wow!"

In my thoughts now, I remember his looking at me from head to toe. I remember his coming close to me, and with one finger, brushing uncontrolled crinkled strands of hair from my eyes. I recall his smell. I'll never forget that. It's mild, expensive, and very masculine. He has a hint of alcohol on his breath that makes him oh so titillating. He moves over to the sofa, takes a seat and crosses his leg. I remember feeling nervous, and not quite sure what to do with myself so I choose to sit a distance from him.

"You aren't nervous are you?" He is so cool…so casual and playful leaning over looking into my eyes.

"No, not really." I lie and fidget. I've never met anyone like him before.

"Do you have to sit so far away?" His voice tone is low, and the sound of it calm…seductive.

"No."

Then come here, girl. I don't bite…not hard anyway." He chuckles and pulls me closer to him.

"I know what can put you at ease." I remember that this is the point where he takes my hand, and the electric shock surprises me as it fires through my body.

"...and what might that be?" I ask breathlessly. I am so nervous.

"A dinner out with me. Do you know a decent place around here where I can wine and dine you in style?...none of Derek's favorite places," he hastens. "...something different ...something unique."

"Sure, I do."

He touches my chin, turns my face to him, and finds my eyes again.

"Well, why don't you take me to one of those places."

Everything he says is deliberate and sounds sexy. Everything he does feels sexy, and I am totally flustered.

"Ok." That's all I can manage at the moment. He is overwhelming me.

When I stand, I remember him standing too and invading my space. I remember him tilting his head and bending down to me. I think he is about to kiss my mouth, but he hesitates just for a second and slightly brushes the side of my chin with his lips. It's a feather touch. He leans back, winks, and smiles like the whole thing is a big joke...it is an "I got you" kind of smile. I remember feeling disappointed, opening my eyes, and bringing my parted lips back together.

"We'll save the best for later," he whispers almost inaudibly close to my ear. He touches my face with his fingers and winks. At that point, I can feel myself falling apart. He has talked the talk on the phone for almost a year, and now he is walking the walk standing in front of me. I feel helpless under his spell. I know it, and he knows it even more than I.

The dinner is great, and he makes me laugh often. At one point, while I'm laughing, he moves to the chair next to me, cups his chin in his hand, and intently watches me giggling at his latest joke. I see his roguish smile melt into a kind of seriousness, and I remember wondering what he's thinking. It is almost dreamlike when he cups my chin with his index finger and thumb, leans over, and brings my mouth to his. I remember that mesmerizing moment, and even now I feel myself flush. Sitting next to him, I'm speechless.

Later that night, I invite him in for a nightcap, and he masterfully spins an artful web around me, and I am helplessly caught in his trap. The lovemaking is absolutely crazy, fun, new, exciting, but unquestionably meaningless. In the morning, he leaves very early with only a kiss to my forehead, and never calls again.

Sitting on the floor now, despairing, I come out of my daydream wondering how in the world I let this happen to me. I can't say I was too young, too inexperienced, too vulnerable, only that I was too foolish and touched my hand to a fire. Derek and I have gone all of these years without a trace of trouble, and now that it is about time to seal the deal, I make a silly mistake and Derek is unforgiving. Well, he'll just have to get over it. It's as simple as that! Two months of him avoiding me, seeing me here and there, talking briefly with me on the phone every now and then is not enough. I'm finally determined that no other woman is going to come between my man and me. There is no way I'm going to keep sitting around here every night crying in my soup. It's getting me nowhere. Nope! Derek is going to tell me something definite tonight. He is going to talk to me and come clean about his feelings, and we are going to solve this. We're going to get passed this, but first I have to find out exactly what is happening in his mind and in his life. I can't keep calling him, begging him, and letting him brush me off. This has to stop because I know he loves me. I want him back, and I'm now resolved to get him back. I'll fight to the death for him.

With my determination strengthening, I jump in the shower, change into a long turquoise wrap skirt and a matching top with coral accents. The low neckline is open and I choose to let the ties with the tassels hang loose. I slip on my turquoise sandals, a gold chain around my neck and throw on a thin matching scarf wrap just in case the ocean breeze is cool. I won't call this time. If he is with someone, it's too bad for him. If he is not at home, I'll wait for however long it takes.

I pull my car out of the park in front of my house and start down the coast for the twenty- minute drive to his part of the beach. I put on our favorite music to make the trip even shorter, and before I know it, I am wheeling into a park right next to his shiny black CTS. The lights are on in the beach cottage and that's sort of a good sign, but I have no fear. This man is mine and has been for a very long time. There is nothing for me to fear. I use our little secret intimate knock on the door and in seconds, Derek is standing quite surprised in front of me. He is dressed casually in his gray slacks, a loose fitting white shirt with no collar, his black sandals and a gold chain around his neck. His hair is loose and hangs casually around his face with those hard to deal with strands that never stay in place kissing his eyelids. My heart is racing now, not only from the surprised look on Derek's face, but also because there he is, all 190 pounds of him right in front of me, and I have not seen him in two months.

"Morgan. What are you doing here?" His eyes show surprise, but also a bit of irritation that I recognize immediately as soon as I see him bite down on the left corner of his mouth. That sign is very clear to me.

"Hmm," I scrunch up my mouth. "That's not quite the way I wanted to be greeted after you have ignored me for so long. I can think of something much more to *my* liking." I playfully poke his stomach, brush pass, and whirl around to face him. I put my arms around his neck and wait just a second for the kiss that I know is coming. Instead, he surprises me. He breaks the embrace and looks at me.

"Morgan, we need to talk."

I hear the serious tone, and I see the slight nervousness in his eyes….that quick blinking thing he does when he's a little on edge.

"I wasn't quite ready for this tonight, but since you're here, we may as well get it done." He takes my hand and pulls me gently over to the love seat that he has in the middle of the floor…the first thing I plan to change as soon as I move in with him. He stops and takes in my total look.

"Man, you look good, Babe, and smell good too."

"Do I?" I make those two words count.

"Yes, you do. Sexy!" He gathers me at my waist, leans back, pushes me out from him, and takes in my whole body with one sweep of his eyes. He folds his lips in and makes his mouth a straight line. He's thinking now, a serious thought, and he quickly breaks the embrace. *I can tell. She slipped into his mind.* We sit together and he takes my hands in his.

"Morgan, you know I still love you despite everything that has happened, and, like I said today, that probably will never change. We have loved each other for a very long time, but there are some things…."

"Yeah, silly," I interrupt. "…since high school. We grew up loving each other."

I try to make my voice light, so light that even I have a hard time thinking that he is about to tell me something I don't want to hear. I put two of my fingers on his lips and look into his eyes. When I move them, I replace my fingers with my lips on his. The kiss starts light, and then I press in with aggression, and I feel him resist his own response, and pull back. *She has control of him.*

"Babe, what is it? I know you're furious with me about that stupid Zack situation. How many times do I have to tell you that Zack means nothing to me? How many times are you going to make me say how sorry I am before you can forgive me? Derek, I never meant for this to happen."

He shifts away from me now, and I read his body language. Because I know him so well, I steady myself for the explosion I know is about to come. I ready myself for the angry voice, and the accusations that will pour out almost non-stop. The tenderness, for sure, will be gone, and each word will lash me like a whip. *The lawyer will be home, and he will take charge.*

"Then why is it that you could let him call you behind my back numerous times, and you not tell me a thing about it? Morgan, you basically let him take my place for a while, and that's why you could let me fly all the way here and never lay eyes on me. You knew what you were doing behind my back, and you couldn't date both of us at the same time. Right? Your allegiance, for a while, was solely with him. You knew what you meant to me, and you let this happen. How am I supposed to forget and forgive that you slept with my best friend? Tell me that Morgan....how? I lost two friends in one horrible moment. How am I supposed to deal with that, and still stay the same? Every time I look at you, every time I talk with you, I see him.

I have no idea what would happen if I tried to make love to you now. My imagination would probably run wild. Your little sexy telephone conversations behind my back…your little quick secret meeting with him, and then the lies you told me afterwards. You did this Morgan… you and Zack, so you have to accept the consequences whatever they are, and you can't play this off like any of this is my fault."

He stops, and looks down at first, and then he looks up at me, and I see tears welling in those beautiful, already misty eyes. The lawyer is gone now, and Derek is back, but I can't find any words at this point. There is nothing else I can say. I have exhausted every excuse, stumbled through every admission, and garnered every manner of apology. I have said it all for the last two and a half months…said it every one of the very few times he would allow me a moment to talk with him; I've written notes, sent gifts, left messages, but nothing has done any good. No matter how hard I fight, it seems virtually impossible to move him out of her arms and back into mine.

"Yes, I'm still angry with you, and I can't say that I will ever forgive you for sleeping with Zack, but I'm trying to let my own heart heal. I won't lie; it still hurts a lot when I think about it, but this is what is important now…this is what you need to know…" He takes a deep breath and exhales loudly. "I met somebody awhile ago, and I guess I should have told you as soon as I knew it was serious, but I was too angry with you."

The word *SERIOUS* cuts deeply, but the defiant voice inside my head screams, "No," this is not happening to me. Derek wouldn't do this to me…not after all of these years even if I did make a mistake. He loves me too much to do this. We can get pass this. We've been through everything together. We overcame Lance Rogers in my life at

136

sixteen, and Darla Simmons in his at seventeen....And then the voice inside my head decides to clam up at the wrong time, and I sit quietly with my hands in my lap. My voice is gone for the moment. I feel my head moving from side to side, and I have no ability to stop it. I suspected all of this, but it wasn't true until the words were formed... until the sound broke its barrier...until the heart began to shatter. In my head, I hear the pieces of glass from inside of me breaking, yielding to the pain, but I can't move. Only my head says no, moving from side to side. Derek is saying something else now. I think it is her name, or where they met, or how surprised he is that this could happen...something. The words are traveling through a fog, and the sound is obscure.

He puts his arm around me and leans forward to see me better.

"Are you all right?"

Four words and the dam breaks. The tears are coming fast and fierce, but the sound is absent, and I am in a lonely place. Minutes pass and he just sits rubbing my back, holding me close to him and trying to explain the unexplainable....and then I hear what I cannot even begin to believe.

"Morgan, if things keep going the way they are now, I know that eventually I'm going to ask her to marry me."

I feel my body, in one motion, twist toward him, and I find his eyes and stare. My mouth is open and moving, but no words come at first....and then suddenly they pour out.

"How can you, Derek? How can you do this to me...to us after all of these years? I've told you a thousand times how sorry I am. I've told you as many times as you would listen that nothing like this will ever happen again. I just got caught up in something that I didn't know how to handle. You know Zack. I didn't. We have been through so much together, Derek. You know me. How can you not forgive this one mistake? I can't believe this is happening…not to us!" My voice can only manage a whisper now and my energy is depleted.

Despite my desperation, despite my uncontrollable tears, despite my fierce fighting to stay with him, he appears serene, his voice composed, and I feel the intensity of his pain and a determination within him to tell me *his* truth. His words come slowly, quietly, but they hit every mark.

"You did this, Morgan.…not me. You betrayed me. You destroyed everything we had. Every thing we built, you tore down in one night, and for what? *You* let Zack mess with us.…and the saddest part of all is that to Zack, it's just a game. He asked you to play, M, and you complied. You played, and we lost. At Zack's games, everybody always does."

I feel the tears begin to burn my eyes, and when I look up at him, I see the beginning of his. In our mingled sorrow, the recognition of all that we have lost flashes in an agonizing moment, and in between us, in full sight, sits the ashes of our TRUST.

In my lost state I lose my voice, my legs, my energy, my sense of self. The world is no longer the place I know. I am in another place far away from dreams of happiness, or fairytale weddings, or prince charming. I try to stand, but my legs are wobbly, and Derek's arms steady me. He is saying something again about staying and sitting, but I find my way to the door. I touch the knob, and when my eyes open again, I see bright lights, dripping tubes, and nurses' white uniforms.

Chapter 10

MY LOSS, HER GAIN

*~Never be so careless with Love as to believe
it is not continuously vulnerable~*

At first the room is a complete blur, and then I see Derek asleep in the lounge chair next to my bed. He is still dressed in the gray slacks and white shirt, but now the sleeves are rolled up and his hair has that bird nest look that it takes on after a restless night when he fails to tie it back out of his face. I watch him sleep for a moment, and then the memory floods my mind and over takes my brief serenity. A choking sound escapes my throat, and Derek's eye open on me. He moves quickly to my side, leans in close to me, and brushes the hair from my face.

"Hey you." His face is close to mine, his voice is quiet, and his eyes are soft. "How do you feel?"

He touches my cheek with his hand, and we lock our eyes together. I feel so many different emotions at this moment, that I can't identify any of them. Is it love, anger, frustration, desire, longing?…What is it? I search Derek's eyes, and in them, I still find love, but something has changed; they're different. With that recognition, I snap.

"What are you doing here, Derek? Why aren't you with your *fiancée* or *whatever*? You need to leave."

I feel weak, and I can't make my voice communicate the anger, disappointment, and frustration that I feel in the very core of my being, so I settle for this hoarse defiant sound that barely captures the depth of my hurt and anger. I so want to be over him right now, but unfortunately, my heart says no. He is patient and seems not to hear me.

"I'll go get the nurse and see if I can get some information about your condition."

I pull the sheet up and cover myself more securely.

"My *condition* will be just fine if you get the hell out of my face. Just go…please."

I feel the tears burning my eyes, but I refuse to allow him to see them. He does not deserve my tears, my heartache, or my pain no matter what I did. Anyone can make a mistake.

"Morgan, don't be silly, he snaps. I'm not going to leave you here alone."

He has that lawyer smirk on his face that I absolutely hate. It's the smirk that says *You're not too bright, or you're too emotional at the moment for credible thought.*

"Why not?" I snap. If I remember correctly, you are leaving me, so why not here?" *OK, wait for it…his logical lawyer lesson…*

"Well, for starters, Morgan, you don't have a car here, and you have no way of getting back to my house to get your car, and I'm not so sure you should even be driving right now. You had a pretty serious fall at the house, and I don't think they are ready to release you just yet. We need to hear what the doctor has to say."

Bingo!…logical thought in between lip biting and abnormal eye blinking.

"Derek, just go. Please! I don't need your help. You don't need to do anything for me…take me anywhere, check on me, care about me. From what I remember, you're done with all of that." I'm looking directly into his eyes now with defiance.

"Morgan, don't."

"Don't what, Derek? Don't act like I can be independent of you? Don't feel hurt that you've given up on us without a fight? Don't let you go? Don't care that you can't forgive me even though you know what Zack is capable of? Don't be angry that you drop this kind of bomb in the middle of my life? Don't take care of myself? What Derek? Don't what? Why can't you remember all the good things I've done for you for so many years?…all the good times we've had….how much we really love each other? You've been everything to me for so long. I have no idea how to live without you, Derek."

The words pour out, the emotion is palpable, and our feelings just hang vulnerably in the air. Derek's lips are parted, but he is speechless, not because he doesn't know *what* to say. He's a lawyer; he always knows what to say. He doesn't know *how* to say what he needs to say without tearing my heart out more. The look on his face speaks volumes. He has someone else falling in love with him, he doesn't trust me anymore, but he still loves me desperately, and he knows that will never go away no matter what. He's keeping secrets too.

I look into his eyes, and he looks back into mine. The look is deep, and in an instant, we mentally share our love together in a kaleidoscopic flash.

"Just go!" I hide my face in the pillows. My heart can't bear that look, and I can't stop the flood of tears.

"Babe?" He tries to touch me, but I shrug his hand away. I hear the name he's called me since high school, and it sounds the same, but I know it is not.

"You went too far, Morgan." His eyes are sad, his voice is weak, and I feel his determination to let me go.

In my anger, I sit up, wipe the tears with the back of my hand, and reach for the phone. I want to hurt him more now because he is making my heart hit rock bottom.

"I don't have anybody to call? I have no way to get my car? I can't get home without you? Is that what you think?"

I punch in the number that I know will hurt him the most…the number that will make him furious, but I don't care.

"*Hey, it's me.*" My voice is deadpan. "*Can you come over to Mercy and pick me up? Yes. I had a little problem at Derek's; I fainted and hit my head. I'm not sure exactly, but maybe in about an hour or so." I look directly into Derek's eyes before answering the next question. "Yes, he's here, but I need you." I emphasize the word "you." "Can you come now? Thanks, love. I'll see you soon."*

I hang up the phone and look straight at Derek again who is pretending now to flip through a magazine with some intense interest.

"Peter, right?" His voice is sarcastic, and he does not look up from his magazine.

"Yes." My answer is quiet and quick, but it crosses time and space and sits stone like in the middle of old arguments and moments of distrust. Immediately, there's the old familiar sign. Derek bites the left side of his bottom lip, and then folds his lips in to a straight line.... *serious thought before speaking.*

"It had to be Peter, right?" His voice is quiet, and he bites his lip again. "It couldn't be your mom or your dad, right? It had to be Peter."

There goes the lip biting again. He still pretends to flip through the magazine without looking once at me.

"Derek, please go." My voice can barely carry the words across the room.

The moment is like time standing still…like approaching a corner before the turn…like seeing the climax of a story just before its resolution. He looks at me, and I look at him, and a momentary silence stills our world…our hearts break secretly together, and then only he speaks to tell me which way the story ends.

"Really?…really, Morgan? Is that what you want? Is that what we've come to for sure? Fine. You think you can hurt me to my core, and I'm not allowed to have a reaction to it? You think I can just forgive everything just like that, and if I don't then it's Peter to the rescue, right?…your Mr. Superman, huh! You hurt me with Zack, my best friend, and then you double down with Peter. Why wouldn't I look for someone else who can genuinely love me? Morgan, you don't love me. You only think you do and even that is part time, because if you truly loved me, Zack would never have happened…couldn't have….and you certainly wouldn't have allowed me to come to see you repeatedly and never even give me the courtesy of seeing your face. Admit it. I'm just your habit, and the sooner you realize that, the freer both of us will be. For me, I'm out. I'm done with this!"

I can't speak. I just watch the close of day.

He slowly and carefully lines up his magazine neatly with the others on the table, looks at me, and I see the lip biting head on. After a moment, he turns and leaves without another word. The door closes quietly, and the dam breaks inside of me.

After a half hour, the doctor comes in and gives me a full report on my *condition.* I have to drink more water…a lot more water, and I have to eat real food. He gives me vitamins to take and a lecture on what happens when you stress out or work too hard on an empty stomach. Even though he tells me I can get dressed and sign myself out, I am still sitting up in the bed, knees bent with my head resting on them. I am so sad. Through the blur of my tear, I see a familiar face. There he is, my very best friend, Peter Lewis Reston IV. He is standing in the open door, seemingly, to assess the present situation of the tiny form before him. I know that I am a crumpled mess, but he is here with his six feet stately stature that towers over me when I stand next to him, his broad shoulders that protect me almost daily, and those bewitching black eyes that sometime appear to look through me to my very soul. Already I feel better just seeing him standing there with his familiar dark curly hair, and the square jaws that twitch whenever I get too close to him. Tears move down my face and meet together under my chin; I swipe them away, and see his grin and that deep dimple that always shows up on the left side of his face just in time to make me smile.

"What's up, baby girl?...been a minute." His greeting is quiet, and his graceful strides are at my bedside almost in one swift move. In an instant, he is sitting in front of me, holding my face and gently wiping my tears away. He kisses my nose lightly and instinctively I move back so slightly that I doubt he notices. He takes a deep breath and lets his eyes fall.

"Derek, right?" I hear the long exhale, nod in agreement, and he puts his arms around me and pulls me close to him.

"Jerk, he mutters in my hair. "Why do you keep letting him make you cry?" His question is sincere, and I can tell from his voice that he really does not understand at all. He knows nothing of Zack or how much I have hurt Derek.

"Where I'm from, love is patient, kind, and does not hurt."

I don't respond. I can feel the steady beat of his heart and his protective arms tighten around me. I hear his soft breathe in my ear, bury my head in his chest, and inhale the sweet smell of him. For the moment, I am content, but only for the moment because reality has a rude way of interrupting the dream, Xing out the fantasy, and halting the fairy tale just to poke fun at the heart that inevitably is still breaking...still shattering into a million little pieces, and still reminding me that this is all my fault. But, I linger in his arms anyway as unfair as that may be.

Within the hour I dress, check myself out of the hospital, and get ready to face Derek again just long enough to retrieve my car keys from the table in front of his couch. Out in the bright noon sunlight, I realize my weakness and steady myself on Peter's arm.

"OK, baby girl?"

"Yeah. I'm good."

"When did you eat last?"

"I can't remember, but I know they gave me fluids at the hospital and some other stuff that I couldn't swallow at the time."

"Well, we'll pick up something light now." In the car, I experience that woozy feeling that tells me something is not all right with the world, and I hold my head and close my eyes to steady myself. Peter drives us to a quiet little oceanfront eatery where we enjoy the fresh mild fish of the day, talk a bit, laugh a lot, and just enjoy each other's company. For a moment, I forget my sadness listening to Peter's corny jokes and funny memories of past instructors, dance rehearsals, and performances. Whenever I watch laughter take over his face, that dimple of his creates a perfect dance going in and out of sight. There's something quite sexy about that look, but I have never been able put my finger on it. For the first time in a while, I feel relaxed and after a little over an hour, we finish our meal, pay the tab, and leave.

It takes less than ten minutes to get to Derek's and on cue, my heart picks up its beat and pounds inside my chest like the beat of an African drum.

"I'll go. You stay here," Peter almost commands.

"I can go, I protest."

"No, stay here." That is a command, and I am too weak to fight this silly battle with his testosterone raging. Peter jumps out of his light gray Wrangler Rubicon and heads up the walkway that seems longer than I remember it. He makes his way to the door, raises his fist to knock, and the door swings open far too fast for greeting a casual visitor. I see Peter throw both of his hands up, and I jump out of the car, and run to his side.

"I don't want trouble man. I just want Morgan's car keys. That's all. Be cool."

"Don't come up to my house telling me what to do." I hear expletives and see the lip-biting thing. I know this is not cool.

"Derek, I just need my keys so I can go home, take a shower, and get back in bed. I'm exhausted. We don't want any trouble. Please."

"If you don't make trouble, there won't be trouble. I just don't want this clown coming to my house, Morgan." Derek's eyes and Peter's eyes have not parted from each other...not one second. It's like I'm a third party that is almost invisible. I see the keys in Derek's hand. I move close to him, take his hand in mine and try to retrieve them, but he jerks away and throws the keys. Peter's reflexes are on automatic and he catches them with one hand. I grab Peter's other hand and pull him to my car. He opens the door for me. I get in, and buckle up.

"I'll be right behind you Mo. Don't drive too fast. OK?" Peter's hand in on the roof of my car tapping out some nervous beat, and he leans in and kisses my forehead.

"OK," I almost whisper. Peter gets in his car, I hear his door slam, and we drive away separately. When I glance in my rearview mirror,

Derek is still standing in front of his house and an odd sense of satisfaction creeps across my face. I swear I can see him biting that bottom lip.

I put the top down so I can feel the cool moist air off the ocean, and after about twenty minutes I wheel into the park in front of my house. Peter parks beside me, jumps out of his car before I can cut my ignition off, and opens my door. Home at last! Inside my safe haven, I turn on the lights, tap my iPad on to music, and let the soothing sounds take over my tense body. When I turn around, Peter is right in front of me, actually invading my space. I let my eyes find his and I know that he wants to kiss me, but I also know, I am not ready for that. He seems to sense my hesitance and just touches my arms instead.

"Mo, come go with me." His voice is almost a whisper, and his eyes are searching mine for an answer.

"My eyes close, my shoulders slump, and I whine, "go with you where? I'm really tired. I just want to take a shower, crawl into my bed, and forget this day."

He leans down a little and pushes me out from him so that he can see my eyes. He cocks his head to the side, gives me that special shy smile he uses to lure his girls, and that cute little dimple shows up just in time to stop my definite no.

"Come on, Mo. I won't stay long," he pleads. "I want to show you something…something beautiful…something calming…something that will put a smile on that face of yours for sure."

I roll my eyes because I can't think of a thing that could put a genuine smile on my face.

"Peter." I draw his name out with a breathy sound so he will know how hard this is for me right now, as if that will make a different to this very determined man in front of me.

I exhale and feel him wrap his arms around my waist and pull me closer. I don't miss that little tugging thing he does to my lower back every time we're close, and he thinks he can get away with that kind of intimacy. I feel the shadow of a smile curling on my lips ever so slightly, and despite the fact that it's a sad smile, it's still a smile none-theless. Peter has worked his little magic again.

"I'm not up for this right now. I'm really not," I whine.

I look directly into his eyes, and he holds me fixed on them. I hear a slow, deep intake of air and see his disappointment. He drops his hands from my waist and moves away from me like a spoiled little brat who is not getting his way. He plops down on the floor pillows, leans back against the wall, and looks up at me with those gorgeous seductive black eyes.

"So ,what are you up for? Sitting here in the middle of a bed with your box of tissues and a face full of tears for that jerk? Is that what you're up for?"

"That's harsh, PeterWe stare at each other for an uncomfortable second or two, and Peter gets up from the floor, and moves over close to me. Without a word, he playfully nudges my shoulder and I nudge back on him.

"Sorry, Mo."

Peter strokes my cheek and brings his hand around to my chin and lifts my face with one finger to see my eyes. "I just don't want you to be alone right now, and seriously, I want you to look at what's in front of you, and stop looking back at some fairy tale ending you've been dreaming since you were a kid. The best medicine for you right now is one good dose of "not looking back" and two tablespoons of charm and good looks. He scrunches up his mouth in that sexy way he has and points to himself. "I can administer that medicine if you let me." Then there is that goofy grin he has when he loses control after his jokes, and I burst out laughing with him in what could have been a very serious moment. Just two minutes ago, I would not have believed that he could pull this kind of laugher from me....not so soon after Derek closed the door behind him and left me crumpled in a hospital bed.

"It's still early...still a little light outside, he urges. Come go with me," he begs in his playful easy-going manner.

"Where?" I ask with exasperation that I certainly hope he hears.

"I'm not telling you where, but I'll tell you this: You won't be disappointed."

I know Peter well enough to realize that when he wants something not much is going to stop him. I'm tired, I'm sad, and I would rather just go to bed, but by now, I know that's not going to happen so I make a final decision: get this over with rather than stand here debating him for another two hours. I know he's not going to go home, so let's just make the best of this. The sooner I go, the sooner I get to come home and bury myself in the sorrow that he thinks I can't wait to experience.

"OK, but I have to take a shower first. What kind of clothes should I put on for this little...outing?"

"Anything comfortable…Jeans…slacks….shirt, whatever. We're not going to a formal dance," he chuckles. He does a formal révérence, and then something else he just creates on the spot to make me laugh.

"OK, you crazy man. Let me get ready. I'll be back in a minute. Make yourself at home, but STAY OUT OF MY REFRIGERATOR!" We both laugh because we both know what he can do to that.

In a half hour, I'm dressed in jeans, a cute pink camisole, my favorite sandals and a long gold chain that Derek had given me on my twenty- first birthday. I put on some small gold dangling earrings, and flat iron my hair straight and keep it down so that it frames my face and falls comfortably down my back. Peter sees me and lets out a playful whistle.

"Wow, girl. You make me lose my mind."

Well, I don't want to do that. One of us needs to be sane. I'm warning you. I am a bit out of sorts right now."

"I know, and we won't be long. I just don't see you sitting here alone tonight dreaming about something you feel could have been that we both now know is not going to be."

I stop dead in my tracks and look directly at him as my temper flares.

"No, Peter. *We* don't *know* anything. Unless you have some kind of crystal ball hidden somewhere, I don't think you know what's going to happen in your own little stupid, precarious life. So don't try to predict mine." I stop and take a deep breath. "Just because Derek walked away today doesn't mean a thing. Anyway, let's just go before you make me really mad, and I change my mind." I snatch up my keys and head out of the door in front of him. He follows behind, and as the door closes I hear him mutter, "Sorry."

The drive up the coast is surprisingly refreshing to me, and we talk about a lot of silly things that make us laugh. During the drive, there are moments of complete silence and surprisingly, they are some of the most comfortable for us. We are so use to each other that words are not always necessary. Before I know it, we are parking and Peter takes my hand and starts a slow run down the beach near Derek's new beach house. He scampers up this rocky place, holds out his hand for me, and we make the short climb together. We cuddle at the top of what Peter tells me is a very special place they call *The Rock*, and when I look out, I see why it's so special. There are at least a million stars twinkling overhead, and the ocean seems to meet them and greet us in all of its own vastness and majestic beauty. The view immediately creates for us a sense of "peace beyond understanding." It is one of the most comforting natural scenes I have ever witnessed in my life; the light from the moon and stars, the sound and the smell of the ocean, our stony seat and the soft breeze kissing my face are all an unbelievable combination of God's creation. The stress melts away, and for the first time in a long time, I feel a complete sense of tranquility. Peter draws me close to him and we sit, for at least an hour, in the midst of God's gift, and it is just what I need at the moment.

Chapter 11

SEARCHING FOR NEW LIFE

~Saying "goodbye" is never the heart and soul of farewell~

It's been two weeks since I left the hospital, let Peter take care of me, sat with him at *The Rock*, and looked out on the most unbelievable natural sight I have ever seen in my life. It is one of those incredible views that make you believe that without a doubt there is a God.

Since then, I have had a much better time on the dance floor. I have settled myself down and actually gotten my groove back. Learning one of the last few dances for our Broadway show has been like child's play, but I still have some major problems. Derek has been blowing up my phone and even though I have not answered one of his calls, I have listened to all of his messages. They have all been basically the same: *"Morgan, pick up. Why are you doing this? We have always been able to talk. I'm not going to stop calling so you may as well pick up. I need to know how you are."* I'm just not ready to take the chance of listening to him right now, and certainly not ready to take the chance of looking into his misty brown eyes knowing that he is in love with someone else. Just the memory of those eyes makes me crumble, so I'm really glad that I have had a lot to keep me busy and glad that Peter has been very attentive to me.

I look at the clock and snap it off before it signals 8:30. I'm happy to have the day off because I have a lot I want to get done so staying in bed is definitely not one of them. I throw the sky blue and yellow satiny spread back and sit up on the side of the bed. I reach for my phone, take it off mute, and see that Derek has already made two calls this morning and left his usual messages. Rolling my eyes is my only response to his persistence. I make the bed and head for the shower. I slip on my brown slacks, a yellow tank, my gold necklace, and brown sandals. I brushed my hair and let the crinkly waves fall where they may. In the kitchen, I make a breakfast of oatmeal, a banana, a boiled egg and juice. When I finish, I put the dishes in the dishwasher and head toward the front of the house. I hear the doorbell.

"I told Peter not to come until 12:00," I mutter to myself. "It's just 11:08."

I snatch open the door all ready to fuss about his being too early when my eyes meet Derek's.

"Hey, what are you doing here?" I can hear the surprise in my own voice.

"You won't answer your phone; you won't return my messages, and I need to know if you're ok." Derek says all of this while brushing past me, and refusing to wait for any invitation to come inside. I close the door, turn toward him, but keep my hand on the knob.

His rant continues. "What, in three weeks you couldn't answer one message? You couldn't just say, Derek, I'm ok. I don't want to talk right now?"

"All right. Derek, I'm ok. I don't want to talk right now. Actually, on second thought, I don't want to talk with you at all...anymore." I release the doorknob and move a little closer to him, and fold my arms in front of me.

"There is nothing else for us to say, Derek." My voice is resigned and he is standing in front of me of course biting the left side of his lower lip.

"Morgan, it doesn't have to be like that. I mean we can still talk." He touches my shoulder, and I look at where his hand is resting.

"OK, Derek. Let me ask you this. Do you want me back? Are you ready to forgive me and let us go back to the way we were?"

"No." I wish I could do that, Morgan. I wish that more than anything, but I can't. You let Zack have what was supposed to be just for me. I can't get pass that, but it doesn't mean that I don't care about you. Heck, I still love you, but everything is messed up now, and as hard as I might try, I can't put it back together. I know we can't be friends, but the least you could do is let me know you're all right. After all, the last time I saw you, you were in the hospital. I admit, I have moved on to some extent, but that doesn't mean I don't care at all about you anymore. I'm not trying to fool myself. I do care, and I always will. I don't think we should try to change that."

"Derek, I know I messed up and that changed things, but you are the one who actually changed partners. Not me. You did that when you fell in love with someone else. I still love you. I still want you. I still miss us, even though you say there is no us....But I'm not going to be used, Derek, and if you think I am, you don't know me like you think you do."

"I'm not trying to use you, Babe."

"...And as of this moment, right here, right now, don't call me that anymore. I'm not that to you anymore. Save that for your new girlfriend," I say with an air of sarcasm, frustration, and what I will admit is a large dose of jealousy.

"See, that's how you want to be."

"...and how is that?"

"You just want to be all hard like you don't care. I know you love me."

Derek moves closer and puts his arms around my waist, and for a moment I let him. I want so much to be in his arms, to feel his soft lips on mine, and to look up into those beautiful eyes of his and see that his love for me has not vanish one bit....but reality stands stiff in all of its arrogance between us, and just his touch is different to me now. It isn't the comfortable feeling of "home." I can tell someone else occupies the space in his arms, and I can tell he really does love her. In that one instant though, when I am in that space that is so familiar to me, my memory sees us dance together, laugh at silly jokes, cry together, play on the beach, nurse each other in sickness, fight over where to eat and what to eat, watch each other sleep, cheer at football games, study together, and sit quietly without one word

156

passing between us. In that one instant, I see, but cannot feel my old Derek. He's gone. Reality, however, tells me that despite his efforts, he is having a hard time not talking with me, not seeing me, not sharing things with me anymore. He misses me tremendously. He wants to move on, but times, experiences and yes, love make this hard for him too. The difference is he wants a new life, and I don't. I made the fatal mistake, he didn't. He doesn't trust me, but I would trust him with everything I have. He can't really get pass my night with Zack, and I could care less about those few meaningless moments.

I gently push out of his arms, but I can't resist touching his cheek, and pushing that stray strand of hair out of his eye…something I've done in intimate moments countless times. I take his hand in mine, bring his fingers to my lips, and kiss them. With my left hand I cover the spot where lips have touched as if to seal the kiss in that place forever, and then I release his hand.

"Derek, you're falling in love with another woman. You have obviously found someone you love more than you love me, and you've moved on. So now, as much as this hurts, and, make no mistake, it devastates me, the only sensible thing to do is to let go and move on also as best I can, and that is what I'm trying to do….nothing more and nothing less. You have to let me go completely or we'll make each other miserable for a lifetime, and I don't think either of us deserves that. I don't know how you let someone else take my place or how you can be so unforgiving, but that is the way it is. So, know that I will always love you, but I have to ask you to go. Don't call me, don't try to see me…just let me go; otherwise, you will destroy me."

I see tears in his eyes, and I feel the burning in mine. Almost without blinking, we look intensely at each other, letting years of love seemingly morph into some crystal cage sitting at the feet of once upon a time. He takes me into his arms and holds me. I feel his grip tighten. I feel the deep breath he takes, and then he bends down and kisses my lips.

"Morgan, I do love you, he murmurs in my ear. He pulls me even closer and kisses me again, then releases me, and walks out of my house. No other words need to be spoken. I feel his love, and I know he still feels mine.

As the front door closes behind him, I hear a car door slam outside. When I look through the window, I see Peter standing beside the Wrangler. I see Derek stop and look at Peter, but without a word passing between them. Derek gets in his car and drives away; Peter turns the knob on my door, and I burst into tears and rush into his arms.

Peter is perfect. He doesn't ask me why I'm crying over *The Jerk*. He doesn't say I need to forget Derek. He doesn't try to convince me that I can just get over it. He doesn't protest Derek's presence. He doesn't do any of that. He quietly comes over to me without a word, takes me in his arms and just holds me. Every now and then, I can feel his hands on my hair, and I feel him lightly kiss the top of my head.

"You said…you said…you had a lot to do today," he whispers in my hair. He tries to pull away and see my face, but I cling to him and hold him firmly to me. He twists me back and forth in his arms.

"Is it all called off?" His voice is soft and caring. Kissing the top of my head he questions, "Are we just staying in now?" Somehow, I find my voice buried in Peter's chest.

"No." I take a deep breath. "No, I've got to learn to live with this. I've got to find my way back to me, and I can't do that isolating myself and hiding away in my house. Derek has moved on and so I will too."

"That's my girl." I feel Peter pull me even closer to him, and I feel his hands moving up and down my back. His touch comforts me.

"So…what are we going to do today?"

I lean back, look into his eyes, and force a grin. "Let's have some fun."

"I'm with that…my ride or yours?

"Neither. Let's just walk down the beach."

"Cool."

I change into my white short shorts, grab what I call my summer bag from the hook on the wall inside my bedroom, and pull Peter out of the door. The summer sun is hot, but the breeze coming off the water is cool, and I barely notice the beads of perspiration forming under my nose. We throw our shoes into my bag, and even though my heart is heavy, we race laughing toward the water's edge.

"Catch me if you can," I yell over my shoulder. I get a glimpse of Peter stopping and standing with his hands on his hips. He looks gorgeous standing in the light of the sun with the mist from the ocean creating what looks like glitter on his chest.

"That ought to be real easy," and it looks like in two graceful steps he's at my heels, grinning and showing those award winning teeth of his. I scream and I feel the air from his hands swiping at me, but I get away. In the water I stop and splash him.

"You're asking for it now," he teases as he tries again to grab me, but I am just out of his reach. He splashes and the water blinds me for an instant and gives him just enough time to reach down and grab both of my legs and lift me off the ocean's floor. He throws me over his shoulder as I fight to regain control of myself.

"Not so brave now are you, Missy?

""Put me down you beast!"

I beat on his back and pull his hair in an attempt to make him lose his balance or just drop me to stop my barrage of licks. Instead, he flips me around so fast that I lose my grip on him, and without losing a beat he swings me around in the water like a rag doll. We are laughing, the water is spraying over us and, for me, it is almost as if time stops and the world goes into slow motion. I see the mist from our motion slowly making its way back home; I hear our laughter echo off the breeze, and I see a mirror beneath us created when the ocean kisses the sun….and then time resumes. Peter puts me down and I am standing in front of him. His alluring black eyes look down on me, and his smile is captivating. However, it is the water sliding down his muscles that really catches my attention, and I can feel myself staring at a Peter that I have never before seen. The water that surrounds us, the sun that beams down on us, and the breeze that fans us all help to accentuate the beauty of his masculinity, and I am transfixed in the moment with my mouth wide open. In those few seconds, he could have kissed me, and I wouldn't have protested….but, he didn't even try.

—◊◊◊—

We make our way out of the water, stumbling, laughing and making deep foot tracks as we go. I grab my favorite beach towel out of the summer bag, and spread it on the sand, and we both plop down.

"So…what now, boss?"

"Boss?"

"Yeah, you're controlling the day, right?"

"Well, I didn't look at it that way. I thought you were just trying to please me and get me out of my Derek mood."

"I think you're right so let's start by not calling what's his name's name….Ever!"

"OK," I laugh. "Cool."

Peter lay on his side and looks directly at me. He props his head up with one hand and uses the other to swipe my nose with his index finger. "How about we go back to the house, get this sand off, and take a little ride."

"So, already I'm not the boss?" I laugh.

"Right. So, pick your little butt up, get your stuff together and let's go," he playfully commands grabbing my hand and pulling me to my feet.

We walk back to the house with me carrying bag and towel and him finding shells and skipping them on the water as we talk and laugh about silly things. We take turns showering, and I change into white slacks and an off the shoulder hot pink blouse that fits at the waist and fans out over my stomach. Peter puts on a pair of clean blue jeans and a light blue collarless shirt that he just happen to have in the jeep or at least that's what he tells me.

161

We race down the highway in the Wrangler toward his next surprise destination. I could care less where we're heading because anything beats sitting around in my tears. After forty-five minutes or so, we pull up to a beautiful mansion where valet parking is obviously the norm. The entire place personifies money, and my mouth drops open in amazement.

"Are we dressed right for this?"

"I think so. If not, looks like there's plenty here, so you can make a change."

"What? You are unbelievable. Is this a party?"

"Get out, the valet needs to park us."

"Peter? Are you crazy? Do you know these people?" I whisper.

"Yeah, I met them once or twice." His answer is very casual and upsetting to me.

"Once or twice? Do they know you're coming…and bringing a guest? See, Peter, this is what I fuss with you about all the time. You never take anything seriously enough. You're not a responsible person. You take life too casually sometimes. Some things are serious. What are you doing? I know people like this. You don't just drop in on them."

"Morgan, just get out. Let the man do his job."

The valet smiles, takes the keys, and is about to say something when I see Peter slightly shake his head no. He grabs my hand, and I reluctantly allow him to pull me up the curved driveway with its manicured lawn and unbelievable landscaping. At the front door, I stand back waiting for Peter to use the magnificent brass door-knocker or ring the bell, but he does neither. Instead, he pushes the door open and peeks in. I am standing behind him now with my hand on his back trying to see around him.

"Peter, you don't just walk in people's houses without knocking or ringing a bell or something. Close the door, and ring the bell," I whisper.

"Be cool. I got this," he whispers back at me. He pushes the door open more and pulls me inside with him. The foyer is huge. The marble tan floor is glistening like new money, and the chandelier above us is crystal with tiny lights that reflect off the glass. The winding stairs lead to something huge above me, but I can't tell exactly what it is. My eyes are about to pop out of my head with both fear and amazement when a uniformed middle-aged lady comes from someplace and startles me.

"Peter, we're so glad you could come. I heard you might not be able to make it. They're both at the pool, so just go on out."

"Hey, Sarah. What's up?" Peter plants a kiss on her cheek, and I can tell she is secretly swooning from it. Her eyes fall on me, and Peter pulls me from behind him.

"She's a little shy," he jokingly explains. "This is Morgan LaRue, a very good friend of mine."

"Well, welcome, Morgan. No need to be shy, dear," she assures me. "It's a pretty friendly down-to-earth bunch here usually." She laughs and shakes my hand.

"Thank you," I manage.

Peter takes my hand and leads me through several rooms, to a huge kitchen with a back wall of all glass so clear that if I had not been with him, I probably would have bumped into it on my way outside. Through the glass, I see the ocean and it is a breath-taking view, one hard to describe in words. Stunning is the closest I can get to its reality.

"Where are we Peter? This is not funny," I whisper. "Look how we're dressed."

"You're fine. You can stop whispering. They know we're here," he whispers back.

"Who knows we're here?...And why are *you* still whispering?" I ask still dragging behind him.

He whispers his answer. "The people I met once or twice. Now, come on. They don't bite or at least they didn't the one or two times I met them."

Outside, we are standing on a hill and stone steps lead to an enormous pool, a hot tub, and a beautifully decorated patio below us, and now I see the two people that Peter has met once or twice. Their backs are turned to us so they make no effort to call to us, wave at us or otherwise welcome us into their private sanctum. While I stand with my mouth agape in awe at the beauty of all that I see, Peter is acting like he lives here and pulling me toward them down the steps. At the bottom, he disturbs the couple's peace.

"Guess who's here? He shouts much louder than necessary even if they are hard of hearing. An attractive lady in her fifties turns first and before I can catch my breath or still my heart from jumping out of my chest she is on Peter, hugging and kissing him. A tall, handsome

164

man also in his fifties follows in his swim trunks and robe slapping Peter on the back.

"Thought you said you couldn't come by this week, but we're always glad to see you, son."

"Yes, we are baby, and who is this gorgeous lady with you?"

"Mom, Dad, this is Morgan LaRue, my new dance partner."

Even though I must confess that I had an incredible evening, adored both of his parents, was fascinated with every inch of the phenomenal Reston Estate, and had the most delectable dinner I've experienced in months, I will guarantee that Peter Lewis Reston, IV will never pull another stunt like that on me as long as life for him exists. Much to his chagrin, I happened to have been in charge of warm-ups and Pilates Class the next day.

Arianna

Chapter 12

ENGAGED

~Love is its own boss, and it will always have its own way~

Both of us find our work in Virginia to be exciting, engaging and down right thrilling, but Derek insists that no matter how busy we are, we must see each other as often as possible. We set a daily date to have dinner together. It's funny that with all of his insistence, he is the one who most frequently can't make the date. We laugh about this, and he always promises to do better.

One Saturday in early December, he calls to set a specific time to be together. It is to be at 8:00 p.m. and he is taking me to an expensive waterfront restaurant. At the appointed time, he is prompt and has reserved an upstairs private corner room that overlooks the ocean. When we take our seats, we see a multiplicity of stars in the night sky and the moon, bright and beautiful. The light reflecting on the water is mesmerizing, and the sound of the ocean captivates us both, and we are silent for a while relaxing in this nocturnal magical beauty. Our table is elegantly decorated with white linens, red cloth napkins, a centerpiece of red roses and white tea light candles. A huge beautiful Christmas tree is lit with tiny white lights and adorns the center of the room. All of this and a nearby fireplace create an atmosphere of enchantment.

Derek is quiet and sitting back in his chair across from me, staring with those bedroom eyes. With his elbows resting on the arms of the chair, his fingers are intertwined and are curled around his mouth. It is as if he is studying me...studying my mood, my feelings and even the very soul of me.

"Are you happy, Ari?" His voice is subdued.

"I have never been happier in my entire life, Derek."

He does not move an inch, and his eyes meet mine, and they are so very serious.

"Are you sure?"

"Of course, I'm sure. Why are you asking?"

"You told me that at one point in your life, you didn't have time to get serious, and, I asked, 'what about now?' Your response was that you would tell me when I had a need to know. Well, I have a *need* to know...now."

There is a very slight smile on his lips, and it is somewhat obscured by his fingers which have not moved.

"What are you doing? I think you're been trying too many cases. I feel like I'm on the stand before some unforgiving judge, and I have to be careful of my answer before the sentence," I laugh. "You're funny, Derek. I am not one of your clients."

"Oh, so you think this is funny, huh? You promise me an answer when I need to know, and now that I tell you my need to know, you laugh it off?" He is not smiling, and the fingers still have not moved.

The waiter interrupts and takes our order for dinner, and Derek orders an expensive bottle of champagne. As soon as the waiter leaves, he assumes his original position with the fingers and fixes his serious look again.

"Now, back to my question. Do you have time for a serious relationship...*now*?"

I crack up laughing at this crazy man across the table from me.

"Yes, Derek. I have time."

"...time for what, my dear?"

"...time for a serious relationship," I giggle.

"That's all I wanted to know," he says in his serious voice. "Why couldn't you just answer that simple question?"

"I guess, Attorney Wellington, because I think it's a...stupid question. It seems like the answer would be obvious to you. You're supposed to be a smart lawyer...a Harvard graduate no less, certainly capable of making simple logical deductions."

"...and maybe it would have been obvious if you hadn't made such a big deal about answering it in the first place way back when I first asked you," he retorted.

I giggle and simply shake my head to express complete disbelief at this foolishness.

He moves from his seat and gently pulls me up from the table, holding my hand and looking into my eyes.

"In light of your answer, Miss Channing, I have another question."

He gets down on one knee, and is now completely serious.

"Arianna, sweetheart, in a very short time, you have easily become the love of my life, the lady of my dreams, and the pulse of my heart; will you marry me?"

"Oh Derek, are you serious? I love you so much, baby. I've loved you from the first night we met. When we're not together, I can't breath. Yes, yes, I'll marry you."

Tears burn my eyes.

Still on his knee, he places a diamond masterpiece on my finger. It is pear shaped, elegantly brilliant and flanked by baguette cut diamonds. The brilliance is almost blinding. When he rises, he takes me in his arms and kisses me with passion and, again, I am totally speechless. The rest of the evening is unbelievable with its excellent food, amazing natural beauty, and this phenomenal man seated in front of me rocking my world again with every word, every gesture, and every nuance of himself. Even with my deep-seated faith, I find this blessing incredible.

I unlock the door to my condo, throw my coat on the sofa, turn my iPad to my favorite playlist and look at Derek. He has already taken off his coat, gone straight to sitting relaxed on the sofa, and is quietly following me with his eyes. Wow! He makes my heart skip beats. I sit down beside him, and put my head on his shoulder.

"I can't believe we're engaged," I gush looking up at him, and holding my hand out to view the beauty of my ring....all of this in six months.

"Do you really like it?" he asks with some uncertainty in his voice.

"I absolutely love it," I reply still examining it. "What's not to love? You couldn't have pleased me more."

"I can't believe it took me so long to put it on your finger. I knew what I wanted very soon after I met you."

"Did you, now?"

"Yes, I did."

"So, what stopped you?"

He pauses and takes a deep breath.

"...a few things."

"Like what, Derek?"

At first he doesn't answer; he simply shakes his head like he doesn't know, and then he responds.

"I just needed to be sure."

"Are you sure now."

"Very sure, baby...so very sure."

For a fleeting moment, I detect something strange in his voice... in his eyes. It's almost as if he travels to another place in his mind. For an instant, he doesn't seem to be completely with me, but I am far too happy to give that a second thought.

"What is it about me that you love so much, Derek?" I ask playfully.

"I love your honesty, your loyalty, your morals. I love your intellect, your sense of humor, your perseverance, and I can't lie; you're extremely easy on the eyes, Baby."

He wiggles my nose between his fingers, and we laugh together.

Wine Time is relaxing and serene. The guitar and saxophone draw us in, and Derek reaches for my hand, pulls me up to dance, and we let the sounds take us to a dream like place. I lay my head on his chest, wrap my arms around his neck, and feel the beat of his heart. I love this man so much; I love being close, and the smell of him immediately transports me to my own microcosmic paradise.

"I miss you." I look up at him. "I miss your misty brown eyes following me around a room, staring at me every hour. I miss our New York leisure days." I smile. "Derek, I never thought this would happen to me. This is what I prayed for and dreamed of for so long, and with all of my faith, I still had some doubts that I would find this kind of happiness. I had no idea that I would actually find my Prince Charming."

"So, I am your Prince Charming. That's very good to know." His smile is subtle and genuine.

"You are my Prince, and you have been for a while now. I appreciate you so much, especially your patience. Sometimes our history makes it hard to believe that really good things actually exist. Sometimes we have no idea what God can do if we give Him half a chance, and get out of His way. Like I said, I never thought this would happen to me."

"I'm the one blessed to have found you, and the plus is that you actually have fallen in love with me or as you say you're 'growing in love' with me." One of his fingers curls under my chin and he lifts my lips to his.

Derek, everyday I love you more than the day before, and these few months have been enough to let me know that you are the one."

"...and you are the one for me."

I move out of his arms and open the draw of one of the end tables. His eyes are following me, but I want to surprise him so I am careful as I take an object from the drawer. I come back to him and reach for his hand. He has a puzzled look on his face when I open my fist and put the cold metal object in his palm. He opens his hand to see the stopwatch that he gave me some months ago. He looks from the watch to my eyes.

"The control is yours now, Baby. I give it to you. Push right here on the top when you want time to stop," I smile as I repeat his words from many days ago.

"You're funny, Ari." He says the words, but does not laugh, and only a small smile curls on his lips.

He slips the watch into his pocket and kisses my forehead.

"I love you, baby," he declares.

We sway to the music, and he kisses my cheek, then my neck. He moves around to my mouth, and I feel more passion in this kiss than I have ever felt since we've been together.

He pushes away from me slightly, and looks directly into my eyes.

"Ari, are you sure about this?...I mean absolutely sure. I don't want you to do anything that you don't want to do." His voice is quiet, sexy, and very serious.

"I could not be more sure. I love you so much, Derek."

He reaches up and begins to remove the diamond studs that decorate my hair, and when all are out, he loosens the fishtail braid and my dark brown locks fall around my shoulders. He finger combs the strands and plays with the hair that naturally curls around my face.

He is so sensual, and our moves are now automatic...no real thought. I know what he wants, and he knows what I want, and our lips tease and meet. I feel the zipper of my dress loosen, and the soft pink material pools at my feet. With one finger he moves a strap off of my shoulder and kisses where it has rested. The music encases us and gently he lifts me and carries me to our bed. There, together, we lay for the first time. We share our love...our passion. We are wrapped up in the ecstasy of that unique place where true love resides...that place where tears of joy and happiness flow because we are one.

In the morning, after waking in each other's arms, after soaking in the bliss of another level to our relationship, after realizing the depth of what has changed, we have a carpet picnic breakfast. We talk, laugh, play, joke, and just enjoy being together.

I shower and dress and follow my lover to his beach cottage. There he showers, dresses and takes me for a walk on the beach. We come to our favorite place that someone has named *The Rock*, and we sit basking in the sun, listening to the ocean, and feeling the winter wind wrap its essence around us.

"It's beautiful here, Derek, and I have known this place for a long time. I spoke of it when we first met. Can we marry here on this spot under God's umbrella sky?"

He wraps his arms around me.

"Yes, it is, and yes we can. I can't wait until you're here with me. I so much want you by my side everyday. I miss that since we left New York."

"Yeah, we did get spoiled there, didn't we?" I reply.

"Very much so. Are you cold, Baby?" He pulls me closer to him.

"Not at all. The wind feels good on my face."

Derek takes a thermos and two cups from his bag, and pours us both a cup of hot chocolate. We sit drinking the hot liquid and feeling the warmth of it and each other.

"Derek, I want you to know how much last night meant to me. Not just because we took our love to another level, but also because you were so patient with me. You never pressured me or tried to force me to move faster than my heart would allow. I will always be grateful for that."

He took my hand in his and played around with my fingers.

"That's because I want your whole heart and nothing less. Ari, I want you to know how much I care about your happiness so that you will care about mine. I want to be gentle with your heart so that you will be gentle with mine.

"I understand that more than you know."

"Yes, I think you do because you've alluded to a few negative things in your past, and I don't know exactly what they are nor do I need to, but what I do know is what I want for us in our present."

"I think you have been showing me a lot of what you want for us. Derek, I can really feel your love and know that it's real."

Love is tricky, Ari. You can try to force it, you can try to wait for it, you can be careful with it, you can try to ignore it, you can deny it, you can try to hold on to it when you know it's gone, or you can just accept it; but the bottom line is, it's always in control of itself. Love is its own boss, and it will always have its own way with you. We're blessed because we're going in the same direction it's going."

Derek is speaking slowly and thoughtfully, looking into the distance without seeing, and I can tell that he is not solely talking with me. I can tell he is remembering something that hurts even now that it glances his memory. I won't ask about it now, because I see the pain just before he drops his eyes. This is the second time I've sensed something odd behind his eyes.

He looks over at me.

"Derek, do I really make you happy? Do you have any doubts about my love for you?"

"Absolutely not....no doubts at all...and you make me ecstatic.

"Do you trust me?"

"Yes, Ari, with my whole heart."

"When do I make you the happiest?"

He smiles and looks down at his folded hands. "They're just little things....like the way you look at me when I walk into a room.

176

Sometimes it's the way you catch my hand when we're together or that little personal thing you do to my back when I kiss you. It's like last night when you put the stopwatch in my hand. That was all about trust....or the day you came to court to watch me. That was all about pride and interest in me. I'll admit, I was nervous that day just because you were watching. I'm glad I was almost over prepared. So... let me turn that question around. When do I make you the happiest?"

"Well, I have something new since last night." I smile to myself, and look down at my hands.

"Last night when you made love to me, I felt so vulnerable in your arms, not knowing exactly what to expect. I saw, in those moments, just how much you love me, and how much I can trust you...your patience, your gentleness, your complete care for me. You make me happy when you look at me like I'm the most important person in the world to you. I'm happy when we do little things together like we are right now....sitting here at *The Rock* looking out at all that God has created. I'm happy when you crack your little corny jokes, give me the last bite of something you really like or take a finger and move my hair away from my eyes. I'm happy just being with you, Derek.

"I love you too, Ari, but most of all I really do trust you with my heart. I want to take you some place special tomorrow."

"Really? Where?"

"I want you to ride with me up the coast to meet my Mom and Dad. It's time. You'll love them, and they will love you."

He smiles and kisses my hand, and we walk back to the cottage and sit together by the fire.

Chapter 13

DIGGING FOR GOLD

~It is impossible to accept the truth when the mind is trapped in a web of misconceptions~

It's the fifth time I've looked out of the window in the last fifteen minutes. Derek is never late so where is he now?…but then actually, he's not late. It's just that I want to get this started and over with. I'm nervous. I have already stubbed my toe twice, bitten the inside of my jaw chewing gum and broken a nail. That might not be so bad if all of that had taken place over a period of two weeks, but for me, today, all of it has taken place in the last twenty minutes.

I take my umpteenth deep breath trying to calm down, and check myself out in the mirror for the tenth time. I brush imaginary lint from my black woolen slacks again, and I straighten my matching black turtleneck top. I love the sheer asymmetric lace inset of this top, and the rhinestone clusters just set it off. It is quite the sensual top, but on second thought, maybe it's the absolute wrong thing to wear to meet Derek's parents, but it's too late to change now....or is it? I don't know. Where is Derek? My dark brown hair flows down my back with a healthy sheen, and the naughty curls that always want to fall out of place are living up to their usual behavior. My makeup is perfect because I have long known how to match the right colors with my cinnamon complexion and big hazel eyes. Derek loves these dangling earrings and they match so...on they go....another deep breath, and finally...the doorbell.

"Derek, what took you so long?"

"...and hello to you too." His sexy baritone voice is lost on my frayed nerves.

"I'm sorry. Hello. What took you so long?"

I think I said one thirty, and looking at my watch now it is one twenty-five. By my estimation, that is on time."

He takes me in his arms and tries to kiss me, but that is not happening because I can't mess up my makeup at the last minute. I hold him around his waist and look up into his eyes that usually melt me, but not today. Today is different. I'm meeting his Mom and Dad, and I have to look perfect.

"No kissing, Derek. I can't let you mess up my makeup. Let's go."

"Baby, you need to calm down. This is not the President of the United States. It's just my parents, and they will love you as much as I do with or without makeup."

He takes the chance of kissing the top of my head and smoothing my hair down around my face. He kisses the tip of my nose and smiles that killer smile. I don't say anything, but I check my hair out in the mirror again before I get in the car.

The drive is relatively short, but in my mind it takes hours. I think in reality it is about forty-five minutes. When I first see the house, I utter one word.

"Wow!"

"You like?"

"You never told me you all were billionaires."

"This is not my house, Baby. It's my parents."

"I know but…"

I get out of the car and throw my coat and scarf around me, and Derek and I run to the door out of the cold. He turns the knob and calls out to his parents. I see his father first. He is a tall stately looking gentleman and I see an older Derek in his face. He and Derek do some secret handshake that is only for them, and, at its end, they hug and laugh together.

"Dad, I want you to meet my fiancée, the love of my life. This is Arianna Channing. Arianna, my father, Derek Wellington."

My…My…My…what a beautiful love of your life. Miss Channing, it is a pleasure.

Thank you, Mr. Wellington. The pleasure is all mine." He takes my hand.

"What a beautiful ring. Derek, did you pick that out or Miss Channing did you have to show him what to buy?" He laughs.

"Funny Dad."

"No, Mr. Wellington. He picked it out all by himself. I didn't even know he wanted to marry me."

"Yes you did."

"No, I didn't."

"He has always been full of surprises, Miss Channing. Well, Congratulations you two. You make a beautiful couple. Come on inside. My wife is around here someplace."

We leave the foyer and enter a theater room and I see Nina Wellington for the first time. She is slim with her hair pulled back and tendrils that frame her oval face. Her eyes are big and dark brown but lack that misty look that is Derek's signature. She is pretty and does not look at all to be fifty years old. She is sitting in a yellow leather theater seat switching channels on a TV almost the size of the entire wall. On the opposite side there are floor to ceiling shelves holding every film you can think of, all organized by genre. The surround sound gives the feel of a commercial movie house and while I take all of this in, I also notice that Mrs. Wellington has not looked at me once. Derek moves over to her side, and she plants a big kiss on his cheek while she smashes his face into almost an oblong shape. I'm sure, as I stand here, that that is something she has been doing since his birth.

"How's my favorite son?" She speaks in simulated baby talk.

"Mom, I'm your only son…actually, your only child." He straightens and takes on a serious tone, but kisses her on her cheek.

"Well, that certainly makes you my favorite," she continues in her baby talk.

His look scolds her, and he quickly changes the subject.

"Come here, I want you to meet my fiancée."

The two of them move over to me, and I smile and extend my hand as Derek introduces us.

"It's a pleasure to meet you, Mrs. Wellington."

"I don't think Derek has ever mentioned you to me, dear." After a moment or two…maybe three, she takes one finger of my hand and shakes it.

"Really?" I look at Derek, and see him exhale loudly and shake his head in disbelief at her comment, and the way she is shaking my finger.

"Mom, you know I have. Remember when I told you that I had met someone?"

"Oh, yes. That was way back in June. So, you're the one?"

"I guess so. I'm the one he was with in June. I don't know about May," I laugh to lighten the mood.

"Well, I do know about May, and I know about April, March, February, January and his whole life, but we won't talk about the months of the year or who was in them with him, dear."

"That's a good idea, Mom. The years fly by so fast it's hard to keep up with who or what or where. Right, Mom?"

"I guess I have a much better memory than you." Her tone is sarcastic.

I know that there is a little secret talk going on between them because Derek seems a bit uncomfortable, and he and his father move over to the other side of the room. I hear Mr. Wellington say something to Derek about his golf challenge. He sets up an inside golf set, and they begin to battle it out. What I notice is that Derek consistently makes two or three attempts to get his ball in the hole to his father's one. They are loud as they challenge one another, and there is a lot of laughing and joking coming from that side of the room. My side is quite different.

"Ariannie, right?"

"No. Arianna."

"Hmm. So where and when did you meet my Derek, Ariannie?"

"Arianna," I correct her again. "At a library in New York City on a Friday night in June." I emphasize the word June.

"Oh, so were you studying on a Friday night or just trying to meet boys who study on a Friday night?"

"Huh! I guess you could say a little bit of both."

"I see. So, you didn't *really* go there to study." She is looking at me with a suspicious eye and shaking her head as if in disbelief.

All of a sudden the room is hot, and I can feel the perspiration rolling down my back. I'm extremely uncomfortable, and I want to escape this house, this woman, and definitely this conversation. I can tell immediately that Nina Wellington does not like me one bit, and I'm quickly developing the same feelings for her. She is circling around me now examining…my clothes?…my body? I don't know which, but I am getting very angry and trying to control my temper just for Derek. If I were anywhere else and with anyone else I might just smack this woman down. She is speaking again, and I already dread listening.

"So, Derek tells me that you are a fashion designer of sorts, and that you have started your own business in the area." Her voice is sarcastic or condescending. I can't tell which because it all blends with her.

"Yes, I am, and I have, but I do a lot more than design."

"Really?" Well, I guess you let your fashion knowledge go out of the window when you got dressed for my formal dinner tonight."

"Formal dinner? Derek never told me there was going to be a formal dinner. He's not dressed formally."

"The dinner is at seven, dear, and Derek has lots of things he can change into upstairs or in his apartment outside." She continues her interrogation. "So...to build a business for yourself, have you always been hanging out in libraries looking to marry big?"

"I beg...your...pardon! If you are implying that I am with Derek for money? tIf so, you are sadly mistaken."

"Really?" Her voice is calm and questioning.

"Yes. Really!" My voice is angry and loud.

I have had it with this woman insulting me, and I raise my voice so that everyone in the room hears me. I have never been so insulted in my life. Derek and his father are so astonished, that they have not moved an inch since they heard my voice. The one about to putt, his father, is still holding the implement to swing. The one looking, Derek, is frozen in place. I break the "sound barrier".

Derek, take me home right now. I will not spend one more second here. Hand me your keys, get my coat, and I'll meet you at the car."

"What the hell happened?" His arms are outstretched in disbelief, and he is looking from me to his mother and back to me.

"Ask your mother. I'm sure she can tell you all about this little poor girl who's trying to "MARRY BIG." I mock and scream the words at her. He is still standing with his mouth open and his father is in the same position.

"I'm not dressed properly for her FORMAL DINNER AT SEVEN, and I have no clothes upstairs or outside in an apartment to change in like you. I storm over to Derek and dig down in his pocket to retrieve the keys while he, to no avail, tries to take my hand out of his pocket. Finally, Derek speaks, but by that time, I am half way out of the door.

"Wait a minute…wait a minute. Everybody calm down. Arianna, come back here. It's too cold outside."

"…and that's why you don't need to take a long time getting outside," I scream over my shoulder as I head to the door. I am mad!

"I don't think Ariannie likes me, Derek."

"Arianna, Mom, Arianna!" He shouts. "What have you done?"

The last thing I see when I turn around just before exiting the house is Derek looking bewildered, his father shaking his head in disbelief, and Mrs. Wellington standing in defiance with her arms folded. I get to the car, fumble with the keys in the December coldness, and I hear footsteps running behind me. I think it's Derek, and I'm yelling at him to get me out of here when I feel a warm hand on mine. It is not my Derek's. It is his father's hand. He takes the keys from me and opens the car door. I get in, and he gets in on the driver's side. I'm shivering. He puts my coat around my shoulders, and I burst out in tears.

"Don't cry, Sweetheart. Everything is going to be all right. My wife is a little over protective of her grown son that she has not realized has become a man and a wonderful man at that." His voice is calm and calming. The tears are still coming, but at least I have stopped the ugly cry with my mouth spread out in some awful contortion. He leans over and takes me in his arms and rubs my shoulder.

"Whatever she said and whatever she did, she didn't mean it. She's just a crazy old woman when it comes to that boy. I've had to endure it for twenty-five years. If you and Derek love each other, as I think you do, then you will get pass this awful Sunday afternoon. She will apologize, and what I can assure you of is that she will mean it. Derek is in there right now telling her what you mean to him, and threatening her within an inch of her life. What I can honestly tell you is that she wants him to be happy above all else. Whatever she can do to make him happy, she will do. Do you understand, Arianna? Do you understand me, Sweetheart?"

"Yes, Sir," That's all I can manage. I see Derek run out of the house over to the car. He snatches open my door and leans as far inside as he can.

"Baby, I'm so sorry. I'll take you home if that is what you want to do. Just tell me what you want, and you'll have it.

Before I can answer I see Mrs. Wellington throwing her coat around her and holding a throw in her arms as she runs towards the car. At first I can't hear her words, but as she gets closer I understand.

"Arianna, wait. Please don't leave...Please don't leave...please don't leave."

Now she is at my side of the car, pushing Derek out of her way and spreading the blanket over my legs.

"Arianna, Please don't go. I am so sorry...so very sorry. I had no right to do what I did. It was a stupid thing to do, and I don't know what got into me. Well, I do, but it is of no consequence. Please say you forgive me or at least come inside, and let me try to redeem myself."

"But your dinner...I don't have the proper clothes."

"What dinner, Mom?"

"I made that up too. It was all pretenses. I'm sorry. I was just being overprotective as usual and acting stupid about this child of mine. You are absolutely beautiful, Arianna, and no matter what you wear, you will make it beautiful too. I can see that. I know that. I just pray that I haven't messed up our relationship. Come inside and try to give me a chance to show you who I really am when I'm not crazy trying to protect this grown man who means everything to me. Ask my husband. He'll tell you that I get a little insane when it comes to Derek. Please...Come on Arianna...Come back inside. Please. Derek will never forgive me if you don't."

"You don't have to go back inside, Baby. I'll take you home. You tell me what you want."

I feel Mr. Wellington's hand on my shoulder nudging me. I look at him, and he looks at me and smiles a Derek smile, and I get out of the car and walk inside with Mrs. Wellington's arm around me trying to love me and shield me from the north wind.

Inside, I feel very uncomfortable, and I just want to be with Derek. Mrs. Wellington is fussing with the throw putting it around my shoulders and trying to usher me toward a fireplace burning in a smaller, cozier room just off from the theater.

"Arianna let me explain why I did this foolish thing. I know some things that you probably don't know, but if you did, you might understand a little better."

Derek can sense my uneasiness and his own and he steps in.

"Mom, she already knows everything she needs to know. That's why she's crying and for goodness sake don't talk anymore about January, February, March, April, and May. She knows you're sorry, and I know it to, but I think right now we need a moment alone. I'm going to take her over to my apartment, and we'll be back."

"All right, son. You do what's best for her," she says looking at me with tears in her eyes. Arianna, please think about forgiving me."

"Don't worry about it anymore, Mrs. Wellington. It's already forgiven. Like Derek says, I just need a moment to pull myself together."

Mr. Wellington has moved over close to his wife and is bringing her to one of the seats near the fireplace. I can tell that he loves her very much and wants to protect her from any additional drama. Derek puts his arm around my waist and ushers me down a rather wide hallway with beautiful paintings on one side and on the other a glass wall that allows a breathtaking view of the ocean. It is absolutely beautiful. He unlocks a door at the end of the hall, and we walk outside, down a short path made of stones, and then enter what looks like another large house. The living room is decorated with earth tones and everything has clean straight lines...a very contemporary look.

With remote in hand, he lights the room, opens the draperies, fires up a fireplace, and turns on music piped throughout the house.

"Wow, again!"

"You like?"

"No. I love." I smile and he takes me in his arms.

"I've never seen you cry before." His voice is soft and caring. He touches my face where the tears have left their stain, and kisses me where the wetness lingers.

"I've never had a reason to cry with you. You make me laugh or just be happy."

"Well, this may be an odd thing to say, Baby, but your teary eyes are beautiful. Your face looks dewy and moist and this look turns me on. You need to wash that look off before I mess up worse than my Mom. You look...Wow!" I hear him suck in his breath.

He kisses me passionately, and right now, I need his kisses, I need his arms around me, and I need this feeling of undeniable protection. I know he loves me. I can feel it in everything he says, and in every move he makes.

He wraps his arms around me even tighter and pulls me as close to him as he can. Bending his head, his lips come close to my ear and he whispers, "I love you so much, Ari. I've loved you since the first time I saw you....and then he straightens and looks directly in my eyes. Immediately I realize that I have never seen a more serious look on his face.

"Ari, don't let anything spoil our love. Ok? Not our parents, not my career, not your career, not any friends, past, present, or future, and definitely not money...nothing...don't let anything come be-tween us...please. I don't think I could bear it."

I hear a slight desperation in his voice and decide to lighten the mood. I pull out of his arms and look up into his eyes with a smile. "So, is that why you don't want me to know anything about January, February, March, April and May? I laugh. Derek had a girlfriend... Derek had a girlfriend," I sing in a teasing singsong voice.

"No. Derek had nothing until he met you....then...Derek has a girlfriend...Derek has a girlfriend," he sings back to me, pulls me back in his arms and kisses my cheek. "I'm so sorry about what hap-pened today. I don't want anything bad to touch you. It's just that Mom is always trying to protect me and keep girls away that just want me for my money. She has no idea who you are."

"And you do?"

"Ari, I keep telling you that I'm a lawyer...Harvard grad, Baby... top of my class. Of course, I know who you are," he says with a cer-tainty that I don't buy one bit because I have never told him one thing about who I am, where I am really from or anything about my family or friends, so I am pretty sure he knows NOTHING.

"So, who am I, Mr. Harvard Lawyer...top of your class?" My voice is coy and impish.

He grabs me around my waist and looks directly into my eyes.

"You are...the second daughter, and the fourth and youngest child of Edward and Elizabeth Channing, owners of Channing Designers International Fashion Houses, located all...over...the...world." He smiles.

"What? You had me investigated? Are you just like your Mom thinking everyone is after your money?" I can hear the anger in my own voice and I push out of his arms.

"Ari, stop being foolish, and get over yourself. Your picture is everywhere," he laughs. All this investigator had to do was read a newspaper every now and then, or pick up a magazine at a barbershop. Nobody has to investigate you. You just stopped modeling last summer. I could be five years old, and know who you are." He is falling on the sofa, and holding his stomach laughing at me. "Were you supposed to be some kind of big secret?"

I jump on top of him on the sofa and try to tickle him, beat him, and do whatever I want to him. We are both cracking up with laughter when I straddle him and hold his hands above his head.

"How long have you known?" I ask in my angriest playful tone.

"Since the second day I met you." He is laughing so hard he can barely get the words out clearly. "I walked downtown and your picture was splashed all over a stupid billboard in Times Square no less, advertising Channing Designs....then a bus passed by me with you and your sister smiling and hugged all up together. Big secret, you are! Daddy's best kept secret!" He is laughing uncontrollably, and so am I. I hit him playfully with my tiny fist.

"Stop before you hurt me with that little balled up thing. That thing is sharp," he laughs.

I get close to his face.

"So how did your Daddy make his money?" I ask in mock seriousness.

"Wine." He laughs. Wine and whisky.

I sit back on him. "Wine? For real?"

"No. Cigarettes." He laughs and dumps me on the floor and rolls on top straddling me. He throws my hands above my head and we are laughing so hard he loses his grip and I throw him off. We are sitting together now on the floor still giggling.

"Cigarettes? Is that the truth?"

"No, silly. You could never be a lawyer, especially a Harvard Lawyer like me," he playfully brags. "You would miss all the evidence. Serial killers would be going free like crazy, even if they had the weapon sticking out of their pocket dripping with blood." He's still laughing but stands up now and reaches down to help me up when it hits me.

"Oh,my goodness! I know! Wellington...Chase Productions... movies...Oh my goodness! I never thought of it. Derek, I never put that together. Derek Chase Wellington, III. I never thought about it. I'm shocked. I can't believe I missed that!"

"I know." Derek is serious again. "It was so funny the first night we met." He touches my face and looks in my eyes with that look that tells me he wants to love me all over. I know that look.

"You talked about my hair, my eyes, my mouth, but never my name...never my famous name, and that is when I began to fall in love with you, Ari. I knew you didn't have a clue, and you began to love me for just me and not at all about the money.

There was a kind of sadness to his tone and I wondered to myself how many times had he been fooled in love. Was that what the months were all about? Had he loved someone from January to May and then got hurt? Had he been hurt because of his parents' fame and wealth? I know I had...at least once.

"Show me your beautiful apartment, Derek. I love what I see."

"Sure. Follow me."

The apartment has two bedrooms with a large bath off the master bedroom, and a smaller one for guests. Both are beautifully and professionally decorated. The tour is fascinating especially the shower that is like a rain forest and the huge closet filled with Derek's beautiful clothes...my specialty. The computer room has every electronic device you can think of and the exercise room is ridiculous....and then there is his theater. I think to myself how I could live here forever...if I didn't have to see Mrs. Wellington.

"So...what do you think?"

"I think you are a very blessed and rich man with outstanding tastes. That's what I think."

"Am I blessed enough to get you to give my Mom one more try?"

I scrunch up my mouth and act like I am in deep thought, but he knows me well enough to know that I cannot deny him another chance with someone so important to him.

"You know I will, but don't leave me alone with her right now," I laugh.

"I won't. Are you ready to go back over and give it another try?"

"I suppose so. I thought I was nervous before, but that was nothing compared to how I feel right now."

We hear a tap on the front door and we both walk back up to the front. I think it's his mother, but he says that he knows that it's his father. He is correct.

"Are you two up for dinner with two old geezers?" His father asks with a quirky smile looking directly at me. Derek saves me and answers before I can speak.

"Are we eating here or going out?"

"Here. Myra has prepared a fine dinner for our guests. We didn't know your favorites, Arianna, but I'm sure you will be pleased. We have quite the variety. What do you say? Nina is really sorry about everything, and she hopes that you plan to join us." He is looking at me and speaking as if Derek is not even in the room.

"Sure, Mr. Wellington. I will be honored to join the two of you."

"Good…then dinner awaits."

"Dad, we will be right there. Give us just a minute. Ok?"

All right, son, take your time."

Mr. Wellington winks at me and disappears out of the door.

"Baby, are you sure you want to do this?"

"For you, yes, but I need you to do one thing for me before we go."

"OK. What's up?

"I need you to go out to the car and bring me my garment bag."

"That's easy…be right back."

Derek runs that short errant for me, and returns with garment bag in hand. I unzip it and take out a long shimmery vest to wear over my black pants and sweater and add new earrings. I decide that it is just right for dinner in this very upscale house with its billionaire owners.

"Wow. You are one knockout, girl."

"Well, this is no time for you to be knocked out. You have to stay alert tonight and in the protection mode. I am at the mercy of your alertness."

"Oh, it won't be bad. I think all is well now."

"Let's hope so." With that, I reach over to him and take his hand, and he immediately lifts mine to his lips. He secures the doors and together we walk the path toward his parent's house.

Inside, the dining room is spacious, but at the same time it has a feeling of warmth and comfort for me until Mrs. Wellington enters. She brings a slight chill to the atmosphere.

"Well dear, I see you have upgraded your outfit for dinner."

"I try. I hope this addition is to your liking," I say with quiet sarcasm.

"Yes, it is....very pretty. As I said earlier, you are a beautiful woman, and you can make anything look good."

The table is elegantly dressed and the variety of food looks delicious and presented with unusual excellence. I must admit even with my frayed nerves, I am both impressed and admittedly ravished. At first it seems that we are all too hungry to have much conversation, and I think to myself how I have never before really appreciated the power of silence until now; however, just as I am settling in to its value and appeal, Derek's Mom speaks, in my humble opinion, with great arrogance.

"Arianna, how sure are you that this business of yours is going to work?"

I see Derek slow his chewing and his eyes are a little bigger than they were before the question.

"I'm actually positive it will work."

"Really? Positive is a strong confident word, my dear. Maybe a little too strong for someone your age?"

"No....not at all. I have a lot of experience in the fashion world, and I've spent a lot of time deciding the direction for my life...actually since my childhood."

"Well, sometime childhood dreams don't work out, dear, and sometimes they are not the most appropriate avenues to follow once we become adults."

Derek is drinking far too much water now and clearing his throat far too often at this point. His father looks as if he is at some old fashion tennis match with his head moving back and forth from me to his wife each time we speak.

"...childhood dreams...hmmm...That could be very true in some cases, but I can assure you that this dream...my dream is materializing with great aplomb without a doubt."

"Well, how much money have you talked my Derek into sinking into this little business venture you are so certain about, dear?"

Derek chokes on the water he is holding in his mouth while his mother speaks and his father seems frozen in time and space with a chicken leg midway his mouth. Suddenly, I turn my body to face Derek.

"Oh my goodness, baby. I'm so sorry. I never even thought to ask you if you would like to invest. I don't generally get too involved in that part of the business, and it never even crossed my mind to ask you. How thoughtless of me! Would you like for me to set up a meeting with you and my financial team? They can tell you so much more about our shares and our stocks, our bonds and other means of making money with us. I turn back to Nina.

Thank you, Mrs. Wellington. THAT was a complete oversight."

I return to my food and put a small amount of rice in my mouth. I need to be prepared for the next onslaught.

"Well, I want my Derek to be very careful with his investments."

I extend my hand across the table and let it rest near her plate.

"Of course, you do, dear," I reply with mock care. You are his MOTHER, but since he is a grown man and a Harvard grad no less, I am confident that this man I am about to marry has the aptitude, the intellect, the astuteness, and the wisdom that caution requires. Mrs. Wellington, I would not have him any other way. I would toss him to the wind if I thought any differently."

"My dear, there will be absolutely no need for wind tossing of my boy since I am also positive that he has all of those qualities, and has had them for a very long time."

I look straight at Derek who has given up eating completely.

"So…Baby, I guess we don't need to entertain tossing you to the wind or your getting hoodwinked, bamboozled, duped, blindsided, swindled, shafted, ripped off, fooled or in anyway taken by your crafty fiancée. Mr. Wellington…" He jerks to attention.

"…would you be so kind as to pass your wife the ground up mincemeat, please?"

"Arianna,...we have a lot of different foods here, but...we...we don't have any ground up mincemeat," he says with hesitation.

"Oh! I thought surely we did at this point, Mr. Wellington. How disappointing. Would you all please excuse me?"

I take a short walk around the house, and I can still hear Derek doing this loud angry whisper at his mother, and I hear her try to defend herself explaining to him how he must be careful of strange women coming into his life...that there is a lot at stake. I hear Mr. Wellington try to assure his wife that Derek is no fool and would never choose someone to marry that he did not fully trust.

In my distress, I purposefully move out of earshot and stumble upon a very special room. In it, I find a variety of instruments. One of which is my favorite...the piano. It is an ebony baby grand, and I cannot resist it. I sit and run my hands, at first, over its smoothness and marvel at its beauty. I realize in an instant how much I miss this old passion and the mistake of pushing it so far out of my present. I touch the keys, both black and white, ever so lightly with respect. I sense and admire the eloquence that exudes from them when masterfully played. This is a fine piece of work. Almost unconsciously, I begin to play an old classical favorite of mine, and am surprised at how well I still remember every note and every rhythmic strand. The music soothes my nerves, and soon I am lost in the sounds of this magnificent instrument and a talent that I have been perfecting since childhood. I am so immersed in the sounds of my reminiscence that I have no idea that the entire family has taken a seat behind me and is listening intently to the beauty and allure of Mozart. I move from him, undisturbed, to Chopin, to Beethoven, to Handel and finally

I stop, still unaware of my audience until their loud and genuine applauses.

Mrs. Wellington is the first to approach the piano and me.

"Arianna that was absolutely magnificent. Where did you learn to play like that...with such mastery? That was something."

"Thank you. I studied for a long time growing up. As much as I love this instrument, it is not my choice for a career, and my parents finally gave me permission to give this up for my passion....New York and the world of fashion. Fashion is in my blood."

"...and so is music, baby," Derek says moving over close to me now and taking my hand in his. "I never knew that these hands could do that. What other fantastic secrets do you have hidden from me?" He kisses my hand and I see admiration and great pride in his eyes.

"I guess you'll just have to wait and see."

"While I'm waiting, I can assure you that I will thoroughly enjoy all that I already know." He brushes my lips lightly in front of his parents, and makes me a little uneasy.

Derek and I spent the rest of the evening playing duets with our very willing audience. The violin, in my fiancée's hands, is sensational and the laughter, singing, applause, and talk of times passed bring us all a little closer together. With the music, the evening seems to rush by, and before we depart, my future mother-in-law and I move just a tad closer to civility.

Chapter 14

GOODBYE, MY SWEET

*~Hushed secrets often find their way from darkness to light,
and shout, without restraint, a verifiable existence~*

A light snow is falling on Christmas Eve. It is both beautiful and calming, but so unlike Virginia especially near the water. I'm juggling two heavy bags of food with the keys in my hand blindly trying to find the lock, and I'm holding Derek's mail with my lips. Seeing the cottage has made me have an urgent call to get to the bathroom, and as if that's not enough, someone has decided to call me at this very moment. I'm sure it's Derek, but I will have to call him back. I finally make it inside, almost throw the bags down, and dash to the bathroom. Now the landline is ringing. What is the big deal? Derek is usually patient, but I guess not today.

Just as I am about to put the food up and start the dinner that I have been promising Derek, my cell buzzes again, and I decide something must be wrong so I dig my phone from my pocket without even looking to see who is it. I get the shock of my life when I answer.

"Derek, why are you blowing up my phone and yours?"

"Hello, Sweet."

The voice is low, calm, and French.

"Jean Paul?"

"What is this I read in the papers today about my sweet getting married…married so soon after we part? Tell me it is not true, darling. *Je t'aime, ma cherie.*"

His calmness, I know is contrived, and my accelerated heartbeat is definitely authentic.

"No, it's…very true." I respond quietly.

"So soon, my Sweet? Why are you doing this to me? You know what you mean to me. Don't make such a problem…mistake…whatever is right word. I don't know. Arianna, I've tried to give you space, but I demand another chance. I will be better. I promise. *Je ne peux pas dire au revoir, mon ange.*"

"Jean, what are you talking about? We already said goodbye. I thought we settled this a year ago."

My heart is slowing its beat now and my determination is strong. I will not be sucked again into his charisma, his intellect, his looks, his voice or his national influence. Above all else, I will push back against his hollow promises and his devilish need and strong desire to intimidate. .

"Everything has been your decision, Sweet. You give me little chance to make amends, you rush to marry someone we don't really know, and you give us no opportunity to show how much we still love each other."

"That's it in a nutshell, Jean. We don't love each other, and you certainly don't love me. You love the idea of me; you love having me on your arm on your special occasions to show me off; you love having me waiting at your house for your return. You want me there to greet and kiss you and pour compliments on you to boost your ego; you love having me stand in the shadow of you. Ask yourself what happens when I insist on my own career. What happens when I am not available for your every need? What happens when I refuse to start a family and verbalize that I will not have your dream of six children? What happens, Jean Paul? *Reponds-moi!*

"See, your problem, my Sweet is that you will not let the past be the past. We should look to the future."

"...and I am looking to my future and you are not in it....but just for kicks, how do you see this new future? How do I fit into it with you, Jean? What would be different?"

"Come back to France and see, my Sweet. You will find a very different person. I know my mistakes."

"I'm afraid your mistakes then were enough to help me realize I can't take another chance on you, Jean. We never really knew each other and you assumed I would follow all of your dictates...what to wear...where to go...with whom to speak and not speak and even how to stand and sit. You want to redo me, Jean. You don't want the me that is inside my own heart; you want to demand existence of the imaginary one in yours." The day you hit me was your last chance, and now, this conversation is over. *Au Revoir!"*

Despite my wish to feel no fear, my hands are shaking, beads of perspiration are forming on my forehead and my heart cannot regulate itself to normal speed. Half of my reaction is fear and half is anger at Jean for spoiling a day so special to me.

"Attendez!" he hastens. It reminds me of so many of his commands, and I snap.

"Wait for what," I scream. It is almost an out of body scream. "Never call me again…never speak to me again…never try to…"

At that instant, I feel the phone being ripped from my hand and for the first time I see and hear Derek.

"Who is this?" His voice is steel like. "…and who is Jean Paul? No, I will not put her back on the phone. You are done talking with her. You talk with me."

Now I am hearing a one-sided conversation.

"No, you have that wrong. She is not *votre amant,* your girlfriend, or your Sweet. "You listen to me and hear me clearly, Buddy."

I see the flash of anger in Derek's eyes and hear it in his voice. He is speaking slowly, far too distinctly, and with every word, his anger accelerates. I can imagine that Jean's voice is even more quiet now than when I was speaking with him. That is the way it is when his anger is at its peak. I know he is blaming me for whatever his imagination can design, and if I were there, I would have a lot to deal with before sanity could return.

"Arianna is very soon to be my wife, and you are never to call her again. Whatever you had is over. Accept it, and move on. She no longer wants to hear from you, and based on what I just heard, you have assaulted her, so I believe leaving her alone would be in your very best interest."

Derek is listening now, and I don't know what is being said. I'm trembling and praying that Jean Paul will not spoil what Derek and I have started to build. Jean is such a liar and manipulator that I don't know what to expect....and then Derek speaks again.

Really? She did all of that? Well, I would say, *mon ami*, you are a very very lucky man to be rid of her for good. I will see to it that she never stalks you again. You have no more worries. Sleep well, *mon ami*, from now on, knowing that I have her in tow. You take care and enjoy your liberty from such a fanatic. *Adieu*."

Derek gives Jean Paul no additional time to speak. At the end of his "*Adieu*" he slides the cell to off and looks at me, his eyes still flashing with anger and then I see that little smile that melts my heart. I throw myself in his arms and bury my face in his wet coat.

"I thought you told me that you left no Frenchmen pining away in France."

I take my face from his coat, and look up at him with tears streaking my face. His thumbs wipe my tears away. He kisses each side of my face and pulls me closer to him.

"Why did you lie to me, Sweetheart? You don't need to do that."

"I know. I'm sorry, Baby." His coat muffles my now soft voice. "...I didn't want to tell you about him because I'm so ashamed of what I allowed to happen to me and I truly want to be your heart, not his. I didn't want to talk about him, remember him or even think one second more about that part of my life. As far as possible, I give him no space now in my mind or in my heart. I closed that chapter over a year ago. I thought I knew him, Derek, but he taught me very well how wrong I was. When we first met, he showed me the world, but later he thought he could control me, and he did until I decided to find myself again, and then, for me, it was over."

"Wow! He really didn't know you, did he? I can't even control you enough to get a decent meal even when it's promised to me. I have to run home to see if everything is all right because you won't answer my phone calls....and now look at my dinner, still in the bags."

I laugh in spite of myself and pull his face down to me. He moves my blouse from my shoulder and kisses it, then my eyelids, then my mouth and lastly, he pecks my nose and tightens his arms around me. I love this man, and I don't want anyone or anything to mess this up.

"Derek, are you mad with me for not telling you everything?"

"No, Ari. We all have a past....Remember January, February, March, April, May...we both just need to leave the past in the past. What I do want is for you to feel free to be honest with me about everything. I don't want you to feel that you have to hide anything. Why didn't you tell me more about him?"

"I guess because he made my life so miserable, and I just wanted to forget. I never knew which Jean Paul would come home each night... the one who love to love me or the one who wanted to fight and hurt me physically and emotionally. Derek, he almost made me a coward. He's such a big figure in France and so many people adore him. I felt helpless to seek any relief from his torment of me."

206

"Well, all of that is over and you are with me now. I feel you shaking, Baby. There is no need for that now, Ari. Hold me tightly and calm down. I'm right here, Babe. He can't hurt you anymore. I'll always keep you safe. Do you believe me?"

"Yes, I do. I know you would always try....but Jean has such long arms, Derek. He can reach me even here."

"Ari, I am a very rich man too, and I know a little something about the law and how it works...how it can track, prosecute, threaten, intimate, and have its will too. Trust me. Secrecy is Jean Paul's weapon. Enlightenment is mine. He would never want those who adore and trust him to know his hidden side, and I would have no problem exposing him to the world. Baby, I'll always take care of you. Don't worry. You have nothing to fear. That is what he wants, but he can never have that from you again. I'll keep a close eye on him at a distance, and that will be enough to know if he even thinks about anything regarding you. Now, what about my dinner, woman?"

"It's coming right up," I laugh. "I love you."

"I'll love you too when you fix my dinner." He swats at me, but I am too quick and he misses.

I put everything I have into making this the best dinner I have ever cooked. The steaks have to be tender; the mashed potatoes fluffy, the string beans tender but not overcooked, the salad crispy and fresh, and the wine expensive and delicious....and then there is the peach cobbler just like grandma Lillie used to make. I set the table with candles and Christmas decorations that create just the right touch for tonight. When we sit down to dinner, I can see that Derek is ravished and enjoying every mouthful. We are barely talking, but there is a certain comfortable feeling in the quietness.

When dinner is over and the kitchen clean Derek wraps his arms around me from behind and leans over and whispers in my ear.

"I have a big Merry Christmas surprise for you, Ari. I hope you love it."

"Well, I already have this beautiful ring on my finger." I spread my fingers out and watch it sparkle in the candlelight. "I'm surprised you didn't make me wait until Christmas for it."

"I couldn't wait another minute to make you mine, baby." He turns me around to him, kisses me and is tucking strands of my hair behind my ears when we hear the knock on the door.

"It's here," he smiles. I can tell that he is excited and anxious.

At the door, the voices are low and I see three men. What in the world can this be...three men?

Derek pulls the door wide and I see the body of an ebony piano. Within a half hour, they have put it all together and I am seated on the bench running my hand over the keys before I bring them to life. My Derek has again found a way to make me love him even more.

When the men are gone, I sit for a moment just remembering the first time, at age five, I touched this instrument; the first time I actually knew that I was making sweet music, the first time I played for an audience, the first time I felt the pride of accomplishment. Derek is silently watching me. I can feel his eyes from the sofa, but they do not disturb my thoughts. I look over at him, sitting relaxed with his legs crossed, two fingers resting on his cheek and his thumb under his chin. His fourth finger and pinkie are slightly curled. His hair is loose tonight and those naughty strands that never stay in place have found their way home over his left eye. That is my favorite look of him. It's the calm sophisticated look and oh so sensual. When I was a teen, I would have seen him and said, "sweet."

I break the silence.

"So, this piece of wood gets to live here before I do, huh?"

"You can live here any time you want, baby. You want to move in tonight?"

I love that he has not moved. I have a chance to look at "the look" longer. He's so sexy.

"You know I can't. Not yet. We have to pick the wedding date, and then we have to have the wedding," I laugh.

"Well, you pick the date, and I'll be there. There is a pause and I look back at the piano.

"Play something for me, Ari…just for me."

I rub my fingers across the keys, and then without a thought I hear the melody that makes me think of him more than any other. The strains of *The First Time Ever I Saw Your Face* take over my fingers, my heart, and my soul. I feel the sounds of the music fill me, but I miss the sight of Derek moving over close to me. For the moment, I am completely unaware of our presence. It is at the end of the song when I see him lean down and kiss me passionately that I realize he has moved from the sofa. He pulls me up from my seat and brings me to him. The passion of his moves, his protection of me today with Jean Paul, the way he stared at me across the table at dinner, his words of comfort, and that little thing he does with my chin when his lips open my mouth to his, all make me want him to a degree that I have not felt before, and I melt into his embrace.

"I can't get enough of you, Ari. I can't get close enough. I love you more than I can say."

"You don't have to say anything with words; I feel it in your actions. Every time you touch me, it's like magic. My worries disappear. If I've had a bad day, all I need is to see that little smile that melts my heart or feel the touch of your fingers to my face, the brush of your lips to mine, the way you play in my hair in an embrace, and your kiss that sends me to a place that only exists where you reside. All those things, Derek, speak volumes to me of your love. You don't have to say a word. Just hold me, baby."

"Come here," he whispers.

I unbutton his shirt and bury my head in his chest. I take a deep breath to smell the sweetness of his body close to mine. I feel his fingers playing in my hair, rubbing my back, and he leans over every now and then to kiss my shoulder. At this moment, in this space and time, he makes me believe beyond a shadow of doubt that he can and will protect me with his life; in this hour, wrapped in his arms, I yield to that feeling of complete security, and all evidence of my fear vanishes.

I look over at the clock and then I look up at him.

"Merry Christmas, baby." I smile.

"Merry Christmas, Ari. This is, indeed, the merriest one I have ever had."

I move out of his arms, reach for my purse and take out his gift.

"For you…"

He unties the ribbon, opens the box, and smiles down at me.

"How did you know?"

"I know you. You love elegance; you love basketball; and you love me. So, there you have it all."

"I do.…a pair of gold monogrammed cuff links with a diamond stone that opens to a picture of the most beautiful woman inside, and tickets to see my Knicks. I could not ask for more."

The night has a mystical feel to it. Everything seems to have a special glow. The snow outside is pure white and cleanses the earth, the fire burning in the fireplace creates a coziness in the room, and curled up on the sofa in Derek's arms is like home to me. Later in the night, when he finally makes sweet tender love to me, I feel like I'm living someone else's charmed life. It can't be mine. Things like this generally don't happen to me, but in this night, something has changed, prayers have been answered, and it is all, very much, happening to me.

Chapter 15

UNWELCOMED VISITOR

*~Anger has the unique ability to take away common sense
in an instant without the courtesy of informing the brain~*

Derek is building up his snowball arsenal, and the neighborhood kids are piling up one to destroy him. Billy, a ten-year old friend, is trash-talking Derek hard, and Derek is answering every threat across their divided line. All the while, the team builds, and Derek, on his own, does what he can to keep up.

"Ari, I need some help over here," he yells. "Look how many they have, and look at my pitiful pile. Eight against one is not fair. Get over here, girl, and give me a hand."

"Derek, I told you when we came out here, I'm not getting in that fight. No snowballs are going to hit this body. I'm making snow angels, and you should come over here and join me," I laugh while I work my body in a steady rhythm. "It's much safer, and a lot more fun than getting hit with icy snowballs."

"You think so?" he yells.

I am spreading my arms and legs back and forth to make the perfect angel when I feel the first cold snowball glance off my coat and splatter on my face. Then I feel another and another and another. I'm getting killed down here, and the coldness is coming so fast I'm having a hard time getting to my feet. When I manage to scramble up, Billy and Shawn call me over, and I scrambled to safety in the arms of my new and very able young team. I look and Derek's pile is quite diminished, and I laugh a wicked laugh and shout, "Look what we have."

We start our barrage, and all Derek can do is duck and try to get off one snowball every minute or so, and since he has no time to aim, none of his ammunition hits a target and almost all of ours do. The laugher is infectious and some of us are rolling on the ground while others keep up the onslaught. The girls go after him with a vengeance.

Derek's pile is soon depleted, and we move in for the kill. We are no longer staying across our line; we are now in his territory, and he is down on the ground laughing and taking his punishment. A couple of the boys are on top of him, and he's trying to push them off, but is weakened by his laughter. I jump on top of him too and try to tickle him through his coat, but that doesn't work.

"Time out, guys. My phone is buzzing," he shouts through his laughter.

No one pays him any attention, and we keep up the attack. Derek gets to his feet and runs toward the cottage yelling over his shoulder.

"Time out, you crazy people. Time out. My phone is buzzing."

He swings the door open and quickly locks it so that his attackers can no longer reach him. He sticks out his tongue at us, and I see him pull the phone from his pocket and answer it, still laughing. Then I see the laugher stop, the smile fade, and that serious lawyer look appear that I definitely didn't want to see on Christmas Day.

"It looks like Derek can't come back, guys. I'll see you all later. It was a lot of fun."

"See ya, Miss Channing. Tell Derek we had fun as usual," Billie calls over his shoulder as they all run down toward the beach.

"You guys be careful and don't stay out too long. It's cold out here," I shout to my disappearing team.

I try to open the door, but it's locked, and Derek sees me and rushes over to let me in.

"Yeah, I know where he was from February to April, but after that it's like he fell off the face of the earth, and we didn't see him again until he was arrested in Florida last month." Derek is pacing back and forth while he talks, and I can tell that something has happened.

"On Christmas day? Yeah, I understand, but that doesn't mean I want to do it. Ok, I'll see you in a few." He sounds disappointed.

Derek slides his cell off and looks at me, and I look at him.

"Come here, babe. I have to go into the office for a very short time, I hope. Our team called an emergency meeting and I have to go. Will you be ok until I get back?"

"What if I say I won't?"

"Then I'll think you're lying, and trying to act all pitiful to make me feel sadder and more guilty than I already am." He smiles while pulling me into his arms.

He leans in for a kiss, and I playfully avoid his lips.

"Come here, woman. I need some loving before I go out to kill a bear and a cow for our dinner."

"I don't like bear and cow," I pout.

He leans in again for a kiss and pulls me closer to him.

"I love you baby. I'll be back as soon as I can." He taps my nose with his index finger, moves my hair away from my eyes, unwraps my arms from his waist, and heads outside. In a moment he's gone, and I'm standing in the living room wondering what to do with myself. I go over to my new piano and begin to play. The music soothes me, and I get lost in the melodies. I guess I've been playing for about a half hour when I hear a knock on the door.

I hope this isn't Derek's mother," I mutter to myself. "Dinner with her tonight is soon enough for me."

When I open the door a very handsome strange guy is standing outside ginning.…just the look of him is jaw dropping.

"Hi," he smiles. "Is Derek here?"

"Hi, and no, he's not." *This guy's look can make your heart stop! Wow!*

"This is where he lives isn't it?"

"…and you are?"

"Oh, I'm sorry. I'm Zack Belford. I was Derek's housemate at Harvard. Do you know when he'll be back?"

"Well, he said not long." *Look at those eyes.*

"Do you mind if I wait for him?"

"Oh, no. I'm sorry. Come in."

From the moment he enters the cottage, I can tell this is a very smooth guy...a take charge kind of a guy. He closes my door, hands me his coat, looks around the room, and decides on his own seat before I can say a word. He's dressed to the nines and his masculine smell is very pleasing. I take his coat, and he moves over to the seat of his choice. *He's watching me.*

"So, what's my buddy doing leaving a beautiful woman like you all alone on Christmas day?"...*Flirtatious, nice touch...not over the top.*

"He just had to run over to a short meeting, and he tells me it won't take too long. Can I get you something to drink?"

"If Derek lives here, I know you have some very good wine, so I'll take a little of that if you don't mind."

"Sure."

"What's your name?"

"Arianna."

"Hmm...beautiful name...beautiful woman... left all alone on Christmas Day. So how long have you known Derek?" *He's quick to move ahead.*

"Not long. We met in June."

"Hmm...June....Interesting month...a lot happened in June."

"Really?"

"Yep," He lets his lips pop out the word. "Really. So, Arianna,...I like that name. It kind of rolls off your tongue, you know. That was beautiful music I heard when I came up to your door."

"Thanks. I didn't know you heard." *Wow! He's smooth.*

"I did....you play classical all of the time?"

"No. I like all kinds of music," I reply handing him his drink.

"So, do you and Derek have a song?" *He's nosey...intrusive...not classy....*

"Hmmm," I smile. "I would say we do, but that I'll keep to myself."

"That's fine....nothing like a little privacy between two lovers," he openly flirts letting his words drag out slowly with obvious innuendos. "I know we just met, but I'd like to hear something for me. Would you do me the honor while we wait?" *Hmm...Narcissistic..."for me."*

"Sure. Anything in particular?"

"I like *Beautiful Liar* if you know it."*...Revealing*

"I do. Is there a reason you like that so much?" I ask. "Are you a beautiful liar?"

"Some would say...I am." *He is so cool. I can tell that anyone who falls in love with him is in a lot of trouble. He's a heartbreaker, and it doesn't take a rocket scientist to tell that. He and Derek are very different... very different.*

I sit at the piano and begin to play, and in the midst of it, I see Zack bring his drink and sit with me on the bench. When I finish, he claps.

"Miss Arianna, that was beautiful. The only thing I ever learned to play is *Chopsticks*. You know it? I'm sure you do."...*his eyes and voice flirt, but not necessarily his words...slick...part of his charm.*

I don't answer verbally, but I start to play the lower chords and Zack jumps in with a very elementary one finger treble part that still sounds relatively good. Just as we near the end of it, the door swings open. I see Derek standing there biting his lower lip, eyes squinting, and a frown I have never seen. I know immediately that he is furious. The *why* is what I don't know. The music stops abruptly.

"Bro...What's up? Been a minute." Zack moves off the piano bench smiling his million dollar smile and approaches Derek enthusiastically with his hand extended.

"What are you doing here?" Derek's voice is seething with anger. "When I saw that car, I *knew* it was you!" He spits out the words with a violent force.

"It's Christmas, Bro. Have we spent one Christmas apart in seven years?" Zack keeps his hand extended and completely ignores Derek's anger.

"I don't want to have Christmas with you." He waves away Zack's hand. His eyes are flashing now and his tone is furious, but I can tell that he is still trying to restraint himself for some reason.

"...but I want to spend it with you." Zack's voice is almost boyish and longing.

"You need to go." Derek doesn't lighten up at all.

"Come on, man. Don't do this."

"Don't be so rude, Derek!" I interrupt, but my tone is cautious.

219

Derek looks pass Zack and directly at me now, and I know imme-diately that I shouldn't have said anything.

"Ari, go in the bedroom." His voice sounds lower and demanding.

"What? Derek, if something involves you, it involves me too. I thought we said no secrets."

"Ari, go in the bedroom, now!"

He is shouting through clenched teeth, his voice is emphatic, and he is addressing me as never before; I don't like it one bit. I'm embar-rassed, angry, and mostly confused. It's too reminiscent of Jean Paul, and I am completely uncomfortable and surprised, but still defiant.

"You can't tell me to go in the bedroom, Derek. I'm not a kid. I don't have to do what you say."

"Ari, I'm telling you. You either go in the bedroom right now, or go home."

He shouts this time even louder and more out of control. His fists are balled up, and his eyes are darker than I have ever seen. This is not the Derek I thought I knew.

"Then I'll go home. You're just trying to show off because your friend is here. Zack, I'm sorry for..."

"Don't talk to him. Just get your stuff and go!...Letting some strange man come in my house and sit on a piano bench with you....a piano bench that I bought and gave you! What's wrong with you, girl?"

Tears are coming fast now as I walk over to the closet, and put on my wet boots and coat; Derek doesn't come over to comfort me. He doesn't say when he will call me. He says nothing. I just hear his heavy breathing and see his eyes locked on Zack who sits quite comfortably on the sofa looking back at him. His legs are crossed, hands laced at his knee, and he is looking so very handsome, cocky, and not angry at all. In fact, he seems quite amused and pretty happy. The dichotomy of their attitudes is confusing.

I open the door, look out at the snowstorm, and back at Derek. His fists are still balled, and his look is defiant.

"...bedroom or home, Ari," he reiterates through clenched teeth. "...Your choice, baby." His head flicks towards the door, and his eyes don't blink.

The word "baby" is not the endearing one I'm used to hearing, but rather, a snapping sarcastic one that bites.

I take a deep breath and make my choice. Not a word is spoken until I pull the door closed and walk away from the house in the heavy falling snow. At my car, I hear more shouting from Derek. The only words I can make out are "why and hell." I start the car, scrape my windshield, then get inside and sit for a minute trying to stop my tears and collect myself. I'm shaking from the cold weather, the lashing wind off of the ocean, but mostly from my concern for what is happening inside the house. I'm not sure that I should really leave Derek alone. Why is he so angry? Zack seems a little over confident, but still friendly and easy-going. Is that really who he is, and, if so, what is wrong with Derek? I decide that he's too angry to hear anything I have to say, and I am very angry about the way he is treating me. Neither of us is able to muster any real communication at this point, so I dry my tears as best I can, and drive away in the storm, barely able to see the road because of both the snow and my tears.

Derek

Chapter 16

MY BRO

~Love comes in different sizes, shapes, colors and forms~

"Bro, you need to calm down." Zack is sitting quite relaxed on the sofa and that alone makes me even madder.

"Calm down? Do you have any idea how much I hate seeing you in my house right now?"

"It's Christmas, Bro. We're always together at Christmas."

Did you come here to see Morgan?"

"Man, you don't get it," he chuckles. "No, I did not come to see Morgan. I haven't even heard from that girl since July when she called pleading with me to talk to you about how she doesn't love me, and how much she loves you. I said, 'you kidding me? You think I'm going to call and tell him that?' Morgan is out to lunch, Bro, to think I would do that. I got too much ego for that crap....but let me be honest with you, Man."

"Oh honest, please, let me hear honesty." I hear how blatantly sarcastic and rude I am, but I don't care how much I insult Zack. He deserves every bit of it.

"Well, to be perfectly honest with you, I've had to tighten security around you, D. I had to keep a closer eye on you cause you're falling in and out of love faster than I can change my pants."

"What the heck does that mean?"

It means what it sounds like it means. You know...You're so in love with Morgan, and then fifteen minutes later, Bro, you in love with New Girl. I had to put more people on you cause New Girl got connections."

"Zack, are you still playing cops and robbers? Grow up! You got people 'protecting' me again? You need to stop."

"On the contrary, my man. I've had to beef things up because you and New Girl are about to be in some deep donkey doo, but old Zack's got your back." He pats me on my back and walks over and sits back down on the sofa.

"What in the name of thunder are you talking about, fool?"

"OK. This is the deal: I had one of my guys just keeping an eye on you every now and then like usual since you're a big time lawyer now, when he realizes that you are actually being followed."

"Followed?"

"Yep, you and new girl. When I found that out, I called in two more of my guys to check it out....The two I can really depend on in a crisis. We've been together since we were kids, and I know how much I can count on them to get things right in a short time. They know people and they can get details."

"What is this cloak and dagger mess, Zack? Does Ari know you're following her? You could scare her, Man."

"Come on, D. That girl is so far up on Cloud 9 with you, she takes absolutely zero precautions. All she knows is that she's in love. See, she left her phone sitting right here on your coffee table, and where is she? You don't know. A suspicious person would never leave her phone, and if you were suspicious, you would not send her out in a snowstorm alone without a phone. Ah, man. You really need me, and you sure need my assistants."

So, I'm supposed to believe that Ari and I are being followed by someone other than your two punks."

"Yep! Actually, now it's four of my people."

""How do I know that this is not one of your little tricks to worm your way back into my life?" I ask with arms folded and a suspicious eye.

"First of all, D, I've never been out of your life, and I never will be, and secondly, I wouldn't tell you a lie like this."

"Yes, you would!" I raise my voice at him. "You love torturing me."

"No, I wouldn't," Zack snaps back. He is losing his patience, and past experiences have taught me that an impatient Zack can be bad for me.

"I need you to stop thinking that everything I do for you has an ulterior motive. It doesn't."

He is in my face now pointing his finger and yelling.

"Stop clouding your thoughts with what happened with Morgan; she did what she wanted to do, so deal with it, and sit you punk ass down." He pushes me down on the sofa.

"You need to listen before you end up getting New Girl in some deep trouble with your arrogant, ignorant self....sending her out by herself in a snowstorm without a phone. I got your back, though." He gives me two very light slaps to my face and grins. "I'll always have your back cause I love you despite what you think. But I'm straight up street, man, and you better know it. Harvard or not! I know what I'm talking about, and this is a time that you better listen."

I take a deep breath, and sit still because there are a few things I do know for sure about Zack: He knows the streets, he always has his ear to the ground, he can win a battle, and sometimes he lacks patience with my "silver spoon" attitude. So, I listen.

"When I found out there were two clowns following you guys, like I said, I had to put tighter security around both of you so I added a few more men and some listening devices...and I don't mean just technology. I got people who know stuff. That's when I found out about this clown named Jean Paul Laurent. He's a rich dude from France that acts like he's got it all together, but the truth is he's nothing but a wanna be thug. He's elementary...second-class...second-rate...

second in everything, and nothing to worry about if you know the right people....lucky you, you know the right people," he chuckles. "This clown had a plan to kidnap Arianna at *The Channing House of Design* right after the holidays. I wish he would try to touch her.... give me an excuse to hurt somebody."

"Are you kidding me?" Zack has just made a believer out of me with this name and the details that he has from the listening devices.

"Naw, Man. Unfortunately, I'm not kidding. He wants that girl back in France ASAP, now that he knows she's planning to marry you soon. My guys told me he went absolutely crazy when he found out about that. I don't know what he might do now, D, but my people are on top of it."

"He called her yesterday and got her very upset. I took the phone from her, and I thought I scared him off, but I guess it's deeper than that." I almost sound like I'm talking to myself.

"Yeah, man. This guy is crazy, but I'm crazier, and he's finding that out as we speak."

"Do your people know where Ari is right now?"

"I don't know. You sent her out in a stupid snow storm driving by herself with no phone." Zack is looking at his fingernails, and acting like he could care less. "Yea, fool, I know where she is. You bet your butt I know where she is, but unfortunately, so does Jean Paul." Zack's phone buzzes. "Hold up, I got to take this. What's up, Bro? Where is she? Yeah, I'm telling him now. Oh wow! That's good. Do you think she'll stay put? Well, tell Angel to keep her there. No, I don't know Angel." He sounds irritated at that. "OK...Ok. I'll check with you soon." He slides his phone off, looks at me, and chuckles.

"Your girl was so mad that when she drove away from here she was driving so fast in the snow that she lost those two French clowns. They called Jean Paul and told him they lost her, and she didn't go home. Dumb punks! How did she learn to drive like that in the snow, Man?"

Ari's live all over the world. She can drive in anything. Where is she?" I ask with some impatience.

"Oh, you want know where she is?" Big man...throwing the girl out in a snowstorm. He's laughing now. "You don't want your girl to talk to "wittle" Zack," he teases in a baby talk voice.

"Man, come on. Where is she?"

"She's at Angel's. She's safe."

"Who is Angel?"

"You're pitiful, Bro. What would you do if I tried to cut you lose like you try to do me?" He shakes his head. "I never met her, but I have the research on her. She's a top model; she's known all over the fashion world, and sometimes Arianna hires her for her most popular lines, especially the new ones, *Sunday's Best* and *Summer Shine*. Recently they've been getting pretty close from what I hear. She never said anything to you about Angel?"

"Nope, I don't think so."

"Not even when you put that rock on her finger?"

"Nope."

"Hmmm...that's strange."

"Where does Angel live?" I ask.

"You don't need to know that right now because you're too impulsive when it comes to Arianna....throwing her out of the house, and now you want to run over there and tell her how sorry you are for acting the fool today. That won't help right now, Bro. We have to keep her safe, and right now, those fools don't know where she is. If they follow you over, then they will."

"Are they watching me now?"

"Yeah, they watch you everyday, all day. That's their job. They get paid big bucks to keep you on their radar."

"So, what can we do?"

"*We* can't do anything. You're going to sit tight until I tell you everything is all clear."

"Well, do you have a plan?"

"Come on, Man...Have you ever seen me in the seven years that you've known me when I didn't have a plan?"

"No. So what's the plan?"

"I don't know that I can tell you the plan. See, you're a man of legal integrity. I'm not planning to go to jail or lose my job. I love Wall Street. I just have to keep at least one foot on the other side of the street, if you know what I mean."

My phone buzzes and Mom's face is staring back at me. I slide my cell on reluctantly.

"Hi, Mom."

"Son, I need to tell you something; it's urgent, and I need you to trust me, and tell me what I need to know."

"What?" I ask.

"I got a call about an hour ago from a very good friend that I've known for a long time. He's looking for Arianna, and he knows that she's your fiancee. She has committed some crimes in France, and he's trying to do his civic duty and help the police get her back in France to stand trial for her crimes. My friend knows that she is not with you at the moment, but can you tell us where she is?"

"Who is this friend, Mom? What's his name, and why is he helping the police?"

"Why is any of that important, Derek?" She asks with impatience. "I just need you to tell me where that girl is. I don't want you losing your license because you're harboring a worthless criminal. You had no problems like this when you were with Morgan." Her voice is getting louder and louder, and I can tell that she is exasperated with me for not telling her right away.

"No, I had worse problems with Morgan," I say under my breath. "Mom, is your friend Jean Paul Laurent?"

"Well…Yes, Derek. How do you know that? Has he called to warn you too?"

I ignore her questions.

"Let me just say that I don't know where Ari is right now, but wherever she is, I want her to stay safe. I want you to know that she has done absolutely nothing wrong. Jean Paul is the one doing a lot that is wrong, and he is the one who may end up in jail. Mom, I need you to trust me when I tell you not to speak with him again. Please don't take anymore of his calls. I don't want you to get tied up in this mess. Do you hear me?"

"Derek, why are you insisting on harboring this girl? She's nothing but a gold digger. I can feel it in my bones!"

Mom, you're feeling arthritis in your bones."

"All of a sudden Derek, you and your Dad make a joke out of everything I say and do."

"No, Mom. This is no joke, and Ari is in grave danger from your friend. He's planning to kidnap her, and only God knows what he will do to her if he gets his hands on her. This is nothing you need to get involved with, and I hope you will stay out of it. Ari and I won't make it to Christmas dinner to say the least, but I'll talk with you later." I slide my phone off before she can say another word.

For almost the entire time that I've been talking with my Mom, Zack has been on the phone too, and my spirits are lifted because he seems happy, and I know he wouldn't be if things weren't going our way. So now I'm trying to listen to his conversation as I finish this up with my Mom.

I'm sitting on the sofa listening to Zack's laughter. He's holding his stomach because he's laughing so hard.

"So, what did he say when you cold cocked his butt?" He is laughing even harder now. "Punk! I want him to call and apologize to my man, and promise to stay out of their lives for good. That's very important to me. Make sure he does that. Has he called his goons off yet? You heard him call them? Oh...you talked to them, and he talked to them. Was our man with them? We didn't break any more hands, did we? I hate amateurs. No challenge! Anyway, good work, dude. Seriously, I need you to stay in France for a while and let your presence be known. I appreciate you, Frank. You're a good man...loyal.

That's what I love about you, Bro. No, he never needs to speak to her again as long as he lives, and you make sure he fully understands the repercussions if he tries. Derek can tell her how sorry he is." He laughs again. "OK. Did you have to break his hand? Oh, he didn't know how hard your chest is." He is laughing again. "Did that fool really break his own hand? Well, take him to the hospital, and get his hand fixed up. We'll pay for that in cash, ok? I need you to take up residence over there for about six months, and don't let him forget who he's dealing with, ok street boy? I'll see you on this side when you get back. All right. Peace out, Dude."

Zack moves over close to the sofa and is looking at me shaking my head.

"Take the boy out of the country, but you can't take the country out of the boy," he laughs. "I love this, man....Espionage, Crime bosses...makes me feel like I'm home."

"I thought you wanted to escape home...the street life."

"Not all of it, Bro. Let's go get your girl. Everything is all clear."

I stand up and face this man with whom I have this love/hate relationship, and I am at the moment sincerely grateful to him.

"Zack?"

"Don't say anything you don't mean. I can get hurt. I'm very sensitive."

"You're stupid, man," I laugh. "No, I just want to say thank you. I don't know what you did to make Ari safe, and I don't want to know, but I'm grateful." I shake his hand, and he pulls me over and hugs me.

"I love you, man, and I'm sorry about Morgan."

Arianna

Chapter 17

THE BLOW UP

Fear, unchecked, locks the heart of progression.

I can barely see the road through my tears. What just happened back there? Why is Derek so angry, and what made him treat me so badly? Unfortunately, I can't answer any of these questions. I can, however, answer how I react to this kind of treatment. I look at the ring on my finger. It's gorgeous, but I won't wear it if I just witnessed the real Derek. I've heard him explode before, but never at me, and he has this uncanny way of changing on a dime. I heard that once on the phone when he thought I was someone else.

I look around and see that almost unconsciously I am driving to Angel's house. She is the closest friend I have here in Virginia, and I need her now. As difficult as the snow makes it, I park in her driveway and walk up to her beautiful home with that unique fountain on this gorgeous hill. The snow makes it even more beautiful…like something out of a decorator's magazine. It's hard for me to believe that she was homeless in her youth. Now look at what she's acquired for herself and a family who struggled to give her the best that they could, despite their hardships. She jokes that this is why they are so close to this day because they lived on top of each other for so long. I ring the bell and I hear her loud mouth as she moves to the door. When she opens it, I immediately notice that she is very surprised to see me standing there shivering in the cold, and when our eyes meet, I burst out in uncontrollable tears.

"Ari, baby, come in. What's wrong?" Her voice sounds extremely concerned.

I stomp the snow off my boots and move into the house and see an exquisite Christmas tree. The lights and decorative colors present a strange blurring image streaking through my tears.

"I'm sorry to bother you on Christmas Day, Angel," I cry.

"No, you come in and tell me how I can help."

She waits patiently while, still crying, I remove my boots and then she takes me to a little private office space with a sofa, bookcases, computer and TV. We sit on the sofa and she takes me in her arms.

"Hush, baby. What happened? Did somebody mess with you?"

"I can't really answer that because I don't understand it." My voice is trembling through my tears. "Derek and I were having fun playing in the snow with some neighbor kids when he got a call to come to his office for an emergency meeting. While he was gone, his housemate from Harvard came by to see him and asked to wait, and I let him. Derek came home and acted like a crazy man when he saw that I let him in the house. He started yelling at me and told me to go in the bedroom or go home so I said I'd go home. Angel, why did he do that? He looked at me like he hates me."

"He doesn't hate you, baby. Her voice is calm and that is what I need. "All of that is something between Derek and that guy. It really has nothing to do with you. Maybe you should have told the guy to come back later."

"Yeah. I'm sure I should have, but that didn't seem too polite for someone I think is Derek's close friend. They were supposed to spend some time together when we were in New York, but they never did so I never met Zack until today. Derek mentioned him one day, and that was all. Look…I see you have company, and I don't want to take you away from them so I'm going to go. I've already ruined my Christmas. I don't want to ruin yours."

"You are going to do no such thing. You're going to stay right here. Go down the hall, and wash those tears away, and come back out and celebrate the day with us."

"No, Angel. I'm not going to intrude on your family."

So, if this had happened to me, would you send me away in a snow storm no less?"

"No," I smile looking down at my hands.

"Would you expect me to leave on my own so that I wouldn't intrude on your celebration?"

"No, but I'm going to go home. It's barely snowing now." I stand up to go, but I really don't want to leave. I need my friend right now, but I don't want to cause any more trouble for people that I love.

"What and sit crying in your condo alone on Christmas? You don't have any business driving around in this snow anyway. I won't have it. What kind of friend would I be if I let you do that? Girl, go wash your face and come out and have dinner with us."

"Are you sure?" I ask quietly.

"I'm positive. Now go."

I go into Angel's beautiful bathroom, and I don't want to touch anything. Everything is so perfect...so pretty. It reminds me so much of my parents' home where everything is always perfect. All of a sudden I miss them, and I'll be so happy when they all come back to the states. My parents, and bothers and sister all love Japan, and they all love living there, but they promise that they are going to come back soon, especially for my wedding if I'm still having one. I wish so much that they were here now, especially my sister. I miss India the most.

I see some fancy paper towels, and I use one to wash my face, but when I look in the mirror, I see how sad I look. I can't bring this face outside and bring everyone down, so I take a deep breath and put my feelings aside for the moment.

Outside the bathroom, I follow the sounds of laughter and Christmas excitement. Around the corner, I see Angel unwrapping a gift, and she calls over to me with childlike exuberance in her eyes. She is caught up in the season, and it is all over her face.

"Ari, come meet my family."

Within a minute her Mom, Dad, and sister are acting like they have known me for a lifetime. They are the type of people who meet no strangers, and they almost make me forget, for a moment, my sadness. We sit down to a wonderful Christmas dinner that is catered. I would expect nothing else from Angel.

"Naw, girl. I slaved over this doggone chicken for hours," she laughs. "...don't even talk about this apple pie...peeling, coring... sugaring it up," she giggles.

"Angel don't get no better, Arianna. She always been a mess, but we love her. That's my baby," her Mom chuckles.

Just as we finish dinner and move back into the den, I hear the doorbell, and Angel goes to answer it. From the den, I hear Angel raise her voice. It's not quite anger, but it is definitely an irritated sound....and then I hear the voice that I know belongs to Derek. I get up, excuse myself, and move out into the hall where I see Derek and Zack standing at the door.

"Ari, I need to speak with you...please."

"It's all right Angel. It'll be fine."

"Look Derek, I don't want her crying anymore."

"...nor do I."

"Well, you make doggone sure of it. Don't bring no mess up in my house today. Now, if you're sure you know how to behave yourself, you two can use this room over here for privacy and...you..." Angel cocks her head and points to Zack.

"Zack, Zack Belford," he replies casually with a charm that isn't lost on me even in my present messed up state of mind.

Angel wiggles her finger at him. "Zack...Zack Belford, you come with me." She is already flirting, and encouraging a guy who, I already know, needs no encouragement to quickly take advantage.

Angel takes his arm, looks back at me, and winks. Zack is a good-looking guy, and I know what she's thinking. I can't help but smile to myself. She never lets an opportunity pass her by, and I can almost guarantee she won't take him in the den with her parents and sister. This is going to be a solo flight.

Derek and I move into a large library that's filled with books and fancy sofas. I quietly close the door and look at him. He hands me my phone, and moves away. We are both silent at first and he drops his head, standing with both hands in his pockets. I know he's sorry so I move over to him and lift his head with my hand, and force him to look into my tear stained eyes. I feel a tear escape, and he wipes it away with his thumb.

"This is not how I pictured today for us, babe. I'm sorry. I'm so sorry," he whispers.

I don't say anything.

"I just got really mad when I saw you sitting at the piano with Zack. I didn't like it. I didn't like it, Ari. Why would you let someone come into my home that you've never seen before? It made me mad."

I still don't say anything.

"What I did wrong was to yell at you, but I was so mad."

"So, is that what I can expect from you when you get mad...ordering me into a bedroom or sending me out in a snowstorm to fend for myself? Is that what I need to learn to expect from you?"

"Not the snowstorm part, but yelling, yeah…maybe…I don't know. I know I don't want to hurt you, but sometimes when I lose my temper, I yell and say stupid things. I know I love you, but I think we have to come to some understanding about what each of us is going to tolerate from the other."

"…and if we can't come to that understanding?"

"Well, I think we can," he rushes to say. "I'm not going to think that we can't. I love you too much to think that."

"Derek, I've already been through the demands, the ordering me around. I can tell you, I won't tolerate that from anyone anymore. That can get scary to me. I can't handle it. I won't even try for you or anyone else."

"I get that. I understand that, but you have to know that I would never hurt you, Ari. I would never put my hands on you. I'm not Jean Paul. The yelling?…I can't promise."

"I thought Zack was a close friend, Derek…someone you lived with for seven years. I didn't think it was a problem to let him wait inside."

"…but you didn't know that to be true. You've never even seen a picture of him. You had nothing but his word, and you let him in my house with you there alone. That's not smart, Ari.…and then for me to walk in and see you sitting next to a stranger, to you, playing around together. That can't happen again. <u>That's</u> my bottom line."

"I get that, and I'm sorry. I wasn't thinking. I'm really sorry. I never want to disappoint you, or hurt you, or make you feel threatened by someone else. I can see Zack. He's a real good- looking guy.

He's flirtatious, funny, charming, shrew...all of that, but he is no Derek Wellington.

I move a distance away from him now, but I turn and look directly into his eyes. I want him to hear my truth and know it to be true.

"You're classy; he only pretends to be. I can see through that. You're sophisticated; he's not. He lacks that inbred thing that comes from childhood training that I know so well....but most of all, Derek, he doesn't have your touch. I love you baby so much. You never have to feel intimidated by anyone where I'm concerned. Zack doesn't measure up to you at all in my eyes."

He comes over to me now, pulls me to him, and touches my face. His eyes, looking directly into mine, say it all. *Thank you for loving just me, for letting me trust you, for giving me the confidence that you are all mine, and I am yours. No one else can interfere.* In that moment, a silent assurance passes between us...an unspoken alliance forms, and I know in that instance an unbreakable bond is knitted together. Despite any future problems, this bond will always stand its ground.

He takes me in his arms, and his kisses are slow, soft, and tender... sincere. I feel every shade and shape of his love in his sensual touch.... the way he casually runs his hands up and down my back and sparks a flame...the way his fingers calmly urge my mouth to his... the way he stops the kiss and lets his eyes, for a moment, lock into mine... the way that our bodies melt into each other. He wraps me up in the depths of his feelings and transmits them to me with every move and nuance of love inside of him. I reciprocate, ridding myself of my disappointment and feeling my anger dissipate.

"Merry Christmas, Ari," he whispers. "You're just given me the best gift any one could ever have: assurance of your love."

There is more kissing; there are more apologies, more hugs, and there is an even deeper bonding formed simply because we've talked this through with complete honesty. Both of us are now acutely cognizant of each other's limits and the barriers never to cross, and that is a step ahead in the progression of our love.

Outside the library, Derek and I walk down the hall hand in hand following Angel's high- pitched laughter. Just as I thought, she is flying solo in the kitchen with Zack. They are having a ball together. Zack is sitting at the bar with a full plate of food, joking, and laughing a lot. She is sitting next to him, and they look very comfortable together, almost as if they've known each other for years.

"Well, it looks like our favorite couple is out of the war zone," Zack remarks as he shoves another fork full of food into his mouth.

"I think so," Derek says quietly, smiling down at me.

"Come fix your man a plate, Ari. There's plenty left."

"Sure. What do you want, baby?"

"Whatever you have. I'm starving."

"Really? It didn't seem that way a few minutes ago," I flirt.

"OK. Tell all of our business."

"Well, not quite all of it," I wink looking up at him, grinning.

I fix a very full plate for Derek, and he takes a seat at the bar, and we don't hear anything but chewing sounds from him for at least fifteen minutes. Since everyone has gravitated to the kitchen by now, there is enough noise. Of course, Zack is the life of the party, and he has everyone almost falling on the floor laughing including me even though I'm a little more restrained than the others. I don't want Derek to get mad with me again, but it's hard not to laugh at this fool. Zack is hilarious. Even Derek can't contain himself at certain points. He makes some comments, and I find out he can be very funny too. With Zack, Derek, and Angel in charge of the entertainment, everyone is having a ball. We end the evening with me at the piano and the rest, of the group, singing carols off key. They claimed they weren't, but I can assure you that they were very much off key. We had a lot of just old- fashioned Christmas fun.

Around eleven o'clock, Angel's parents retire, her sister, Bria, is picked up by some other friends, Angel and Zack decide to go clubbing together, and Derek and I go back to the cottage. I can only wonder where the Zack/Angel relationship is going to end up. Like I said before, I can look at Zack and tell that he's a heartbreaker....but their future is the least of my concern.

I park my car in front of the cottage. It's been a rather hard day, and I'll admit it: I'm tired. I turn to face Derek who is staring again and reaches over and takes one of my hands in his. He raises it to his lips and kisses first the backside and then each fingertip without taking his eyes from mine.

He opens the car door and comes around to the driver's side and opens my door, but I don't move. I look up at him.

"What's wrong? Aren't you coming in?"

"No, Derek. I'm going to go home tonight."

"Why? Are you still angry with me?"

"No."

"…then why? I want you to stay with me tonight," he whines.

I don't say anything.

"Well, if you want to go home, is it all right if I go with you?"

I look up at him. "Derek, I…I need a moment."

"You're still mad," he says emphatically.

"No, I'm not. I just need a moment."

Both of us are silent, and Derek is still holding the door.

"Will you come in, and let's talk about it?"

I take a deep breath, and I know I'm not going inside to stay or talk about it, or do anything. I know I'm going home. I have to wrap my head around what happened yesterday and today, and I know I can't do it with Derek. I'm too weak around him, and he'll have me in his bed before I can utter my own name.

"No, Derek. We've already talked."

"Well, obviously not enough."

"No, it was quite enough."

"Do you still love me?"

I smile a quiet smile and look up at him standing there holding the door wanting me to come in, wanting to make love to me, wanting everything to be all right.

I look directly at him. "Derek, everything is fine. Yes, I love you more than I can say, but tonight, I need a moment, and tonight, I'm going home."

"You're going to go home and spend Christmas night alone. Great. That's just great, Ari. Perfect...Brilliant idea!" He slightly shoves away from the car in his exasperation.

"It's not Christmas night anymore, Derek. Check your watch."

"Whatever." *He's irritated now, and confused.* "I'm not going to beg you. Will I see you tomorrow?" he snaps.

"Yes."

"Promise?"

"Yes."

"...and you're not still angry?"

"No. Not at all."

"...and we can't talk about this?"

"Maybe tomorrow."

He takes a deep breath.

"OK."

He leans into the car and lightly kisses me, touches my face, and taps my nose.

"I love you, Arianna Channing. Just remember this: When we get married, you won't be able to run away to your own little private place. We'll have to work things out together. That's what we should be doing now. Drive carefully, and call me when you get home."

"All right. I love you, Baby. Good night."

Derek closes my door, and I drive away feeling tears sting my eyes. I have to go for the moment so he won't see just how scared I am of being alone with men who yell....so he won't know the horrible secrets and scars left from a relationship that I have physically escaped, but one that still keeps me mentally bound. What I can't share with him is the shame of being in a situation I allowed for more than two years. I never want him to think that I equate him with Jean Paul in any way because I don't, but, somewhere deep inside me, I have to face this fear and stop it from continuing to master me. Tonight, I'm not there, but I love Derek enough to know that one day I will be.

Derek

Chapter 18

DOWN MEMORY LANE

On the wings of Memory, emotional thoughts and feelings
takes flight and breathe in new life.

When I walk into the house, I feel the weight returning that I'd felt way back in May. The last two days have been filled with tension. Jean Paul calling and upsetting Ari, Zack showing up, Ari sitting with Zack in my absence, finding out about the Faux Cops and how much trouble Ari could have been in, and now not being allowed to help Ari through all of this simply because she won't let me.

I take off my coat, turn on some music, slip off my shoes, and lie down on the bed. I feel bone tired...too tired to undress. I let the music wrap itself around me and begin to lull me to sleep. I feel my phone and dig it out of my pocket.

"Hi baby. I'm home, safe and sound."

"Good. I miss you already." I can hear my sleepy voice and so can Ari.

"You sound so tired, Baby. Get some sleep, and I'll see you tomorrow."

"Good night, Love. Don't forget. Dream of me."

Almost before I can turn the phone off, it buzzes again, and I think Ari forgot to tell me something.

"Yeah?"

There is silence.

"Hello."

"De…De…Derek?"

"Yes. Who is this?"

It's…it's me." The words are almost unclear.

"Morgan?"

"Hey, baby, I gotta tell yah."

"Morgan, are you all right? Are you drunk?"

"Derek, man, I still love you so much, man."

"Morgan," I say it again louder. "Morgan! Are you drunk?"

"Nawww, baby, why would you say that? I love you so much."

"Morgan, where are you?"

"Derek, babe, don't you miss me? I want you so bad right now!"

"Morgan, are you alone? Where are you?"

"I'm right here, Babe, waiting for you." Her words are slurring badly.

"Tell me where you are Morgan." I sound anxious and nervous.

"OH EM GEEEEE, Derek! You don't understand! I miss you."

"Morgan, please tell me where you are?"

"I love you Derek…so much, I love you, I mean…I reallyreallyreally love you."

"Ok Morgan, ok," I say changing my tactic. "I love you too. Tell me where you are so I can come get you."

"I'm out here…waiting for you, Baby."

"Morgan, look around and tell me what you see so I'll know where you are."

I'm trying desperately to sound calm, but my heart is about to jump out of my body. This girl does not drink anything stronger that juice, and I am scared to death at the moment. Who got her drunk, and why is she alone?

I hear her take a deep breathe, and I try to wait patiently for her response. I think she's trying to pinpoint a location to tell me exactly where she is and then I hear snoring.

"MORGAN!!!"

"DEREK!" She shouts back, startled. "You called me! I'm so happy! I love you so much!"

"Morgan, Babe, tell me where you are so I can come pick you up."

"I'm by the big tree and the little tree, Derek." She yawns. "I'm gonna go to sleep now."

"Morgan, stay awake and tell me where you are."

"You know silly! That big tree…the big one."

"Morgan do you see a street sign?"

Street sign?…Yeah." There is a deep sigh.

"Read it for me, Morgan. Read the sign."

"Ah…Dock…Dockside. Derek, it says Dockside."

"OK. I know where that is. Stay there, Morgan. Stay there. I'm coming to get you. Stay on the phone with me."

"Babe, I'm cold. I forgot my coat. I left my coat…I left it, Derek."

"OK, Babe. I'll be right there. I'll bring you a coat."

I throw on my shoes and coat, grab another coat from the closet, and dash out to my car. *How could this happen? Why is Morgan out at this time of night alone in all of this snow? How did she get drunk? Where is Peter, Mr. Hero?* I turn on the car phone and try to keep her talking.

"Morgan?" No answer. "Morgan? Do you hear me?"

I hear light snoring.

I drive as fast as I can to Dockside, which is close to where I live. When I get there what I see scares me to death. Her car is parked in the middle of the street. I swing to the side of the road, jump out, and run to open the door on the driver's side and try to wake Morgan who is now fast asleep. I lift her out of her car, and put her in mine then drive her car to the side of the road. When I get back in my car, I see her beautiful face for the first time in over two months, and my heart skips a beat. I drive to her house, find her keys, and carry her to her bed. She wakes up as I put her down.

"Derek, I was trying to find you, Derek. I couldn't find you, Derek. I couldn't find you."

"I'm right here, babe. Go back to sleep."

"Derek, don't leave me. I don't want you to leave me. I miss you. I lu- you, Derek. Do you know I love you, Derek?"

"Yes, Babe, I know you love me. I'm right here, Morgan. I'm not going to leave you."

"You love me, Derek? I love you. You love me, Derek?"

"Yes, Morgan, I love you. Now go to sleep." I try to close her eyelids with my fingers.

Her beautiful, big eyes pop open again. "You love me? I love you too."

I pull her to me and take off the coat I brought for her, slip off her shoes and dress, and put her under the covers. The soft light in the room creates a special glow on her beautiful smooth skin. I look at the lips I have kissed for years that are now strangers to me. She is asleep in no time, and at first, I sit in a chair near the bed and try to fall off to sleep. The chair is just too uncomfortable, and I'm very tired, so I think about it for less than an instant, and decide to lie down on the bed next to her. I grab the throw at the foot of the bed and pull it over me. That is the last I know until I see the light of the morning sun filtering through the bedroom blinds. Without moving, I look at Morgan sleeping next to me, and memory floods my mind. I very lightly touch her face and take my hand back quickly almost like I've touched something hot. She stirs, but doesn't wake, and I continue staring at this woman I thought, for years, would be my wife. Her long crinkly hair is falling over the pillow just right, and her breathing is soft and calm; she looks beautiful and so small, vulnerable, and innocent....and then I see her slowly open those gorgeous gray eyes of hers.

"Hi." Her sound is sleepy and sexy.

"Hi, yourself," I respond. We are lying facing each other and looking at and, I know, admiring each other's eyes. We always noticed the eyes...her eyes like her father's and mine like my mother's.

"What are you doing in my bed?" she asked calmly without moving.

"The chair was too hard. I'm not use to sleeping in chairs."

"That's a pretty flimsy excuse to get in my bed. Aww...my head... hurts."

"Yeah, you really tied one on last night."

"It feels like I did. So...what are you doing here in my bed?"

"You don't remember?"

"No. Did you make love to me?"

"No. I'm not in the habit of making love to intoxicated women."

"Oh, how disappointing, Babe. I'm not intoxicated now."

"You called me, and I came." I touch her face and smile. "Why were you out last night by yourself? Where was the dancing Superman?"

"You're funny. Peter is in New York with his parents. They opened a new show last night. They invited me to come, and Peter was upset that I wouldn't, but our show just ended in New York, and I didn't want to go back, so I stayed here. I missed home. But it was Christmas, and after he called, I was lonely so I went out and ended up in a bar for some reason."

"Why a bar, Morgan? You don't drink."

"Sometimes I do now."

"Why are you doing this to yourself?"

"Babe, I miss you so much, and I still love you as much as I ever did. Why can't you forgive me, Derek?" She touches my face and moves a little closer to me.

"I have."

"You have?"

"Yes."

"Enough to come back to me?" She moves my hair from my eyes, and that floods memory.

"No. Morgan, it's over for us. I'm engaged. You know that."

"Well, you can get unengaged."

"Why would I do that? I love her very much." I see her flinch, and I know my words hit a mark and sting.

"Remember the first time we kissed, Derek?" We are still lying side by side looking into each other's eyes, and I touch her face again.

"Yes. I'll never forget that, Morgan. That moment will always be special to me."

"Do you still love me?" She covers my hand with hers and moves my fingertips to her lips, and kisses each one.

"Babe, I've told you over and over. I will never stop loving you."

I see the tears forming in her eyes, and I see them begin to drop on the pillow. I gather her in my arms and kiss the top of her head and her cheek. I get off the bed and stand looking down at her.

"Morgan…none of this is about whether I love you or not. I do love you, and I always will. This is about betrayal, and that is what I can't get over.…betrayal for almost a year with my best friend. It might not be as hard if it had not been with Zack."

She throws the covers back and sees that she's wearing only her slip and panties.

"Did you look at me, Derek?"

"Yes, but I promise you one thing. I didn't see anything I hadn't already seen."

"Are you sure?" She scrunches up her face and smiles.

"Positive…Absolutely positive," I say with great certainty, and a full- face grin.

She's on her knees in the middle of the bed, swats at me, and I dodge the lick. We laugh, and that feels good. She heads to the bathroom, and I hear the shower running. When she comes out, she has on a white see-through robe with a bra and little bikini panties underneath. Her crinkled hair is beautiful, framing her face, and I will be honest and just say it: I almost lose my mind. I know I have to go, and I have to go NOW. I am sitting on the bed, and she walks to me and stands between my legs.

"Derek," She whispers my name in a pleading, crying, sensual way, and I close my eyes and take a very deep breath.

"No, Morgan. This can't happen," I say looking up at her.

I stand up, and she pulls me to her, but I gently push away.

"I'm going now. You're fine, and I have to get home."

"To her?"

"Yes...Maybe. She wasn't there when I left."

"Why can't you give me another chance?" she pleads.

"Stop. Don't do that. I don't want you begging me because you changed everything, Morgan, and you can't change it back. All the pleading in the world is not going to make a difference. My mind goes to too many dark places when I think of you with Zack. Remember, I know him. I've been with him when he is around other women. I know what he's capable of doing, and I know what he does. So now, I'm in love with Arianna, and I want to marry her. I don't want to betray her, and I don't want to feel guilty about anything when we say our vows." Despite myself, I squeeze Morgan's hand as I have done so many times before.

"I want you to take care of you," I whisper. "...and no more drinking. You parked your car last night in the middle of the road. You could have been killed."

"Really? Well, thanks for rescuing me. You're still my hero," she smiles.

"Do you want me to take you back to your car now?"

"No, you go. I'll get it later."

"All right. It's on my end of Dockside."

I touch her nose and hug her a little longer than I should. In that moment, memories flood us, and I know for sure, and she knows too that I still love her so very much. Our eyes meet in recognition, and we hold a stare that clearly communicates the love between us. I drop her hands and quietly walk through the house alone, out of the door, and home to Arianna.

—◊—

When I drive up to the cottage, I see Ari's car, and I have no idea how long she has been there.

"Oh great!" I mutter to myself. "I hope I don't have a lot of explaining to do, especially since I have on the same clothes from yesterday. Oh great."

I take a deep breath and sit in the car a minute longer to try to gather my thoughts, but no thoughts come. I'm too tired for sensible thought. Being with Morgan this morning was hard. I know I still love her, but I also know that I can't be with her. Love is not enough in this case.

I'm tired, stressed, and don't feel like a scene with Ari, and I know I'm not about to tell her anything specific about Morgan. That little secret is going to stay in my pocket a while longer. That would just open up too much that I am not ready to share.

I open the door and see her sitting on the sofa looking refreshed and beautiful. *Please don't ask me a lot of questions, Babe. I can't handle much more right now, and I don't want to lie to you.*

"Hey."

"Hey yourself. You look like you need the three B's."

"The three B's?"

"Yeah, a bath, a breakfast, and a bed," she laughs.

"I do. I need the three B's badly." I can hear my own exhaustion.

"Well, why don't you start with the bath, and I'll start you a breakfast."

"That sounds like a plan." I hesitate. If it is necessary, I want to get whatever is going to happen on the table now...no more surprises.

"You're not going to ask me where I've been?"

"Should I?"

"No, I guess not."

"Derek, I trust you, and wherever you've been, it doesn't look like you had too much of a good time. So, let's not burden you with an inquisition. Let's just start with a bath and breakfast, and then I'll think about kissing you good night for an hour or two."

I smile at this fantastic woman standing in front of me, pinch her nose and head to the shower. Inside, I can't believe what a shower is capable of doing when you need it as badly as I do. The water is warm and refreshing. The tiredness, sore muscles from tension and the guilty feelings melt away, and I wash most of it down the drain. When I come out, Ari has a full breakfast on the table of eggs, bacon, pancakes, coffee, and juice. I can't believe how blessed I am.

"Wow! Look what you've done for me. I think you do love me, girl."

"I keep telling you."

"When you left last night, I wasn't so sure."

"I just think that yesterday and the day before were very hard on both of us. I needed some space, and it looks like you did too. Derek, I think both of us need to heal our hearts from other places we've been. You know about Jean Paul, and now I know a little about Zack. I know enough to realize that there is cause for a lot of anger there. I can see it sometimes when you look at him, so we both need to heal, and maybe we can help each other."

She gets up from the table, walks around to where I'm sitting and pulls me up to her. She pushes strands of hair away from my eyes, smiles, and kisses me with all the warmth and love that two hungry people can muster at a breakfast table waiting with delicious hot food.

"I'll help you, and you help me," she murmurs burying her face against my chest.

I pull her closer. "How in the world did I get so blessed? God is being so good to me."

"I feel the same way, and I don't want anything to spoil what we have. Sometimes if we look too closely into the past, we find things that we really don't need to know, and certainly don't want to know. For today, let's call a truce on our troubled past, and just live in this day and be happy."

"That, babe, is a deal I can live with easily."

I kiss her again, and we sit and eat, laugh, share our thoughts and even talk about our upcoming wedding. We both want it in June on the beach. We both want it to take place at *The Rock,* and we both want to be barefoot in the sand.

Chapter 19

THE PARTY

A past, haunted by tears and distress, finds immeasurable comfort in a peaceful present.

Ari is bending over putting the last dishes away from breakfast, and I'm just sitting and watching her every move. That's one of my favorite things to do. She relaxes me.

"You know you look really sexy to me putting those dishes away."

"Derek, I look sexy to you when I'm just breathing."

"True that. I won't deny that at all. You know what I think?

She looks over at me. "I think you ought to bring your little sexy self over here and give your fiancée some good loving."

"You know what I think? I think my fiancée would stand a much better chance of that if he would get his lazy butt up and help me with these dishes. That's when a *man* is really sexy. Did you know that?"

"Nope. I think that bit of trivia slipped pass me," I laugh.

"Well, try it out and see what happens."

"No, you try out coming over here and giving your fiancée some good loving like I said before."

She turns around, puts the dishtowel on the counter, puts her hands on her little hips and teases. "My fiancée is acting and looking like he's about a hundred years old today, so I don't think he's up for the loving of a twenty four year old strong sexually alive woman."

"You come over here, and I'll show you what your fiancée is up for."

"No. You walked in here like you haven't seen a bed in fifty years…looking all old and beat down like somebody stole your bike on Christmas Eve. You got to prove yourself to me. I'm not coming over there to some worn out old man and get disappointed. If you got so much then catch me if you can," she giggles.

"Ahhh…you like the chase, huh?"

"Yeah, when I know I'm gonna win, and with your tired old depressed self, I know I'm going to win," she chuckles.

Oh, you think you're gonna win? You think I'm tired. You think I'm too old, huh? So…since I'm all that, if I have to chase, that's double loving. Girl, I can have you in my arms and across my knee in a split second.

"Promises, promises," she teases smiling and shaking her head.

I leap from my chair, but she is quick and dashes behind the sofa. When I try to reach her, she runs to the other end, and then there is a stand off.

"See, now that's gonna cost triple loving," I tease.

"All this energy you're wasting old man means no loving," she giggles.

"Trash talking…now, that's quartriple loving." I dash again and miss.

"See you can't even count, old man…quadruple comes after triple," she is holding her stomach laughing at me.

"I knew that…I knew that," I say quickly. "Whatever comes after quadruple is next for correcting me." We are both losing it now, and I fall on the sofa laughing, but she makes a mistake and leans on the sofa. Before she can blink an eye, I have twisted around, have her by her waist and pull her full force over the sofa and in my arms.

"Ahh, you wanta correct me now, Miss A+ student? Huh? Huh?"

I'm tickling her in all the spots that I have learned she can't stand to be tickled. She is laughing uncontrollably and wiggling trying to get out of my grasp, but that is not happening.

"Now woman, I want my loving!"

"See, if you weren't so old, you'd be *acting* instead of still *asking*," she laughs emphasizing the words acting and asking.

"You're right." I stop laughing, and I look seriously into her gorgeous hazel eyes, and we both melt in that moment, and our lips passionately meet in mutual desire. However, at that very instant, just when I have won my prize, at the very minute my dexterity has paid off, at the split second I am about to prove my virility and that I am far from an old, worn out, depressed man, my phone buzzes. Damn!

I reach in my pocket, still holding Ari down and see Zack's ugly face staring back at me.

"What, man? What do you want now?"

"Hey, D I thought we were cool!"

"Zack, what do you want?"

"Angel and I were thinking about coming over and spending the day with you guys."

"Why?"

"Well, we thought it might be fun to just hang out a while with old friends."

"Really?"

"Yeah, really. What do you say? Come on, man. It'll be fun."

I let Ari up now, and she's laughing again because she can tell what's happening and finds it so very funny.

"Not half as much fun as what I was planning, but all right. I'll see you in a few."

"Great. We're on our way."

"No need to rush. Take your time."

I slide the phone off and look at Ari. "We're having company now, but be warned: They will not save you forever. They will leave at some point."

"You think? Who's coming?" she laughs.

"Zack and Angel."

"They're still together?"

"I guess so. I'm going to change clothes."

First of all, I try to figure out what to wear since I have no idea where this day is going to lead. Are we staying in or going out? Who knows! Finally, I settle on a pair of black slacks, a white shirt and a pullover black sweater. I can't go wrong there. I clasp on my gold chain bracelet that immediately makes me think of Morgan and the day she slipped this little gem on my arm for my twenty-third birthday. It was good seeing her, lying next to her, but no time to ponder that. I have Zack to contend with now.

"Ari. Ari," I call coming out of the bedroom. Standing at the window looking out is Zack instead.

"Hey, man. Where's Ari?"

"How should I know? That's your lady. All I can tell you is when we drove up she asked Angel if she wanted to ride with her, and Angel hopped out of my car into hers. Arianna let me in, and they took off."

"She didn't say where she was going?"

"Nope."

I dig my cell out of my pocket and call her. "Hey, where you going? Oh, good idea. Thanks. See you in a few."

"They're going to get refreshments for our unexpected company," I say as if this is a confidential reveal.

"Unexpected company? Who's coming?

"You and Angel," I say bluntly.

263

"Man, you always got jokes."

"Yep, I'm a regular little standup comedian sometimes."

"Sooo...Mr. D...you really liking New Girl, huh? He moves away from the window and faces me.

"Zack, I'm engaged to Ari. I think that raises the bar a bit. Don't you?"

"OK. So, you love this girl, right?"

"Yes, I do...very much."

"More than Morgan?"

I turn away from him, take a deep breath, and try to figure out how not to answer the question, and end this discussion at the same time.

"To be very frank with you Zack, I try not to think about Morgan much."

"Really?"

"Yep, really.

"When was the last time you saw her?"

"This morning."

"This morning?"

"Yep, and that's all I'm saying about that."

"But you just said you try not to think about her that much, but you saw her this morning."

"I also said that's all I'm saying about that. Changing the subject, I have something for you, and I don't want you to read more into this than is real. Don't use your imagination, and don't try to build it into something that it's not."

"Something for me?"

"Yes."

"Something like what?"

"It's a Christmas present."

"Bro, you got me a Christmas present?" He asks in total disbelief.

"Yes, but like I said, don't read more into this than is real."

I go over to the corner of the room where we have our little Christmas tree and pick up a small exquisitely wrapped gift and hand it to Zack. That's when I see them...the tears in his eyes. I hand it to him, but he doesn't move to take it. He just stares at the gift in my hand.

"Take it," I urge as I push it closer to him.

"You're giving *me* something? Wow! Bro, I don't even know what it is, but it already means everything to me."

"It's not that much, Zack, but I want you to know how much I appreciate what you did for Ari and me. She was scared to death, man, and you helped change that for her, and I'll always be grateful to you for that.

"You know I'm always looking out."

"Yeah, I know that, but at some point, you need to get rid of the faux cops," I laugh. Seriously though, this time, I'm glad they were around."

"I'm always glad they're around. They have my back and yours too."

"Now…despite what you did to my relationship with Morgan, I want you to know that you'll always be my Bro. I don't think anything can change that, Zack, just like I'll always love Morgan. Nothing can change that. But just because you love someone, it doesn't mean that you accept everything they do, and you need to understand that. There are always consequences to actions. Things that you do can't be undone. You can't un-ring the bell. You hurt me, and you hurt me badly. Both of you did, but somehow I've found a way to forgive you guys, but I'll never forget it. Anyway, I got this for you a while back, but I couldn't give it to you until today. I love you, Man and I hope one day you'll really love me. Open it."

The tears slide down Zack's face, and he no longer tries to hide them. He wipes a few with the back of his hand and stands looking down at the gift. It almost seems like he doesn't want to open it… doesn't want to disturb the beauty of it just as he doesn't want to disturb the beauty of this moment. Inwardly and secretly, he has looked forward to this for a very long time. For seven years we didn't exchange gifts at his request, and he said it was because he hated Santa Claus and never wanted to be reminded of him. Then he would laugh. For seven years we made a pact not to exchange gifts, but this year I had to break it. Now I see like everything else about Zack, that this too, has been a deception. He probably thought I wouldn't get him a gift, and he didn't want to be disappointed, so he took the control, as usual.

"I do love you, man in my own little crooked way, and it took all of what happened for me to realize that I've got to straighten out the crooked spots. I've been doing some growing up…and I'm starting to understand what it means to have somebody in my life like you, D. I never knew anybody like you before." He is looking in my eyes now, and I can see the sincerity of how he feels.

"I thought I had lost you, but I was never going to give up trying to get you back." He looks down at the gift in his hand. I look at the expensive diamond ring sparkling on his finger and realize that everything he has, he has bought himself. None of it has been given to him by anyone else, and that is what he's thinking. Reality suddenly hits me like a ton of bricks, and I realize that this is probably the first gift he has ever received in his entire life.

"I never had a gift like this before, man."

"You don't even know what it is," I chuckle.

"...but look at how it's wrapped." He speaks quietly, slowly, and is completely serious.

With those few words, I understand a little more the depth of my friend's deprivation. In my own head, I've never given wrapping a second thought. Wrapping to me simply meant tear it to shreds as quickly as possible to see what hides inside....but to him, in this moment, it means something far different. It means someone thinking of him, someone providing for him, someone giving time to him, someone caring for him, and someone realizing they even love him. He feels all of this before ever seeing what is inside. In this moment, my Bro teaches me a very important lesson.

"Open it," I insist.

He looks at it again and starts on the ends carefully pulling the tape away without tearing the paper. When both ends are loose, he turns the gift on its back and stops when he tears a small piece of the paper. He tries a different angle and moves the paper apart.

"It's heavy," he says looking up at me.

He removes the box.

"I'm never throwing this box away. It's beautiful."

He runs his hand over the top of it, and I can tell that he is valuing every second of this time.

"Dag man, you make a real production out of opening a gift," I chuckle as I sit down on the sofa trying to lighten the mood.

He looks around at me. "Look Silver Spoon, I know this doesn't mean anything to you, but it means everything to me." I know that right now, he couldn't be more serious.

He moves over to the sofa and sits beside me. Finally, he lifts the lid from the box, only to find another inside. He lifts out a black velveteen box, opens the lid, and moves the tissue aside. He lifts out the gift.

"Wow!" D, you got this for me?...after what I did to you?" His tone says this is unbelievable.

He looks at the gift, turning it in every direction, and then he looks back at me. He looks again at the gift and back at me. He places it in front of us on the coffee table and sits back in his seat admiring it.

I look at the black marble nameplate with its unique crystal white streaks. The letters of Zack's name are etched into the marble and each letter is filled with gold.

It reads: Zackary T. Belford

Junior Wall Street Project Manager

Zack reads the inscription aloud slowly, and again I see the tears. We both sit totally comprehending the depth of this event. We remain in a comfortable quietness until we hear the girls and a key turning in the lock.

—⁓—

"Your lines are really climbing, especially *Sunday's Best*. I don't think I have ever seen a new fashion house climb so fast," Angel remarks as they juggle the bags, purses, and keys.

"You're making it happen with *Sunday's Best,* and *Summer Shine* is not far behind. My accountants assure me that we're showing big profits right now with both of those lines. Hey guys," Ari calls.

I jump up to help with the packages and Angel sets hers down and moves quickly over to the sofa.

"Hey, baby….miss me?" Zack stands up and kisses her.

"You were out of my sight weren't you?" He smiles and holds her around her waist.

"Yep, I was." She breaks the embrace. "What's up, Derek? Are you staying out of trouble with my girl?" Her voice is loud and friendly, and I turn to give her my full attention.

"I'm doing my best to stay out of trouble, and you look like you're what's happening," I smile. I see you and my Bro have been connecting for the holidays….hugging and kissing and stuff."

"Yeah, it's been *real* nice. Right, baby?" She looks around at Zack who is back on the sofa.

"You know it, I know, and now the world knows," he chuckles.

Angel walks over to the sofa and picks up the nameplate. "Wow, look at you. Zackary T. Belford. Junior Wall Street Project Manager," she reads with a sense of pride. Now that's something. What does the T stand for?"

"Tyler."

"Nice. Mr. Zackary Tyler Belford. Ari and Derek give you this?"

"Yes, they did. First gift I ever got," he says looking up at her.

"What do you mean the first gift you ever got? You mean the first gift you ever got that you really liked…that had your name on it?… that Derek ever gave you? What do you mean this is the first gift you ever got? That sounds stupid."

Zack looks up at her, takes the nameplate from her, turns it around in his hands, and drops his head. He now has everyone's attention.

"No, I mean this is the first gift I ever got in my entire life. There was never any Santa Claus for me. Pops says I was always naughty, and Santa didn't visit little naughty boys. This is it, and Ari, like I told D, I'll never forget this. This means more than you will ever know… more than you *can* ever know. Thanks."

The room is silent for a moment, and every one takes a deep breath trying to figure out how to change the mood. Ari is the first to speak.

"How about we get this party started? Do you guys know how to play Pinochle or even Double Pinochle?"

"Heck, yeah. Actually, Zack and I played Double P with some of my friends the other day and whipped them good."

"Yeah, you don't want to mess with us with Pinochle. Right D? I beat him all the time," Zack brags.

"I don't know about all the time, man. Let's just say, it's not my best game."

"Well, it's mine so you stick with me baby, and I think we can take these two chumps," Ari giggles.

"I got a game room in the back. Let's see if we can even the odds."

Zack picks up the gift from the table and tucks it under his arm.

"Let's do this!" He rubs his hands together and his mood seems to change immediately. His thoughts are back from his trip down memory lane, and he is now ready and seemingly even happy. We move to the game room and Zack is impressed.

"Wow!...a man cave. Black and red...nice colors...pool table, game table, trophies, bar, darts, theater, music, the Knicks on the wall. This I nice."

"Thanks. Sit your butt down, and let me beat you in my nice man cave."

"In your dreams, baby...in your dreams. Come give me a little inspiration, baby."

"You got it. Angel moves over to Zack and kisses him a bit too long for public affection, but then I know that's just Zack.

The game is full of trash talk, laughter, idle talk, and food. Time passes quickly. Before we know it, darkness has set in and four games have produced a tie. We decide to leave it at that.

"Y'all want go with Angel and me to this dance club tonight? We went Christmas night and had a ball."

"What do you want to do, baby," I ask Ari.

"Sounds good to me."

"OK, let's get changed and check it out," replies Zack rubbing his hands together.

"Angel, I'll get our stuff out of the car and D where can we change?'

"Guest bedroom...to your left will be fine."

After about an hour Ari steps out in a plum velveteen tunic with a drawstring at the waist and beaded fringes on the cuffs and the hem. Underneath she sports silver jeans, and high heels. Her earrings and bracelet are silver and plum. She decides to let her hair go free tonight so her dark curls frame her face and move down her back.

"Girl, woo." I suck in my breath. "You take my breath away. You stay close tonight. I'm not taking my eyes off of you."

"Until you see someone prettier," she smiles and grabs me around my waist.

"There is no one prettier."

"Wait until you see Angel. I'm going to see how long it takes you to take your eyes off of her," she laughs. "Remember, she's my top model, so be careful."

I take Ari in my arms and look at her beautiful face. "Baby, you have nothing to worry about. You have my heart."

The club is jumping with music and the crowd is having a great time. We start off dancing to a house beat, then a little hip hop before we decide to take a break. Talking is next to impossible so we move over to the bar so that I can get a Scotch and Ari can have her regular ginger ale. We spot Zack and Angel on the floor and they look great together. They are easy to spot in black and white and their energy and good looks draw everyone's attention.

"Baby, excuse me a minute." Ari almost screams over the music. "I'm going to the lady's room." I nod and watch her move with grace across the crowded room....and that's when I spot her. There she is... Morgan, on the dance floor, swinging her slim hips to the beat and looking like a princess on stage...her home. I can't help myself. She is both beautiful and alluring like the mythological Sirens. I move almost like I'm caught in some dreamlike state until I'm standing next to her. I touch her shoulder lightly, and she turns around to me, then waves her partner off. She is so close...touching me. She's just a hair from being in my arms. I lean down close to her ear. My heart, for some reason, is out of control.

"Having a good time?" I try to sound calm.

"Yeah, she mouths the word with a big grin that makes her look even more beautiful. Then she gets close to my ear. "Don't worry, I'm not drinking tonight," she laughs. You want to dance?" I nod yes, and we swing to the heavy beats of hip hop. She is laughing and really enjoying herself and for a minute, so am I. When the music changes, I bow slightly, smile, and release her hand.

"You here alone?" She yells.

"No." I shake my head and let my lips form the word.

"Well then, I'll see you when I see you." She cocks her head to the side and looks sad, puts her hand on my arm, turns, and disappears in the crowd. She vanishes as quickly as she appeared. The dancers on the floor seem to engulf me now, and I start looking for Ari above the crowd. I feel a tap on my shoulder, and it's Zack.

"I saw that, he yells in my ear. "You better change that look on your face before Ari sees it. We need to talk." He moves away, and we both see Ari and Angel at the same time.

"Ladies, meet us at the bar in ten. OK? D, give me a minute." We move across the floor toward the restrooms and away from the loudest music.

"Man, I saw that. What are you doing?" Zack's eyes are serious. "You're not me, D. You can't do this. What do you think you're doing?"

"Nothing, man. I saw her, and I just spoke. That's all." My voice is quiet.

"Naw, you did more than speak. You can't fool me. I saw you with the baby browns. This is Zack, Bro, and I know what I see. You crossed the room for her! You still love that girl. What are you doing marrying Arianna when you still love Morgan? Man, you should have seen your face. *I love you* was written in red."

"You exaggerate everything. I love Ari a lot."

"Enough?"

"Yes, more than enough. I trust her and she trusts me."

"Should she?"

"I hope so. I never want to hurt her. Oh man!"

"Why did you see Morgan this morning?"

I exhale loudly. "She was drunk. She called me to pick her up because she was lost. When I got there, she was parked in the middle of the street, Zack. You know what could have happened." I take another deep breath. "I picked her up, took her home, and I was too tired to drive back so I slept on her bed, but absolutely nothing happened. I swear to you, man. Nothing happened. I even told her that nothing could happen. We talked. I left, and drove home. That's it."

"Arianna is good people, man, and I'd hate to see her get hurt. I know this is all my fault. I know it, and I'm more than sorry about that…but like you said, you can't un-ring the bell so there's nothing else I can do but say I'm sorry…but you? Now that you've made another choice, I think you have to make good on it, Bro."

"I plan to," I say with clear irritation in my voice.

OK, then. You good? Can we go back out there now? I had to get you away. Your face was telling the story, baby."

I take a deep breath, and look at Zack. "Here's what I know. I know I love Ari. I have no doubt about it. It's just that when I see Morgan, memory won't turn me loose, man. Good memories and bad memories. They…they collide. This morning when I was with her, our past was racing through my mind like a runner on a track. I've been thinking about her all day. My voice cracks, and I feel the onset of tears burn my eyes.

"I guess you need to decide if the bad memories outweigh the good."

"They do," I answer pensively, and I feel my head shaking in the affirmative. "I have no doubt about that either. I know you take a lot of the blame, as you should, but she has to take most of it because she could have said no if she loved me enough."

After an hour or so, the four of us leave, and in Zack's car, in the back seat, I take Ari in my arms and kiss her passionately. Butterflies flutter, and something wonderful, in that moment, tells me again that I'm home.

When the party is over, when our guests have gone, and when we are all alone in what will soon be our home together, we lay. I feel the calmness settle over me; I recognize Doubt's attempt to take flight, and in the bliss and tenderness of our lovemaking, I know that I love this woman in my arms, and I can barely wait for her to be my wife. But...if I'm completely honest with myself, I know, too, that Morgan is not just a distant memory, and somehow I think she never will be.

Chapter 20

NO LOOSE ENDS

~ Lies, even to oneself, weigh on the heart and soul
with unrelenting and inescapable guilt~

The winter months whiz past us so fast that they are almost a blur. I'm extremely busy with court case after court case, trials, research, consultations and just trying to be the best lawyer I can be, and keep my head above water at the same time. Bill and Shawn Brollen trust me more and more and give me responsibilities that I only dreamed I might have in the years to come. Ari's fashion house is flourishing, and her lines have gone worldwide in the blink of an eye. While her parents are helping a little, her own creativity and expertise have been remarkable. Angel is now her top model for *Sunday's Best* and *Summer Shine*. She and the staff have taken it to new heights, and now Ari is concentrating on her new collection, *Champagne Elegance*. It's proving to be even more popular than the first two. Between fashion shows, designing, meeting with New York and International staffs, and keeping every other detail together, Ari is spending a lot of time planning the wedding. I do what I can when I can to let her know that I want this day to be perfect…the happiest day of her life. I know that her designers are putting a lot of time into her dress, and I know that she will be a stunning bride. Every time I see Ari now she tells me that she has checked the weather again for our day, and we laugh.

A week before the wedding, I meet her family when we pick them up from the airport, and fortunately for me, our first meeting is nothing like the one Ari experienced with my Mom. Her family is friendly, carefree, and fun, and absolutely no one thinks that I am digging for gold even though her brother, River, asks me more questions than any of us think necessary.

"Are we going to hold up a sign?"

"I think not. It hasn't been that long, Derek. I think I can still recognize my family. The only one questionable is River who changes his hair constantly, but even he can't fool me."

I smile at this woman I love so much and watch her expressions that communicate how anxious she is to see her family. I can tell she is a bit nervous, but more excited than I have seen her in a very long time. I see the group, and recognize them immediately even though I have never laid eyes on them. They are all beautiful/handsome…a family that demands attention just from their looks. Her sister spots us first and runs the rest of the way to hug the sister I can tell she has missed more than anything. If I didn't know better, I would think they were twins. The only difference is that India has obviously cut her hair somewhat short and is wearing it natural in twists that fall just right into a natural style. She is beautiful too with the same hazel eyes, a copper tone complexion, and wide smile.

"Look at you, girl." Her hands move in the shape of a woman's body. "I can tell you have a man. You exude beauty," India teases and they hug long enough for the rest of the family to join the group.

India walks around me as if examining me for approval. "So, you're Derek, huh?"

"Last time I check," I smile.

"Wow! Sexy too! Listen to that voice." She is grinning. "I like that hair." She gives my hair a flip and tried to move the naughty strands that always fall over my eye, but her touch is too flirtatious for me, and I move out of her reach.

Ari is busy giving everyone a hug, but Mrs. Channing does not miss the show that India is putting on.

"India, stop giving Derek a bad impression of us," she laughs.

"Mom, Dad, this is Derek...the man who will be my husband in a week! Wow! I love saying that...my husband," she laughs with a little playful jump.

"We've read a lot about you, son, in Ari's emails, and when we get her on the phone, she can't stop telling us everything about you," her dad remarks. Both of them have warm smiles, and I can feel myself relax.

"I hope its all been good."

"It has except for that one little thing," India responds quickly before anyone else can say a word. She's walking around me again trailing her finger around my shoulder. I turn with her and with my eyes ask what is the one little thing.

"India, stop it!" Ari hits at her sister. "You're just trying to pay me back. I did this to her little sixteen year old boyfriend when we were kids, and now she wants to pay me back ever though we're supposed to be ADULTS now! I was only twelve then."

"You scared him off," she laughs…just wanted to check to see if Derek can be scared off as easily."

"Not a chance, India. I love this woman too much to let a little family intimidation frighten me, and I'm certainly not sixteen." I pull Ari close to me and hold her around her waist.

"What kind of lawyer are you, Derek, and how long have you been practicing?" Connor is the oldest son and he's sizing me up to protect his sister, I'm sure. I already spied him checking out my outward appearance so now he begins the questions that will tell him something about the person I am on the inside. I don't have a sister or a brother for that matter, but I get it.

Oh, this is Connor, Derek, my oldest brother, but then you probably already know that, right," she says with a sly wink. Ari playfully brushes her hand over Connor's close- cropped hair, and he tries to lean out of her reach.

"Stop, Ari. You still play too much."

"…and you're still too serious."

"I'm a defense attorney, Connor."

"I see," he responses as he continues to size me up.

"And this is my youngest brother, River," interrupts Ari.

CHAPTER 20: NO LOOSE ENDS

"It's great meeting all of you. I've looked forward to this for a while. Ari and I thought you all might be hungry when you landed so we have reservations if you're up for it."

"I sure am. Nice looking out guys," remarks River.

"Looks like you haven't changed a bit either. You're always hungry," Ari said jabbing her brother's stomach.

"Yeah, nothing has changed, and I hope you have some real food at that wedding."

"I think you will be very pleased," she smiles and hugs her brother. I can already tell there is a special connection with the two of them. I guess it's the closeness of their ages.

At dinner everyone has a great time. We talk about Ari's fashion house and its success, and of course, her Dad has some special Daddy advice to make the house even better and more successful. He talks about the fabrics that they are shipping to her from Japan, and a few samples that they got on a trip to Spain. I can tell Ari is taking it all in and planning to use all of his ideas. I can also see how much respect the kids have for their parents, and how much love and respect the parents have for their kids. I am, indeed, impressed that Mr. Channing has been reading the newspaper clippings about the cases I have won with my firm, and he remarks about one in particular. Every now and then, I look over at Connor, see his brown eyes staring at me, and the lawyer in me says he wants to know more about me, but is hesitant to ask.

"Derek in a tense, professional career like you have, does everything stay calm and cool or do you ever get yelled at?" River asks with a mouth full of food. Ari's look tells me immediately that she disapproves of River's inquiry.

"That's an odd question to ask, River. You don't need to answer that Derek."

"I'm just saying…I know everything can't be perfect. I get yelled at everyday. I just want to know what happens when something goes wrong in a court." River seems quite sincere, and I feel compelled to answer.

"I don't mine answering, and I'm afraid I have to answer that in the affirmative, River. We were trying a case not too long ago, and I really didn't bring my "A" game to court. I didn't even bring my "B" game. I made some major mistakes and the firm was not happy. I didn't think what I did was a mistake.

"Were you right?" The entire table is quiet waiting, and only Ari and I know how delicate this moment is. She knows how upset I have been since Shawn confronted me and accused me of embarrassing them in the judge's chambers during a private consultation. I look up from my plate and put my fork down. Just the memory of it disturbs me greatly even now.

"No, River. I was wrong. I was very wrong, and it almost cost an innocent man his life, but I learned a very good lesson that day. When you work as a team, you have to trust your team and do everything you can to support. I overlooked some very important information in a couple of depositions, and I missed a very important meeting. On top of that, I was extremely arrogant, and I refused to see my own errors. I was completely unprepared. Thank God my team was on top of things. I'll tell you this. I won't make those mistakes again. I have people's lives in my hands and that is so serious…nothing to be taken lightly. I won't think again that just because I usually win that I can't lose. I know I will make other mistakes, but it won't be because I'm unprepared. That experience has been quite humbling."

After that answer, Ari tries to lighten the mood because she knows how much this incident still hurts, and how many times I have continued to apologize for it. We finish our lunch and go back to the cottage together. After an hour or so, I pull Mr. Channing aside for a private moment…a very important moment.

He is a tall, slim man with serious eyes, but the business side of him can put you at ease in a minute or intimidate you for the entire space of time that you are in his presence. When I look at him, I see Conner the most. They have the same brown eyes that penetrate into your soul and the same olive smooth skin and facial structure. He is very handsome and very poised. In front of me is a man who knows what he wants, and I can tell he is a man who goes after it with passion. That is where I see my Ari in him.

"I know that I'm doing this a bit backward, Sir, but you left the country, and I couldn't easily reach you," I laugh. For the first time today, I'm nervous, and I think it shows.

"I love your daughter, Mr. Channing. I think I've loved her from the first moment I saw her, and I can't wait to make her my wife, but before we marry, I would like to ask you for your daughter's hand…I ask for your blessing."

"Ari has told us a lot about you, Son, and I have no doubt that she loves you with her whole heart, but I have to say this."

Before he speaks again, he takes a seat on the sofa and laces his hands together. He seems to be in very deep and serious thought.

"You and Ari haven't given this a whole lot of time, Son. I think this marriage is a bit rushed." He is looking directly in my eyes, and I see a seriousness there that fails to produce that unique twinkle…that sparkle I saw he had when he first met his daughter today.

"Derek, my wife and I have been married for thirty-four years, and we know each other very well. Sometimes we can finish each other's sentences. In these thirty-four years, there have been a lot of ups and downs…a lot of them, Derek….but never once have we tried to work out any of our problems hastily or without the other completely involved. Our children were born soon after we married and relatively close together. They transformed our relationship to some degree. Some of the time, we were very frustrated and stressed. That's what small children do to you even through you love them with everything inside of you."

He is speaking very slowly, and I can tell that his mind is far back in the past, but at the same time here, very much in the present with me. I'm looking at this father seated with me on my sofa and not quite able to understand his feelings about me. I'm thinking that he wants to trust me, but he's not quite sure if I will ever hurt his little girl in a place that he cannot reach to fix; I see and feel that this frightens him in a deep place that I have not yet experienced, and cannot until I, too, am a parent.

"You know, when your kids are little, Derek, you teach them so many things, like how to laugh at themselves, how to cope when the tears comes, how to be humbly successful, and how to get up when they fall. My wife and I worked hard…very hard, to make our children feel secure no matter what we were going through at the time. Sometimes, when things were hard, we made them easier by

284

sincerely loving and leaning on each other. As the man of the home, I always felt it was my responsibility to make sure that my wife and kids were all right first...you know...comfortable about whatever we were doing, and I almost always knew what made them comfortable.... no secrets...always clearly communicating. Yes, we had money pretty soon after we started our fashion business, so fortunately, finances were not a problem for long, but life can throw a lot of curves at you where money can't really help. Sometimes people don't believe that, but I'm sure you know that to be true."

"Yes, I do, sir. I know that very well."

"As the head of the home, you have to make sure that your family is taken care of physically and emotionally. You're pretty young, Son. You and Ari are just getting your lives started. But the thing that worries me the most is what I will call a father worry. You haven't known my daughter very long; therefore, I think you have a lot to learn about her before you can make her genuinely happy. Are you going to love her and care about her enough to know very soon how to finish her sentences...know what's inside her heart and provide what makes and keeps her happy? Are you really ready to do this, Derek? Are you really ready to take a wife, with all of its complications, and be completely faithful to her for the rest of your life? Are you really ready, son? Are you ready in case children come early...before you actually plan them? You're a good-looking, intelligent guy, Derek. I suspect you haven't been alone just waiting around for Arianna to show up. So... Do you have any loose ends out here you need to tighten up before you do this thing, Son?"

"I'm ready, Sir...I'm really ready, and there are no loose ends to tie."

"No loose ends?…not even one, Derek?…good-looking , intelligent, rich guy like yourself? He asks and raises an eyebrow.

"No, Sir.…no loose ends.…not even one."

He is silent for a moment, just looking at me.…searching my eyes and, I think, even my soul, giving me time, if necessary, to tell him the truth. I can tell that he does not truly believe me.

"Ok…Ok, then." Mr. Channing is shaking his head affirmatively, as if he is still thinking, but at the same time having no choice but to accept the words that I have spoken to him. I can tell that he's sizing me up…trying to decide, from the day that I was born, if I have been taught integrity, and if, after being taught, I stand on those principles.

"Well Son, I take you at your word. You have my blessing, but I want you to know that my children are everything to me, and if you hurt Arianna, I'm coming after you…just so you know. She's my baby." He chuckles and lightens the mood.

We shake hands and move back to the game room.

"Arianna, I see this beautiful piano out here. Come play something for your Daddy. I haven't heard you tickle those keys in a long time."

And so the evening ends with music, laughter, singing, and a feeling of close family unity. All evening, I look at this man who is entrusting his precious daughter to me. I see the pride in his eyes when he speaks with her, sings to her music, and throws his head back in laughter with her. Watching them, I know so very well why I cannot shake the one question and my answer. They both continue to gnaw at me well after the Channings leave my home.…no loose end…not even one? No.…no loose ends."

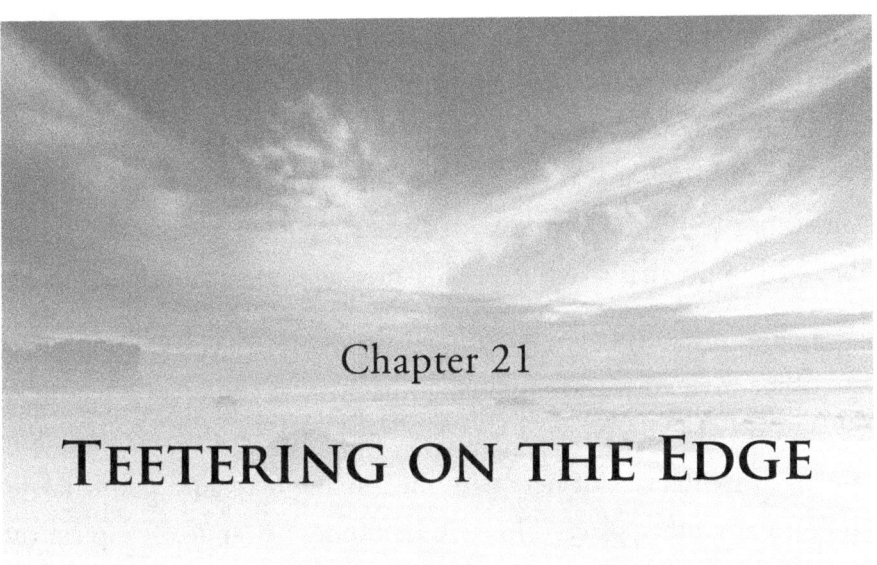

Chapter 21

TEETERING ON THE EDGE

~Temptation loses its sparkle in the radiance of Deep Respect~

Somewhere in the back of my mind, I realize that I have now read this page three times, and I still have no idea what the words are telling me. Every time I start over, my mind drifts again to Ari and the wedding. I keep imaging our day on Saturday. I know that she's going to be unbelievably beautiful. I also realize that while the dress will be stunning, she will put it to shame, and I can barely wait to make this fantastic woman all mine. Her family has been here for over a week now, and I really miss her. I understand her spending time with them. She's missed India most of all, and they have been trying to catch up. Despite my impatience, our special day is coming fast, and Ari is putting the finishing touches on the wedding and still trying to help run a business. Even knowing and understanding all of that, I can't seem to concentrate. I saw her for about five minutes yesterday and not at all today. When she called earlier, she thought she might be able to drop by, but warned me that she might not show up because something had gone wrong with India's Maid of Honor dress, and they had to get that fixed before her mother had another nervous fit.

I close my notes allowing myself the excuse that I will be out of the office for two weeks anyway, and someone else on the team can take up my slack in court. I lean my head back on the sofa and close my eyes to visualize Ari here with me...living here, and never having to go to any other place. This will be home. I hear a soft tap on the door, barely audible.

"There's my baby," I think to myself....but then, , I wonder why she doesn't just use her key. Grinning to myself, I bounce up, open the door, but then immediately see that it's not Ari at all.

"Morgan, what are you doing here?" *I'm puzzled.*

"Derek, can I come in?" *She's serious.*

"Of course, you can." I step aside and let her enter.

"What's up?"

"Time. Time is up, Derek. You've got to tell me...is it really too late for us? Has time run out for us?"

"Morgan, what are you doing?"

"Derek, I'm not going to pull any punches with you. Here is the honest truth. I love you. I never stopped loving you. Even when I made that awful mistake, I still loved you, and I don't understand how you can do this to us."

"Morgan, how many times do I have to tell you that there is no us anymore?"

Now I see the tears, and I don't want to go through this again. I don't want to hurt Morgan, and I don't want to be tempted to do anything that I'll regret. I step back away from her and try to get some distance from her tears and my fear of betrayal.

"Morgan, you have to understand that this thing has been over for quite some time now. I've moved on, and I'm looking forward to a marriage with someone else. You have to try to understand that. You can't just come in here and try to resurrect the past. That part of my life that you keep remembering is over. You have to stop living a dream, baby."

"Derek, it's a dream we had together. We both had it."

"But the operative word here, Morgan is "had."…past tense. It's over, and I don't like you coming here trying to make me feel guilty about something I didn't do. You and Zack did this. Suppose Ari had been here when you came knocking on my door. You're being down-right selfish, Morgan. You messed us up, and now it seems like you don't care if you mess this up for me….talking about how much you love me. Where was all that love when you were sneaking behind my back secretly building a telephonic relationship with my best friend? Where was all that love the night you slept with Zack? Where was it when you stood in my hospital room sway in his arms when you thought I was knocked out cold and would never know about your little indiscretion? Girl, you just need to leave." I can feel my anger building with the memory of what she has done to me…to us…to our relationship.

She moves over close to me now, and I see her flushed face and dewy eyes that make her look so beautiful, so vulnerable, so hurt, so helpless and small. I know she sees this as a last ditch effort, and even in my anger, the sight of her breaks my heart. It's so hard for me to see her this way, and so...I can't help myself.

"Come here." My voice is soft. I take her in my arms. *Mistake.* I hold her. *Another mistake.* I pull her closer and kiss the top of her head. *Major mistake. Loose ends come to mind.*

"Babe, we can't do this," I whisper. I hear my voice crack.

"I love you so much, Derek. At least, just give me tonight....just one more night. That's all I ask, and I'll leave you alone. I promise. I thought I could move on and just forget. I can't. I tried."

"Baby," I sigh a deep sigh. "I'm getting married in two days. I can't do this."

"Just one night, Baby....just one night."

I look in her teary eyes and shake my head no.

The tears are moving slowly down both cheeks now, and I wipe them away with my thumbs, and pull her to me again. My heart is breaking, and I can feel my love for her. I don't want her to hurt. I don't want to hurt, and somewhere in the zone of my brain that is still thinking, I know more than anything else that I don't want to hurt or betray Ari.

"Come sit with me, babe." I whisper close to her ear.

We move over to the sofa, and before I can take my own comfortable position, Morgan is kissing me and trying to unbutton my shirt. I feel myself being taken in by the lips that I still miss, by the passion from someone I have loved for years, and, honestly, by the just plain male lack of good common sense when it comes to sex with a beautiful woman, especially one that you love like I love Morgan. But somewhere, I can't tell you where, I get the strength to stop her. I get the common sense to push away. I find the power to stand up and out of her immediate reach.

"Morgan, stop it." My voice is gentle, but firm. "I'm telling you, this is not going to happen. I can't do this to Ari. I can't do this to you. Yes, I love you enough to say no because if we do this, it won't stop with us tonight. You know that, and I know that, and there is nothing but more hurt at the end of that road."

"Then why with all of this uncertainty, Derek, would you get married? If you know it wouldn't end tonight, why would you not give us another chance or at least wait a minute?"

"Because I know me, and I would always think you might cheat again, and I would have betrayed Ari in the process. I don't want to do that."

"Derek, we went together for nine years, and in all that time, I never cheated once…I never even thought about cheating. I made one mistake, and I can't for the life of me understand why you can't find it in that heart of yours…that heart that still loves me, to forgive." I hear the irritation and impatience in her voice, and I feel the irritation coming in my own.

"I told you. I have forgiven you. I just can't do this again with you."

Standing so close to me, and hearing those words cause a reaction I don't expect. Suddenly, she's pounding my chest with her sharp

291

boney fists, and I grab her wrists. Holding her there, we are both very still. I'm looking in her teary eyes; she's looking in mine, and in that moment of stillness, we are acutely cognizant of the secret we share. I want to kiss her so badly that the feeling surprises me, but we know that if I do, it won't stop there, so I don't.

"Derek, you are not over me, and I'm definitely not over you, so why are you doing this? Why can't you wait and be sure that you really want Arianna? That's fair."

I move away from her now, and sit on the sofa again. She sits next to me, and I pull her to me. She lays her head on my shoulder and for a while we say nothing. We sit in a comfortable silence that we know so well. In this brief serenity, we view scenes of our past and remember all of those feelings. I'm the first to break the silence.

"Morgan, you're going to be fine. I know that you and Peter are close, and he'll take good care of you."

Morgan pushes up, and glares at me. "Don't say that, Derek. Don't tell me that. Don't let those words be my memory of you. Since we were teens, you've been the one for me, and that has not changed even if you want it to change."

"Morgan, if you love me like you say you do, then you'll let me go, so I can let you go. Baby, here's what I know for sure: A part of me will always love you. I know that's never going to change. However, I also know I can't go back to where we were. That place is gone. For me, it's dead. There is no way either of us can fix this. It won't happen. What you did hurt me and disappointed me to my core, and I can't forget it. I know that those thoughts won't go away, and I won't be able to be what you need me to be. You won't be able to be what I need you to be. I know that. We would fail each other miserably even though we wouldn't want to fail. I don't want to wonder where you are if you're late coming home from work or wonder if it's the truth when you tell me you have a late rehearsal. I don't want to think you're betraying me if you're not where I think you should be. I want you to be happy, Morgan, but I have to be able to trust my wife.

She looks at me, and with those words she stands and pulls me to my feet. She wraps her arms around my neck and looks up into my eyes.

"Then let me say this to you: 'You reside in my heart with purity, an undeniable authenticity.' Remember when I wrote that to you?"

"Yes, I carried it in my wallet and in my heart all of these years until you hurt me."

Well, it still stands whether you carry it or not. I love you, Derek Wellington with my whole heart, and no matter where we end, who we are with, where we go, what we do, how far the distance, our love will be..."

With her hands placed on each side of my face, she pulls me to her and lightly kisses my lips, lets her hands slide to my shoulders, and then to my hands. She squeezes them in our old familiar way that says take care, releases her hold, gathers her things, and leaves without another word.

Chapter 22

OUR WEDDING DAY

~There is no greater love than one without conditions~

~ Derek ~

"You need anything now, D? Some water, wine, a smoke?"

"Zack, I don't smoke," I say with mild exasperation.

"I know that. You need anything else?"

"Yeah."

"What? What? What?" Zack is a wreck!

"For at least the next fifteen minutes, Bro, while I'm getting dressed, I need you to stop asking me if I need anything," I laugh.

"You always got jokes. I can't help it. I'm nervous."

"Why are you nervous? I'm the one getting married in an hour. All you have to do is walk out with me, stand beside me, and remember the ring. That's it."

"Ah, man!...the ring. Zack is patting all of his pockets and turning one inside out.

"Man, don't tell me you can't find the ring. I just gave it to you ten minutes ago. What could you have done with it in that short time?"

Now I'm nervous, and I'm standing in front of this clown watching him searching for my baby's ring.

"Ha, Ha, I got you back." He points at me. "It's right here in your Bro's top pocket, safe and sound."

"Man, don't do that. Somebody is at the door. Now you have something to do. Get that for me, and stay out there with them, please."

"Sure thing. Nothing to it, but to do it." Zack does a little dance, makes a twirl turn, and heads to the door.

I hear loud voices and none of them sound friendly. *For heaven sakes! What now. It can't be loud mouth Angel. She's supposed to be with Ari. What in the world is this mess on my wedding day?* I'm muttering to myself and trying to finish tying my bow tie at the same time. Zack yanks the door open, and I see fury or fear in his eyes. I can't tell which. Maybe it's both. I don't know.

"You got trouble, man...big trouble. That's your Mom out there demanding to see you, and she's got Morgan with her."

"What? Are you kidding me? Morgan?"

"I wish I were kidding, but I'm not, D."

I push past Zack and see Mom and Morgan standing in the front room. The first thing I notice is that Morgan looks beautiful in a lacy tight fitting short white dress, and I see the scallop edged hem and wonder why is she wearing this. Why is she wearing white? She is not the bride. I smirk to myself walking down the hall and wonder if she has a veil somewhere in her purse to whip out at the last minute. My mother and Morgan both are insane.

"Ma, what is this about? Hey, Morgan. What are you doing here?" I say as calmly as possible.

My mother jumps in immediately with her most serious scolding tone…the one she used to use when I was about ten or eleven…the one that had that index finger pointed straight at my forehead and would punch me if I didn't straighten up fast.

"We're here to give you one last chance to act like you have two grains of sense, boy. You know good and well you have no business marrying that girl. You and Morgan have been planning this wedding since you were in high school."

"No. Mom," I say as calmly as possible. "We haven't. You have been planning this wedding since I was five years old. Well, it's not going to happen. I'm marrying Arianna today in about forty-five minutes, and there is absolutely nothing you can do about it."

"We'll see about that," she said with a major frown on her face. "I don't think you've started hating money yet, and you are putting your inheritance on the line, boy. I will not give one dime to that little gold digger girl you're trying to marry today."

I take a deep breath. "Where's my Dad? I need somebody in here with some good common sense."

"I have good common sense, and I tried to get him to come in here and talk some sense into you, but he wouldn't budge. The last time I saw him he was outside sitting in a seat trying to act like he doesn't know us. But that's all right too. This wedding is not happening, Derek, and I told him so. I thought you would see the light before it got to this. That girl is a criminal and wanted in France. I will not have my son married to a jailbird."

My mother is pacing around in circles and waving her hands about like a crazy person. I know her. She is dead serious, and it will be hard to talk sense into her now. Frankly, I'm not about to try at this point. This is my day, and I don't plan to have a round table discussion with her or anybody else.

"You need to calm down. Arianna is no criminal. I thought you would have figured this out by now or that Dad would have told you or something, but I guess I was wrong on both fronts, so I'll just tell you now."

"Figured out what? Tell me what? You can't tell me anything now, Boy, but that you're going out there and tell that girl the wedding is off."

I take another deep breath, and speak slowly to keep my temper in tact. "The wedding is not going to be called off, Mom. Arianna is heir to the *Channing Fashion World of Design*. She is the youngest daughter of Edward and Elizabeth Channing who have far more money than we ever thought about having. She does not need to steal any money from anyone, and she certainly does not need my meager inheritance."

"Do you mean the Channing's who rule the fashion world?"

"Yes."

"You mean the Channing's of *Channing International Fashions*?"

"Yes, Mom...the very same. I don't have time to explain this to you now. I have a date with a minister, a beach full of guests, and the love of my life. So, bye! I'll see you outside."

"Wait a minute, child. Why didn't you tell me this a long time ago?"

"Simply put, Mom, Ari wanted you to accept her for herself not her money."

"But Jean Paul told me..."

"Look, I told you Jean Paul was trying to kidnap Ari because he's in love with her and wants her back in France, but that's not happening either."

"Now, Morgan, why are you doing this? I thought we settled this together privately Thursday night." I'm looking at Morgan now, and I walk over closer to her. I take her hand in mine. "Don't be a part of this."

"She is a part of this. This should be her day."

"Well Mom, it's not, and it's not going to be," I say emphatically looking directly into Morgan's eyes.

I see Morgan avert my eyes, and she and Zack exchange glances, and that's when it happens. Morgan releases my hands, moves away from me, and stands in front of Zack.

"This is all your fault, Zack." She spits out the words quietly. "You did this to me. You took my life away." I see the intense anger in her face, and her voice gets louder and out of control.

"You took everything from me." I see her jab him in his chest. "You knew exactly what you were doing. You may as well have killed me."

Morgan is screaming and crying. In a flash, she is all over Zack, pulling at his clothes, scratching his face, and kicking his legs. I'm trying to get her off of him, and Mom is just standing there with her arms folded letting it happen. Zack is yelling at Morgan and everything, for the moment, is again totally out of control.

Zack is screaming now and trying to fend off the blows.

"Did I rape you, Morgan? Did I tear your clothes off of you or did you tear mine off of me? Did I push you down on the bed or did you push me? Answer that! Answer that for D. Answer that for the man you claim you love! Answer that for his Mom, cause you know the answers."

"Look, I shout above the fray. Everybody calm down. This is my day. Not yours, Mom…not yours, Morgan as much as you may want it to be…Not yours, Zack. It's mine! It's Ari's and mine, and if you all care one little bit about me, you will respect that. Zack, go get cleaned up and let's go. The rest of you either go outside and sit in a damn seat and be quiet or go home. Morgan you shouldn't even be here, but if you want to put yourself through this, then stay at your own risk, but do not ruin this day for me any more than you already have."

I am moving over to the door to usher them out when I see my Dad quietly open the door and enter the room. Everything and everybody stops. My father's voice is calming and slow when he speaks.

"I just thought I'd better come over here and rescue my son."

"That's what I'm trying to…"

"Hush, Nina. This is my time to talk, now. I'm sure by now you've had your say." He closes the door and walks over to me. On this my wedding day, my father takes my hand, shakes it, squeezes it a little, and looks directly in my eyes.

"Son, you've chosen this amazing woman you want to spent the rest of your life with, and unlike some other people in this room, I trust your judgment. If you tell me that you love Arianna and you want her to be your wife, I'm here to support that decision."

I see a hint of his tears.

"You're my son, and you've never disappointed me once…never embarrassed me once…never disrespected me once…never given me one minute of trouble, and on this day, your day…one of the most important days of your life, I want you to know that I honor you with my loyalty, my respect, and most of all my undying unconditional love."

He releases my hand and turns to my Mom and Morgan.

"No one is going to mess this day up for my son who has done nothing but love us and give us all, and I mean all…everybody in this room…a reason to be proud of him. Nina, you're my wife, and I love you, but today, if you can't honor our son the way he deserves to be honored, you can't stay here. Morgan, I have loved you since your birth, but if Derek has decided to marry someone else then you have to respect that and move on, Sweetheart. Now, you all can do one of two things, and I have never been more serious in my life: Hug this man, wish him well, and go outside and sit down and watch him marry the woman of his choice, or I can have our driver take you and/ or Morgan wherever you wish to go....but let me make myself clear: neither one of you will continue to try to mess this day up for my son. Do you understand me?"

"Chase, I wasn't trying to mess up his day."

"Well, good. Son, we'll see you outside."

My father, the man I have loved and respected all of my life, opens the door, stands back for my Mom and Morgan to leave, turns, winks at me, and quietly closes the door behind him.

"Whew! Man, what a scene. I had tears in my eyes, Bro. See D, that's...that's what I'm talking about...right there...what just happened...what your Pop just put down...that's love, Bro. That's the stuff I never had."

I take another deep breath.

"Go get cleaned up and let's go, Zack."

In the bathroom, I see him running water and wiping the blood from his face and trying to patch his torn skin.

"Well, it's a good thing you don't have to wear white today. That girl was all over your face, Bro," I laugh.

"You need to quit with the jokes. I'm not in a joking mood right now."

"You deserve those scratches, man, and more than that."

"You're right...I do. Come on. Let's go get you married so I can get me a nice stiff drink and heal my wounds."

"Look, you better not get drunk on my wedding day."

Zack slaps me on the back. "Wait, man. I got something to say."

"Oh, Lord. What now?"

"Naw, nothing bad. I just want to say that I'm happy for you, Bro...happy that you found someone who puts that smile on your face every time you call her name. I can look in your eyes and tell that you really love Ari. For a while, I wasn't sure, but I am now.... and like I told you a while ago, she's good people. She's the kind of girl even I can't do anything with, and it ain't many of them left....but you can trust her. She's not looking anywhere pass you, Bro. You're a lucky man."

"No, Zack, I'm a blessed man...very blessed. There's a difference. I'll tell you about that one day when we have more time, but right now, I want you to help me go get married."

We walk out of the cottage together. I'm dressed in all white and Zack in a light gray tux, white shirt, a deep turquoise cummerbund, matching bow tie and gray shoes. The sun is just right in the June evening sky as it thinks about sinking into the waiting ocean. Despite the scene with my Mom and Morgan, I am overwhelmed with joy, and I can tell that Zack and I look mighty good walking to *The Rock* where the love of my life will meet me.

~ *Arianna* ~

India is still fussing with my hair and Mom is checking my dress again. She thought she saw a spot on it an hour ago, and a half hour ago she thought there was a tear in a small piece of the lace around the hem. Now she's checking the train and she thinks maybe it's too short.

"Mom, come here." She checks the dress and gives it a final brush with her hand the way that only a mother can do and comes over to the dresser where I sit getting tired of India fussing with one or two strands of my hair.

"Everything is perfect, Mom. The dress is outstanding. Our people put everything into making it absolutely magnificent. Stop worrying and go down on the beach and wait for me." I push India out of the way, and get up and hug her.

"Thank you, Mom for everything. You and Dad have made my life a joy, and I only hope that I can do for my children half of what you're done for me."

"I'm so proud of you, baby. Before I go, I have something for you, and one day I want you to give it to your daughter or son to give to his daughter."

Mom reaches for her purse and takes out a small black box that shows its age, and she lifts the lid.

"I want you to wear these today as something old."

The earrings are small teardrop diamonds that just happen to match perfectly the beautiful new diamond necklace from my siblings.

"Oh, Mom they're beautiful."

"They belonged to your great grandmother, and I wore them on my wedding day, and now, I'll see them sparkle in the evening sunlight again on your day."

I put them on with pride, and turn to let Mom see if she approves.

"My, My, you look absolutely beautiful." She hugs me and crosses the room.

I know that this is a very special moment. I realize in this instant that the next time I speak with my Mom, I will not be Arianna Channing, her little girl. I will be Mrs. Derek Chase Wellington, III, all grown up and married. As a result of recognizing that, I look, now, at her every motion. It's like taking a snapshot of the moment, and I know that I will always remember how beautiful she looks today in her gorgeous turquoise gown with the hints of silver in all the right places. She turns and takes one last look at me before she leaves the room, and I snap my own mental picture.

One by one my father, and my brothers come in to see me and wish me well. River and I have always been close because of our age and even though I know he will never admit it, I see a glimmer of tears even as he hits at me and tells me my face is still ugly even on my wedding day.

The professionals come in and help me into my dress and make sure that everything fits the way it should. I think to myself that I can't gain a pound if I want this dress to fit even through dinner today. I check myself out in the full-length mirror and see the stunning beauty of soft white lace fitting over my curves, and how the hemline moves so smoothly into the stunning train. The one shoulder lace piece is adorned with a scattering of diamonds that I know will glitter in the sun. The headpiece is lace and satin. The narrow band fits across my head and the satin flower with scattered diamonds caps over the top of my right ear. I am pleased.

I move down the steps and on to the beach. My Dad meets me, and we walk barefoot down the white aisle runner decked with roses. Then I see him….my Derek, matching me in white and looking so handsome waiting for me with Zack and our minister under the arch of flowers. I hear the symphony. I see the ocean, and the quiet waves make a perfect backdrop of sight and sound. I see the white seats filled with our guests, the arch with beautiful pink and white roses. I see Angel and India take their places in fantastic turquoise dresses that almost match the ocean. When I finally reach Derek, we cannot stop smiling. I can barely wait for the part where my father gives me away so that I can take his hand. Derek has not taken his eyes from mine, and when we get to the vows, I listen so intently to his words.

Ari, today I stand here, in front of this company, asking you to be my wife. You found me a year ago at a very low point in my life. It was 8:15 on a lonely June night in a dusty old New York library. On that night, when I felt friendless, your playful gaze caught and saved me, and you became my friend. That night you stared and noticed my hair, my eyes, my lips, and then, some weeks later, you found my heart. Since then, Baby, you have become my very best friend, my soul mate, and the love of my life. Ari, you've taught me patience, how to wait for things that are important…how to stand still and not rush in to destroy what can be so beautiful if we would but give a few extra moments in time…how to take the time to look at a blade of grass, a flower, run my hand in the water of a brook, and hear the song of birds. You've taught me to appreciate what God has created that surrounds me, and each moment in time He gives me. Because of you, I now appreciate how important those quiet moments can be. You've taught me to trust again, and you've helped me see that God opens windows of escape when we least expect them. Baby, I promise to love you with my whole heart, trust you with each aspect of my life, and respect you with every fiber of my being. Know that you are my heartbeat, the breath that I breathe, and the one who brings me life and happiness. You're home to me. I love you, Arianna, far beyond these words I speak ,,. and I promise to love you forever.

Tears are in my eyes listening to the man who will very soon be my husband, but at the completion of his vows and just before I make my promises, I hear a disturbance, see a lady in white push through her row and run down the beach. I wonder to myself if she might be March, April or May in Derek's life, but the day is too wonderful for me to ponder that, so I simply and immediately dismiss her from my mind, and make my promise to this man I love standing before me.

I say the vows that I hope are as sincere and meaningful as Derek's, and the ceremony is beautiful, touching and exemplifies the moments in life that we know we will never forget. We exchange the rings, say the prayers beneath *The Rock* and finally hear the pronouncement of husband and wife. When we kiss, we know we hold it too long, but for us, it's perfect. He is my husband now, and I am his wife.

In the moonlight, the reception is exquisite with its candles lighting the beach and the music that touches our heart. We dance and sing and play on the beach, and the dress that I wanted to be so perfect is full of sand and misty water from the ocean, and I don't care. If

I didn't know better, I would think that Angel and Zack have a better time than Derek and I, but that's impossible. I even notice both of our parents dancing, talking, and laughing together. The meal is delicious or at least that's what River says, and everyone has a wonderful time.

The evening wears on and after all the toasts, well wishes, and congratulations, Derek and I say our goodbyes. I see the attorneys from his firm slap him on the back and wish us well and tell him that his work will be waiting for him when he returns. They laugh and tease him good-naturedly. We talk together with my parents who tell us how beautiful the wedding has been. We spend a moment with Derek's parents who assure us that they will collect all of our gifts and take them to their home for safe-keeping. I hug my sister and make her promise to come and work with me if only for a short time. I hug my brothers and tousle their hair again just because I know how much they hate it. We catch up with Zack and Angel and know that we are disturbing them, but we don't care. We want to say goodbye, but they wave us away as if we are annoying small children. We dash to the cottage, kiss, hug, change clothes, and drive to the airport to catch our flight and start the honeymoon of a lifetime.

~ Derek ~

When we land in Hawaii, my father has another plane waiting to take us to a private island that he recently purchased. We are both exhausted from the long trip, and can't wait to arrive at our final destination. When the plane lands, we're taken to the house and its beauty is unbelievable. The back is all glass with a view of the ocean that will greet us every morning inside our elegant master bedroom.

"Wow! Your dad out did himself, Derek. This place is awesome."

"Well, it fails in comparison to this lovely lady in front of me. "

"I'm too tired to be awesome," she laughs.

I take my new wife in my arms and kiss her. "Never. Nothing can match my lady."

The first day, we sleep in, and that is lovely. It has been a long time since we've had nothing special to do, no place to be, and no particular people to see. It's been a long time since we could have breakfast together, sit and talk about things that don't really matter, and just laugh with each other. We play a few games, take a walk on the beach, and just spent time relaxing.

In our little kitchen, Ari decides to make dinner for us, and she spends time fixing things that she knows I will enjoy.

"You're such a good cook, Ari. When did you ever have time to learn how?"

"I told you...my grandmother taught me. Don't you remember? I told you the day we went to my little secret place."

"Yes, I do remember now. Well, I'm glad you spent so much time with her. This meal is delicious."

"So...Derek, who was the lady in the white dress at our wedding? She seemed so sad."

"Just an old friend."

"Why was she so sad?"

"Was she? I don't know. Sometimes people just get sad at wedding."

"Are you sure you don't know why? I think you do."

"Well, I certainly didn't get an opportunity to ask her, and I was too busy paying attention to my new wife to worry about somebody not having a good time. I was having a great time!"

I get up from the table and pull my wife up to me. "Why would I ever pay attention to some other woman when I have this in front of me?" I kiss her passionately and hope the kiss will divert her curiosity about Morgan. I don't want to explain the past on my honeymoon, and Morgan is not important to me anymore. Ari is.

"Why do you think she was wearing white?"

"Ari, have my kisses gotten that boring already? Pay attention."

I kiss her again, and this time it works. The second kiss is a charm and moves us to other heights and not another word is spoken or another thought given to the sad lady in white.

Our honeymoon is fantastic, and we get a chance to do a lot of things that we enjoy and some that we have never done before. Ari tells me her favorite was the day we went to a beautiful waterfall and spent a lot of private time picnicking, swimming, laughing, talking and just being in love with each other. I think I enjoyed the hike to the top of what I called a very huge hill. The view at the top person-ified serenity. We actually said a prayer up there because we felt so close to God...so grateful to Him for everything, and then it was time to leave for home. The flight doesn't seem as long as it did coming, and before we know it, I'm picking up my wife and carrying her over the threshold into our home.

Two weeks off make both of us have to dive head first into work. Like my bosses told me, none of my work was done, and I have quite a few witnesses to interview for our pending case, and then there is also the research on the suspect. I can tell that we both have missed our work, and Ari is full of conversations about fabrics, showstoppers, new models, new lines, colors, textiles, and a bunch of stuff I don't even understand. ..but I listen because she is my wife, and I am interested in everything that involves her.

Time passes fast and before we know it, we have celebrated our first anniversary, and our connection grows stronger everyday. During the year, Ari has taken at least three trips, two overseas and one to New York, and they only served to prove how much I never want to be away from her. All of my cases have been successful, and life is good…but then, in late October, I hit a major snag.

Chapter 23

END OF THE ROAD?

~Truth is defined by honesty first to self, and then to all others~

"Derek, your Mom is on line 4."

"Thanks, Sara."

"Hey, Mom. This is a surprise. What's up?"

"Hi, Baby. I was just wondering if you could come by the house today. I need to see you."

"Sure. Is everything all right? Is Dad ok?"

"Yes, everything is fine. I just need to see you. What time do you think you can be here?"

"I'm not too busy right now. I'll drive over and see you in about an hour, Ok?"

"Sure, that will be fine."

"Mom, just checking…you're not matchmaking again today are you? Ari and I have been married for over a year now, and you keep trying to put me with someone else. Is Morgan there again this time?"

"I'll see you soon. Bye."

I hang up the phone, grab a few things since I won't be coming back, and head out for the forty-five minute drive to Mom's. Every now and then she's been setting up what she calls 'these friendly meetings' with Morgan and me, and I can't lie, I have enjoyed Morgan's laughter, our talks about old times, and her crazy way of teasing me. I've missed all that. I do feel very guilty though that I'm meeting her behind Ari's back, but I keep telling myself that it's all right if we remain just friends. I know very well that Morgan wants to be more than friends. She, at least, wants the friends with benefits kind of relationship. We've shared a few kisses, and that is as far as I'm willing to take this, and I know that she and Mom are wishing for a lot more. The last time I came about two weeks ago, Morgan kept asking me to show her my apartment outside the main house, even though she has seen it a thousand times. I refused. I'm not willing to go that far.

The evening is pleasant, and I pull into the driveway and immediately feel the guilt. Morgan's car is parked out front. I knew it would be. In the house, I move toward the sound of laughter coming from the theater room and poke my head in.

"Good evening, ladies."

"There's my baby." Mom jumps up from her seat and rushes over to hug me. "You look good, son. I guess Arianna is taking good care of you after all."

314

"She is. Hi, Morgan. How are you?"

"I'm good, Derek. Like your Mom said, you look good. It's great seeing you again. I was hoping you would come."

"So, ladies...what is this little reunion all about this time?"

"Well, I was missing you, and Morgan was missing you so....we thought why miss you when we don't have to anymore. We can just call you up and have you come over for dinner. Good idea, right?"

"Not a good idea, Mom. We can't keep doing this."

Morgan gets out of her seat now and comes over to me. "Are you angry that we keep calling you?"

"No, not angry. This is just not a good idea."

"Well, I think it's a great idea, and I have all of the foods you like prepared for a special dinner for the three of us."

"Three? Dad's not here this time either?"

"Oh, he's sorry he couldn't be here. He's in LA signing contracts and setting production for several films. He's busy."

"Yeah. I'm sure he knows nothing about this little dinner you've planned or your other little quiet meetings with me."

"Oh, those are just minor details, son. He's not interested in the day-to-day things around here even when he's home. I'll go check on the dinner and then we can eat, and the two of you can have a nice little visit."

My Mom knows nothing about cooking or checking the dinner. She's leaving the room on purpose so that Morgan can have a little private time with me. It's so obvious. Morgan seems a bit nervous and not sure at all if their little plan will continue to work. She moves over close to me.

"Can an old friend have a little hug?"

"Of course, you can." We hug and she smiles up at me.

"Sorry if you really don't think this is a good idea, but just to be clear, these meetings have not been my idea. I come by to say hi to your Mom. I do that at least one or two times a month. I see no reason why we have to miss each other even if the two of us are not together. She's like my second Mom."

I move over to the sofa and sit down. "You're right about that, but I think you're coming now for more than just a visit with my Mom. Anyway, how have you been?"

She smiles slightly and comes to sit next to me. "Not as good as you, Derek." She puts her hand on my knee. "I still miss you a lot. I still love you a lot. Like I said last time we met here, I thought I could move on, but that just doesn't seem to be happening."

"Even now?"

"Even more so now that I know you will come to see me sometimes." Her hand moves to my face, and I take it away.

"So, Morgan, what about Peter. Is he still around?"

"Yes, but he can never take your place, Derek. Even though you always thought that he could."

"Well, a lot of times you made me think that he could. How's the dancing?"

"The dancing is great. You should come and see me sometimes. You already know that I have the lead, and it's everything I always thought it would be. I just thought I'd be sharing my success with you. It's a lot of hard work, and a lot of jealousies that cause stress, but I love to dance, so it's all good."

Her voice softens and her quiet tone takes her away to memory.

"I used to look for you, Baby…every night." Her speech slows, and she smiles. "For a long time, I had it in my head that you wouldn't be able to stay away, but I was very wrong." My voice seems to snap her out of the memory.

"I've thought about it. I still think about you a lot more than I should, but then I considered how Ari would feel if she ever knew I was taking her to see my old girlfriend…didn't think that would be respectful."

"Hmm…Your old girlfriend, huh? Is that all I am to you?"

"Morgan, we've had this conversation. I'm a married man now, and have been for over a year. What else can you be?" I look down at my laced hands then up at her with my sexiest look. "What do you want to be?" I know that this last question is a major flirt and will lead her on. I can hear the seduction in my own voice.

She looks at me and slowly traces my lips with her fingers. "I want to be your wife. That has not changed for me, but I'd settle for being your lover." Her hand comes to rest over my lips, and I kiss her fingers.

"Huh! Really?" My mind warns me. *Back off.* Instead, I take her hand in mine, and let my voice play with her.

"Well, the sad thing for you is that it has very much changed for me. I have a wife. I love her, and I don't need a lover." For a second, I bite the corner of my lower lip. *Stop teasing her. Why are you flirting?* "I don't plan on changing any of that. So, all the little tricks and schemes that you and my mother cook up won't make me change my mind about that." I tap her nose with my index finger.

"If you're so strong in your marriage, Derek, what are you doing here now? You knew I would be here."

"That's a good question, Morgan, and I guess the answer is simply that I still miss you. I can't say that I ever really got completely over you. At first, I was extremely angry, then disappointed, and even a little revengeful."

"Is that why you married Arianna so soon?"

"No. I really love Ari a lot. She's an amazing woman, and she loves me for sure. My marrying her had nothing to do with you or our break up."

"Really?" Her voice has a touch of sarcasm, and I don't respond.

I am sitting relaxed with my arm stretched across the back of the sofa, and Morgan takes that opportunity to quickly take a seat in my lap, pull my arms around her, and really kiss me. The move is very slick, and to some extent, it surprises me, but I don't dump her off of my lap. The moment is good. I don't tell her to stop, and I don't stop my hand from moving up her back and pulling her closer to me. Mainly, I don't stop the passion in the kisses. They are long and thorough, and I let them run their course. I don't do a lot of things that I should have in those ten or fifteen minutes. When the kissing stops, she looks at me. I look at her and know immediately that there is a lot still there in my heart for this girl that should be totally off limits to me now.

"I knew it. I knew it the last time you came. You still love me, Derek. You can't help it. We have too much history for you to just forget everything we mean to each other. Why do you want to keep giving Arianna just a part of yourself?"

"Get up, Morgan. Get off of me. I knew this was a bad idea when I saw your car."

"Why Derek? Why is it such a bad idea? If you don't love me, and you don't want me, what harm can there be in having a little dinner together?"

"...but you see, that's just it, Morgan. You can't leave it at a little dinner. You have to come on to me, kiss me, and dredge up a lot of old feelings that need to stay buried. I never said I didn't love you. I always say I love you, and I've always said that I don't see those feelings changing. Look, I've got to go. I should never have gone along with this. Sometimes I'm just so stupid."

"This is your second time coming, Derek. This is the third time we've kissed, and this time was very different. It was like old times. You know why you come."

"Tell Mom, I'll see her another time when it's just Dad and her. I'm not doing this again, Morgan. It's not fair to Ari, to me, or to you. This isn't going anywhere."

"Derek, please..."

"Morgan, I'm married. We can't do this anymore. You have got to move on. I have, even if I have been playing this little game."

"Have you, Derek? Have you moved on? Are you sure?" I don't think so. Look at what just happened. Her voice is high pitched and angry.

I stop and look at her, but I don't respond. I just cross the room as fast as I can, and get out of the house. I almost run to my car, but not before I hear my Mom calling after me. I pay her no attention. I slam my car door, and drive away at a very high speed.

The drive home is miserable. The guilt is eating me alive. I guess this time bothers me more than ever because I knew Morgan would be there. The first time, I didn't. This time I really kissed her back, and I felt the passion, and now I know where all of this can lead if I'm not careful. In my mind, I'm honest with myself. I didn't want to stop kissing her. I wanted more…a lot more. It took everything in me not to take what was so very easy to have. I ask myself how am I any different from any other person who cheats on his spouse? I have no excuse for my behavior. I can't blame it on knowing and loving Morgan for a lifetime. I can't blame it on my Mom. It's me, all me, and that's the honest truth. I didn't choose her so what am I doing now? I hit the steering wheel hard to relieve my stress, and I curse myself under my breath. I feel tears sting my eyes. I know I love Ari so why am I letting this happen?

—⚬⚬⚬—

At home, I sit in the car for a moment, and try to compose myself so that I can act natural, and when I think I can, I go inside.

"Hey Babe." Her voice is bright. "I was getting worried. You're very late. It's already dark. Where were you?"

I take a deep breath. "I went to see my Mom."

"Oh, how is she...still pining away to see me?" She giggles. Her laughter is carefree, and I can tell she is in a great mood and glad that I'm home.

"Did she tell you to bring me over soon?"

"You're funny."

"What's wrong, Babe?"

"Nothing."

"No, something is wrong with my baby. I hear it in your voice, and I see it. Did she bad mouth me again to you, Derek? I told you not to worry about that."

"No, she didn't. Actually, she said that I look good, and you must be taking good care of me after all." I laugh to cover how nervous I am.

Ari comes over and wraps her arms around me.

"I'll always take good care of your, baby." She lifts her head, kisses me, and buries her face in my chest like she has done a million other times.

"Hmm, that's some strong perfume she put on you. Is that your Mom's perfume?"

"What are you trying to say?" I can hear the irritation in my voice.

"That you smell like perfume, and I hope it's your mother's." I hear her sarcasm and change of attitude.

"Ari, I don't need this. I'm tired. I'm hungry. I've had a hard day, and I'm going to take a shower."

"OK. You got to wash somebody off, right?

I don't answer. I look at her, smirk, and push her a little hard out of my arms.

I walk down the hall with GUILT riding my back. After a refreshing shower, I go back to the front to try to make amends with Ari, but I see her standing with my phone in her hand and tears in her eyes.

"What, Ari? What are you doing? What's wrong?" My voice sounds irritated when I see my phone in her hand.

She looks at me, and her stare is hard. I can tell that she is furious.

"Sometimes you forget what my profession is, don't you?" Her voice is cold.

"What do you mean forget what your profession is?"

"Derek, I deal everyday with women's products. I knew that wasn't your mother's perfume. I've smelled your mother's perfume. It's soft... expensive...not like what you were wearing. Where have you been, Derek?"

"I told you. I went to my Mother's."

"You told me a lie. Now, let's try the truth this time." She's staring at me, and she is very angry.

"I'm not lying to you. Call her. Ask her." My voice is casual and nonchalant.

"I don't have to. You have a text. She waves my phone in her hand.

"...a text?"

"Yes, a text. I'll read one of them to you. I read them all, but this is the latest…the one you got about five minutes ago that you haven't seen."

Her voice is slow, angry, and full of hurt. I'm nervous now and feel water already building on my forehead and palms.

"i still miss you, Babe. 2day, your kisses were everything i remember and more, and so were the others we've shared recently, but I need more, and I know you want more. I knew it when your arms tightened around me, and I felt U again.'"

Ari is crying and her voice is angry…breaking…choking as she reads. Tears are streaming down her cheeks when she stops reading and looks up at me with a sadness I've never seen in her beautiful eyes before now.

"What the hell, Derek? Who is this?…and don't lie to me." Her voice is trembling, and she is crying harder.

I look at my Ari, and I see the questions in her eyes, her slumped shoulders, her confusion, her sadness, her disbelief. I see profound hurt, and, in that horrific moment, I have no idea what to do or what to say.

"Come sit with me, Baby, and try to calm down…please. I'll tell you everything that I should have told you a long time ago." I exhale loudly. "Her name is Morgan LaRue."

"The dancer?" she asks in disbelief.

"Yes. You know her?"

"No, not personally, but her name is quite well known. You're cheating with her?"

"I'm not cheating, Ari.

"Yes you are. I just read it."

"No, I grew up with Morgan, and basically, we broke up the night I met you."

"So, I was your rebound, Derek? Oh, this is great! This story is going to be just great. I might need popcorn for this one." Her voice is extremely sarcastic and angry.

"No, not to me...no rebound. Today, my Mom called and asked me to come over."

"Your Mom. I should have known she helped." The sarcasm is heavy.

"When I got there she was there with Morgan. She had prepared a dinner for us because she still wants me to be with Morgan."

"I prepared dinner for you, Jerk."

"The perfume was on me, Babe, because Morgan sat in my lap and kissed me. I don't love her, Ari. She just can't get over the fact that I've moved on."

"You've moved on, but you go to visit her, she sits in your lap, and the two of you share kisses that tell her you want more? You're moved on?"

"Well...Well, it's not like what you think. I haven't seen her often.

"Are you kidding me? Once is too often." I hear the hurt in her voice that overpowers the anger. "So, she was the lady in white at our wedding, right? She's March, April, and May."

She is almost talking to herself as if this question has never left her, and now she finally has her answer. I swallow hard before I speak.

"Well, more months than three, but yes."

"Why did you lie to me about her?"

"I didn't really lie. I just didn't tell you everything. Who wants to talk about an ex on their honeymoon?" My voice is just below shouting.

"Her message doesn't sound too much like she's an ex."

"Well, she's very much and ex, but…she's kind of a friend."

"A friend? She can't be your friend, Derek. That's stupid. You make me sick."

Ari stands up and makes a call from my phone.

"Who are you calling?" I ask chancing some irritation in my own voice, hoping that it's not Morgan. I know that could be a scene even on the phone and reveal far more than I want her to know.

"No Nina, it's not Derek. This is Arianna." Her voice is calm and cold, but I see her hands shaking.

"I'm just calling to tell you not to set up any more dates with Morgan LaRue and my husband. If you do, let me assure you that you will be very sorry." There is a brief pause. "No, I'm not threatening you. I'm promising you… and yes, '*your baby*' is sitting right here… for the moment."

Ari closes off the call and throws the phone hard at my head. I duck, it hits the wall hard, shatters to pieces, and she goes into the bedroom.

I follow and see her crying, sitting at the foot of our bed.

I sit beside her and wrap my arms around her. I pull her to me, she pulls away, but then, when I insist, she rests her head on my shoulder.

"Baby, don't do this. You know I love you with everything in me. I don't want anyone else. You are all I want...all I need. I love you. I married you. Even with Morgan coming to our wedding dressed in white, I married you because you are the one I want. I'm so sorry I did this, and I'm sorry I've upset you. The whole thing was just stupid."

So, now I know why your Mom hates me so much. You didn't marry her choice."

"No, I didn't. I married my choice."

"I just don't understand why you couldn't have been honest with me from the beginning."

"Because of what's happening right now. I knew it would upset you...make you have doubts about me, and I didn't want you to have any doubts."

"I don't have doubts, Derek. I know for sure. Your Morgan texted it, and now you've told me. You're been sneaking behind my back having an affair with your ex girlfriend, and anyway, what's the difference between having doubts then and being sure now? How could you do this to me, Derek? Running around kissing her and then coming home to me. I thought you loved me." I can see that verbalizing it is making it even more real to her. She's looking at me crying, and I see her heart breaking.

"Baby, I love you more than I love myself. I know that's hard for you to believe right now, but I do. I don't want to hurt you. You know me, Ari."

"...know you well enough to think you'll tell me the truth like you did when you first came home tonight? You come in here late with your head bowed down to the floor, barely able to look at me, smelling like some dime store perfume and telling me you were with your mom. Do you think I'm stupid?"

"No, Ari. I know you're not stupid."

"You're damn right; I'm not stupid. I checked your phone, Derek, because I could feel the lie. It's the first time I've ever felt the need to check your phone. I put in your password, and I saw her name, I saw her picture still on your phone, and then I read all of her messages... how you've been sneaking off putting her to bed, dancing with her, paying her visits and kissing her...and there's no telling what else you've been doing behind my back. How much of an ex is that?" Her words spill out almost faster than I can think.

She jumps up from the bed and looks at me.

"You still love her, don't you?" Her voice is accusatory.

I don't answer, but she does. She slaps my face hard twice, pushes my head hard with her fist and walks out of the room. I follow her.

"Tell me this, Derek: When she kissed you, did you kiss her back? Did you hug her and tell her how much you still love her? Did you tell her to stop? Did you protest in any way? When she was sitting on your lap did you throw her butt on the floor? Don't lie to me." She looks me directly in my eyes, and for the first time since I've known her, she screams at me. "Tell...me...the...damn...truth!"

"No, I didn't stop her," I yell back. "I didn't protest. She was sitting on my lap, Ari, and I didn't dump her butt on the floor, BUT," I yell,…"I told her this couldn't happen, and I did leave right after that. I didn't stay and have dinner, and I didn't stop when my Mom was calling me to come back."

"So, you got your kisses, but not your dinner. Oh, so you're supposed to get a prize for that, right? Why did you need to run?…because you love her, right? You love her, right? You didn't trust yourself, right?"

"Since I'm being honest Ari, I guess I'll always love her to some degree; I grew up with her, but she's not my wife."

"Derek, I grew up with a lot of people, but I don't sneak around behind your back kissing them."

"Ari, she's not even my real friend. You are. I love you."

"I'm not sure anymore. I think maybe you want to love me. So… tell me, what broke you two lovebirds up, anyway?"

"Ari, don't. I'm not going through that with you."

"…and I can't go through this with you when you're not sure who you really love. Obviously, you two have a history and never got the closure you need. I was just a rebound."

"What are you talking about? I got closure. You were not a rebound. I married you."

"Stop telling me you married me like that's supposed to be some… some kind of trophy for me. Marrying me doesn't make you sure you love me. If you were sure, you wouldn't be running around visiting her, and you certainly would have stopped the kissing or never allowed it to start. You would have dumped her butt on the floor today, and left. I believe you want to be sure, but now I know that you're not. If you loved me so much, you would have brought your butt home."

I try to pull her close to me and smother her with my kisses despite her protest...despite her constant yelling...hoping that the kisses will be enough to take away her doubts...enough to calm her down and let her know that she is everything to me. However, even as I try to make love to her later in the night, I know when she refuses me again and again and again that things for us are definitely not the same. The realization is like a death to me. My heart breaks, but I know it's all my fault.

The next morning, I see her swollen hazel eyes, her slumped shoulders, and a beautiful body that looks beyond weary. She tells me that I need to deal with this mess I've made. She informs me that she's leaving. It shocks me! I spend the day and a night trying to talk her out of separating, trying to persuade her that I know exactly what I want. In the end, after all the tears, all the yelling, all the pleading, she reminds me that I did not come even close to convincing her that I don't still love Morgan so...there is nothing that will convince her now to stay. I tell her not to pack...not to go, and that I will leave our home instead, but before I do I make one last plea. I had to try one more time.

With a few things packed and the bags at the door, she lets me take her in my arms.

"Ari, don't let me go. Don't make me go. Please...I adore you. You have to know that. I'll make this up to you, babe. I promise you I will if it takes the rest of my life. I'm so sorry."

"Derek, I love you, but I can't do this now. Please don't ask me anymore. This is the hardest thing I've ever done in my life, but, as I see it, I have no choice. You need to go and find out what you really want, and maybe I'll still be here when you find out."

"Ari, I know what…"

"No, Derek, You don't," she interrupts. "If you did, we wouldn't be standing here like this now with your bags at the door and us saying goodbye. You wouldn't have the need to run around kissing other women, and wanting more of them. You don't know what you want, and I can't live with you if you don't. I won't share you, and I'm not going to live a lie. I told you that a long time ago. I tried to make it as clear to you as possible. You've got to go. Goodbye, Derek. I'll…I'll see you."

"When?"

"Don't ask me that," she whispers.

With those last words, and the little peck she allows on her cheek, I realize I have lost my wife, and I leave wondering if this is the end of the road for us now…wondering if I will ever get the chance to return to the love of my life.

Arianna

Chapter 24

OUR TEST IN TIME

~Romance has the capacity to soothe an angry heart~

I'm finding out that fixing and eating dinner alone is hard to get use to when you're been married for almost two years. When I'm at work, the day moves faster, but it's the nights that are so hard. I set the table, and more times than I want to admit, I set a place for Derek, and then I remember and move the plate to the counter. I sit and push the food around and only allow a few morsels to actually find their way to my mouth. When I realize that trying to eat is useless, I begin cleaning up the kitchen and then look forward to another night of solitude. I pray a lot for peace of mind now. I don't cry anymore, and I guess I can say that is some kind of improvement, but despite my prayers, the sadness seems to have taken up residence in my heart.

I reach for the phone to call India and then change my mind. She'll just ask me a million more questions about what happened and try to get me to ask Derek to come home, but I'm definitely not ready for him to move back. I put the phone down, hear a light knock, and I open the door.

"Arianna?"

"Yes."

"I'm Morgan LaRue. May I come in for a minute? I have something I need to tell you. I know I'm the last person on earth you want to see, but this is important."

Her words come fast as if she feels she has to push them out quickly before I slam the door in her face. I'm shocked at first and just stand in the open door looking at this very beautiful woman who has taken so much from me. I'm remembering her face at my wedding and seeing again in my mind her sadness that was so apparent on that day. There is a lot about her look that makes me think of the singer, Rihanna...the eyes...the shape of the face...the long light brown hair...her size...her natural beauty....

"Please...just for a minute, and I promise I'll go."

My curiosity gets the best of me so I step back without a word and let her enter.

"What could you possibly want to tell me? You're destroyed my marriage, my husband is gone, and I'm extremely sad. What else do you want?"

"I don't want any of that. I don't want to destroy your marriage, I don't want your husband to be gone, and I certainly don't want you to be sad. I know my words may seem meaningless at this point, but I want you to know how sorry I am that all of this has happened, and I certainly hate the part I played in it."

"Well, Derek is free to see you now. He's free to do whatever you and he want to do. I'm trying to move on with my life, and I hope he's doing the same." My voice is deadpan as I move over to the sofa wondering to myself why I have let this woman in my house.

"Derek and I are not seeing each other because he loves you... very much."

"Well, if he loves me so much what was he doing playing tonsil tag with you?"

"It wasn't like that."

"Well, what was it like, Morgan? You're here. You want to talk. Well talk...Tell me what it was like with him putting you to bed, or dancing in your arms, or kissing you until the both of you want more. You wanna talk? Talk!" My voice is obviously angry and exasperated with my unwelcomed guest.

"Derek and I grew up together and even when we were young our parents seemed to believe that we would end up as husband and wife. As we got older, we fell in love, and we believed it too. I know we would have stayed together if I hadn't messed everything up, but I did. At this point, I feel like not only did I mess us up, but now I've taken away his wife, and I don't want to do that. I don't want to be responsible for that. I don't want to be this person anymore. I feel like I've been so selfish, and I've hurt Derek even more. Arianna, I want to fix this if I can."

"First of all, let's get something straight. You didn't *take* anything; I let Derek go. And as far as fixing this marriage, it won't be you to fix anything. If it gets fixed, it will be Derek and me who will do the fixing. So, let's just get that clear first. You interfered in our marriage, but it could only have happened if Derek allowed it to happen, and he did, so, if at all possible, he has to try to fix the mess he's made, not you. I could care less about your part in this."

I'm getting very impatient with this woman thinking that she can waltz in here and tell me anything about my husband or my marriage, and my impatience becomes extremely apparent.

"Did Derek send you here to plead his case? If he did, he's making another huge mistake, and I'll deal with that too when I see him."

"No, he didn't send me here. He has no idea that I'm here. Actually, no one has seen Derek for over a month, and we're kind of worried about him. Have you heard from him at all?"

"No, I haven't, but what do you mean *no one* has heard from him? Doesn't he go to work?"

"No, but they are not telling us anything either, and Derek won't answer his phone."

"Do they know where he is?"

"We think they do, but they won't confirm or deny that."

"Morgan, should I be worried?" For the first time since this woman came into my home, I'm really listening to her and growing more and more concerned by the second.

"I really don't know, but I am. He's never done anything like this before...just disappear and not communicate. Arianna, I've known

Derek all of my life, and I had this image in my mind of a happily ever after, but like I said, I messed that up. Now he's gone, and we don't know where he is, and I'm worried."

She's rambling on and on, and I'm about to panic, but I don't want her to see me panic so I hold it together.

"Derek was very happy with me at one point, but I disappointed him with his best friend so he lost both of us at the same time."

"You were with Zack?"

"Yes, I was, and I'm certainly not proud of that. Then when he found you, he was happy again, and even though you say I'm not, I still feel some responsibility for the problems you two are having. Both of us are now out of his life, and I don't know how he's handling you not being in his life because he loves you so much, and he's lost so much. Look, I didn't come here to worry you, and I know half of my rambling doesn't make any sense. I just want you to understand that Derek loves you, and he is devastated over losing you. I feel like I have hurt him again, and that is the last thing that I want to do. If there is anything I can do to get you two back together, I'll do it. I'm not going to lie to you. I love Derek, but I understand that he loves you, and he has told me a thousand times that I need to move on. Well, that is what I'm doing now, and I don't want him to lose his wife because of me."

"I think you are a little late for that, but regardless of your part, I blame Derek. He could have said no, but he didn't."

Morgan stands up to go, and I stand with her and move over to the door. I want her to leave so I can see if I can find Derek. What she has said disturbs me greatly, and I have to know if he's all right.

"Arianna, I'm really sorry about this. I hope that you and Derek can work this out, and I hope when you find him that he's all right."

"OK. Bye."

My heart is pounding as I close the door. I immediately pull my cell from my pocket, and call Derek. Thank goodness, he picks up on the first ring.

"Hey, Babe. You finally called me." I can hear his smile.

I take in a big gulp of air. "Derek, where are you?"

"Arlington. My case was moved about a month ago. Right now, I'm sitting in my hotel room waiting on the verdict."

"How long have you been waiting?"

"Since yesterday. The jury asked to review some of the blood evidence, so that was a bit of a hold up, but enough of that. How are you?"

"I'm lonely and sad."

"I think I can fix that if you let me." *Wow! Listen to him. He sounds so good…so good.* I want to say come home, baby, so badly, but I don't. That would be a very wrong move.

"Why didn't you tell me that you were out of town?"

"I tried."

"You did?"

"Yes."

"When?"

"Over a month ago."

"Over a month ago? I don't remember that."

"You wouldn't because when I called, you barely let me say hello, and these were your words to me: 'Derek, don't call me, don't text me, and definitely don't come over here. I need some space.' And then you hung up in my face so you didn't let me tell you anything. I wanted to tell you that I was leaving town, and I'd probably be gone for at least a month."

"Why didn't you call me back?"

"You said don't call, don't text, don't come."

"Derek, you can't listen to everything I say. Sometimes, it's just emotion talking... hormones. I don't mean everything that comes out of my mouth." I laugh, and I can hear Derek's chuckle.

"It's so good to hear that giggle. I haven't heard that in a long time, and I miss it. Baby, I miss you."

"I miss you too, but I think this separation is good for both of us. It gives you time to decide what you really want."

"I know what I really want, and I'm going to do everything I can to make you believe I know what I want."

"You made me *believe* it once. You've got to make me *know* it now. There's a big difference." Both of us are silent and the pause is uncomfortable, so I break it. "Changing the subject, why are you not answering your phone?"

"I am answering my phone when it's someone with whom I want to speak. Everybody else is off my list."

"Your own mother is off your list?"

"Did she call and complain to you?"

"No, but I know she's worried about you and doesn't know where you are."

"Who told you that?" He laughs and his voice indicates that he doesn't believe a word of that.

"Morgan."

"Morgan?"

"Yes."

"You went to see Morgan?"

"No. Are you kidding me?"

"Then how did you talk to her?"

"She just left here about two minutes ago."

"Why was she there?"

"Wow! You really sound like a lawyer right about now. You're getting a lot of practice in Arlington aren't you?

"Come on, Ari. Stop playing. Like your brother said, you play too much. What was Morgan doing at our house?" I insist.

"She says she came to apologize to me for breaking up my marriage, and in the meantime, she tried to find out from me where you were, but I didn't even know you had left town. She said your mother was worried, and your office wouldn't give her any information so I guess she and your Mom put their heads together and decided to try me."

CHAPTER 24: OUR TEST IN TIME

"I see. It sounds like another one of their little schemes to find out where our marriage stands. I think they want to know if you're talking to me now, or if we are still separated. They're full of little tricks. Be careful, Ari. Are you all right?"

"Yes, why wouldn't I be? I'll admit when she told me you were missing, it frightened me, but I stayed cool while she was here. As soon as she left, I called to see if you would answer me, and thank goodness, you did."

"You bet I did. I thought you would never call. I even checked my phone once during the trial, but my team noticed. The Brollen boys threatened to take my phone if I didn't pay more attention, so I stopped," he laughs. "I was paying attention, but I mean the case is in the bag, so I thought, what the heck. Babe, my closing argument was so tight," he brags. So, I was checking my phone to see if you called. It's so good to hear from you, Baby. Just your voice makes me feel better. Ah, man, I needed this." He was rambling in his excitement.

"Yes, I kind of like hearing your voice too, Attorney Wellington."

"May I call you sometimes now so you can hear it more often?'

"Yes, I'd like that," I giggle. "When are you coming back?"

"I wish it could be this minute, but I can't really answer that. Like I said, we're waiting on the jury, but I don't suspect they should take much longer. I know we won the case. Our evidence was solid, Babe, so maybe in a week after we tie up everything here."

"Good. I don't like thinking that you're that far away from me."

"That's good to hear even though Arlington isn't very far. Are you letting me come home?"

"No, Derek. We're not there yet." My voice is quiet, but serious.

"Well, I like the 'yet' part."

"You're silly. Goodnight, Derek. You take care of you, ok?"

"I'll do my best."

"Do you want me to call your mother and tell her where you are?"

"My Dad knows exactly where I am. He could tell her, and probably has, but I'll call even though she doesn't deserve it. Goodnight, Babe."

After we hang up, I hold the phone in my hand for a moment. It is my first connection with Derek in quite a while, and the call makes me realize how desperately I miss him. I walk to the back, take a shower and dress for bed. I slip down in the covers and smile thinking about my husband. When my phone buzzes, it pulls me out of my daydream, and I look over to see Derek's smiling face, and my heart leaps.

"Yes?" I ask with a tinge of sexiness in my voice.

"I just want to say goodnight."

"You already did about thirty minutes ago," I giggle.

"Well, I want to say it again. Ari, I've missed this so much that I actually bought a journal so I could write my goodnights to you every night before I close my eyes."

"Really?" I asked.

"Yes."

"Read me the one from last night." I can't stop my very wide grin.

"For real?"

"Yes. I want to hear what you said to me last night."

"OK."

There is a pause, and I can hear him turning pages in the book.

"I said, 'Goodnight, my darling Ari. I cannot wait until the time when we are lying face to face again in our bed, and I can reach up and touch your beautiful face. I can see me now plant a kiss on your nose, and move to the lips that I miss so much. Until that time, this will have to suffice. Goodnight, my love. Have the sweetest of dreams.'"

A smile is plastered on my face. "You're such a hopeless romantic, Derek. I want to hear more. Read the one from night before last."

"Ok. It says, 'Ari, I miss you. I miss your smile, your sweet smell, the way you flirt. I miss you holding me...I miss feeling your face in my chest. I miss your music, your voice. Ah...I miss all of you. If God blesses me again as He blessed me before, I will have all of that back and more, cause according to Job, that's the way He rolls. I love you, Ari...so much. Take care of you until you let me take care of you again. Good night.'"

Hmm...thank you for reading that to me, and you have sweet dreams tonight."

"I can assure you that I will. Goodnight, Babe."

Chapter 25

UNCERTAIN TIMES

*Casual flirtatious moments can create
unnecessary stumbling blocks.*

Who would have ever thought even a month ago I could be sitting comfortably on a sofa in my beach cottage with another man...the handsome Bran Mathersen? But here we are relaxing with an evening glass of wine, candles flickering, and some soft sexy musical strands almost mesmerizing us after a pretty active day. We are both fairly tired and the coziness of the cottage is soothing. Our friendship is growing, and both of us feel at ease just being ourselves joking about our little special outing.

Early in the day, we take a short ride up the coast, have a light lunch, and duck into a few unique shops in the area. We play catch- me

-if -you -can on the beach, kick the waves at each other, play a cat and mouse game in the cool water, and then he catches me, swings me around, and we fall together laughing and holding on to each other. The result of that is a lot of sand and salty water all over us both; we are a mess, but it makes me forget my troubles momentarily, and I am a different person for a minute. During the early evening, we spend a little time just talking and teasing each other sitting cross-legged on a pier. The breeze coming off the water is refreshing, and we find ourselves engaged in a lot of meaningless chatter that makes us giggle like silly teenagers with secrets. It's just pure fun. Bran is such a good listener, and I wonder if he has an old girlfriend he practices on every now and then. This man is quite unique, and I won't lie. Even though I am still very much in love with my husband, I can't help noticing his beautiful sexy smile, the water glistening and dripping off of his muscular slightly hairy chest, and those strong arms that can make any woman's heart skip beats. Bran is definitely very easy on the eyes. Later in the day, we enjoy dinner at a little beach grill that I discovered recently on one of my alone getaway days when I couldn't bear bumping into Derek....one of those days when just a glimpse of him would practically undo my twenty-six year old self for the rest of the week.

This day, however, has been just a brief time to get away from work, stress, and my ongoing problems. I'm just not willing to share Derek's heart with Morgan while he pretends or simply lies that he's all about me. She, no doubt, will always say she loved him first, and stake some kind of false claim, but I can't play these hurtful games. Even though Derek and I talk now, our separation has lasted months because I can't be sure exactly where our relationship stands. I hear his words with my ears, but not yet with my whole heart. I want true commitment; if I'm completely honest with myself, I'll have to admit that I still want and demand the fairy tale, the part where we live happily ever after. I'm not looking for perfection because I have sense enough to know that no one is perfect, but I do demand fidelity, respect, and honesty. If I can't have that with him, then it's the end of us as a couple. Our separation will certainly end in divorce.

"What are you thinking about?" Bran searches my eye to check my mood since I am so quiet.

See? That's my Bran...a perfect friend for me right now. He knows exactly when I need a distraction. Derek is worming his way into my almost perfect day, taking over my mind, but Bran breaks the spell just in time, and, for now, I slam the door on Derek thoughts.

"Just our day," I lie.

"Hmm, somehow I don't really believe that." He smiles at me, reaches up to touch the top of my head and lets his fingers play with a few strands of my hair.

"What are you doing?" My impatience is obvious. I jerk my head out of the way, put my hand up to remove his, and inch away from him. He can't think falling for me right now is going to work because it isn't. Derek still holds the key to my heart, and there is no doubt about that at all. Being without him Christmas and New Years proved that. It was horrible just seeing him a short time here and there, but it was all that I could and would permit. I know that right now, Derek is the only one who can quiet this constant gnawing void in my chest. It's there when I sleep, and it's still there when I wake. It's there when I work and when I play.

Bran wants to get close to me. I know that almost more than he does because I watch his every move on me. I know I need to keep him at arms length right now because in my heart there is no room for anyone but Mr. Derek Chase Wellington III, the

man I love almost more than life itself. Even though he and Morgan are no longer seeing each other, I feel that I have to put some time between him and her...some time for me to try to heal and forgive a husband who kept so many dark secrets. A lot of hurtful things have happened to me in the past year, and I know I need to be sure of where his heart is now.

Bran is my saving grace. It's so odd how he just shows up in my life just at the right time. I notice him one night waiting tables at *The Surf Rider*, an oceanfront restaurant; a few days later we actually meet. He's tall and muscular with an olive complexion that accentuates his beautiful green eyes, long alluring eyelashes and those neat light brown dreadlocks that just make him drop dead gorgeous. I hire this twenty-six year old a week or so later to model my men's fashion line at *Channing Designs*.

In the process of my investigation of Bran, I find out some very interesting facts. In actuality, he is a very rich guy from New York City who works on Broadway with his father. He is the only child of a famous star, director, and producer. In our many conversations later, I discover that he wanted to move out on his own in search of a woman who would love him for himself and not for the money and fame that follow him in those New York circles. He is looking for the lady of his dreams. He says moving to the Peninsula and getting a job waiting tables has been both cathartic and quite a change of pace from acting and the glitzy world of the Broadway stage. He has sort of melted into welcomed obscurity, no longer being known only by his father's name, money, and prestige. Here in the shadows, on the beach, he is just Bran, working at an oceanfront restaurant serving others. Despite his desire to get away from the limelight and blend into a more simplistic everyday life, he could not resist my offer, and we have fast become great friends and almost constant companions, but for me absolutely nothing more than that.

"Did you enjoy yourself today?" he inquires, his voice relaxed, sultry, and with a hint of an ulterior motive.

"I did, Bran. What about you?" My tone is light. Can't let him get any ideas that his sexy voice can control me.

"Ari, I always have a great time with you. But then…you know that, don't you?" He raises his eyebrows and lets that playful smile of his take over his handsome face. There is no sense at all in denying that if I were not so in love with Derek, this man would rock my world. He turns to face me, and those eyes of his melt into mine, and even though I try to look casual, I'm like a captive bird in his gaze. There's something about those glassy green eyes and those naturally long eyelashes that just draw me and hold me. He leans in a bit closer, as if he hadn't been close enough, and ever so lightly tilts my chin, and lets his fingers linger there. "I think I could make you a very happy woman, if you'd give me half a chance."

"Well now, that seems to be your problem, wouldn't you say, Mr. Mathersen?" I try to sound as sarcastic as I possibly can as I push myself up from the sofa and move

to the kitchen area. Bran has this uncanny way of taking me off my game sometimes, and making me a bit unnerved. Can't let him see that. I start putting away the dishes that I left out earlier as my excuse to get some distance from him.

"You know I told you, Bran, I'm still very much in love with Derek."

He follows me into the kitchen, takes the dishtowel from my hands, and turns me to face him. He wraps his arms around my waist, and leans in unsuccessfully

for that elusive kiss he so badly seems to want. Even though his strong and alluring sex appeal is not lost on me, I take the chance of looking directly into those mercurial green eyes with a seriousness that is not missed on him. I gently push him away.

"Not even those stunning eyes of yours are going to change a thing. It's not going to happen, Bran. I told you. We are just good friends. Can you handle that?" I continue to put up dishes because I know I need something to help me avoid direct contact with this gorgeous man standing here in my kitchen desiring me.

"We will see. I don't give up very easily and when I *really* want something, I can be a real first class pest about it," he teases with a mischievous glint in his eyes. "With your little investigation, you dis-covered my secrets. So now you know that I've been given everything I've ever wanted all of my life so…just know, I have my methods."

He's flashing that winning smile, showing most of his beautiful white perfect teeth.

"And so do I," I retort with a chuckle that says I know something that you don't. *Does this boy really think he can get over on me?* I smirk and take the bait. I'll play at *his* risk. I get right up in his face playing that assertive woman shaking my head I'm sure of myself game.

"Don't forget, I was born rich too, and I have always…always gotten everything I've ever wanted. I have my methods too, and right now, I still want Derek." I move away from him and the joking eyes are gone. I am serious.

"Bran, even though Derek and I have been separated for several months now, and I still can't honestly say I trust him, I very much want to be able to go back to him one day." My eyes find his, and I feel the burning that comes just before the water brims. I shake off the feeling as best I can, but not soon enough to avoid knowing that just saying the words makes everything so real and conjures up that nagging spot in my chest…the ache that is a constant in my heart.

Bran can feel himself becoming slightly irritated, but he knows he has to keep this light. He is determined not to let the tears affect him…determined not to go down for the count.

"Ari, I…I know what you're telling me, but I just don't understand it. I don't buy what you're selling. You're a beautiful, intelligent, classy, rich woman who can basically have any man you want. Why do you insist on waiting around for something that might never happen for you guys and missing out on great opportunities like this lovely face right here?" He chuckles, picture framing his face with his hands.

"Not finished yet, huh, Mr. Mathersen? OK. Two can play this game." I flirt with him.

"Maybe I won't miss out on it. I don't have my crystal ball with me tonight so who knows what the future holds for me." I pretend to slip by him, but stop at the right place to tickle him on his right side, a spot I found on the beach that makes him giggle and crouch down like a schoolgirl. I saunter back toward the sofa laughing at him when I hear this very soft knock on the door, and then we both hear his voice.

"Ari?" It's Derek, and I snatch a deep breath.

In that instant, my heart skips a noticeable beat and those darn butterflies begin their wild unstoppable dance in my stomach. I move over toward the door, but take the time to look back over my shoulder at Bran, pull a few strands of my long brunette locks between my teeth, flash my sexiest smile, and ready myself to deliver the knock out punch.

"See. I told you." I emulate the sexiest voice I can find at the moment, trying to hide from him the uncontrollable excitement in my body. "I have my methods too when I want something, and I, too, don't give up easily." Bran drops his eyes and looks away. I know it would have been easy for me to see his great disappointment if I had not turned so quickly to open the door for the love of my life.

"Hey"

"Hi, you busy?"

"I have company, but you can come in."

"You sure?"

"Ah…Listen guys," Bran interrupts coming out of the kitchen area. "I was just about to leave anyway. What's up, D?" I hear a little nervousness or something different in Bran's voice, but not enough for Derek to notice.

350

"Not much. Just needed to put my eyes on my baby." Derek moves into the room and those beautiful brown misty eyes of his never stray from mine. It is as if suddenly we are the only two people in the room.

"Hey…guys…I'm out." Bran knows he is interrupting something special, but he moves over next to me anyway and casually puts his arms around my waist and takes my eyes from Derek's to his.

Yikes! A little too close in front of Derek, I think. Knowing our situation, this is a bit disrespectful. I calm myself and think how it's just better to go with the flow.…not the time to make a big deal out of anything…don't want any bad scenes.

"I had a great time today, Ari." His voice is quiet and sincere. "You stay cool, babe," and he smiles and releases me.

"I'll try." I give him a little punch on his forearm and a genuine smile. "I'll see you tomorrow, Bran."

"Yes, you will. Ten thirty scheduled shoot with Shawn." "Later, D."

"Later."

With that, Bran exits the already open door.

Chapter 26

A MATTER OF TRUST~

~Trusting: Allowing you to take my heart inside of yours knowing,
without a doubt, you will eternally shield it~

Within the nanosecond that it takes for the lock to click behind Bran, the temperature rises more than a hundred degrees in my living room. Well, that's an exaggeration, but Derek is standing in front of me, all 5'11 inches of his fine twenty–eight year old handsome self...that self that makes my heart pound with just the thought of him. His smooth skin, those misty bedroom eyes, and new well-trimmed beard give him that distinguished sexy look. He's wearing his dark brown slacks that fit so smoothly over his slender hips, his light blue shirt open at the collar showing the brown beaded cross necklace I gave him, and those brown sandals that just say Derek to me.

His medium brown shoulder length hair is loose tonight and those few sun-kissed golden strands, as always, are falling carelessly over his right eye. Wow! Just the slight tilt of his head, the longing look in his eyes as he brushes a light kiss on my lips is enough to send my mind reeling back in time and space. There is no doubt at all. Even after all the pain we have experienced over these past few months, I love this man with every beat of my heart. I want to believe I know him like the back of my hand, but unfortunately, he has already proven this is not true. The slight downward tilt of his head looking for my lips, his right thumb resting near them, and his index finger tilting my chin is his invitation to me. It says, *"Come to me, baby,"* and I'm not going to lie; it puts me on automatic. I don't have to think to know what he wants from me. I know immediately and respond with a familiarity that only a constant lover knows. Our memories create the moves. It's like a graceful dance of love performed to perfection for a million years. But memory, too, is cruel and two-faced. While one whirls in my mind and causes the heat to rise, the other sits stoically at a distance in the corner of my mind mocking and reminding me that these touches have not been for me alone. The lips that are brushing mine so softly now, have touched Morgan possibly in the same way. The look, the sincerity in his voice, the quickness of his breath, and most of all the love in his heart have all so recently been for two of us, and that one cruel thought springs a new icy response to life, and I push out of his arms. Even though my hands still rest on him, and my lips are still wet from his kisses, there is this new distant look that burns through touch. There is no doubt. The invasion has already taken place, and Derek knows instantly that despite the fact that he has tried to convince me now over and over for the past several months that he is totally in love with me and me alone, trust is hard for me to find.

Tonight, as much as I may want to commit again to this relationship, it's still too soon for me. I am reminded yet again that Betrayal, a hard and ruthless game, sucks the life out of promises.

He pulls me back to him, and touches my mouth with his. "Hey, you." The sound of his voice is almost inaudible, but I feel the words on my lips.

He leans his head back and looks me in my eyes. "Ari, let me come home, baby...please. I miss you *so* much. Every morning that I wake up without you next to me, and every night that I go to bed without you in my arms is like....it's...it's like hell. Right now, I'd give anything to go back and get what we had, but I know that can't happen." He touches my face. "I messed that up...I messed that up badly, and I have no idea what made me act like such a fool. I knew Mom wanted me with Morgan. I knew she had Morgan at the house. Why did I fall into that trap?...but I'm not blaming anyone but myself and I'm so sorry, baby. Just let me come home. I'll make it all up to you. I promise. *"Betrayal sucks the life out of promise."* Please. Please, Ari. I need you. I'll do everything I can to make this up to you."

My eyes fall, and I know I can't answer him now so I just let the moment take charge. He's looking at me now without passion...just pure sorrow, and it breaks my heart. His eyes are writing the passages of regret that emit from his heart. His silence, as he waits for my answer, is communicating louder than the capacity of any words. He holds me, and I feel his hands moving along the center of my back, and his hands come up to hold my face close to his.

"How are you?" His voice is soft and filled with concern. It's a simple question, but the answer is far from simple because I know that it's not just about the moment. It's much more complex than that. It's about everyday since we've been apart…everyday that I've suffered this loss…everyday that I've searched for the man I thought I knew…the man I loved before his transgressions…everyday that I've searched for my husband who completely lost my trust. I take a deep breath and blow out the stress that the answer demands.

"Well, I…I can't tell you that I'm fine because that would be a lie. The truth is I'm…I'm sad. I'm very sad, Derek, and the sadness seems to want to live here now." I slightly pat the place where my heart sits…that place he used to own. He shifts his stance, sighs deeply, and I feel his despair. He reaches for my hands, and he entwines his with mine and holds them at our side. I lay my head on his chest and allow the familiar scent of him to make me feel at home because that is what he is to me…HOME.

The music filling the room seems to draw us closer, and we allow it to create a calm around us. Derek pushes away just enough to see my face, and he smoothens my hair down with both of his hands, holds my face close to him, and allows what he calls my 'beautiful hazel mirrors' to caress him. He smiles that old familiar way of his, that quiet smile that barely moves his lips, the one that releases the truth behind the misty eyes, and makes my heart flip every time. He kisses the tip of my nose, and with both of my hands in his, he sways back a bit, cocks his head to the side and looks at me from head to foot.

"You are stunningly beautiful, Ari, and it makes my heart ache to even think that you might no longer be mine." With that and a slight rub of my hand he goes to sit on the nearby sofa.

Without a word, I light a few more candles, refresh the ice bucket, and put in a bottle of champagne. Derek is sitting with his right ankle crossed on his left knee. His right arm is stretched out on the back of the sofa, and I can feel his eyes follow me around the room. Every now and then, out of habit, the tips of his fingers tap, tap, tap, the back of the seat. *Damn, he's beautiful!*

"So...tell me about your day, baby." His voice is soft and a little cool when his eyes meet mine. Immediately, I'm on guard because I know that this is not a simple request or a passing interest in my normal daily activities. I know exactly what he wants to know, and he knows I know. I take an inaudible breath and move to sit next to him. I casually reach for his hand and play with his fingers.

"Bran and I just rode up the coast for the day. It was fun. The water was cool, and we ate out at Benny's, but you know, it was just something different...something to do." I sound very natural, nothing to detect the slight nervousness that I actually feel working in my stomach.

"Hmm, something to do," he murmurs. It sounds like something that he detests hearing, but since it's just an old expression, I can't tell why he sounds a bit angry.

"So...this something to do with Bran..." He hesitates and looks down at my hands playing with his fingers. Then, with trepidation, he lifts his eyes to mine.

"Is it serious?"

I look down at our hands entwined together and a quiet smirk takes over my face. Sometimes I just can't believe this man. I glance up into those beautiful dreamy eyes of his, and they almost become my undoing...almost but not quite.

"Are YOU serious?" My voice holds a degree of sarcasm, disbelief, and, yes, a little anger.

I'm calm on the outside, but I feel a slight boiling on the inside. He's the one who cheated, not me. He's the one who should explain his actions, not me. I'm the one who has every right in the world to be suspicious, not him!

He steps out on a dangerous ledge.

"You know he's crazy about you." His comment hangs in the air waiting for my response.

"His little goodbye scene was pretty serious, don't you think?"

Still there is no comment from me. He releases my hand, sits up straight, and looks me in my eyes.

I look down, shake my head, and smirk.

"You don't know anything about Bran so how can you claim to know how he feels?" Now I've given Derek some fuel, and he's going to walk the ledge without caution. He's going full steam ahead, recklessly.

"Because I'm a man, and I can tell when another man is hot for a woman, especially one as fine as you. Look at you!...white short shorts, tie up red blouse, stomach showing, bare feet. Come on, Ari."

That disturbing crease comes to his forehead and in between his eyes. I hear the anger?... jealousy?... exasperation?...whatever it is in his voice; I don't really know exactly what it is, nor do I care. What I know is I'm not about to back down or give him one inch.

"Well, maybe your concern ought to be how *I* feel about Bran, since it really doesn't matter how *he* feels about me if I don't feel the same about him."

I know Derek has been stewing about this since he walked through the door, so I'm on guard for one of his little tirades. He takes one look at my face and decides to change his tactic. All of a sudden, his voice is low and sexy, and I know he thinks this will catch me off guard…a fight using the unexpected. Really? Are you kidding me? He's got to do a lot better than that, *Mr. Prosecutor.* After all we have been married for almost two years, and I know all of his little tricks.

"So tell me, Mrs. Wellington, III…How *do* you feel about him?"

"You know what, Derek? I'm not doing this," I snap. I feel the heat smoldering that causes my eyes to widen and my head to shake without any real assistance from me. "You're not coming over here and upset me with this crap. I'm not doing this."

"I can't ask you anything about him?" he snaps back.

I glare at him, and at first I don't answer. I let the silence speak volumes for me….and then, as if I have a second thought, I answer with all the sarcasm I can muster.

"You know his name. You know he was here, and you know he left. That's all you need to know."

I see the muscles in his jaw tense, and I can feel his anger building.

"I know you spent the day with him, and I know I don't like it. I don't like it, Ari, and you're still my wife."

"Well that might change too, and what makes you think I give one twit about what you like any more?"

He shrugs his shoulders and stares at me like he can't believe what I just said. I can feel the heat of his anger, and I can tell that he's searching for some words that are not immediately available to him so I decide to give him *my* truth, and maybe calm the situation a bit at the same time.

I'm quiet now, and I take his hands again, and let my eyes find his.

"I'll tell you this Derek Chase Wellington, The Third: I love you. I love you very much, and that's never going to change. I've never cheated on you, and never thought about cheating on you because, unlike you, I'm not playing games."

Tears begin to well in my eyes as I continue.

"I think it might be a very good idea for us right now not to talk about Brandon Mathersen. Know that he models one of my lines, we're very good friends, and that is all it is for me right now. Don't come in here questioning me and trying to intimidate me like some slick lawyer about my friends because if you do, that will be your quickest route to the other side of that door. I mean that. You lost your right to do that with me."

There is finality to what I have to say, and I can tell immediately that it is not lost on Derek. He completely understands that he cannot risk playing with my emotions at this point. He knows that I am tired. He snatched the life out of me in late October and he knows it has been a long five months for me.

I slightly tighten my hold on his hand. "I just need a little time. *We* need a little time. I think if we had done that before we got married, we wouldn't be caught in this awful spot now. I'll admit it. You swept me off my feet, Derek, and we were married far sooner than we should have been. You needed time to decide your true feelings for Morgan. But now, we don't have to repeat that same mistake. We can take our time and really assess where we are and what we really want."

Derek presses his lips together...an old habit he seems to rely on whenever he's thinking about something serious. He looks at me, and I see that his anger has diminished. He reaches to touch my face.

"Baby, you have to know that I love you...that I've never stopped loving you one second, and that I will always love you."

I hear his words, but what *he* doesn't realize is that this is a serious matter of trust. I no longer know deep in my heart that he never stopped loving me one second. It seems that he did. It seems that he stopped loving me for a lot of seconds; otherwise, how could he have hurt me so unexpectedly, so callously, so deeply? How could he have betrayed everything that we built...how could he keep up these secret meetings with an old sweetheart? I don't think I can ever understand it. I don't understand how you put your marriage, something so important, at risk in exchange for a few stolen moments....but still... despite it all, I let him pull me into his arms now and hold me close to him. We sit together in a comfortable silence that most husbands and wives have perfected. The music seems to soothe us both and quiet the mood, and we close our eyes and let the melody take us to old familiar places. Every now and then, Derek brushes my hair with his hand, and our lips touch or he kisses the top of my head. I know he just wants to be near me, touch me, and be reassured that he has not lost me completely.

During the five months of our separation, he never fails to try to explain that he and Morgan have a history *[insert knife]*,...that even though he betrayed me [*push knife in deeper*], he never stopped loving me. He talks about his confusion *[twist knife]*...the length of time that he and Morgan have been together *[twist knife more]*...that both of them experienced great difficulty completely severing their relationship knowing that they could never just be friends *[smile while twisting knife]*. Somewhere in the back of his mind, he still believed that Morgan was his soul mate; *[pull knife out quickly and see the blood on the floor]*...but now, if I can believe him *[while still greatly feeling the pain]*, hopefully time and his indefatigable love for me have schooled him differently. If I had my greatest wish at this time in my life, I would somehow be able to communicate to Derek just how much it pains me hearing his explanations....the excuses for what he has done to us. I wish he could understand how my mind works even as he is kissing me now...holding me now...loving me now. My mind wonders back....July 4th, when he was so late for our dinner date. Was he with her then? Did they celebrate before he came to me?... moments when I found him completely lost in thought.... Was he thinking of her then?...times he made excuses for coming home so late...did he stop by her house first to spend time with her? There is this seemingly never ending list of events that I can point to, question, and forever wonder about the validity of his explanations. I wish he could understand that.

As I try to shake these thoughts, I hear the music change. Robin Thicke's rhythmic beats do almost the impossible. They find a way to pull us out of our seriousness and sit us smack dab in the middle of a better mood. Out of habit, when we hear the beats, we start one of those things we used to do. We begin what we called seat dancing with arms and legs flying here and there, laughing and pushing on each other. Derek jumps to his feet, grabs a make believe microphone and begins a playful karaoke: The music is blasting that we have "got to get it together." He pulls me to my feet, grabs my hand and swings me out in an old style 60's dance move. I let go of his hand, put my hands on his shoulders and sway my sexy narrow hips to the beat. I take over the Faith Hill part. Derek holds his make believe microphone close to his mouth and looks in my eyes singing Robin's part. Then we join in unison grinning, singing, dancing and just plain acting carefree and crazy. It's exactly what we used to do when we were really together. We had so much fun entertaining each other, and just being in love.

The rhythm takes us over, and we throw away our mics and rock to the beat with hips gyrating, arms flaying, and hair swinging. In the end, hugging and laughing, we fall back on the sofa.

"We're still pretty good together." Derek is out of breath and even that is funny to us. "We might need to find an agent," he jokes and we giggle momentarily out of control.

"Don't quit your day job just yet big boy," I tease in a Marilyn Monroe like voice, and I hug him. In that moment, we throw caution to the wind, and kiss passionately; we look into each other's eyes, and then just fall out giggling like the carefree kids we used to be.

As if the playlist knows what to do next, it skips to a more serious tone, and the music of Mariah Carey's "My All" almost automatically brings us back to our feet. Derek stands first, and without a word offers his hand to me. He pulls me up to him and wraps his arms around my waist. I put both of my hands around his neck and rest my head on his shoulder. I take the chance of letting the sweet familiar smell of him send me into that distant world where I know passion resides. He pulls me closer and bends his head to kiss my waiting lips, and our bodies seem to melt into each other. Derek holds me close, and the slow rhythm moves our feet, but the alluring voice of Mariah, and the words she sings sear into mind, body, and soul.

I feel desire mounting, going where I have refused to go for so long….a place where not even my mind has dared to touch in fantasy. Derek releases my waist and takes my hand, presses the music repeat button, and attempts to lead me away to love, but caution invades the mind, fear gnaws at the base of common sense, but miraculously anger simply fades away. In each other's embrace, sorrow melts like the fleeting symmetry of snowflakes touching the surface of earth, and we are drawn to each other like moths to a flame. The distance that has ensnared us for months appears far too weak now to battle at this meeting. Melodic strands pluck at our heartstrings and memories gently nudge us back to that sacred place of love. The physical meeting, however, must wait. I love this man in my arms, and he is offering me his heart, and pleading for a second chance, but TRUST must first take its rightful place of honor and tonight is not the night.

Chapter 27

SEARCHING FOR ANSWERS

~Answers from God are never late; His timing is perfect~

"What took you so long to open the stupid door? I thought I was gonna have to call the doggone rescue squad."

Angel pretty much always storms into the house like some whirlwind from a tornado or a freight train running loose on the tracks. She has on those high wedge heels that push her all the way up to her intimidating six feet. Her neat skinny jeans fit the contour of her hips like they were melted on and her silk white blouse with its scoop neckline hangs loose at the waist. Of course, she hasn't left home without her many gold bangles or the long expensive chains that hang around her neck. She has streaked her light brown hair with that green dye again, and with all of that, she still pulls off this astonishing beauty…one of the most gorgeous models I have ever seen in my life. She throws her oversized orange bag on the sofa and stands looking at me still at the door.

"So, what's up with King Casanova? What'd he do now?…sorry tail fool! I keep telling you to leave him alone….got me over here in the A.M….Really?…like I don't need sleep. I know he did something else stupid, and then said he was sorry two second later with those fake tears trying to fall. 'I'm sorry, Ari. I didn't mean it.'" Angel goes into her cartoon like imitation of Derek's voice.

"Can you just stop and calm down?" I have to laugh at her especially at her version of how Derek sounds. I finally close the door, but not before she continues with her all assuming tirade.

"I told you to stay away from that fool. Heartbreaker…no count, sorry tail man."

Angel is waving her hands around, starts to pull out a cigarette, but I wave my index finger "no" before she can light it.

"Oh yeah, that's right. This is the no smoke zone…at the home of Ms. I Can't Stand A Little Ash on the Floor…But you're still my girl. So, go ahead. Talk to me. What's up?"

I inhale and exhale loudly, and bite the corner of my lower lip.

"Derek came over last night."

"Heck, I *know* that. I can look at your face and tell that."

This is Street-wise Angel, and she seems her usual impatient, feisty self, but I still take my time to continue. I speak quietly and seriously despite the tone Angel always sets.

"I love him, Angel. I don't think I can fight it. I love him so much."

"Oh, my goodness. I gotta pull out the *heavy* artillery today. What the heck did he do to you?"

She stops and holds up her hand. "I'll tell you what…this is crazy, and I think it's about to get madhouse nuts up in here, so before you spill it all out, let's just take a little walk down the beach and sit on *The Rock*. That always seems to help for some unknown reason."

The Rock has been my favorite place even before I moved here with Derek two years ago, and I know very well why it calms me. It is the best place to see the ocean, the best place to watch the sun go down, the best place to see the moon rise over the water, the best place to kiss the one you love, and at *The Rock* is the absolute best place to get married, and touch the face of God.

Without another word, I throw on my green paisley caftan, put my hair in a ponytail, and grab my green sandals just in case. Angel is busy checking out my music and dancing to the beat of whomever is next on the playlist.

"Cut that off and let's go. I have to be at work by 9 for a shoot with Bran at 10:30."

Angel presses the iPad off and follows me out. The morning sun over the water is breathtaking, and the cool breeze off the Atlantic is just what I need to relax. The two of us walk down the beach in an unusual quietness, and I so much appreciate Angel just being by my side. We find *The Rock* and climb it to the top and sit together with the March wind whipping our hair and the sound of crashing waves

367

playing their own special earth melodies. We sit still for a moment just taking in what God has blessed us to see.

"So…what are you thinking?" Angel looks out at the ocean and speaks quietly, breaking into my thoughts.

"He wanted to make love," I muse somewhere between thinking and speaking aloud.

Angel turns and looks at me askance. "I sure hope you turned that fool down. We gotta get him checked out first. We don't know who he's been messing with."

I laugh for the first time this morning, and playfully smack at Angel's shoulder. She leans away from me to try to miss my hand, and we look at each other and burst out laughing again.

"You know I'm telling the truth. You can't trust anybody these days. If you're thinking about making love, you gotta get the fool checked out."

"Angel, don't be silly," I laugh. "That Christmas you spent with Zack…you didn't get him checked out. Nothing's wrong with Derek, and he's not messing with anybody now. He wants me back too much to mess up again. Besides, he's Mr. Careful personified. I knew that right after we got engaged."

"Oh, you did?" She raises an eyebrow.

"Yes, I did," I say with some finality. "I know now that making love as soon as we were engaged was a huge mistake. I knew then, and I know even more now that we should have waited until marriage. Everything in me told me to wait, but I didn't. By then, I thought I was deeply in love, and I let my heart control me. I've learned that the heart and the brain don't always cooperate with each other."

"What's that word you use when you tell me the Lord is warning you about people or situations? What's that word?"

"That word, Angel, is discernment, and unfortunately for me, I didn't use it this time."

"That's it! You've talked to me about that quite a bit, and I have used it."

"I should have. I thought I knew Derek, but I didn't....not much at all. He was able to fool me when I stopped listening to God, and was just listening to him and my heart. That was the mistake. The heart has no common sense, and it will let you down every time," I muse.

Angel is looking out at the water now, and a deepening shadow veils her gray eyes, and they seem darker. Her mood has changed. This is "Serious Angel." Somehow, I know that she no longer is seeing the ocean or hearing the sound of the waves. Her mind has gone to some other distant place and time and she speaks slowly and thoughtfully.

"Love is a funny thing, Ari. The mind knows when relationships are not right even when the heart tells us to keep trying to force them or go with the flow. There's that thing that keeps gnawing at us that says something isn't right. Somewhere in your mind you could discern that things with Derek were not completely honest. You told me once something about April, May, and June in his life, but you also said you were going to ignore that. Instead, you should have forced him to level with you. I think that was God prompting you to look a little deeper."

"Yes, there were several times that I had the opportunity to ask him to explain that, but I didn't. I knew I should have, but I was not obedient to God's voice. I was too busy having a good time."

"Ari, when we do listen to that inner voice, we know when things are not right or when the relationship is completely over...that everything is finished...that if things don't change for the better, there is practically nothing that can solve the problems or...erase the pain or...bring back the spark. You can be assured that God will let you know whether you listen or not."

She stops and closes her eyes for a brief moment. "The brain can decide it's time to move on...that you can build a new relationship with someone else, forget about the past and let memory fade." She moves nervously on *The Rock* just slightly. "But when the heart says no to logic, there is very little...very little that the brain can do unless you have very strong FAITH and use it."

The end of her sentence seems to almost drift off to the water's edge, and in that moment, I know that there is a lot of my friend's past still hidden in the recesses of her mind, and not at all shared with me.

"You sound like you know what you say from experience. Do you?"

"Unfortunately, I do, Ari."

"Are you in love with him still?"

"Very much so, and no doubt I will be for the rest of my life. I have fun with other men, but he's never far from my thoughts. Even Zack can't push him away, and he gives his best shot," she slightly chuckles. She looks longingly at the water, and I see the tears forming in her eyes, and she lowers her head.

"Is he married now?"

"No, and I don't think he ever will be." She almost whispers and shakes her head. "One day I had to decide if it would be brain or heart, and I chose brain." She inhales deeply and looks at me with the most serious look I have ever seen in her eyes. "That is what *you* have to do, Ari, and you have to try desperately not to make a mistake."

"Did you make a mistake?'

She shakes her head no. "It's just that my heart won't shut up." She laughed a little and reaches over and hugs me.

"As much as I call Derek a fool, I know he's a good man. I know he loves you deeply, and I know you love him, but you have to be able to trust him, Ari, and he has to love you enough that you can. If you find that you cannot trust him, you'll have to let the brain control or the heart will continuously be broken."

There is silence except for the wind and water surrounding us. Angel and I look out at the ocean and take in the beauty of that little spot of earth, and both of us think about the men who hold our hearts. Angel has made a decision using her brain, and I need to make a decision one way or the other. Limbo is suddenly not working for me. We sit together on *The Rock,* as close to Jesus as we can physically get, with God's creations surrounding us, and I silently pray fervently for His guidance. We sit contemplating our futures until the present takes control.

"Come on, Sweetie. It's time for you to get ready for work."

We climb down *The Rock* and walk silently back to the cottage, and Angel and I seal a quiet bond of best friends forever. She stops at the door.

"I'm not coming in, Ari; I have a few errands to run today so I gotta get going.

But you take care of you. Do you hear me?" Her expression is serious, and I know she's worried about me more than she's willing to admit.

"I'll be fine. I'm good. I'm good." The last "good" comes out a little too accentuated and Angel cocks her eyes and raises an eyebrow, and I know exactly what she's thinking.

"Look, I leave for Spain in a couple of days with the company I signed with in LA, and I'll only be there for a little over a week. I'm not even going to be that busy because six models are going and three of us have one all day shoot each. The other days are kind of light.... just a few group takes. Why don't you come with me? It would give you a welcome break from work and worry, and we could have a lot of fun on my off hours. Come go, go with me."

"For real?"

"For real." I can get everything set up with Dominic....No problem. He's absolutely nuts about you. He's always talking about my friend from Virginia with the hazel eyes, the long legs, the curves in all the right places, and he goes off on what he calls 'those gorgeous locks flowing down her back.'"...and then he *always* closes his eyes and adds 'hmm.'" We both laugh and the release is refreshing.

"I don't know, Angel. I'll think about it. I have a meeting set up next week with my designers in New York, but I could easily do that in a couple of days. I know I have to talk with them to see how our new luxury line is rolling out, but that's easily taken care of...I can Skype it if I want...so, I'll think about it. Maybe I could even find some unique fabrics in Spain. I need something different for a new idea I have rolling around in my head. My Dad gave me some, but I could look for more. Thanks for the invitation and thanks for this morning. I really needed you. Maybe you should think a little more about your guy. That doesn't seem to be over."

"Naw." She hesitates only a moment. "It's...It's over. Remember what I said about the continuous broken heart?" She scrunches up her mouth as if she is in some very deep thought. "Well, I think too much of my heart to put it through that for the rest of its life. I can't constantly live on the edge. I need a firm foundation under my feet. Sometimes, Ari, the hardest thing to do is the most necessary." Angel rubs her folded arms as if she feels an invisible chill. "This is the first time I've even been able to voice my feelings out loud. It's so difficult for me to let him go, but I have to because I know my needs. When things get hard in my life, I want a shoulder and strong arms, and I don't want to have to go searching for them in another woman's bed or even wonder if that would happen."

She looks at me with a sadness that I have not seen in the time we've known each other. Angel is looking out toward the water again, but I know the only thing she is seeing is the man who stands invisible now holding her heart.

"When I wake every morning and go to bed every night, I don't want my partner to be the very personification of lies, manipulations, and deceit. When you *know* that's the path, when you *know* he can't make up his mind, when you know he really doesn't love you enough, then you have to let it go. So, don't worry about me, Sweetie." She smiles a rather sad smile, that kind of smile that reveals the depth of hurt and pain, but recognizes its necessity, and accepts it. "I've got some distractions…good looking ones too like Zack. Heck, Zack might be my Mr. Right one day. Who knows?"

"Now that's some wishful thinking bordering on insanity," I chuckle.

"I'm sure you're right. He's not even close to settling down, but he is a lot of fun."

We hug, and Angel turns toward her new red convertible Lexus and waves bye with that money making smile that has her at the top of the modeling world, that smile that has her face plastered on almost every magazine I pick up. I can hear my phone ringing so I dash inside and grab my cell, and Derek's picture grins back at me.

"Good Morning." I'm sure he can hear my smile.

"How is my lady?" His voice is low, quiet, and sexy and has that lazy hoarseness that tells me he's just waking.

"I'm fine. I took an early morning stroll on the beach, sat at *The Rock*, and now I'm about to get ready for work."

"Oh yeah….that's right…the 10:30 shoot with my fav, Bran. Right?"

"Well, I didn't know he was your fav, but yeah." There is a silence at the other end, and because I know him so well, I know that the memory of my connection with Bran irritates him.

"Well, listen, Ari, I'm not going to hold you. I have to go too. I'm due in court soon. I called to ask if you'll let me take you out tonight?

I miss you. I want to see you so badly, and you'll make my day if you say yes." There's that voice again, and there goes my heart skipping beats and butterflies winging their way whimsically through my body.

"I would love to, Derek. I want to see you too." *Did I just say I would love to go out with him?…that I want to see him too? Of course, I did. I said last night that I don't play games.*

"Great. You make me a very happy man, Baby. I'll pick you up at 7:00. Wear…*Sunday's Best.* I love you. Talk to you later."

"You're so cool…wear *Sunday's Best,* I repeated with a little giggle. I can do that. Later, Babe."

It's so perfect that Derek should ask for *Sunday's Best* because it sums up my many visits with God, my many hours spent asking for His Guidance, His Strength, and His Unconditional Love. I hang up the phone with an overwhelming confidence and an undeniable sense of peace wrapping itself around me, and I know that God has answered my prayers. I honestly feel like I'm floating on some distant cloud. My heart is in springtime where fantastical flowers bloom and the scent of them is clean and fresh and new. Somewhere between the time of *then* and the hour of *now,* a reality enters majestically, like the freshness of morning dew, and I no longer doubt that my husband loves me. Somewhere in the middle of *I'm not so sure* and *I recognize and believe the validity and veracity of his love,* my husband enters my heart again and makes his indelible mark, one that was not there before. This one is new, honest, and well defined.

When I am finally seated in my car ready to drive to work, I ponder this awesome feeling for a moment. When I come back to myself, I question how I got ready for work so quickly. My mind has been preoccupied with nothing but thankful prayers and the joy of knowing what possibly lies ahead for me, and the man I love. I thank the God of my Strength knowing that only He can give me the patience to wait until seven tonight.

Chapter 28

A GOLDEN NIGHT
TO REMEMBER

~Never stop searching for the Wonders of God~

I realize when I leave home that I won't be able to stay at work all day. I know it as well as I know my name. I can tell within a few minutes of being at work that my team knows it even more clearly than I. They want me to leave as soon as possible. *We can handle everything,* they keep repeating. *You just need to go home and get some rest.* I keep telling myself that I'm not doing that badly today. I'm doing ok. So what if I ruined two dresses adjusting the sleeves, sent an important fax to the wrong address, and forgot a planning meeting with my designer team preparing our new male line. Oh well, we all have our bad days, and we all make mistakes....maybe not that many in one day, but oh well. Anyway, I get through the first half of the day, and now I'm on my way home to calm down and dress for my evening with Derek. I'm nervous, excited whatever. I don't know, but I'll get it together. I keep wondering where he's taking me on this date night, anyway. He's such a hopeless romantic so I know it will almost make my heart stop, but the main thing is I can't wait to see him. To me, it's almost like a first date.

My closets are filled with amazing outfits of every color in the rainbow, and I have the task of choosing just the right one for tonight. I'll think about it a little longer because it has to be perfect. I shower, wash my hair, and roll my wet locks in a towel for now. I polish my nails, apply my makeup, and sit watching one of my favorite shows while my fingers and toes dry. I blow dry my hair and curl it so that my long brown tresses fall just right down my back and the intermingling lighter streaks that frame my face accent my smoky hazel eyes. They seem to create an allure that many say is unmatched. Derek wants me to wear *Sunday's Best* so I decide on a cute little black number that can't go wrong in any setting. The scalloped neckline matches the hemline of the dress that comes just above my knees, and the little one shoulder sleeve gracefully caps the top of my arm. The dress fits the curves of my body perfectly. My sheer silky barely black hose and the four inch Christian Louboutin black heels with a lace flower to accent the dress are stunning. I fasten the three-stone drop diamond pendant around my neck, add the matching earrings, and slip on the diamond tennis bracelet Derek gave me on our first anniversary; that completes the trio. Two of these are extremely expensive birthday gifts from Derek, and they, most definitely, add the final touch of elegance. I check myself out in the full-length mirror, and with satisfaction, decide that I will probably knock my husband off his feet, and that is my intention.

I walk up to the front to relax and wait, but I'm still too nervous. To fill time, I opt to create a new playlist on my iPad instead.... anything to take my mind off of waiting. However, there is very little wait time when I hear a knock on the door, and I open it to the most handsome man I know. My Derek is dressed in a black three-piece suit with a light grey shirt, striped black and grey tie and matching handkerchief. His black shoes are shining like new money, and he smells divine. His medium brown hair is slicked down without one strand out of place and he has it secured in one of his fancy knots behind. His trimmed beard is perfect and makes my heart skip.

"Wow Ari, you never fail to take my breath away, girl." I see him take a very deep breath.

"You're not so bad yourself, Mr. Wellington." My voice is quiet, and I can feel that my eyes are wider than normal.

Derek is still standing in the threshold of the door, I'm still holding the doorknob, and we are both caught in a brief trance. The butterflies in my stomach have gone absolutely wild. They have no sense of direction and their flutter is far harsher than I ever remember. I inhale, hold my stomach as if that will help, and finally manage to speak and move aside.

"Come in, Babe."

"No need. Do you have everything?" *Wow! His voice.... I have got to get it together.* I see him slightly shake his head and take another deep breath as if ridding himself of the cobwebs clouding his mind.

I know that we are both enraptured. I turn, grab my purse and wrap and see the white limo and driver dressed in all white, waiting.

"Well...this looks extremely special," I smile up at him.

"Every minute with you anywhere is extremely special to me," he replies with that little smile and a voice that makes my butterflies lose their mind.

"This is all very interesting. Do you want to tell me where we're going?" I am indeed intrigued, and feeling quite exceptional. He stops, pulls me close to him, turns my face to his with one index finger as if he is about to kiss me and says, "No."

"No?" I grin up at him.

"No, it's a surprise."

"As hungry as I am, dinner is a surprise?" I laugh.

"This dinner is," he winks as he taps the tip of my nose and brushes a kiss on my lips.

"It's a good thing I have extra lipstick with me or you'd be in a lot of trouble at your surprise dinner."

"Yeah, well...I'm lucky that way. Good things happen to good people," he smiles, "and I'm good people."

In the car, I see that we are heading north. I let the music soothe my nerves and enjoy sitting close to Derek and feeling secure with his hand holding mine. After about fifteen minutes, the driver pulls up to a group of new condos, and I wonder again where we are. Before I can ask, Derek jumps out of the car and signals to the driver not to bother to get my door. He comes around to my side, lets me out, and I look around at the beautiful landscaped grounds and the condos that have about four different sizes and designs.

"Where are we, Derek?" I ask while silently admiring the natural beauty surrounding me.

"Be patient, Babe. You'll see in a minute." He smiles and catches my hand and brings it to his lips as we walk.

He takes keys from his pocket and opens the door to one of the smaller condos, and when I enter, I know immediately that it is *his* place. The decorations are professionally done so the rooms I see are outstandingly elegant. There are pictures of our wedding, our honeymoon, our anniversary dinner, the two of us together on the beach in silhouette, and me with him in New York. They are all expertly framed and displayed creatively in clusters on several walls, and expensive artwork adorns strategic places. There is a single picture of me on a coffee table flanked by two blue and white beach shells. The furniture sits on glistening hardwood floors and the accent pieces are all white with touches of a very soft blue. Of course, the total look is contemporary with clean lines, and everything is spotless. There is no clutter. This place is Derek personified.

"So, this is where you hide out," I manage through my amazement. "It's beautiful and it's so you."

"Yeah, but it's not where I want to hide out. I like living on the beach in a comfortable cottage with a certain beautiful woman named Arianna....you know her? You know the place?" He asks. I smile up at him.

He moves in front of me and touches my face and lightly kisses my lips. When I open my eyes, over his shoulder, I see the dining room table elaborately decked out with decorative white and gold place mats, Bone china, elegant gold flatware, and gorgeous crystal glasses trimmed in gold. Two tall crystal vases hold a single long stem white flower in each and Derek moves over to the table and lights the candles that add a very special romantic touch.

He picks up a remote, and instantly Lionel Richie's *Lady* fills the room. When the music begins, it is as if every move is choreographed. At the start of the melody, he takes my hand and momentarily looks at me with a passion that I have not seen in his eyes for a while. Slowly, meticulously, when the artist begins to sing, Derek takes me in his arms. The music, the words, and the smooth voice of the singer move us away to that romantic place where enchantment resides, and the moment easily captures us. We barely move in our dance, and I am mesmerized by my closeness to him...by the masculine smell of him. It is that intimacy that translates the power of the message in the song and Derek's overwhelming desire that these words communicate his feelings and bring me completely back to him. Not one note, not one word of the message is lost on me. I let the voice, the melody, and words melt into me and consume that place in my heart that has been vacant for too long. At the end of the music, we kiss with passion, and then he leads me over to the table to take my place. Before I can sit, however, he puts his hand on my waist and turns me to face him.

"Ari, welcome to my temporary home." He grins, kisses me on my forehead, and helps me in my seat. He disappears momentarily and comes back with a waiter, and introduces him to me. Derek takes his seat, and we are served a delicious meal of Seared Salmon with Balsamic Glaze on a bed of brown rice pilaf. On the side are a zesty broccoli casserole and a few other delicious choices. My drink is a tangy peach tea, and the dessert is peach cobbler that I know Derek has added just to remind me of how often we have shared this special Grandma Lillie dish together.

After dinner and light conversation, I see him sit back with his hands laced under his chin studying me. It's one of those quiet sexy looks that can throw me off guard, so I occupy myself by continuing to push food around on my plate. Tonight, I can tell that he has a lot on his mind, and he's trying to figure out the best way to address whatever he is thinking. I can also discern that he's feeling some sense of fear because every now and then I see him bite the corner of his bottom lip. That's never a good sign, so I set out to lighten the mood.

"Did your mother ever teach you that it's impolite to stare?" I asked with a coy smile.

He smiles that smile that barely moves his lips. "Did your mother teach you that? If she did, then she did a very poor job because, as I recall, that is how we met...you staring at me." He shifts his position and looks at me with those misty brown eyes almost not blinking. For the first time today, despite his mood, I am relaxed and feel like I'm where I belong, in the presence of this man that I know I love with all of my heart. He continues to stare, at first without a word. Then, as if he has been waiting for just the right time, he speaks.

"Ari, I want to ask you something important...something kind of personal. Do you mind?"

"Derek you can ask me anything you want to ask, and I will answer you as honestly as I possibly can. I have no secrets from you anymore."

"Hmm, I like that answer. I want to know…I want to know where you see yourself ten years from now?"

"Wow." I smile slightly to myself and nervously adjust my napkin in my lap to give myself an extra few seconds. It's not that I don't know my answer. I do. It's that I want to be clear in my explanation after I give my answer. I know my husband, and he will never stop with just one question or one answer. The lawyer will inadvertently show up, and I will need to be sure, clear, and credible.

"I see me happily married, with at least two children, and *The Channing House of Design* extremely successful. That's what I see in ten years."

"When you see that portrait of you and your children,…is there even a slight chance that I'm in that picture?"

Now it's my turn to take a deep breath. "I don't know, Derek. I hope so. I can't see a complete picture yet. You hurt me. You hurt me badly, and I'll be very honest with you. It has taken a lot of prayers, a lot of sermons, and a lot of meditation to get me to this point where I am right now, calmly sitting here knowing without a doubt that I love every breath you take. The hurt was so unexpected, Derek, and that made it very deep. I didn't see it coming. You blindsided me, so, I hope you're in my family portrait. I want you there, but I have to know that I can trust you. I can't wonder when you're late, if you're coming from being with Morgan. I can't wonder when I smell perfume on you, if it was just a grateful client who hugged you or if you stopped by to see Morgan and she sat in your lap or was all over you in different ways. I can't worry when I'm out of town about what you're doing…if you're spending hours with her because you know I won't be coming home. I can't live my life like that…I won't, and I can't let my heart be broken over and over again. I think too much of myself...too much of my own heart to have it mistreated repeatedly." His eyes are down, but I am looking directly at him, and I see his nervousness and even a sense of fear.

"I want these jagged edges in my heart to heal, Derek, and afterwards, I want my heart to stay whole. "Baby?" He looks up and our eyes meet. "If I take you into my heart again, I have to be able to believe you. I have to be able to trust that you will handle my heart with great care. I have to know that you recognize and respect its fragility."

I stop and continue looking at him. He drops his eyes and is almost absentmindedly moving his thumb on the smooth surface of the table. Then he looks up at me again.

"Ari, I know that you believe in God and the power of His promises, but do you believe that He sometimes allows us to go through tests and hardships so that we can actually find Him?"

"I do. I know that's true. I know I talk to Him more frequently now and ask Him to help me more. My personal relationship with Jesus is much closer now than it was when I first met you.."

He slightly shakes his head. "Yeah, mine too. I take knowing Him far more seriously now. Do you think that even through all of the hurt...the pain that we go through in life, we can learn and become much better people?"

"I do believe that, Derek, but it is only if we really want to learn and grow."

He sits back in his seat and for a moment he's quiet and seems distant. He's biting that bottom lip so I know that in his mind he's going to a place that he does not visit often...a place he is trying to forget. It's a painful place, and I see it in the way he shifts his position, but mostly I see it in his very sad eyes. He starts to speak and his words come out slowly almost like he's in a dreamlike state. His eyes are focused on some distant object in the room, but I know that he's not seeing it at all.

"When Morgan betrayed me with Zack, I felt...Huh!...I felt completely unforgiving, and I judged her harshly without ever giving her another chance to show me that she was sorry. Ari, I was so angry with her...so angry with both of them...so embarrassed at what they had done to me."

There is a long pause before he starts to speak again. "I was so disappointed in Morgan. I knew Zack was capable of almost anything, but...Morgan surprised me beyond belief, and I judged her for something that I ended up doing myself, actually with her." Now his eyes find mine. "I hurt you as deeply or more than she hurt me. I've learned something through all of this, and I think that's what life is about, Ari...growing, changing, and becoming better people. We go through this life judging others, refusing to forgive, and we're capable of doing the exact same things, but God forgives us every time."

"Yes, He does. What else have you learned? Is that all?"

"No." He reaches across the table, takes my hand in his, and brings my fingers to his lips. He looks deeply into my eyes. "I've learned how very important and how valuable it is to have someone's trust in your hands, especially someone like you. I'm going through this pain of not knowing if you will ever be able to forgive me and take me back....the pain of knowing how much I hurt you. Beating myself up over and over for keeping secrets that should have been told soon after we met...being completely dishonest with you....But dishonesty, betrayal and deceit have taught me their rewards. I know quite a bit now. I know the pain of leaving our home and coming to it seeing you happy with someone else there...in my place. I now know the pain of not seeing you everyday...not sharing our lives together... not hearing your voice for months...the pain of hearing you cry...the pain of not having you close to me at night or waking and seeing the morning light wash over you, and slowly seeing your eyes open to a new day. I know that pain, Ari." He is rubbing my hand and holding it a bit too tightly so I know from his touch just how nervous he is.

"I know all of that pain, and I'm sorry that I caused it. You asked me if that is all I've learned, and the answer is definitely not. I've learned something far deeper. God does allow us to go through some awful things sometimes, but in the end, if we look close enough, we can see lessons that He's taught along the way, and we can be far better than we were before. We grow through the pain. I've grown. I never realized that before this happened to us. I would be so much more cautious now, Ari, if temptation were in my view. I never want to see the hurt I caused in your eyes again as long as I live. Baby, I grew up. I can only hope and pray that you see my growth, and give me a second chance. I'm on my hands and knees to you for that, Babe, because I caused this. I put no blame on anyone but myself....not my mother...not Morgan...not Zack...just me. I'm the one who could have and should have said no. I know that I love you far more now than I did when we stood at *The Rock* and exchanged our vows. My love for you now is far more earnest, more meaningful, and much more real to me. Whether I'm with you in that family portrait or not, that will never change."

Derek gently squeezes my hand to express his sincerity, and I feel, in this touch, the veracity of his words. He sits back momentarily and takes a deep breath, and I know immediately that there is something else important he plans to say. Then, I hear the words.

"Now…" There is a pause, and I see him bite that lower lip. "Arianna, I need to tell you something else. I need to let you know how completely honest I'm willing to be now, in this moment, and for the rest of our lives."

With that one last sentence, his voice is different, but I can't quite put my finger on what it is that's making it different, but what I know is that he is extremely uncomfortable.

"Baby, you can tell me anything. What is it? You look different… worried." I feel the awkwardness of this moment, and it makes me a bit nervous, but because I am beginning to know that this man loves me, I take the chance of walking out on that ledge again…going blindly to the edge…trusting that he won't let me fall. He pauses again, and then I hear his voice, quiet and careful, like he's walking on shattered glass.

"Morgan…Morgan came here late last night. She was waiting here when I came home from the cottage seeing you." He takes my hand in his again, and the words hang in the air like a too heavy overcoat… too heavy for me to move. My heart seems to stop momentarily, and I cease breathing in that instant. *I thought that was over. I thought she had stopped trying. I thought she was sorry.* I hear her empty apology in the back of my mind. I take a sip of air through parted lips and teeth, take another step closer to the edge…trusting…and manage two simple words.

"She did?"

"Yes." His answer is a whisper, and it's quick, but the "s" sustains itself in the air.

"Why?"

"I don't know."

He is tiptoeing now, and I sense his fear. It's standing stiff and stoic between us.

"You don't know? What did she say? What did she do?"

I'm looking in his all too moist eyes again, and he's trying to talk with them. They seem to say that whatever I say here, Arianna, is truth, and his words pour out non-stop like a flood.

"She tried to kiss me, and I pushed her away, Ari. She told me again that she misses me, and she wants me back...that she can't live without me....that we have too much history between us to part. She was pleading with me...crying. Ari, we loved each other for a very long time, and she said she still loves me, and she can't let go. She admitted that she has lost weight, can't eat, can't sleep, and can't get over me....but I know that she can, and I know that in time, she will. I know that she must! I took her to the door in all of her tears and agony, and I confess to you, it was hard, and I was very gentle with her...very gentle, because I care about her, Ari, but I was firm too, and I told her she had to leave. I told her that it's over, that I want my wife back more than anything in this world. I told her I will not stop until I get you back in my arms. This will sound pretty corny to you, but I don't care. I'll climb whatever high mountain you want me to climb, Babe. I'll swim whatever deep waters you want me to swim in. Whatever you want me to do, Arianna, I'll do if you will just love me completely again. I told Morgan that, and that's when she left. For me, Baby, it's…it's over…completely over. I promise you, for me, it's over." On the last four of his words, he briefly squeezes his eyes shut to emphasize the depth of their meaning.

That's when I look up and see them glistening across the table. At first they are toying at making an appearance. I see them progress and simply well up in a pool almost ready to spill over.…and then, for the first time in my life, I witness his full tears dropping and sliding down his face, and they touch the very essence of my heart.

"Derek. Baby." Through his tears, he looks directly in my eyes. My voice is quiet…serious. "There's no need for tears. I am so in love with you. I've known it with absolute certainty since this morning when you called. I don't want to spend one more day, not one more hour, not one more second without you close to me. I had no idea how much I love you until right now, this very moment, and I know that is an answer to the prayers I've prayed for us. We both have grown. We have grown in a meaningful love. We are both new because Jesus cares so much for us in our weaknesses and in whatever strengths we have. I forgive you, Derek. I forgive you completely, Baby, and I do trust you again with my whole heart, and I give it back to you."

I stand up and hold out my arms waiting for him to come around the table and fill them…to fill my heart again…to get rid of the emptiness that has invaded for so many months, but he does not move from his seat. He looks up at me…at my outstretched arms waiting, but his tears continue, and I hear a choking sound. In that instant, I feel his relief. I feel his melting pain, his momentary lack of strength, his joy, his exhaustion, his exuberance, his honest love. He looks directly at me and speaks rather slowly from his seat.

"Ari, I have to warn you. If I manage to get up, if I manage to come around this table, and take you in my arms right now, I'm home for good, Baby....no more waiting. I am at the cottage tonight."

I can't wait any longer. I can't listen any longer. I take two giant steps, a skill I mastered in childhood games, and together with Derek's swift motion, we meet, and he sweeps me up from my feet and brings my body into his. He opens my mouth with his and with that one passionate kiss, the jagged edges of our hearts repair and are made smooth, the rough places are no more. For the very first time, we are one. I take my thumbs and wipe his tears, and he kisses mine away.

Close to my ear, he whispers, and I hear his voice break again.

"Let's go, Ari. Our limo is waiting, and your husband is coming home tonight."

Call to Me, and I will answer you,
and show you great and mighty things,
which you do not know.

— Jeremiah 33:3

ABOUT THE AUTHOR

Doris H. Dancy is an accomplished and award-winning educator, writer, speaker, playwright, novelist, a church officer, and a member of the Lambda Omega Chapter of Alpha Kappa Alpha Sorority, Inc. She received her BA Degree in English and Spanish Education at North Carolina Central University in Durham, North Carolina, and her MA Degree in English Education from Hampton University in Hampton, Virginia. Dancy has been a Teacher of English, High School English Department Chairperson, English Teacher Specialist, and Supervisor of English K-12 for Hampton City Public Schools. She is the author of the Redemptive Love Series: *Jagged Edges, And the Word Became Flesh* and *All Other Ground*. Each novel has received numerous awards.

Mrs. Dancy is married to Willie Dancy, Jr. and they have two daughters, Monica Dancy-Hayes and Tara Dancy Abaya. They have three beautiful granddaughters: Cadence, Tali, and Zoey.

To learn more about Doris H. Dancy,
please visit: www.dorishdancy.com

ADDITIONAL TITLES

By Author, Doris H. Dancy

The Redemptive Love Series

All Other Ground

My website:
www.dorishdancy.com

Awards

1. Readers' Favorite Five Star Award
2. USA Best Book Awards Finalist
3. International Book Award Finalist
4. 3-in-1 The Voice Book Award for Christian Writers
Available At: www.dorishdancy.com

394

www.ingramcontent.com/pod-product-compliance
Lightning Source LLC
Chambersburg PA
CBHW060811030726
47503CB00002B/445